THE PUZZLE OF A BASTARD

LINDA RAE SANDE

ALSO BY LINDA RAE SANDE

The Daughters of the Aristocracy

The Kiss of a Viscount

The Grace of a Duke

The Seduction of an Earl

The Sons of the Aristocracy

Tuesday Nights

The Widowed Countess

My Fair Groom

The Sisters of the Aristocracy

The Story of a Baron

The Passion of a Marquess

The Desire of a Lady

The Brothers of the Aristocracy

The Love of a Rake

The Caress of a Commander

The Epiphany of an Explorer

The Widows of the Aristocracy

The Gossip of an Earl

The Enigma of a Widow

The Secrets of a Viscount

The Widowers of the Aristocracy

The Dream of a Duchess

The Vision of a Viscountess

The Conundrum of a Clerk

CHAPTER 1

ALONE BUT NOT LONELY

ate December 1838, Woodscastle Manor, Chiswick

The sound of horse's hooves had Emily glancing up from her book. Ensconced in the library since breakfast, she had become so engrossed in *The Story of an Earl*, she had completely lost track of time.

Not that she was expected anywhere. Or expecting anyone.

She straightened on the long leather sofa and directed her gaze towards the leaded glass windows that faced the front of the house. Even as she stood to discover who might be outside, she heard Humphrey, the butler, open the front door.

The horse, a beautiful bay with a white blaze and black stockings, stood alone in the crescent-shaped drive. Footprints in the snow showed its rider had already made his way to the front door, but he couldn't be seen from her vantage.

A stable boy hurried to take the reins and to lead the horse to the stables, but he was apparently ordered to remain in place for the time being. The boy offered the beast a carrot as a few snowflakes fell from the sky.

Perhaps it was just a delivery then. A courier or a footman sent with a note, probably for her brother, Thomas.

Curiosity had Emily setting aside the book on the library table beneath the windows. She made her way out to the hall and the entry beyond to see a rather tall gentleman standing just inside the front door. He was dressed in riding clothes, and Humphrey was speaking to him in his usual quiet but impressive baritone.

Pasting a pleasant expression on her face—her mother had taught her and her four sisters the importance of a welcoming expression—Emily said, "Good morning," as she made her way past the round ebony table that marked the center of the large entry to Woodscastle. Her slippers barely made any sound on the black and white patterned marble floor.

"Ah, I had hoped to find Thomas at home," the visitor said as he turned his attention to her.

Emily's first thought was to ask if he wanted her uncle, Thomas Wellingham, or her brother, Thomas Grandby, but then she recognized the man. "James? James Burroughs?"

His eyes widened, but he paused a moment before he said, "I know you're not Ariel or Sarah, so you must be... Amy?"

Grinning, Emily shook her head.

"Christina?"

She shook her head again. "Emily," she offered as she dipped a curtsy, impressed that James Burroughs could remember all of her sister's names and the order in which they had been born.

"Well, that would have been my next guess," he claimed as he stepped forward and took her proffered hand to his lips.

Emily had to resist the urge to pull her hand from his gloved one, so startled was she by the courtesy. She had expected to simply shake his hand—she hadn't had the back of her knuckles kissed in several months.

"We haven't seen you in an age," Emily said as she regarded him with a brilliant smile, "although Tom mentioned you would be returning to London soon. Were you on the Continent?"

James had the bearing of one who had served in the militia, but he had instead followed in his father's footsteps and become a banker. Despite his occupation, he was still trim, his broad shoulders emphasized by the very latest in men's fashionable top coats. The dark green riding jacket he wore was pinched in at the waist and featured a pleated skirt that nearly reached his knees. His buff-colored trousers disappeared into the tops of black Hessians. Although they had probably been shined just that morning, a sheen of melting snow covered them now.

"Nothing that far away, I assure you. I'm just back from Bath," he said, tucking his top hat under one arm. "Father wishes to retire, so there's finally a position for me at the Bank of England."

Emily reached out and placed a hand on his arm. "Can you stay for tea? I was just about to order a tray be delivered to the library, but we can certainly take it in the parlor." She noticed Humphrey hurrying off towards the kitchens, secretly glad the servant wouldn't hear every word of their conversation. At twenty-four, she had decided she no longer required a servant be present when a member of the opposite sex paid a call, especially one to whom she was distantly related.

James looked uncertain for a moment, but then allowed a grin. "Of course. I could use some refreshment," he agreed, deciding not to admit he hadn't yet had breakfast. "And a chance to catch up on the Grandby family antics." He allowed her to take his riding crop and hat and watched as she carefully placed them on the half-round table next to the front door.

Emily grinned as she led him to the parlor, a ground

floor room on the opposite side of the front entry from where the library was located.

A fire was still going in the fireplace, a clear sign one of the servants had thought she would be spending her morning in the peach and green parlor instead of the wood-paneled library.

Ever since the rest of the Grandby family had departed for Derbyshire for the Christmas holiday, the usually bustling household was unusually quiet. The servants seemed uncertain as to which of the public rooms to keep heated for her use.

"You must have come looking for my brother, Tom," she said as she indicated an overstuffed chair near the fireplace and then took the one opposite. The low table between would allow her to serve the tea.

"I take it he is in town?" James asked as Humphrey entered with the tea tray.

Along with the pot of tea and cups and saucers was a plate of biscuits and several small cakes. Emily knew the cook, a recent hire, was using his recipes instead of those left behind by the prior cook. With most of the family gone, he was expecting her and the servants to weigh in with their reviews of his latest creations.

"Almost always these days," she affirmed. "Tom took a room at one of his men's clubs—"

"*One* of his men's clubs?" James repeated, the sound of disbelief evident in his voice. "How many does he belong to?" Given the cost of annual dues, most men belonged to only one—if they could gain membership.

"At least two?" she guessed. Emily dimpled as she placed a cake on a small plate and offered it to him. Starving, James gladly took it and then watched as she prepared the cups for tea.

"I think just the two," she continued. "He was concerned the one was becoming too political, and the other offered apartments and a dining hall so he would not go hungry at night." She poured hot water into one of the cups and swirled it around to warm the porcelain. "He rarely comes to Woodscastle anymore. I think because he prefers a quieter environment."

James was about to argue—Woodscastle was six miles southwest of London and surrounded by trees and parkland—but then he remembered Emily had siblings. Lots of them, including some who had married and were raising their families at the large manor house.

"So... Tom is still not married?" James guessed. He had seen the capitalist in the past year when Tom was in Bath on business, but he knew first-hand how quickly a young man's circumstances could change.

"He is not, and he's been making comments that suggest he may never," Emily said with a shrug. "I cannot tell you how many of my friends are heartbroken. They had hoped he might take notice of them. I suppose with his fortune, he would seem a desirable catch." She said this last as if she couldn't agree. "Do you still take milk in your tea?"

James allowed a half-grin at hearing her claim. "A bit of milk, yes," he replied, surprised she would remember his preference. It had probably been twelve or more years since he'd had tea with the Grandbys. "Aren't you being a bit harsh when it comes to the opinion of your friends? I should think Tom a desirable catch even if he didn't have a fortune."

She allowed a slight giggle of delight. "I admit I do not know him as well as when he used to spend more time here at home. Perhaps he is no longer so serious as to seem stuffy."

"Stuffy?" James repeated with a chuckle.

Her smile bright, Emily nodded. "So much so, I tease him about it. He's even on the board of the British Museum, if you can imagine."

His eyes widening at hearing this tidbit, James was about to admit that the museum was one of the topics he wished to raise with Tom. Instead, he ate his cake as he watched Emily pour the tea and then add the milk, his gaze on her slender fingers and the perfect oval fingernails at their tips.

No rings graced either hand, but he noted that a gold ring was threaded on the chain she wore around her neck. There was a gemstone embedded in it, but given how it hung from the chain, he couldn't see its color. "And you? You must have two or three of your own children by now," he guessed.

Emily offered him the cup of tea on a saucer. "I do not, actually. Like Tom, I am not married—"

"*Wot?*" James nearly spilled his tea at hearing her comment. "But... but you're spoken for, surely."

Long ago, Emily had learned how to keep the pleasant expression pasted on her face even during discussions like this one. Despite how the topic rankled her—a broken heart seemed to take forever to heal—she was usually able to claim that no one had yet captured her fancy and then would simply change the subject.

From James' look of shock, she almost wished she hadn't extended the offer of tea. "I am not," she said, just before she lifted the plate of biscuits and held it out in his direction. He took one, although he didn't seem to pay attention to his choice.

Emily furrowed a dark blonde brow at seeing the reddish-brown biscuit he took. "I thought you didn't like Dutch biscuits," she commented, just before she set down the plate, added another cake to his plate, and took a sip of her tea.

His gaze going from her hands to his own, James regarded the ginger-flavored biscuit as if seeing it for the first time. "I do not," he agreed. "How is it...?" He rolled his eyes. "I cannot believe you remember that I don't like molasses and ginger."

Emily grinned, leaned over, plucked the Dutch biscuit from his hand, and lifted the plate of biscuits in the other. "I remember only because Father used to give you such grief over it. He couldn't believe you would not prefer Dutch biscuits over the lemon ones."

"Because he knows my father loves Dutch biscuits," James said as he helped himself to the lemon equivalent. "Apparently they used to fight over who would get the last one."

Emily could easily imagine what he described. Like most in the extended family that had begun with Margaret Merriweather Burroughs, Dowager Duchess of Ariley, their fathers had grown up in Merriweather Manor with dozens of cousins and aunts and uncles.

"You mentioned he wishes to retire from the banking business," Emily prompted, referring to Andrew Maximillian Burroughs. "He cannot be *that* old."

"Six-and-fifty," James countered, his eyes widening with the claim. "He wants to take my stepmother and their son to the Continent while he can still walk." He said this with a hint of humor, suggesting his father was actually in robust health. He tucked into the second cake, secretly glad she had seen to serving him more without even asking him if he wanted another.

"Andy will love it," Emily said, referring to the son. Her eyes rounded. "Why, he's twenty now. The perfect age for a Grand Tour."

"So... you know my half-brother?"

Emily allowed a chuckle. "Since he was born. He has always lived down the road at Merriweather Manor." She paused as she considered his query. "Didn't you?" She knew James was much older than she was—mid-thirties—but he was still young enough to be in school when his father, a widower, had married Jane Vandermeer Fitzpatrick during the banker's extensive renovation of Merriweather Manor. That had been twenty years ago.

"Only when I was home for the holidays. I was at Eton

and then at Cambridge, and then working in Brighton before Bath."

"But... you have a room there," Emily hinted.

He pretended shock. "You say that as if you have been in it," he teased.

Her grin faded as color suffused her porcelain complexion. "Your stepmother gave me a tour of the house several years ago, so... yes, I admit to having seen it."

Rolling his eyes, he said, "Lady Andrew has kept it exactly as it was when I was still in school, which is to say, more elegant than I probably deserve."

Thinking she shouldn't have mentioned the bedchamber, Emily dipped her head. "I am sorry about your older brother. Pneumonia, was it not?"

She tried but failed to hide a wince. She knew very well Henry Burroughs had died of pneumonia. She had sat by his bed for an entire day and night as she had watched him succumb to the illness. Heard his feverish words of what had happened to his mother. His pleas that his real father be forgiven for what he had done to his mother. His vows to God should he be spared.

His vows to her.

James straightened, surprised by the change of subject. "Thank you. I cannot say I was surprised, though. Like my mother, Henry was always on the sickly side." He was about to say more, but thought better of it.

"But your sister, Sophia, is doing well," Emily said, hoping to lighten the mood. "I played cards with her at a party just last week."

Rolling his eyes, James said, "I cannot believe she has four children."

"I cannot believe how much they look alike," Emily said with a grin. She waited for him to respond and then waved a hand in the air between them, thinking he was suddenly lost in thought. "Don't you agree?"

James gave a start, as if pulled from a reverie. "Truth be told, I haven't seen them since they came to Bath a few years ago," he replied, looking ever so sheepish.

Emily furrowed a brow. "So... you're not staying at Merriweather Manor?" Sophia, her husband, and their four children had apartments in the sprawling manor home.

James' eyes darted to one side. "I am, but... I've managed to avoid being seen by anyone just yet."

Her eyes widening in disbelief, Emily asked, "How is that even possible?" She knew at least three families lived at Merriweather Manor as well as an army of servants. "There must be fifty people living there." Then her eyes widened in delight. "Does Merriweather Manor have secret passages, too?"

James blinked. "Not that I know of," he replied. "But they certainly would have come in handy last night." He paused a moment. "I take from your question that this house must include a few?"

Her eyes darting to the side, Emily leaned forward and said, "I can get from my bedchamber all the way around the house to my aunt's bedchamber almost without being seen," she claimed. "My father can get from his study into the kitchen using a secret staircase."

Grinning, James said, "Now that's more useful, I should think."

"So how is it you weren't discovered last night?"

"I arrived and told the butler not to tell anyone I was there," he said in a quiet voice, as if he feared being overheard.

Emily giggled and then leaned forward. "Is there a *reason* you are lying low?" she asked in a whisper.

He grinned and shook his head. "I have become so used to a quiet life. Alone, but..." He sighed.

"Alone, but not lonely?" she offered.

His eyes widened. "Yes, *exactly*. How is it...?" He shook

his head again and his gaze suddenly darted to the door. "Where is... where is everyone else?"

Emily dipped her head, just then noticing his teacup was empty. She quickly refilled it and added some milk. "Most have gone off to Cherrywood in Derbyshire for the holiday. And lately, my aunt and uncle—the Wellinghams—have been staying in their townhouse in Kingly Street—"

"I suppose it is rather dark when they finish work in town," James commented. "They still run Wellingham Imports then?"

"They do. And as you now know, Tom has flown the coop."

"Leaving you all alone in this huge house."

She shrugged. "There are the servants, of course," she reminded him.

"I'll have you know, I am jealous," James remarked.

"Jealous?" Emily angled her head to one side. For a moment, she thought he might be referring to something else. Someone else. Then she remembered they were speaking of the house and aloneness. "If you'd like to move in, I know of an available bedchamber in the Wellingham wing."

"The *Wellingham* wing?" he repeated, his face lighting with humor.

Emily blinked, wondering how it was she hadn't noticed his handsome features before now. There was the faint resemblance to two of her brothers, his dark hair the same shade of brown cast with strands of gold, his eyes the same hazel, his cheekbones not yet sharp, his jawline square and centered by a chin that would never appear weak.

Try as she might, she couldn't find any of his late brother, Henry, in his appearance.

She used a finger to point up and toward the back of the house. "My aunt and uncle have their suites up there, and all the rest of us have our suites on that end of the house," she explained as she redirected her finger.

"Are you quite serious?"

"About the offer of a room?" she countered. "Yes, of course. No one else is using it—even when everyone is home."

"And... when will that be?" he asked, straightening in his chair.

One shoulder lifted. "End of January at the earliest. Mayhap end of February, depending on how much snow is still on the ground at the time."

James Burroughs regarded her for a long time before he finally gave a nod. "It would just be until I can find something in town," he said. "I could almost do what Tom has done and get a room at a club, but I think—"

"Oh, you would do better with a townhouse," she suggested. "Lots of little rooms and your own study to hide in when you return home from the bank."

"I was thinking of my own library."

Her eyes rounded. "A man after my heart," she teased. "Until you have your own, you're welcome to use the one here. Do you have a valet?"

He shook his head. "My last valet didn't wish to leave Bath. Perhaps I'll take on one when I live in town," he replied.

"Well, should you decide to hire one before then, I know of two empty quarters in the servants' hall," she offered.

James leaned forward, his arms resting on his knees. "Are there rooms you prefer to keep to yourself? Where you might not want my company? I shouldn't wish to impose."

She shook her head. "The library is quite large. There's a music room, the dining room, and this parlor. The snow is kept swept off the paths in the back gardens. Why, it's doubtful we would even see each other except at breakfast and dinner," she said. "Would you like to see the bedchamber?"

"A vantage looking over the front of Woodscastle?" he half-asked. "No need. I couldn't ask for a better view."

Emily grinned in delight. "Then I'll have Mrs. Elliot, the housekeeper, see to preparing the bedchamber above us for you." After a pause, she asked, "And that beautiful horse you rode here?"

James' attention darted to the window, although the horse was beyond its vantage. "He is my own, but I'll need to see to a town coach. I'll have to get to the bank every day, and I cannot do it riding a horse," he replied.

"You can use the one that's still here as well as our driver," she offered. "No one else is."

He gave her a look that suggested he didn't believer her. "Not even you?"

"I have a phaeton," she said with an arched brow. "And I know how to drive it."

James blinked and finally allowed a grin of his own. "You saucy wench," he teased.

Continuing to grin, Emily replied. "I am, and don't you forget it."

CHAPTER 2

A RHYTON IN RUINS

eanwhile, at the British Museum in Great Russell Street, London
The wooden crate landed with a *thud* at Gabe Welling-ham's feet, and he winced. "Have a care!" he cried out, incensed at the lack of regard the two barrel-chested delivery men showed as they moved to lift another crate from the back of a dray cart. "These are priceless antiquities."

Clouds of white air appeared and disappeared in front of his face, his exhalations of breath freezing due to the chilly temperatures. With the large doors open to accommodate the dray cart, the entire receiving area at the back of the museum was cold.

From his vantage, Gabe marveled at what lay beyond the doors. What was once called Long Fields and then Southampton Fields—the site of numerous duels and the Field of Forty Steps—was now covered in building materials for the museum's ongoing expansion. The ingredients for concrete as well as cast iron, stacks of stock brick, and blocks of Portland stone were neatly arranged and spread out as far as the eye could see. A pile of timber was diminishing with each passing day as carpenters built display cases.

From the largest building site in Europe had come the new East Wing, where the King's Library and some of the museum's senior staff were housed. One after the other, new exhibit halls were completed and quickly filled, and yet one of the workmen had said it would be more than a decade before Sir Robert Smirke's design for the grand neoclassical building would be complete. That would happen when the South Wing was built with its planned colonnaded portico.

Intended to make for a grand entrance on the side of the quadrangular structure facing Great Russell Street, its construction wouldn't start until the original Montagu House was demolished, and its demolition wouldn't begin for another few years.

Gabe wondered if he would still hold his position as an archivist of Greek antiquities when all of it was finished.

The last crate was set down atop the first one, its *thud* only slightly less loud than the first. Once again, Gabe winced and managed to catch the attention of a nearby carpenter.

"Sir?" the carpenter said as he approached. He carried a box of nails under one muscled arm and a hammer in the other. His dusty trousers, work shirt, and plain brown waistcoat were at odds with Gabe's light trousers, shawl-collared waistcoat, and long topcoat.

"How do, Barstow? I could use a strong arm," Gabe said as he indicated the two crates. "Our newest acquisitions from Greece," he added.

One of the benefits of the museum's ongoing construction meant there was always a carpenter nearby to help with prying the lids off the shipping crates.

Gabe hefted a pry bar and handed it to Barstow before helping himself to another. The two worked the sharp edges under the crate's lid, and soon the nails securing the wood gave way. Barstow helped to move the top crate off the one below it and they pried the lid off of it.

"Thank you," Gabe said as Barstow gave him the pry bar and went on his way.

Gabe took a deep breath and used his hands to move aside the excelsior that protected the first crate's treasure—an ancient Greek krater that featured a scene with the god Apollo. He lifted it from the bed of packing material, awestruck. The krater was intact. No obvious chips on the rims. There was a slight imperfection in the figure of Apollo, but he knew that could be repaired.

The museum employed an expert in pottery restoration. He hadn't yet met the man, but the evidence of his expertise could be seen by the trained eye in several of the artifacts already on display in the museum.

Setting the krater on a nearby table, Gabe turned his attention to the other crate. Pushing aside the lengths of wood strands, he frowned when he couldn't find what the packing list claimed was inside—a rhyton. The conical drinking cup wouldn't be especially large, but it should have been evident in the crate.

Gabe continued to push aside the packing material until his hand intersected something.

A shard.

He winced as he pulled out the dark brown curved piece of pottery. He pushed his hand back into the crate, reaching to the bottom to discover that the entire rhyton was in pieces.

Had it broken en route? Or had it been shipped this way?

He finally started scooping excelsior from the one crate into the other, moaning when he discovered the remaining pieces of the rhyton at the bottom. "Dammit," he muttered.

"Really, sir, it's not as bad as that," a voice said from his right.

A female voice.

One he was sure included a very slight Stoke accent.

Gabe straightened to regard the owner of the voice—a

dark-haired woman who might have been his age. She was wearing a huge apron and sporting a bun atop her head that was sprung so tight, he was sure her facial features were pulled out of their natural shape. Her gloved hands were both fisted and resting atop her hips.

He gave a bow. "My lady?" he replied. "Isn't it... ruined?"

She rolled her green eyes. "It won't be after I'm finished with it," she said as she held out her right hand, intending to shake his. "Mrs. Longworth. I perform the restoration on pottery."

Gabe immediately bowed over her hand and brushed his lips over her knuckles, noting the gloves were not silk, but rather cotton, and slightly soiled from what might have been clay.

Frances Longworth gave a start, jerking her hand from his hold. When she realized she had overreacted, she stepped back and managed a curtsy. "Apologies. I... I just wasn't expecting... *that*," she stammered.

"Gabe Wellingham," he said, rather wishing there had been someone to do the introductions. "Archivist. I've recently been hired to catalogue the Ancient Greek antiquities."

The woman's gaze took in the cut of his clothes, the perfectly tied cravat, and the simple but expensive waistcoat that peeked above his fashionable black wool topcoat. One that was pinched in at the waist and then flared out in perfect pleats to the sides and back. "It's very good to finally meet you, sir," she said, as she moved to the side of the crate holding the shards that had at one time made up a brown rhyton.

"You, as well, my lady. How is it I haven't made your acquaintance before today?"

Lifting the front of her apron into a makeshift hammock, Frances carefully scooped the pieces into the apron and dipped a curtsy. "No need, I suppose. Good day." Cradling the pottery shards as if they were a baby, she turned to go.

"Wait," Gabe said as he moved to follow her. "Where...where are you taking them?"

Frances allowed an expression that suggested she thought him daft. "To my workroom, of course."

"But..."

"I'll have the finished piece delivered to you when it's reconstructed," she added, just before she left the receiving area.

Gabe watched her go, realizing two things at once.

Mrs. Longworth wasn't the man he had thought she was, which had him wondering if others in the museum's employ knew M. Frances Longworth was a woman.

And she would be positively lovely if her bun wasn't so damned tight.

CHAPTER 3

APHRODITE ARRIVES

eanwhile, at Wellingham Imports
"Has it truly arrived?"

Tom Grandby regarded his uncle and namesake, Thomas Wellingham, with an expectant expression as he struggled to catch his breath. He had practically raced all the way to the brick building housing the offices and warehouse of Wellingham Imports in his high-perch phaeton, making it from his office in Oxford Street in under a half-hour. "I was in a meeting when your caddy dropped off your cryptic note."

The older gentleman—sixty-two years old but still seeing to the day-to-day operations of his import and export concern—grinned at his nephew's enthusiasm. "Just this morning. Came on the *Sea Breeze* a day ahead of schedule," Thomas Wellingham replied. "These winter winds have played havoc with shipping lately." He waved for Tom to follow him. "What do you hear from your mother?"

Christiana Grandby was Thomas Wellingham's sister, and he hadn't seen her since she and most of her brood had departed Chiswick to spend the holiday at the Burroughs' family country estate, Cherrywood. Tom, her second oldest son, had elected to stay behind, claiming he had business to attend to in London.

Tom gave a short laugh. "Although she dearly loves spending time in Derbyshire, she misses Aunt Emma and Emily."

Thomas stopped short. "Emily?" he repeated. "Didn't she go to Cherrywood with the rest of the family?" Although Emily was four-and-twenty, Tom's youngest sister hadn't yet married.

"Surely you would have noticed. She's staying at Woodscastle," Tom replied, referring to the sprawling manor home the Grandbys and Wellinghams shared in Chiswick. "At least, I thought she was," he added as a frown furrowed his brows. "Should I be worried that she might have been whisked away by some devious rogue intent on marrying her for her dowry?"

As far as he knew, Emily wasn't being courted by anyone, more because she wasn't actively seeking a husband than because there were no interested men. He hadn't thought to ask her why, deciding it was more his mother's concern.

Thomas shook his head as they made their way to a crate in the warehouse. "She's no doubt there. *I* just haven't been," he said. "Emma and I have been spending our evenings here in town, at the townhouse in Kingly Street." He paused as an expression of worry darkened his face. "I don't miss the seven-mile drive from my office after dark, but the fact that you haven't seen Emily of late means *you* haven't been staying at Woodscastle, either," he accused.

Dipping his head slightly, Tom said, "I have not. I took a room at one of my clubs—Arthur's, in fact. For the very same reason you have been staying in town at night," he added. "I thought my business would slow when the snow started falling, but I seem to have more clients now than I did before Father decided to retire."

His father, Gregory Grandby, had spent most of his years

helping others invest their funds into profitable ventures. Having inherited a princely sum from his late father when he was but four years old, Gregory had learned early on how to choose investments that would pay handsomely, although not always quickly. His last large investment had been in several railroads, and it would be at least a decade before those would show a profit.

"Perhaps you should take on a partner," Thomas suggested. "Best thing I ever did for this business."

Tom chuckled. "As I recall Father telling me, you had to marry Aunt Emma to make her a partner," he accused.

"That's because she owned a good deal of this company's stock," Thomas said, *sotto voce*. "My decision to marry her was the best decision I ever made, and not just because she was already an owner." He paused a moment. "She is the joy in my life."

Tom noticed the gleam in his uncle's eyes and he grinned. Then he sobered when he suspected the reason for his uncle's words. "I am not *courting* anyone. I am not *looking* to court anyone, and why is it you still think I should *marry*? I'm... I'm rather too *old* to consider matrimony now, don't you suppose?"

Thomas let out a laugh. "Since when is three-and-thirty too old to wed?" he countered. "Your cousin, Milton, Earl of Torrington, didn't get married until he was—"

"Six-and-forty," Tom interrupted, his eyes rolling as if he'd been reminded of the earl's late marriage to Adele Slater Worthington many a time. "I just do not think it would be fair for me to wed and then not be able to spend much time with my wife," Tom explained, just as they stopped before a wooden crate. "All my travels. My time at the office. It would be unfair to her." His eyes widened. "This is it?"

His uncle nodded and pushed aside the lid, its nails having been removed upon its arrival earlier that day. "I'll let you do the honors," Thomas said as he stepped aside.

Tom took a deep breath and leaned down to push aside the mounds of excelsior that filled the wooden crate. When his hand touched something hard, he paused and took a breath. He spread the curled wood shavings aside and reached down with both hands to grasp the object. "It's intact," he murmured in awe.

"Well, I made sure of that before I sent word of its arrival," Thomas said with a laugh. "I admit I was surprised of your interest in something from Greece. The last vase we brought in for you was from Wedgwood, was it not?"

Tom nodded. "That particular work of art has a prominent place in my office," he replied. "The craftsmanship is excellent, as is the design featured on it. In fact, I think it rivals anything that's coming from the Continent these days," he said of the Wedgwood vase.

"And this one?" Thomas asked as he indicated the terra cotta pot his nephew was still working to free from its bed of excelsior.

"I expect this one shall become my new favorite." As Tom lifted the item from the crate, he held his breath and finally allowed a long sigh. "It's heavier than I thought it would be."

"How old do you suppose it is?"

"Two... three-thousand years, perhaps?" Tom guessed as he held out the large, black Attic vase in front of his body. The detailed design that graced the vessel seemed entirely untouched by age. As to the figures featured in the painting, Tom was fairly sure one was Aphrodite. The others were all men, but he could only guess one might be the god Poseidon. As for the others, he didn't know which mortals or gods they might be.

He hoped Gabe Wellingham would know.

Tom finally set the vase on the edge of the crate, but continued to support it with both hands.

"How do you expect to confirm it is what *I* think it is?" Thomas inquired.

The younger man finally allowed a huge grin. "With any luck, your cousin's son will know."

Thomas furrowed a brow, deciding Tom was referring to Gabe the Younger, the illegitimate and oldest son of Gabriel Wellingham, Earl of Trenton, and his countess, Sarah. "A student of Greek antiquities, is he?"

Tom nodded. "No longer a student, but currently employed at the British Museum as an archivist. He catalogues the Greek artifacts they've been acquiring by the ship full, which means he will have work for several years."

Thomas nodded his approval. He was impressed that the earl's son was working rather than living a life of leisure. Gabe could do so given the young man would claim his inheritance when he reached his majority. "Like you, a wise young man."

"He is, and I've sent a note that he needs to join me at White's tonight for a brandy. Would you care to join us?"

Thomas shook his head. "Thank you, but I find I am in need of Emma's company this evening."

Allowing an expression of worry, Tom asked, "Is everything all right?"

His uncle nodded. "Always. But she's spent the entire day in the accounting office, which means I haven't seen her since we arrived this morning."

Tom couldn't help the red that suffused his face. "You're as bad as Mother and Father," he accused.

"I am in love with my wife, and have been since..." He paused and gave a slight shake of his head. Perhaps it wasn't love at first sight, but his regard for Emma Fitzsimmons had developed over a period of less than a month. "Since I hired her to perform an audit of the company ledgers," he added. "Your father knew it, damn him. Pretended he had developed a *tendré* for Emma even though he was secretly in love with your mother at the time."

Grinning, Tom turned his attention back to the Greek vase.

"What are your plans for it?" Thomas asked. He thought it odd that his nephew would acquire such an artifact when he had no townhouse of his own in which to display it.

"There's a caryatid in my office," Tom replied. "This will be perfect sitting atop it."

"Your office?" Thomas repeated in disbelief.

"In Oxford Street. I spend more time there than anywhere else these days," he said. "And I always admired Uncle William's office at the bank. He surrounded himself with beautiful things. Still does."

Thomas rolled his eyes, remembering his one less-than-pleasant visit to Sir William's office at the Bank of England. That had been ages ago, and despite his having lived for ninety years, Sir William III was still alive.

"Do you wish to take it with you?" Thomas asked as he indicated the vase.

"I do, but... I only have my phaeton."

"I'll have one of my men follow you with a dray cart," Thomas offered.

Tom thanked his uncle as he helped to repack the vase, thinking that even if he didn't have a wife, he would at least have Aphrodite for the rest of his life.

CHAPTER 4

THE RIDE HOME

*M*eanwhile, in Chiswick

James Burroughs mounted his bay and made his way back to Merriweather Manor, an unusual sense of calm having settled over him.

Perhaps it had been the morning ride through the falling snow, or the quiet that surrounded him as if every sound but those of hoofbeats were swallowed up by the white carpet.

It was certainly a marked contrast from the sound of chatter and the thumping of footfalls that had awakened him that morning at Merriweather Manor.

He arrived from Bath much later than he expected the night before—the hired coach in which he rode had been delayed at one of the coaching inns due to snow.

The delay had allowed his horse to rest, though. Once they reached the outskirts of London, he'd been able to arrange for his trunks to be delivered to Merriweather Manor before he rode there with only a valise stuffed with some essentials.

The thought of facing any of his relatives that morning had him skulking down the servants' stairs and out the back door to the stables, deciding he could delay making his presence known until after a ride.

Despite the travel the day before, his horse, Neptune, seemed anxious for more exercise today. Even if he hadn't been, James knew he could borrow another from the stables. His father kept a half-dozen or more for riding.

However he managed it, he had wanted to see Thomas, to commiserate and to catch up.

His father's decision to retire could not have come at a more opportune time. The situation in Bath had grown untenable. Given his age—there were some there who thought him far older than his six-and-thirty years—and his lack of a wife or evidence he was at least courting someone, he knew some believed he was a molly.

He had staved off rumors for a time with hints of a betrothal to a lady in London. He had employed a mistress for a few years, though, but not having produced his betrothed for any of the entertainments in Bath meant the rumors would persist.

It was past time to leave Bath behind.

Since his brother's death last spring, he had no other member of the family—close to his age—who could empathize with his continued bachelor status.

He had qualms about taking a wife.

Every woman he met seemed intent on marrying him for his fortune.

Just once, he would like to have met a woman who had no idea he was rich. Who might show an interest in him for who he was rather than what he could buy for her. Who might be attracted to him for his other qualities—loyalty, steadfastness, his pleasant disposition—rather than the handsome features sported by every man in the Burroughs family.

He knew his distant cousin experienced the same difficulties. He had put voice to his complaints the last time Thomas was in Bath on business, half expecting Thomas suffered the same problem.

Tom, he amended, remembering how Emily referred to her second-oldest brother.

His thoughts turned to her, and he slowed his mount. Despite her age, Emily had seemed so at home running the household while everyone else was away. She had been dressed in a bright gown the color of violets, her fitted bodice and bell-shaped skirt suggesting a pleasing figure and long legs. Her simple jewelry—pearl earbobs and a string of tiny pearls around one wrist—was perfect for her age and coloring. Only the ring on the gold chain had seemed out of place.

She offered her hospitality so easily. Drawn him in with her easy smiles. Plied him with tea and cakes and offered a place for him to stay. Never once had she seemed motivated to do so by his fortune.

Because she probably has one of her own.

He blinked and then rolled his eyes.

Did she have the same issues with her suitors? Did men only show interest in her in the hopes of gaining her dowry?

She was quite attractive, but not in the elegant, overdone manner of his last mistress, Marjorie, or any of the Burroughs women he could claim as aunts.

Emily's features were softer, her dark blonde hair highlighted by strands of gold, her green eyes filled with mischief, her easy grin highlighting a dimple and lips he just then thought of kissing.

He allowed a sound of surprise that must have startled Neptune, for the bay suddenly quickened his step to a trot. James pulled back on the reins, not wishing to arrive at Merriweather Manor just yet. He wanted a few more minutes of quiet. A few more minutes of solitude before facing a houseful of people.

He almost turned around and headed back to Woodscastle. There was solitude there.

Well, not complete solitude.

Emily was there. Probably back in the library, reading a book.

The thought had him trying to remember her age. Had she already reached her majority? Opted to take her dowry and forego marriage in favor of the independent life of a spinster? If that was the case, she wouldn't still be living at Woodscastle.

Would she?

Four-and-twenty.

The age came to him in a flash.

He had been twelve when she was born. Despite the chaos of all her older brothers and sisters, Emily had always been the calm in the middle of the Grandby storm of children. Quiet and reserved, watching as if she was on the outside looking in. Joining the fray when invited, but always the first to step out.

Just like me, he thought, which had him coming to his senses to discover he was already in the half-round drive of Merriweather Manor. Despite wishing for just a few more minutes of quiet, a few more minutes of time by himself, his arrival had been noticed. Besides the groom who hurried up to take his horse, several happy children were spilling out the front doors to greet him.

Well, he had sent word ahead that he would be coming to stay for a night or two. Perhaps his trunks had already been delivered.

The memory of Emily's brilliant smile had him pasting on one of his own as he accepted the cries of welcome and the hugs of nieces and nephews and his father and stepmother.

Later, though, he would make his way to town and look for Tom at White's.

At least he was still a bachelor.

CHAPTER 5

RECONSTRUCTING A RHYTON

*B*ack at the museum

Sweeping into her cramped workshop and shoving the door shut with one foot, Frances allowed a sigh of relief as she settled her back against it. For nearly a month, she had been avoiding any contact with the newly hired Mr. Wellingham, sure he would take issue with her sex.

By timing her arrival in the receiving area to coincide with the dray cart she had seen pulling onto the museum grounds, she knew she could catch him—and her newest project—on neutral ground.

The last thing she wanted was to have him seeking her out in her workroom, or for her to have to meet him in the office he had been assigned upon his hiring—it was smaller even than her workroom!

She had seen him before, of course. Watched him make his way from the museum entrance to the hallway leading to the Greek and Roman exhibits. He had probably seen her before, but simply thought she was a patron there to view the artifacts.

From the cut of his clothes and the crown of blond curls

that topped his perfectly chiseled face, she knew Mr. Wellingham had attended university.

Probably Cambridge.

Had probably studied the Classics.

Add to that his voice, devoid of a regional accent, and she was sure he was the son of some landed gentry, or worse, the nephew of a wealthy merchant or tradesman and raised here in London.

He probably even had a membership in one of the men's clubs.

She considered how he had reacted to her appearance, and then wondered at how he had addressed her.

My lady.

As if.

But what had surprised her most on this day was what he hadn't done. He hadn't put voice to any shock or taken umbrage at learning she was a woman. In fact, he seemed far more concerned about what she planned to do with his rhyton.

Just the year before, the man who had hired her had certainly been surprised by her sex. She hadn't given him a chance to take issue with it, though.

Frances had appeared before Evan Shoemaker, an updated character in hand along with his letter she had received the week before, offering her the position of Pottery Restorer.

"You're Mr. F. Longworth?" he had asked in dismay.

"Mrs. Frances Longworth, yes. Pleased to make your acquaintance, sir," she said as she held out her right hand. "If you'll just show me to my workshop, I can get started right away."

She had learned years before to simply take charge of the awkward situation, act as if she knew what she was doing—because she did—and get on with her assignment.

"But..." he had started to say, finally noticing her hand. He had given it a half-hearted shake.

"Yes, I'm aware I am a woman, but my training is quite extensive. I have learned from the very best, and you'll find my skills exceed any man you might have employed in the past for the same position."

She remembered how he had blinked. How he had been so tongue-tied, he had simply turned and led her to some stairs.

Down they had gone until they reached a poorly-lit corridor in the basement. A series of doors on either side reminded her of the hotel in which she had taken a room for her first week in London.

Here, the floors were concrete, though, while those in her hotel were carpeted. The workroom he opened was probably the same size as her hotel room, although it felt far more crowded given the shelves of pots, a tall worktable, a potter's wheel, and the general mess that had greeted her that day.

"Where's the kiln located?" she had asked, her entire body turning to take in the workroom where she would be spending her days, hopefully for a very long time.

She'd had no intention of returning to Staffordshire.

"Kiln?"

"The oven. For firing pottery?" she had clarified. "For creating the patches necessary to fill in any gaps in the event there are pieces missing from an amphorae or a krater."

Mr. Shoemaker's eyes had darted sideways. "I am not sure we have one," he had replied.

She remembered having done a quick inventory as the man spoke. She had found some clay that wasn't yet hard as a rock, a tray of powdered pigments, oil paints, brushes, protein glue, and plaster. "Is there waterglass?" she remembered asking. "And kaolin?"

From the expression on Evan Shoemaker's face, she doubted he even knew what she was asking about.

"There is a clerk that sees to ordering supplies, of course," he had finally replied, perhaps realizing he needed to simply allow her to do the job for which he had hired her.

She had to be better than the potter who worked there for the past few years. His restorations had been so poor, the curators had threatened to accept positions in Paris. "Just down the hall. Mr. Peabody. He'll see to whatever it is you need."

"Does that include my pay at the end of the month?"

Frances wanted Mr. Shoemaker out of her workroom, but she didn't want him to forget he had hired her, nor did she want him lowering her agreed-upon salary just because she was a woman. "I trust the position still pays what you offered in your letter." She had made sure not to make this last comment a question.

She didn't want him reconsidering anything.

"Mr. Harris will see to setting everything up," Mr. Shoemaker had replied, the slight sigh at the end of his words suggesting he had decided to give up on arguing with her. "The uh.... those pots on the shelves behind you are the priority," he stammered. "Mr. Harris has done the initial work to catalogue them, but he will need to finish the paperwork for them before they're given to the curator for display."

"Very good," she had said, giving the Greek pottery a cursory glance. "I'll get started on them right away. Now, I've probably kept you entirely too long, sir. Thank you for your time. Good day."

That's when she had undone the buttons of her redingote and revealed the enormous apron that covered the front of her gown. An apron that had paid witness to hundreds of reconstructions and restorations and, despite frequent washings with lye soap, had the clay and pigment stains to prove it.

"Good day, Mrs. Longworth," he had said, and then took his leave as he muttered to himself.

.   .   .

*F*rances settled her makeshift cradle of pottery shards onto the worktable and began setting them out in an orderly pattern. This was her favorite kind of puzzle. Three-dimensional, usually with a piece or two missing, with little variation in the decoration.

This particular puzzle featured light, evenly spaced swirls that covered the exterior of the brown pieces. The pattern made it fairly easy to determine which edges belonged together.

Using a compass and a ruler, she determined the radius of the top opening and the approximate length of the cone-shaped object. To reassemble it, she required a slightly thinner but taller cone on which she could arrange the shards, one she could remove once the shards had been glued together and any cracks or missing pieces repaired.

Having made many over the past year, she already had clay conical-shaped models on her shelf. They were solid cones of various widths, pricked with a series of pinholes, that she had created on the potter's wheel and then baked in the kiln Mr. Harris had discovered in the boiler room.

Placing the cone on its flat head near the edge of the table, she carefully covered the pointed bottom with the intact bottom of the rhyton. Then she began piecing together the rest, supporting the shards with sewing pins she poked into the seams and then into the pinholes of her cone. The slant of her cone helped to keep the ancient pieces in place as she worked her way down.

Once she had every piece in place, she carefully turned the cone, studying all the edges to discover what might be missing.

That's when she realized that not only was the rhyton complete, the edges of the shards matched almost perfectly. There was no evidence of erosion. No evidence the rhyton had broken a thousand years ago and then been discovered *in situ.*

A knock on the door had her calling out, "Come," before she considered who might be on the other side.

As she feared, the blond curls and chiseled face of Mr. Wellingham poked around the edge of the door. "There you are, my lady," he said, his gaze going to the cone. "You've already repaired it?" he asked in awe, stepping the rest of the way into the cramped workroom.

Frances inhaled slowly. "It still has to be glued together, of course, but... not much will have to be done to it after that."

She watched as Gabe moved closer, his attention on the rhyton and the seams of all the shards.

That's when she noticed his blue eyes.

Bright blue eyes, which were perfect with his blond hair and fair complexion. She also noted that his face wasn't as angular as she had first thought. It wasn't yet chiseled, exactly, but might appear that way in ten or twenty years. The line of his jaw and shape of his cheekbones suggested they might have been chubby when he was younger.

He had probably looked like Cupid's brother when he was a child.

And then the scent of his cologne drifted past her nose, and she inhaled softly. Sandalwood? A hint of spice? No amber and no citrus, but then it was winter. Men didn't have to cover their body odor with the scent of limes during the colder months.

"Your reconstruction technique is remarkable," he murmured. "Your cone looks as if it works no matter how tall a rhyton is."

Frances straightened, stunned to hear his compliment. "Thank you, sir," she replied, although she kept her guard up. At any moment, she expected him to add, "For a woman."

"What is your opinion of the breakage?"

Her eyes widening—no one ever asked for her opinion—Frances said, "Recent. Either in shipment or during packing."

His attention darted to her for a moment, but he quickly redirected it to the rhyton before she could catch him watching her. "My thoughts exactly. There is no sign of wear on the edges. No evidence of weathering." He allowed a sigh of disappointment. "It's really too bad. It might have made for a good exhibit piece."

Frances furrowed her dark brows. "What do you mean, *might* have?" she challenged.

Gabe knew he had mis-spoke the moment she spoke. "I just meant that... the breakage will be apparent—"

"Not when I am finished with it," she countered. Her hands went to her hips. "If that is all, Mr. Wellingham, I'd like to get back to work now."

Knowing the sound of a dismissal when he heard it, Gabe gave a bow and moved toward the door. "I... I meant no offense, my lady," he stammered, just before he took his leave.

Frances took a deep breath, wishing she could have responded with an explanation of what she planned to do rather than lashing out at the man.

I've been on the defensive far too long, she thought as she moved to mix a batch of glue.

CHAPTER 6

A STEPMOTHER'S APPEAL

Later that afternoon

"Must you go so soon?" Jane Vandermeer Fitzpatrick Burroughs asked as she accompanied James up the east wing stairs of Merriweather Manor. "You've only just arrived."

James paused before the carved door of his bedchamber and regarded the woman who had owned his father's heart from a time long before Lord Andrew Maximillian Burroughs, had gone to university.

"I'll just be down the road at Woodscastle, my lady—"

"*Mother*," she interrupted. "You can call me mother," she insisted.

"All right. Please, do not take offense, Mother, for none is intended, I assure you. But I find I have a need for… for...." He paused and seemed at a loss for words.

"Quiet," Jane finished for him, her head angling to one side. "You are so used to living alone, this household must seem terribly chaotic."

He dipped his head, secretly glad he wouldn't have to explain himself to Lady Andrew.

Back when he had first learned from his father that his

mother hadn't been the man's first choice to marry, James had felt sick. Vowed he would never feel anything but contempt for Jane Vandermeer.

But after meeting her and seeing the change in his father —Andrew's status as a widower had been going on for nearly seven years when he returned to London from the Continent and married Jane—James slowly warmed to the dowager countess. She seemed to be genuinely in love with his father. And her skills at running his father's household were evident in how clean and tidy all the rooms were, in how the meals were prepared and served, and in how happy the resident families seemed.

If he didn't feel so overwhelmed by the sheer number of people who lived at Merriweather Manor, he knew he would be comfortable staying there.

"Exactly," he said, sighing with relief at knowing she understood his need for quiet.

"Well, perhaps your presence at Woodscastle will help Miss Grandby," Jane said then. "I have been so worried for her."

About to open the door to his bedchamber, James paused and regarded his stepmother with a furrowed brow. "You mean because she's there alone?" he asked. "I rather doubt we'll spend much time in each other's company," he added, thinking it wouldn't really be appropriate for them to be in the same room together without a chaperone.

Jane stared at him a moment and then gave her head a quick shake. "I apologize. It's really… it's really not for me to say," she stammered. "I'll have the carriage brought 'round to take you to Woodscastle, and be sure your horse is ready, too," she said. She dipped a curtsy before heading for the stairs.

James managed an awkward bow and then watched as she barely lifted her skirts to descend the stairs.

Whatever in the world did she mean by her comment?

Help Miss Grandby? In the short amount of time he had spent with Emily earlier that day, he hadn't been left with the impression she was in need of any assistance. Despite the rest of the family having departed, there was still a staff of servants at Woodscastle.

"Mother!" he called out, hurrying to join her.

Jane paused at the top of the stairs, turning to face him when he halted alongside her. "Is there something I should know about Emily?"

Her eyes darting to one side, Jane countered his query with one of her own. "I suppose that all depends. What do you know?"

James shrugged a shoulder. "She's always just been little Em," he replied. At Jane's arched brow, he added, "Well, she's not so little anymore, of course. She's grown into a fine young woman."

"One you might...?" Jane squeezed her eyes shut.

"Mother?" he asked, worry etching his face.

Jane reopened one eye. "Do you suppose there's any chance you might one day decide... *she* is the one?"

James jerked back as if she had slapped him. "The one?" he repeated.

Now Jane's fisted hands went to her hips, as if she had to put them there or risk punching him in the face. "Really, darling. How thick *are* you?" Despite her words, a grin appeared at the corners of her mouth and she was suddenly struggling to keep from laughing. "Oh, forgive me. I cannot believe I just said that to you."

"Well, neither can I," James retorted, allowing his own humor to show. He sobered as he scratched his forehead. "This is about me getting married, isn't it?"

Jane sighed. "You're the oldest now," she said quietly. "You're heir to your father's fortune—"

"You mean he has some left after what he's done to this place?" The words came out harsher than he intended.

Jane rolled her eyes. Perhaps she might have to slap him after all. "He does, actually, and with Henry having died, *you* need an heir, which means *you* need a wife. You're not getting any younger."

And there they were. Spoken aloud not by his father but by his stepmother.

The two requirements for any man who found himself to be the oldest male in the family along with a reminder of his age.

Marriage. An heir. You are getting old.

"I thank you for the reminder," he said quietly. "And I'll be going now."

Looking as if she was about to cry, Jane said, "I'm so sorry. I shouldn't have been the one—"

"Father wouldn't have said a word, and you know it." He took a deep breath and let it out slowly. "Will you tell me what it is that Emily needs help with?"

Jane stared at him a moment and finally said, "A broken heart, I think."

Remembering how Emily gripped the ring that hung from the chain around her neck, James nodded. "I will see what I can do."

He doubted he could do anything for a broken heart, but he could spend some time with her. Make sure she wasn't wallowing in pity. She certainly hadn't seemed out of sorts when he'd left her.

But then, neither had he.

CHAPTER 7

AN INVITATION ARRIVES

Trenton House in Curzon Street, Mayfair, early evening

Barclay opened the front door of Trenton House and quickly stepped aside to allow Gabe to enter. He was followed by a blast of cold air and a flurry of snowflakes.

"Much obliged, Barclay," Gabe said as the butler took his top hat and greatcoat.

"Cook can have your dinner ready at eight, sir," Barclay offered. "If you'd like it earlier, you only need tell me so."

Despite the pangs of hunger he had been feeling for the past half-hour, Gabe replied, "Eight is fine, although seven would be preferable in the future. I find myself growing rather hungry before I've even taken my leave of the museum. Is there any correspondence?"

"Indeed. I've put yours in the study along with the earl's. And a note was delivered by a courier earlier this afternoon. I believe he was from Mr. Grandby's office, sir. He didn't wait for a reply, of course, so I left it with the letters."

Gabe nodded, knowing immediately that Barclay referred to Tom Grandby. He had remained in town for the holiday, claiming he had business. But then, Tom always had business. As an investor, he spent his days in search of the next important venture or invention that might prove profitable in the future.

Gabe wondered if there might be a different reason Tom had decided to remain in town. Perhaps he would learn what it was once he read the missive.

"I could do with a cup of coffee," Gabe said as he headed for the study. He secretly wished for a cup of chocolate, but he knew how much trouble it would be for the cook to make it. Given the rest of the family was away, he didn't want the servants to have to do more than they already were on his behalf.

"Right away, sir," Barclay replied as he hurried off toward the kitchens.

Gabe raised an eyebrow at the sight of the silver salver on his father's massive mahogany desk. It was piled high with white envelopes. From their formal address, most were probably invitations to events sponsored by the aristocrats who remained in London for Christmas.

He knew his father, Gabriel, Earl of Trenton, and his mother, Sarah, Countess of Trenton, had originally intended to remain in town for the holiday. That is, until Gabe's sister, Anne, suffered from love at first—or rather second—sight and quite suddenly married George, Viscount Hexham, the heir to the Torrington earldom.

Having helped the viscount gain his sister's hand in marriage, Gabe knew the attraction was mutual. Neither wanted to navigate the choppy waters of the Season and the Marriage Mart, and both were eager to start their nursery, so opting to marry before Parliament reconvened in March meant they could instead board a steamship and head to the Kingdom of the Two Sicilies for a wedding trip.

At the same time, George's sister, Angelica, had married Sir Benjamin, an astronomer and heir apparent to the Wadsworth earldom. They were on the same steamship.

Not to be outdone, both sets of parents and Gabe's brother, William, had joined the happy couples on their wedding trip, which meant Gabe was left to his own devices. Given his position at the museum, he found he hadn't yet missed his family.

Except at dinner.

In a room that usually vibrated with good humor and constant conversation, Gabe found the silence in the dining room deafening.

When Barclay delivered his coffee, he asked that his dinner be brought to the study.

"Very good, sir," the butler acknowledged as he set the coffee and a tray of walnuts and biscuits on the front edge of the desk.

Having been given orders by his father to answer any invitations with his regrets, Gabe opened all the missives and took to penning responses. For those that included him, he replied that he would attend alone.

When he found the missive from Tom, he sat back and grinned as he read the script.

Dear Gabe,

You're either hosting a raucous house party or you're experiencing profound loneliness. If the former, I am offended at not having received an invitation to join you in merriment. If the latter, I expect you to join me this evening at White's where we can wallow in self-pity at having to spend the holidays alone.

I look forward to seeing you and to learning how it goes at the museum. Have you met any mummies to your liking? If you're not careful, you could find yourself wrapped up in a linen bandage, preserved for all eternity. Or perhaps all those statues of Aphrodite have you falling in love?

I've acquired an Aphrodite and wish to engage your services in determining her worth.

Brandy at half-past nine. My treat.
Thomas

Gabe allowed a chuckle at reading his cousin's note. He checked his chronometer, deciding he could eat quickly and make it with time to spare. "Barclay!" he called out, not surprised when the butler appeared only a few seconds later. "I'll need the town coach at quarter of nine. That missive was from Cousin Thomas."

"White's, sir?"

"Indeed."

"I'll see to it right away and have dinner served just as soon as possible."

Gabe nodded as he returned his attention to writing responses to invitations, wondering at Tom's mention of Aphrodite and her worth.

Was the man finally considering marriage?

He also wondered at Tom's comment about wallowing in self-pity, but he decided he had no intention of doing so.

He would be spending too much time thinking about Frances Longworth.

CHAPTER 8

COUSINS UNITE AT WHITE'S

*H*alf-past nine o'clock, White's in St. James Street

Tom Grandby allowed the butler to take his hat and greatcoat as he perused the first room past the entry. Although there was no sign of Gabe Wellingham, the man who caught his eye had a huge smile aimed in his direction.

"Where have you been?" Tom asked as he joined James Burroughs, his right hand stretched out to shake hands.

"Where have *I* been?" James countered as he slapped Tom on the arm. "I tried to pay a call on you at Woodscastle this morning, only to discover you apparently don't live there any longer."

Tom dipped his head as they moved to take two nearby upholstered chairs. "Apologies. I should have mentioned in my last letter that I was taking a room at Arthur's. Saves me at least an hour of travel each day."

"No harm. I got in late last night and sneaked into Merriweather Manor like a thief in the night. Told the butler not to tell anyone I was there. Then I sneaked out this morning to look for you."

Tom angled his head. "So... you must have seen my sister?"

"I did," James agreed. "Had a very pleasant conversation with her over tea and cakes, in fact. She was an excellent hostess. Must have known I hadn't eaten any breakfast. Why, I can hardly believe she was once little Em."

A guffaw escaped Tom just as a footman arrived to take their drink order. He turned his attention back to James. "I didn't intend to leave her out there all alone with the servants. I thought she would go with the rest of the family to Cherrywood," he explained. "Not sure exactly what happened to make her want to stay, but... Mother seemed to think it was acceptable for her to do so." For a moment, his expression indicated he hadn't given his sister's decision a second thought, but now he might.

"Well, if it's any consolation, she won't be there all alone any longer," James replied as he noticed a blond man waving in their direction. His first thought upon seeing the young man was that Cupid had grown up and put on some clothes. "Do you know him?"

Tom had furrowed a brow at the odd comment about Emily not being alone, but then followed James' line of sight. He smiled and stood up when he spotted Gabe Wellingham. "I do indeed," he said. He shook hands with Gabe once he had made it through the crowd. He turned to introduce him to James.

"Gabe Wellingham, this is your banker's replacement, James Burroughs," Tom said with a grin. "His father, Lord Andrew, has decided to retire, which means James can finally be a banker here in London instead of over in Bath."

Laughing as he shook hands with the younger man, James said, "No one calls my father 'Lord Andrew' these days. Will I be staying in a bedchamber near yours for the next few weeks or so?"

Gabe and Tom exchanged quick glances, and Gabe was

the first to ask, "Have you offered him lodging in Trenton House?" When he paid witness to Tom's look of confusion and quick shake of his head, Gabe added, "It's all right if you have. There are plenty of guest rooms."

"Trenton House?" James repeated, just as two footmen added a chair to their group. He suddenly rolled his eyes heavenward. "Oh, good God. You're *Trenton's* boy! Gabe the Younger?" he teased as he settled back into his chair, realizing he had been confused as to which Wellingham family the young man belonged.

"I am," Gabe admitted, knowing the 'Gabe the Younger' reference was not only because he looked so much like his father but because they shared the same given name.

"I apologize," James offered. "I thought perhaps you lived at Woodscastle. That's where I'll be staying starting tonight."

"Ah, that would be the house belonging to my father's cousin, Thomas," he replied. "I've never been, but I expect it's rather well appointed." He nodded in Tom's direction. "A bit surprised *you're* not living there any longer. Didn't you live there growing up?"

"Wait," Tom said as he spread his hands out in front of him. "Yes, I can claim Woodscastle as my home—I lived there until just a few months ago—but now *I* am the one who is confused," he announced as he sat down. Hard. He turned to regard James. "Why are *you* staying at Woodscastle?"

James accepted the glass of brandy from a footman and allowed a brilliant grin. "Because this morning, I had an offer I could not refuse."

Tom absently took his drink from the footman, his mouth slack. "Emily offered you a room at Woodscastle?"

"She did, bless her heart."

"What about Merriweather Manor?" Tom countered. "Your father spent a fortune renovating that pile."

"Two decades ago," James said, surprising even himself at

how long it had been. "And yes, it's a magnificent estate now, but given the number of people who live there these days, I thought it best I find someplace a bit more... *private*. Just until I can secure a house in town, of course."

"Is it your stepmother?" Tom asked in a whisper, immediately assuming his friend was uncomfortable around the woman who had been Lord Andrew's first love. He had intended to marry Jane Vandermeer long before she ended up betrothed to another, a marriage arranged by her father.

James' eyes darted to one side. "Not at all. Lady Andrew is a lovely woman. I adore her. I *do*," he emphasized when he noted Tom's look of doubt. "I just... I don't adore the crush of cousins, and nieces, and nephews. I had dinner with them this evening, and I found I could not think. I could not breathe, there were so many people."

"This need to be alone—have you experienced it more of late?" Gabe asked as he leaned forward. "I ask only because... I find I do not miss my family since they departed for Italy. I rather prefer having Trenton House all to myself." He paused and then added, "Well, except at dinner."

James nodded. "I admit I had such leanings whilst living in Bath," he replied. "But I gave them no thought."

"Do not get too comfortable at Trenton House," Tom warned, his attention on Gabe. "Especially if it's entailed."

Gabe knew exactly what Tom inferred by the comment. Although his parents were married now, he had been born a bastard and would not inherit any of the entailed properties of the Trenton earldom. His younger brother, William, would have that honor.

Or that curse, Gabe thought, rather glad he would be allowed to pursue his interest in Ancient Greek artifacts—for the rest of his life, if he chose. Once William took a wife, Gabe expected he would have to find his own townhouse, or take rooms at the Albany.

A fleeting thought of Frances Longworth had him thinking the townhouse would be the better choice.

"I do not know what has happened to me of late, but I find I prefer a quiet environment," James said in a low voice. "One that doesn't require me to converse or answer inane questions."

Tom was about to say that he might be required to do so at Woodscastle, but then he remembered Emily's penchant for quiet. She was always satisfied to just *be* while those around her insisted on being noticed or noticing those around them.

"So... who did all the talking while you were with my sister this morning?" Tom asked, not intending for his query to sound as if he were suspicious of his friend.

James blinked. "Hmph." He gave his head a quick shake. "Both of us, actually. We had the most pleasant conversation. Not the least bit stilted. She's... well, she's an excellent hostess and knew exactly how to make me feel at home," he claimed.

"Am I going to have to move back into Woodscastle to act as a chaperone?" Tom asked.

His words sounded light—teasing, almost—but Gabe furrowed a brow when he thought he detected an undertone of suspicion. "It sounds as if they are almost brother and sister," he offered in James' defense.

"Exactly," James replied. "Besides, it's quite obvious she has her heart set on another."

"*Wot?*"

The word of astonishment came from Tom, and its volume had several nearby club members turning in their direction.

"Apologies, but if... if Emily has her heart set on someone, *I'm* certainly not aware of just who he might be," Tom said in a hoarse whisper.

Was that why Emily had elected to remain at Woodscastle instead of going to Cherrywood with the rest of the family? Because she was secretly seeing someone? Because she was carrying on a clandestine *affaire*?

For a moment, Tom knew his expression would frighten off anyone who didn't know him, and he struggled to erase the evidence of his sudden anger.

James and Gabe exchanged quick glances. "She wears a ring on a chain around her neck," James said with a shrug.

The air seemed to go out of Tom all at once. "Oh. I'm aware of it. I think it's just a... a family heirloom," he said. "Something our mother probably found in her jewelry box."

Although James didn't agree, he had no real reason to counter Tom's claim. "Probably," he said, thinking the ring might be a topic of discussion during a dinner at Woodscastle. He turned his attention to Gabe. "So. Who have you decided to make Mrs. Wellingham?" he asked boldly.

Gabe's eyes rounded into saucers. "I'm only one-and-twenty!"

Tom cleared his throat.

"Oh. Two-and-twenty," Gabe amended. "Far too young to have set my cap on anyone."

"And yet... you have your *mind* on someone," James accused.

Gabe furrowed both blond brows and regarded his new acquaintance with a less than amiable face. "Not that I'm aware of," he argued. Then the image of Mrs. Longworth's too-tight bun flashed before his mind's eye and he blinked. "Well, I might occasionally think of one particular woman, but not because of what *you're* thinking."

Tom straightened. "Now you *do* have to share," he insisted, a teasing grin lifting the edges of his lips.

Gabe shook his head. "She's merely another employee at the museum. I met her just today."

"The museum?" James repeated, straightening in his chair. His gaze darted to Tom and then back to Gabe. "The British Museum?"

"Yes," Gabe replied. "I'm an archivist there. I specialize in cataloguing the Greek antiquities."

James turned back to Tom. "And you're on the board?"

Tom furrowed a brow. "My sister told you that, didn't she?"

"Yes. Seems you've become stuffy," he teased. Before Tom could put voice to a protest, James said, "It's rather fortuitous I've met you both here this evening then."

"Why is that?" The query was said in unison by Tom and Gabe.

"I came into possession of some Greek urns whilst in Bath. I'm not sure of their worth, but I accepted them in lieu of blunt in a game of whist."

"Copies? Or... or originals?" Gabe asked as he leaned forward.

James shrugged. "I've no idea."

"From whom?"

His gaze darting to one side, James leaned forward and said, "A rather bombastic baron who acquired them whilst he was in Greece last year. Most of them seem in good condition, except for a slight alteration made on some of them."

"Alteration?" Gabe repeated, his excitement waining.

"The wiggly bits on the men have been painted over with little fig leaves, if you can imagine."

"Oh, that's actually quite common," Gabe said, somewhat relieved. "The tastes of some collectors have me flummoxed at times."

"Anyway," James went on, "I've no place to display them —my father's office is already quite well appointed with his collection of Roman artifacts—so I thought to just give them to the museum."

"But, surely you'll want them for your own house, once you've settled in one," Gabe argued.

James winced. "I rather doubt it. I think there must be

eight or nine of them. I prefer more modern pieces. Like those ceramic urns they make up in Stoke."

Gabe immediately thought of Mrs. Longworth and then wondered why it was his cock responded as it did. He shifted in his chair.

"I think you stunned poor Wellingham into silence," Tom said to James. "As a board member, let me assure you your donation would be greatly appreciated. Most especially if they are originals."

"How would that be determined?" James asked.

"I can usually tell right away," Gabe said. "And if any are in need of restoration, we have an excellent person for that at the museum. She's quite good."

"*She?*" James repeated.

"A potter, yes," Gabe said quickly.

"A potter?" Tom repeated, straightening in his chair. The talk of Greek pots reminded him that he needed to ask if Gabe could appraise the vase that was now mounted on a column in his office.

"Mrs. Longworth is an expert at pottery restoration, if you must know," Gabe said quickly, hoping they would drop the subject.

They didn't.

"*Mrs.* Longworth?" Tom repeated, his brows quirked. His eyes widened. "Wait. M. Francis Longworth is a... a *woman?*" From the manner of his query, it was evident he was as surprised as Gabe had been upon meeting the prickly woman.

Then Gabe's eyes widened. "How do *you* know of Frances Longworth?"

Tom set aside his brandy. "As a member of the museum board, I authorized his... or rather, *her* hiring," he replied, obviously still surprised at what he had just learned. "M. Francis Longworth," he went on. "Formerly of Wedgwood's factory, *Etruria*, in Staffordshire."

"I *knew* it," Gabe said, his face brightening with excitement. When he noted the looks of confusion on both Tom's and James' faces, he added, "She is quite skilled. I sorted that she had to have come from one of the studios specializing in high-end ceramics, and given her..." He allowed the sentence to trail off and then lifted a shoulder. "Wedgwood's factory was the only one that made sense."

Another expression of pain crossed Tom's face. "You believe her work is good enough for museum pieces?"

"Oh, I do," Gabe assured him.

Truth be told, until he could see the final version of the rhyton she was restoring, he wouldn't know for sure. But it seemed imperative he defend her just then. Or at least her skills. Surely there were other artifacts she had repaired that were already on display in the museum. He had the impression she had worked there for some time.

"She's reconstructing an Ancient Greek drinking cup for me right now," Gabe explained. "One that arrived literally in a dozen pieces. She had it reassembled on her workbench not even ten minutes after we took it from its crate, a veritable puzzle all ready to glue together."

James arched a brow. "You're smitten with her," he accused.

"I am not," Gabe replied, a bit too quick with his response. "With her skills, perhaps. She's quite good, but... she is far too..." He paused, not sure how to describe the prickly chit whose bun was too tight.

"Beautiful?" James offered, the brandy attributing to his general good mood.

"Vexing," Tom put in.

Pointing at Tom, Gabe said, "*Vexing* is a good word."

"Contrary?" James offered.

Gabe grimaced. "Not exactly."

"Prickly." This came from Tom, and Gabe's eyes widened.

"Indeed," he agreed. "I want nothing more than to pluck

the pins from her hair so..." He paused and placed both hands against his cheeks and pushed them back so his facial features were distorted. "So I might see what she really looks like," he finished before allowing a laugh.

James turned his attention on Tom, who glanced at him and then nodded. "You're in love," they announced in unison.

Gabe's eyes rounded into saucers. "But... that cannot be. She is nothing like my mother, and I am most determined that whomever I fall in love with will be like her in every conceivable way," he argued. "Besides, I am only two-and-twenty," he reminded them. "And..." He paused to be sure their attention was firmly on him. "She is unavailable. She is already married."

Tom narrowed his eyes. "I distinctly remember from reading the character that M. Francis Longworth was *not* married and was unencumbered by any attachments."

Frustration had Gabe shaking his head. "Perhaps at the time," he argued. "That's been... how long ago? And for whatever purpose does it serve for her to go by 'missus' if she is not married?"

The other two gentlemen shrugged. "The housekeeper at Woodscastle goes by Mrs. Elliot and she has never been married," Tom replied.

"It is the same with the housekeeper at Merriweather Manor," James offered.

Gabe thought of Mrs. Thorton, the unmarried housekeeper of Trenton House, and knew his argument was moot. He was about to concede defeat on the matter when Tom held up a finger.

"I suppose she could be a widow," Tom offered. "It would explain much," he added, his thoughts not entirely on the matter at hand.

Gabe was determined to put to rest the suggestion he might be interested in the potter in any way but that of a professional association. "Either way, I do not believe Mrs. Longworth is looking for an attachment, and I am certainly not," he stated.

Tom once again turned his gaze on James. "Six months, do you suppose?"

James shook his head. "Four, tops." He glanced around. "Shall we put it in the betting book?"

Gabriel rolled his eyes. "Gentlemen, have a care," he whined. "Unless you truly want me to end up with even more blunt than my father has seen to settling on me."

For a moment, he couldn't believe what he had just said. He never spoke of the fortune he stood to gain when he reached five-and-twenty, nor mention the allowance his father settled on him despite his protests that he didn't require the funds.

The brandy had not only loosened his tongue, but he could no longer feel his knees.

His protests were too late, though, for Tom had already made his way to the adjoining room and was recording the bet in the huge betting book. James joined him, writing in his own bet.

When the pair returned to their seats, Gabe said, "It's your blunt now, but it shall be mine in four month's time."

James grinned and said, "Time will tell." He pulled a pocket watch from his waistcoat and frowned. "I should take my leave. My first night staying at Woodscastle. I shouldn't wish to have to wake the butler to gain entry."

"He's up until midnight every night," Tom said, but then his brows furrowed. "As is Emily. Reading. Do give her my regards if you would. But that is *all* you will give her, if you take my meaning," he warned.

"I will, and I shall be the perfect gentleman as I always am." He turned his attention on Gabe. "I shall arrange for the delivery of those Greek urns to the museum in the next day or so. To your attention."

"Thank you," Gabe replied.

"No offense, Wellingham, but you are doomed."

With that, James took his leave of White's.

Struggling to keep a straight face, Tom finally said, "I wondered if I might prevail upon you to take a look at my newest acquisition?"

"Acquisition?" Gabe repeated.

"An Attic vase. It's in my office in Oxford Street."

The younger man's eyes widened. "Who did you buy it from?"

Tom leaned toward Gabe and said, "Lord Henley acquired it on my behalf from a private collector in Athens. It arrived on the *Sea Breeze* this morning—"

"Intact?"

"Indeed. I am fairly sure the woman in the design is Aphrodite, but I'm afraid I cannot identify anyone else, nor am I sure which mythological story it's meant to depict," Tom continued. "It's possibly the birth of Aphrodite. Would you be up for the challenge?"

"I would, indeed," Gabe replied, a grin appearing. "It would have to be outside of museum hours, of course."

"Of course," Tom replied. "Perhaps you could stop by on your way to the museum in the morning?"

Gabe thought a moment and asked, "Is eight o'clock too early?"

"Not at all. I have a meeting scheduled a bit later than that. Would you like a ride to Trenton House?" Arthurs' was only a ways down in St. James Street, but Tom felt honor-bound to offer his coach.

"I came in the Trenton town coach," Gabe said. "But thank you for the offer." After another moment, he leaned forward and asked, "Pray tell, who is it that warms your bed these days?"

Tom arched a brow, at first tempted to reply that it was none of Gabe's business. But he saw that Gabe wasn't asking for the purpose of teasing him. "Unfortunately, no one," he replied. "Or perhaps it is fortunate. The pursuit of the perfect woman for me is proving rather difficult. So much so, I have ceased thinking about it."

His face displaying a look of disbelief, Gabe said, "You do realize that once you find her, you'll have to chase her until she catches you," he warned.

His brows furrowing at hearing the odd comment, Tom finally allowed a chuckle. "Perhaps that is what I am doing wrong. I will see you in the morning. Good night."

Gabe watched the older man take his leave of White's before he settled back in his chair. Try as he might, he couldn't *not* think of Mrs. Longworth.

The woman was proving to be vexing even when she wasn't in the same room.

And he rather doubted she was chasing him.

CHAPTER 9

A HOMECOMING OF SORTS

An hour-and-a-half later, at Woodscastle
Having finished another chapter of *The Story of an Earl*, Emily was about to close the book and head to her bedchamber, but she instead poured another cup of luke-warm tea. She sat pondering the leather-bound book, dimpling at the thought that she had determined the identity of the actual earl on whose life the book had been based.

Written nearly twenty years ago, *The Story of an Earl* was Lord Sommers' follow-up to *The Story of a Baron*. Both tomes were filled with thinly veiled characters based on real-life aristocrats, so half the fun of reading the stories was trying to determine who was who.

Emily was fairly certain she had figured out the main characters, but then an odd comment or unlikely event would have her second-guessing her choices.

Thinking of taking the book with her to bed, Emily stood up and dared a glance out the windows. She had deliberately remained in the library all evening. Should James Burroughs decide to begin his tenure at Woodscastle this night, as he had implied during tea earlier that afternoon, she wanted to be awake to greet him.

Or perhaps Lady Andrew had talked him into staying at Merriweather Manor, at least for one more night. Emily could imagine how much Jane would want her stepson to remain close. He had just returned from having been away for a long time, after all.

The sound of horses' hooves and a town coach had her smiling in anticipation. For some reason she could not explain, her brief visit with her distant cousin had left her feeling lighter than she had in some time. She had thought at first that ever seeing him again would merely prove painful, a reminder of why she had been so heartsick this past year.

Instead, their conversation had been easy. She had remembered his preferences for milk in his tea and his distaste for Dutch biscuits as if she had learned of them only the day before. She had even teased him about his choice of biscuit, wondering if a gentleman could change his opinion of a particular flavor. Now she knew it was unlikely.

Despite being Henry's brother, James was nothing like him and yet was just as easy to be with.

A sudden lump in her throat had her fighting back tears, and her hand clutched the ring that hung from the gold chain around her neck.

The sound of the front door opening had her straightening, determined to greet James as if he was the long-lost cousin he was.

Rounding the corner from the library to the entry, Emily watched as two footmen carried a trunk between them. "I can escort you," she offered, curious as to why James hadn't yet appeared at the front door.

She made her way up the stairs, glad she had ordered the sconces remain lit in the hallway above. The footmen followed her into the bedchamber, depositing the trunk at the end of the bed before turning to head back down the stairs.

As she was about to go back down, James was making his way up. "Welcome to Woodscastle," she said.

James grinned and took her hand in his. "I am glad to be here," he replied, and then lowered his lips to the back of her hand. "Your brother sends his regards."

"Ah, so you found him," she said as she dimpled.

"He was at White's," he affirmed, offering his arm as they made their way to the bedchamber.

Emily placed her hand on it. "As were many others, no doubt."

"It was quite crowded."

"Did you see many of your old friends?"

He frowned. "No, I did not," he replied, in a manner suggesting he hadn't given it any thought before her query.

"But you made new acquaintances," she said, not making it a question.

"I take it you are familiar with Gabe Wellingham?"

Emily stopped just inside the bedchamber to turn up a candle lamp. Intending to show him the dressing room and bathing chamber, his comment had her regarding him with surprise. "I am, of course. He is my mother's cousin. Ever so polite. I last saw him at a dinner party I attended at Worthington House just a few weeks ago." She paused before she turned to regard him. "I take it he was at White's tonight?"

James nodded as his gaze took in the bedchamber. "I think we may have teased him overmuch."

A musical giggle erupted from Emily. "He no longer looks as much like Cupid as he used to," she claimed.

Allowing a chuckle, James said, "I thought at first he did look like Cupid. But, no, our teasing was over one of his co-workers." He did a quick survey of the chamber. "This will do nicely," he said, moving to stand next to her by the fireplace. Although he had ridden in the town coach from White's to Merriweather Manor, he had elected to ride his horse from there once his trunks were loaded on the coach.

"A co-worker at the museum?" Emily asked, wondering why Gabe Wellingham would be teased if not for his blond curls, blue eyes, and resemblance to Cupid.

"Indeed. A potter. Your brother and I may have placed bets on his bachelor status ending as a result of her. It was silly, really."

Emily couldn't imagine Tom being so frivolous with money. He rarely placed bets, even during horse races.

"This woman would have to be just like his mother for him to even look at her twice," she said.

James' brows arched in surprise. The earl's son had made the same claim earlier that evening. "*Humph.* Then I will lose my bet in four months' time, for I was not left with the impression that Mrs. Longworth is anything like the countess."

Emily blinked. "Mrs. Longworth?" she repeated. "The potter you speak of is... is a *woman?*"

It was James' turn to blink. "Apparently so."

"The potter who does the restorations at the museum?"

James regarded Emily for a moment, amused by her expression of shock. "You speak as if you have met her but thought she was a... a man, perhaps?" he guessed, just then remembering Tom's reaction when Gabe had spoken of her.

Giving her head a shake, Emily said, "I haven't had the pleasure, but I have read the character. I remember Tom asking what I thought about his... *her* qualifications when he was deciding whether or not to approve her hiring at the museum. I had no reason to suspect she was a woman when I read it."

"Well, apparently Mr. Wellingham didn't either. At least until he discovered he's vexed by her."

Emily dimpled. "I rather doubt anything will come of it. As I recall, she had a good deal of experience at one of the largest pottery factories in all of England, so she's probably much older than him. Besides, he's far too young to be thinking of marriage."

"And yet three of your contemporaries have seen fit to marry recently," he countered. He had learned earlier that day that the Grandby twins, Angelica and George, and Gabe's younger sister, Anne, had married only the week before.

"One of them to one of yours," she replied just as quickly, referring to Sir Benjamin, heir to the Wadsworth earldom. He was in his mid-thirties.

"Touché," James said, acting as if he'd been stabbed. "Ben had to, though. He's due to inherit and will require an heir."

Emily smiled, and James grinned at seeing the delight in her eyes. Did she have any idea how happy she made him when she found humor in his antics?

"Lady Angelica will make him the perfect wife," she assured him. "I was at the dinner party where he announced he was going to propose. And then, apparently he did once all of us had taken our leave that night."

"He is a better man than I," James remarked. "Cupid will have to empty his quiver and not miss a single shot to have any effect on me," he claimed.

"Well, Society will not let you go unmarried for long," Emily warned, a grin still teasing her lips. "You are the grandson of a duke. I can hardly believe you haven't yet been caught in the parson's mousetrap."

He pounded a fist against his chest. "You wound me, my lady," he replied, pretending offense. Then he straightened, his eyes widening. "Society will demand the same of you," he countered.

She shook her head. "Not if I choose the life of a spinster."

James sobered. "You wouldn't."

Emily was about to explain herself but decided it was a

discussion best left for another day. "Did you find the bank agreeable?"

Shrugging, James said. "It's much the same as when I was last there, but the area around it looks as if change is imminent."

Furrowing a dark brow, Emily realized what he meant when she remembered the nearby church. "They're going to tear down St. Bartholomew's, probably in a year or two." She was about to say more, but Humphrey appeared at the door.

Suddenly aware she was in the guest bedchamber with James after midnight—without so much as a servant to act as a chaperone—she said, "I will let you get settled, Mr. Burroughs. We can continue this discussion over breakfast." She dipped a curtsy and then hurried from the room, hoping her reddening face hadn't been apparent to James.

Directing a neutral expression in the direction of the butler, James said, "Humphrey."

The butler gave a slight bow. "Are you in need of anything before you retire, sir?"

James' first thought was of Emily, but he quickly erased the image from his head. "Peace and quiet is all I require. Good night."

Humphrey bowed and shuffled back the way he had come, leaving James suddenly all alone, and the room very quiet.

Well, he had what he claimed he wanted.

So why was he looking forward to breakfast with Emily?

CHAPTER 10

APPRAISING APHRODITE

*T*he following morning in Tom's office in Oxford Street, London*

Having never stepped foot into Tom's office before, Gabe Wellingham took a moment to survey the posh hall just inside the door. Thick carpet swallowed up the sounds of traffic in Oxford Street. The walls appeared polished—wood paneled on the lower half and silk-covered up to the mould-ings. The deep green of the fabric reflected a moire pattern that moved with his every step.

"Good morning, sir," a secretary said from where he sat behind a marble counter.

"Morning. I am Gabe Wellingham, here to see Mr. Grandby."

"Ah, you're here about the vase," the man said. He stood and moved to a door on his right. A moment later, and Tom appeared.

"You found the place," Tom said as he held out his hand.

"Wasn't hard, but didn't this used to be a solicitor's office?"

"It was," he acknowledged. "Father had the office next door, and when I joined the business, he bought out the solicitor and we combined the two. Six months of renovations gave us both good-sized offices, but now that Father is retired…" He allowed a shrug. "His office has become a show place for the pieces he's collected on his travels."

Gabe glanced across the hall and caught a glimpse of what Tom meant. "I imagine his study at home must be full of artifacts as well?" he guessed.

Tom agreed. "A veritable museum."

"Will you look for another partner?"

Shaking his head, Tom said, "I'll let Father see to it. It's possible one of my younger brothers will join me." He waved Gabe into his office.

"Now *this* is an office," Gabe said with appreciation. "Mine is but a tiny room in the basement of the museum." His gaze fell on the caryatid that held the Greek vase, and he made a sound of appreciation.

"I have to admit, my reaction was the same," Tom said as he admired his acquisition.

Gabe stood before the black Attic vase featuring red figures and stared in wonder. "She's beautiful," he breathed. "And she's definitely Aphrodite."

"Indeed," Tom agreed. "What else can you tell me?"

"Its shape is what we call a *pelike*—"

"Not an amphora?" Tom asked.

"Similar, because amphorae also have the two handles and the narrow neck. But pelike are distinguished by their belly," he explained as he traced the curved outline of the near-spherical pot. "Where an amphora is wider near the top."

"Ah, I see," Tom replied.

"The style of the art would suggest it's from the Classical period," Gabe continued.

"And who are the other characters featured in the scene?"

Holding a magnifying glass between his face and the vase, Gabe studied one of the males depicted in the artwork.

"The one flying near Aphrodite's head is Eros," he said quietly. "The one with the trident there on the right is Poseidon. You can see there's a fish there, too."

"I thought so," Tom murmured. "And then who is the one on the right?"

Gabe chuckled. "That would be Hermés. He appears to be resting on a plinth." He pointed to the staff the character held. "That's a *kerykeion*. A herald's wand," he said as he straightened. "I have to admit, I'm quite jealous."

Tom dipped his head. "I'm sure you can afford one should you decide to start collecting them," he said.

"Not this one," Gabe replied, his manner most serious. "That cockle shell she's standing behind? That represents the castrated member of Uranus."

Tom winced. "I think I recall that story."

"Then you must recognize what this image depicts," Gabe prompted.

"Is it truly the birth of Aphrodite?" Tom asked in a whisper.

"It is. Did you have reason to think otherwise?"

Tom shook his head. "When I sent word to Lord Henley that I was in search of such an artifact, he wrote back that he thought it would be easy to find one. I, of course, thought he was boasting."

Gabe continued to study the decoration around the edges. "No doubt there are others just like it or similar, but this one is in exceptionally good shape. I cannot imagine Mrs. Longworth having to use any of her skills to improve upon it."

"How old do you suppose it is?"

Gabe stepped back and regarded the entire piece. "Probably from around 350 BCE," he replied. "May I ask how much you had to pay for it?"

"It was equivalent to about a hundred pounds, plus the

cost of shipping it here," Tom replied. The way he said the words suggested he was pleased at the price.

"Did you have Wellingham Imports handle it for you?"

"Of course," Tom replied. "My uncle would have been offended if I hadn't."

"You did well. Had I been the owner, I would not have parted with it at all. But knowing what the museum has had to pay for some recent acquisitions, you might find its worth closer to two-hundred pounds."

Impressed, Tom straightened. "I shall take very good care of it," he promised.

"You may wish to find a more secure mount for it," Gabe suggested. "I would hate to hear that someone had knocked it off its pedestal."

Tom pointed toward the shelves along the short wall of his office. Books filled the outer edges of the shelves, but sculptures were on display in the center of each. "I'll move it there. Place it right in the middle," he said.

"And insure it if you can," Gabe said as he turned his attention back to the pelike. "Seeing this makes me wonder what other treasures we're going to receive from the hold of the *Sea Breeze*," he said. "So far, I've only received three items."

"How many more are you expecting?"

"At least seven," Gabe replied. "And I'm hoping they will all arrive intact."

"And if they don't?"

Gabe allowed a shrug. "Mrs. Longworth will be very busy," he replied. "Which reminds me. I need to take my leave. I'm expected in my office shortly, and I will have to pay a call on the potter."

"Oh?" The word was accompanied by waggling brows.

Gabe gave him a quelling glance. "It's just a query I have about a krater."

Tom nodded. "Oh, of course. Well, thank you for

coming. Drinks will be on me the next time we're at White's."

Grinning, Gabe said, "Aren't they always?"

He took his leave and climbed into the Trenton town coach, his thoughts more on Mrs. Longworth than on Aphrodite.

CHAPTER 11

BREAKFAST FOR TWO

*B*ack *at Woodscastle*
Having given precise instructions to the cook earlier that morning regarding breakfast, Emily was relieved to see a buffet had been set up on the sideboard in the dining room. She had no idea when James might come down for the morning meal, or even if he would, but she wanted him to be able to choose from a variety of foods.

She filled her plate, delighting in the ability to select both a slice of ham and a rasher of bacon to go with the poached eggs that floated in hot water. Buttered toast was displayed in a rack, and sections of oranges had been arranged in a flower pattern on a tray.

About to ruin the symmetry of the flower by taking one of its petals, she paused when James appeared on the threshold. "Why, good morning, Mr. Burroughs," she said brightly.

James gave a slight bow and joined her at the sideboard. "It is a good morning," he agreed.

"I do hope it's because your accommodations are agreeable?" she half-asked.

"Very. I slept like the dead."

"Oh, good, because it's not really a very good morning, I'm afraid. It's snowing again," she complained with a sigh. "Will you need to go into town?" She moved to take a place at the table, opting for a seat adjacent to the carver at the head of the table, hoping James would know to sit there. "I can let Humphrey know to have the town coach readied for your use."

James reviewed the foods on the sideboard. "I will, and thank you for the offer of the town coach. I need to go to the bank—let them know I've arrived and can start—as well as see to some personal business." His plate filled, he turned and regarded the table. For a moment he seemed flummoxed.

"Please, take the carver," Emily said, just as the butler brought in cups on a tray. "I neglected to ask your preference for coffee or tea in the morning, so I had Humprey bring both."

Humphrey set down the tray and headed back to the kitchens as James settled himself at the head of the table.

"You needn't have gone to the trouble on my behalf," he said. "But coffee is welcome in the mornings. And yours smells especially delicious." He was used to coffee with a much stronger odor, one that suggested the coffee beans had been roasted until they were burnt.

"Our new cook has brought with him skills our last cook lacked," Emily replied as she poured him a cup. "Do you take sugar or milk?"

He shook his head. "Let me try it first. I was finally used to the dreck they served in coffee shops in London before I moved to Bath, and then I had to get used to a completely different flavor once there."

"I haven't been to Bath in an age," Emily said. "Father took us there—four traveling coaches, if you can imagine—"

"It must have looked like an Eastern caravan," James remarked as his brows lifted.

"Children of all ages, trying our best to behave ourselves

despite how excited we were because he had told us the story of the Roman baths."

James grimaced. "You must have been so disappointed."

"There wasn't a single pig to be found," she agreed with a giggle, referring to the ancient story of how a pig herder had discovered his pigs' skins were soft after they wallowed in the muddy spring. That had led to the building of the pools and steam rooms that made up the heart of Bath.

"I do hope you have been there since," James remarked as he tucked into his breakfast.

"I have not. A couple of my brothers went again just before Milton had to go off to Eton for school."

"He is the youngest, is he not?" James asked.

"Indeed. He'll be finished at Cambridge this year. That is, if he's not kicked out before then."

James' eyes widened. "Whatever has he been doing?"

"Nothing good," Emily replied, a grin displaying her dimple. "He's always been mischievous. Vexes my mother something awful. But Father always just grins and says he's behaving just like his namesake."

Resisting the urge to laugh out loud, James knew exactly who she meant. "The antics of Milton, Earl of Torrington, in his youth are legendary," he agreed. "Although my father implied his father's early death helped to make him mend his ways. I believe he inherited when he was but sixteen."

"He was the oldest and the heir, so I would hope so," Emily remarked. "Our Milton is the youngest of ten, terribly independent, and I think he will struggle to find his calling in life."

James considered her comment a moment. "Perhaps he will become a banker. Help Tom figure out what to do with all the blunt he's been creating these past two decades. I would love a crack at it, of course, but I know I would have to prove myself before I would ever see a penny."

Emily stilled, her eyes darting to one side. "Roger is a banker," she said, referring to her oldest brother.

James straightened, another frown making him appear rather imposing. "With a competitor?" he guessed, knowing Roger Grandby wasn't employed at the Bank of England.

"Barclay's. He lives a very staid life. Has a townhouse in Whitechapel. I rarely see him."

"But he doesn't handle Tom's accounts," James said, not making it a question.

"Your father has had that honor—or that burden—for the entire time Tom has been investing clients' monies. Which means *you* may end up with the account if what you say is true about your father retiring."

James' eyes rounded. "He never said a word of it," he claimed. "I would love the challenge, of course. Tom is... he's a master at making money. It's as if he has a crystal ball and can see the future."

Grinning, Emily finished her breakfast and said, "His crystal ball is blind in one respect."

"Oh?"

"He has not seen a future for himself with a wife, and yet I know he would like one," she replied.

Furrowing a brow, James said, "There are those of us who have avoided the Marriage Mart for so long, we missed our opportunities with the young ladies who would have made perfect wives for us. Now, none of those fresh out of the schoolroom hold any appeal, and all the older unmarried women have declared themselves spinsters and are not interested in taking on a husband."

Emily looked both left and right. "I have made no such declaration."

James made a sound of disbelief. "Then... how is it *you're* still unmarried?"

It was Emily's turn to make the throaty sound, and she

lifted a hand to grip the ring that hung from the gold chain around her neck. She hadn't expected him to simply ask outright. Not yet, anyway.

"My betrothed saw fit to die before we could exchange our vows," she replied, wincing as she heard the sharp words. The familiar lump developed in her throat, and she struggled to breathe.

Setting his coffee cup on the table, James stared at her. "I'm so sorry," he whispered. "I... I had no idea you had accepted an offer of marriage." Not once had Tom mentioned anything, nor had James' father or his stepmother.

His gaze went to her fist, the one that held the ring. "Your betrothal ring?" he asked in a whisper.

She nodded. "I tried to give it back, but... the family would not take it."

"Trying to give it back was the right thing to do, of course, but it is yours," he murmured. "I am sorry for your loss."

Emily angled her head to one side, realizing he had not guessed the truth of the matter. "Thank you."

At that moment, Humphrey appeared at the door. "Pardon, my lady, sir, but the town coach is ready."

Pulling his timepiece from his waistcoat pocket, James' eyes widened. "I apologize, Miss Grandby, but I really must be going."

"Of course. You cannot be late on your first day," she said, her face once again displaying a pleasant expression. "Shall we expect you for dinner?"

James was about to say that he would eat in town, but he changed his mind at the last minute. "Yes. I'll try very hard to be back by seven."

Emily smiled. "Then I will be sure dinner is ready shortly thereafter. Have a good day."

He nodded. "You as well." With that, he gave a bow and took his leave of the dining room. A few minutes later, and Emily heard the front door open and close.

Although she struggled to hold back tears, a few escaped. Men could be so blind. And deaf and dumb.

CHAPTER 12
A BOLD MOVE

In the pottery restoration workroom, British Museum
Trying to act as if he was on a mission when in fact the subject of his mission hadn't yet made it back to her workroom, Gabe pretended interest in the sheaf of papers he carried in one hand.

He reread a paragraph he had perused earlier that morning. One that inferred a particular red and black pot was probably from the Hellenistic period rather than the Archaic period.

What could the Keeper of Ancient Roman and Greek Artifacts be thinking? The krater at the heart of the discussion was clearly Archaic. The art depicted in the scene that decorated the circumference of the pot wasn't of the same level of detail as Hellenistic art.

So engrossed was he in reading the Keeper's notes, Gabe didn't notice Mrs. Longworth entering her workshop. It wasn't until the door shut that he realized he had missed her arrival.

"Dammit," he muttered, realizing he would have to meet with her on her turf rather than in the neutral territory of the corridor.

He paused before knocking on her door. There was a long wait before he heard her call out, "Come," from the other side.

What had she been doing? She hadn't been in the room that long.

He gingerly opened the door, glad when she didn't present a sour expression upon seeing him as he poked his head around the opening. "Good morning, Mrs. Longworth. I wondered if I might be allowed to take a closer look at one of the pots scheduled for your artistry?" His gaze went to the krater that sat on the worktable in front of where she stood. "In fact, that may be the one right there," he added.

Frances sighed loud enough so her annoyance was evident. "Yes, of course. I was just about to get started mixing some glue." Several black shards surrounded the mostly-black krater. "Do you think you will be long?"

Gabe stepped all the way into the workroom and took the two steps to the table. "Not if you're able to assist."

Her eyes widening in surprise, Frances struggled to return an impassive expression to her face. "What is it?"

He held up the papers. "I disagree with Mr. Harris' assessment of this krater, but perhaps my memory of its art is flawed. I hoped to take a closer look..." His voice trailed off as he studied the krater.

"Well, it's clearly Archaic," Frances announced, her arms crossing in front of her apron.

"My thoughts exactly," he agreed. "But Mr. Harris thinks it is Hellenistic." He glanced up. "I left my gloves in my office. Might you... rotate this so I can study the other side?"

Frances resisted the urge to sigh and simply did his bidding. The series of figures on the krater paraded past as she turned it, the scene depicting an alternating series of men and women.

Although the women's hairstyles were meant to appear elaborate, the details were somewhat muddled, as if in the firing process, the clay didn't take on the correct coloring. Each man depicted was engaged in kissing the woman located next to him.

All except for one man, who stood behind a figure that was bent over.

Gabe arched a brow. "What are your plans for altering the art?" he asked, worry evident in his voice. Despite what appeared to be chaste kissing and no evidence of exposed genitals or naked breasts, there was the clearly sexual scene she might have to hide.

"Other than filling the voids with these pieces, nothing," she replied, one eyebrow arching suggestively.

"Your words are a relief to my ears. I feared you would have to obliterate this scene."

He couldn't help but notice how her face took on a pinkish cast. "That particular scene can be construed as one quite innocent," she remarked.

Gabe's eyes widened. He wasn't sure what she saw, but he knew what he saw. "And the kisses? Not too passionate?"

She allowed a sound of disbelief. "Hardly. They are rather chaste, really. A surprise given the women are clearly prostitutes."

"Hetaira," he corrected her as he took a seat in a wooden chair. "More like mistresses," he added, his own face reddening. "I do hope you're not offended by having to work on such a piece."

She straightened. "The artwork on pottery does not offend me in the least. Besides, I have worked on far more revealing pieces than this, Mr. Wellingham." She remembered wishing she didn't have to cover over any of the suggestive scenes, believing she was performing the equivalent of vandalism.

"Have you ever had to cover scenes of this kind of kissing? Due to its lascivious nature?"

"Lascivious?" she repeated. "I cannot recall this level of art having the ability to impart such a thought."

"But it's clear to me," he argued. "There is passion here. These women are important to these men. Perhaps they even have feelings of love for them," he murmured as he studied the artwork more closely. "Kissing can be so much more than the simple touching of lips. So much more than—"

"Really, Mr. Wellingham. You speak as if you think I have never been kissed," she remarked.

Gabe's eyes widened. "Have you?" Challenge tinged his voice.

Frances rolled her eyes. "Does not the fact that you call me *Mrs.* Longworth suggest that I am or have been married?"

Straightening in the uncomfortable wooden chair, Gabe regarded her with surprise. "I call the housekeeper Mrs. Thorton, but she is not married," he countered. His brows furrowed. "*Are* you married?"

About to answer that it was none of his business, Frances instead allowed a sigh of defeat. "I am not, but you will keep that information to yourself."

"So... you haven't been kissed."

Her shoulders dropped as she let out a *humph*. "Whether I have or have not is none of your concern, Mr. Wellingham," she stated, her annoyance most evident in her pinched expression.

"Do you wish to be?"

The question was so unexpected, Frances stepped back as if she'd been slapped. Before she could respond or run from the room, Gabe dropped his head into his hands. "Forgive me, my lady. It *is* none of my concern," he said. "I do not know what compelled me to ask."

Frances wrapped her arms around her middle, giving a feminine shape to the form beneath the oversized apron she wore. "Why do you call me that?"

Gabe lifted his head and shook it. "What?"

"*My lady*. You've used the honorific nearly every time you've addressed me—"

"Habit," he answered quickly. "I was raised to do so in a household where..." He paused, just then remembering he had never mentioned the identity of his parents. "Where I was expected to address all the women as 'my lady,'" he explained. "Would you prefer it if I did not refer to you by those words?"

Frances considered all the reasons why Mr. Wellingham might have been required to use 'my lady' when addressing women, finally deciding he must have been the son of a servant employed in a lord's home. Or perhaps a footman who had been given the opportunity to attend university. Or mayhap he had been employed in a shop that catered to ladies of the *ton*.

"I rather like it, actually," she murmured. "Makes me sound as if I'm... worthy of... consideration."

Gabe furrowed both brows and stood. Frances looked as if she would take another step back, but she held her ground. "Why would you think you are not?" he asked.

Inhaling sharply, she allowed a shrug. "I am not of noble birth—"

"But you are educated," he argued.

"I am a commoner who happened to have a father who..." She stopped speaking.

One of Gabe's eyebrows arched up. "Who was your father?" He took another step in her direction. Her bottom was now pressed against the shelves. If she leaned too far back with her head, an intact Roman glass vase from the first century would be in danger of tumbling from its perch and ending up in a thousand tiny shards on the floor.

"He was a potter," she stated, as if she had come to the same conclusion about the Roman vase and decided it best to remain where she was.

Gabe angled his head to one side. Her slight Stoke

accent, frequently heard in those who spoke a Potteries dialect, had him jumping to a conclusion. "He worked for Wedgwood." After his discussion with Tom at White's, he had begun to piece together just how it was Mrs. Longworth might have gained employment at the factory.

Nepotism.

Frances' eyes widened. "How... how did you know?"

Gabe shook his head. Wedgwood's factory had been one of the few that had survived the recession, all because its owner and founder, Josiah Wedgwood, had invented cost accounting. By creating pottery for the masses in volume and a few select high-end pieces for the well-to-do and royalty, the business had thrived. "I've seen you work with plaster. With clay. Only someone who had grown up watching an artisan work his magic would develop the skills you have," he claimed, deciding she was far too young to have become such a craftsman of her own accord.

Her expression softened. "You think I have skills?" she whispered in reply.

"You would not be employed here if you did not. Your skills are exquisite, my lady," he replied, "Even if you are required to use them to obliterate beautifully rendered genitals from Greek antiquities."

She winced, both at his easy use of the word 'genitals' and because his claim was true. "Not by choice, I assure you," she replied, her face once again taking on a pinkish cast.

Staring into her bright green eyes, Gabe wondered if she would wish to obliterate *his* genitals after what he was about to do to her. "I'm going to kiss you now," he whispered.

Her eyes rounded, and Gabe thought of saying how she reminded him of a doe that frequented the Trenton property near Wolverhampton. Instead, he lowered his head to hers, until their noses touched. "Close your eyes," he breathed, his own lids lowering over his blue eyes.

. . .

*F*rances swallowed. Despite his command, she kept her eyes wide open as his lips took hers. *How could a man be blessed with such long lashes?* she wondered as she opened her lips enough so his lips could take purchase.

This wasn't a kiss of claiming, or the kiss bestowed by a lover just before bedtime, or even the innocent kiss of two young lovers.

She had experienced all three in her lifetime.

This was far different.

A kiss of exploration. Of determining whether or not future advances would be welcome. Of whether or not she might be considered a candidate for his bed. Of whether or not he might be welcome in hers.

The thoughts had her nearly pulling away.

"Your eyes aren't closed, are they, my lady?"

His quiet query had Frances suppressing a grin, especially when his forehead continued to rest against hers. "If they were, I could not admire your long eyelashes."

His eyes shot open even as his brows furrowed. "Eyelashes?" he repeated. "My lady, you're supposed to be admiring my... *skill* at... at kissing," he murmured, just before he settled his lips on hers again.

She ended that kiss quickly and said, "I can do both at the same time. Did you know your lashes have golden tips?"

Gabe blinked. "My eyelashes?" He pulled away slightly and made a sound of disbelief. "I hadn't noticed, my lady."

This time she was the one to pull away. "Oh, surely you've seen them. In a mirror, whilst shaving," she argued. When she noted his look of denial, she added, "Certainly a man who notices the tiniest detail on an Attic black and red pot would notice such a detail on his own person."

He was about to argue—he only noticed the tiniest

details on items that were of special interest to him, and his eyelashes weren't of special interest—Gabe instead said, "Yours are dark and curled into perfect little arcs."

He positively loved how her expression changed just then. How her lips parted and made it possible for him to take up where he had left off with the kissing.

After a moment, she pulled away again. "You did that deliberately," she accused.

"Did what?"

"Complimented something on my person so that I would..." She couldn't finish the complaint when his lips settled over hers again.

When Gabe finally ended the kiss, he allowed a sigh of frustration. "I must end this."

"Must?" she repeated, not sure if she felt disappointment or relief at hearing his words. At any moment, someone might come into the workroom and discover them.

"I'll have you thoroughly ruined if I do not stop," he murmured, hoping she hadn't noticed how aroused he had become in the short time he'd been kissing her.

What was he thinking to accost the poor woman in her workroom?

"Thoroughly?" she repeated. She gave her head a shake. He would think she was a parrot if she continued repeating his words. But 'thoroughly ruined' implied something far more scandalous than the kisses he'd been bestowing on her. Something that might involve unobliterated genitals.

"I know you may find this hard to believe, my lady, but I am a man." At her arched brow, he added, "I suffer the same effects as most men when in the company of a female I've been guilty of kissing."

Frances blushed as if she was a chit fresh out of the schoolroom. Did his words imply that he was aroused? And if so, was he frequently in the presence of females upon which he bestowed kisses?

And did he kiss often?

"You do this often?" she asked, anger bubbling to the surface.

He shook his head. The one atop his neck. "Not of late, my lady," he replied, noting her rising color. "Which might explain why it is I thought to kiss you." Even as he said the last, he knew she would not understand his meaning.

"I do believe I am offended, Mr. Wellingham," she stated as she whirled around and moved to her counter, busying herself with the scattered puzzle pieces of a Greek amphora. "Thoroughly."

"My lady, I…"

"*Out*, Mr. Wellingham," she ordered. "I have work to do."

Gabe allowed an audible sigh before he gave a bow and took his leave of her workroom.

*O*h, how Gabe wished his mother was still at Trenton House instead of on a steamship bound for the Kingdom of the Two Sicilies. Surely *she* would know what words he could use to make things right with Miss Longworth.

Settling onto his uncomfortable wooden chair in his small office, Gabe regarded the other krater that had him heading for Miss Longworth's workroom in the first place. He was sure she would know how to repair the tiny crack and replace the missing divot that occurred in the middle of the image of Apollo.

He could release the piece to Mr. Harris, knowing it would gain a place among the other ancient Greek treasures that populated the wing devoted to Ancient Greece and Rome. But Apollo was the most important figure on the Attic krater, and the flaw across the middle of his body would be apparent to anyone who viewed the piece up close.

Gabe set the krater aside, thinking he could simply bring it to Miss Longworth's attention on the morrow. Perhaps by then, she would have forgotten his ill-mannered behavior.

He rolled his eyes.

By tomorrow, she would have had twenty-four hours to think about what he had done to her. Twenty-four hours to fume and pontificate. Twenty-four hours to make him into the world's largest ass.

"Really, Mr. Wellingham," Frances said from somewhere to his left.

Gabe nearly knocked his chair over as he quickly came to his feet. "My lady?" was all he could manage to say.

She angled her head to one side. "I do hope you weren't thinking to give that krater to Mr. Harris for display?"

Shaking his head, Gabe said, "No, my lady. There's a crack—"

"And an unfortunately placed piece missing right in the middle of Apollo," she remarked as she studied the krater.

Gabe felt a combination of relief and trepidation. "I was hoping you could repair it. It's one of the reasons I went to your workroom in the first place," he said, unable to meet her gaze.

"Well, of course I can repair it," she huffed.

Gabe watched as she lifted the piece into her arms and carried it off to her workroom.

He watched her go, admiring the sway of her skirts as she walked away.

Prickly and proud, he thought to himself.

Well, at least she was still speaking to him.

CHAPTER 13

DINNER FOR TWO

ater that night at Woodscastle
Emily regarded the opened tome on the library table and allowed a sigh. Although the copy of *Debrett's Peerage & Barontage* wasn't current—this one was from nearly five years ago—it included enough information on the Burroughs family for her to sort the relationships.

She expected James for dinner, and she wanted to be sure she knew all the names in the event he might mention any of them. Emily traced the line from her grandmother, Sophia Burroughs Grandby Simpson, back to the Burroughs' tree. Then she used the charts to discover her paternal grandparents' place in the family that included Mary Margaret Merriweather, Fourth Countess of Torrington, as its matriarch.

Emily took a deep breath as she mentally worked through all the relations.

She felt a slight headache coming on when she realized she and James were second cousins, straight across.

Not sure why she felt disappointment at learning they were related at all, she closed the book with a *thud* at the very moment the front door was doing the same.

James.

She lifted her head and attempted to see beyond the library window, wondering how she could have missed the sound of the town coach as it rattled into the drive.

The oddest sensation gripped her chest just then.

Between arranging the menu for this week's dinners and ensuring the household was in good stead, she had spent the entire afternoon preparing for his return.

She had looked forward to his arrival.

Imagined what it might be like to welcome him home.

Could she do what her mother did whenever her father arrived? Hurry out to the hall and bestow a kiss on his cheek? Ask how his day had been. Ask if she might fetch him something from the kitchens. Mention that his posts were on a salver in his study.

Even though there was no mail for James, Emily was about to head for the hall to welcome him home when she found her feet wouldn't move.

Which was probably just as well. She was about to make a fool of herself.

She wasn't married to James.

But the idea of *being* married to him seemed so right. Even more so than marriage to Henry. Especially after what she had learned about him.

Did James suffer from the same character trait? Would she discover he wasn't the perfect gentleman she had imagined him to be? The perfect friend? The perfect mate?

Well, even if James wasn't perfect, he was still her guest. Greeting him at the door would be the sort of thing a good hostess would do.

Her feet finally obeying, she waltzed out to the hall, allowed a brilliant smile upon seeing James, and moved to join him as he gave his hat and topcoat to Humphrey.

"Good afternoon. How was your first day at the bank?"

James regarded her with a grin and afforded her a bow. "Better than I could have expected," he replied.

Emily curtsied. "You must tell me about all of it over dinner," she said. "I expect it will be ready in less than a half-hour. I hope that's not too soon?"

"Oh, not at all. I'm starving, but I wish to take a moment to change for dinner," he replied.

"Of course. Would you care for a brandy before dinner? Or a coffee?"

He shook his head. "Whatever you're having will be fine." He bounded up the steps to his bedchamber as Emily watched from the hall.

"Would you like me to summon a maid to help you dress, my lady?" Humphrey asked.

Dress for dinner?

Emily hadn't dressed for dinner since the rest of the family had taken their leave the month before. "No, thank you. I'll manage," she replied as she headed for the other set of stairs.

The entire way to her bedchamber, she imagined what she looked like in every dinner gown she owned. When she opened the wardrobe door, she knew exactly which gown to pull out. She gave the coral confection a quick shake, hoping the silk wasn't too wrinkled from its weeks of hanging in the wardrobe.

Stepping out of her day gown was easy. Getting into the dinner gown was easy.

Doing up the buttons at the back proved impossible.

She knew she had missed at least two, possibly three, but there wasn't time to put on a different gown.

She moved to the dressing table and repinned her hair into a simpler style, her gaze briefly falling on the reflection of the gold chain that hung around her neck.

The ring was still hanging from it, but given the shape of the neckline of her gown, the ring fell behind the edge of the lace trim and wasn't visible. It was just as well, since the dark blue gemstone set in the ring didn't suit the gown.

About to leave her bedchamber, she paused to change shoes and took one last look in the mirror.

*J*ames regarded his reflection in the mirror over the bathing chamber sink, secretly glad his beard was blond. Given its coloring, he could forgo another shave and instead use the limited time to take a quick sponge bath.

Like Bath, London was a city. Unfortunately, it was far dirtier, and James felt as if soot covered his entire body. At least the town coach was clean, as was the bank. Every other place he had called on that day suffered the same effects of a cold winter day—slush and mud.

When Humphrey appeared and asked if he might see to his muddy boots, James was quick to take him up on the offer. He pulled a pair of shoes from his trunk.

"Are dinners on the formal side here?" he asked of the butler.

"Probably not as formal as you are used to, sir," Humphrey replied.

James felt relief at hearing the words. After spending time in so many offices, meeting so many people, he looked forward to an evening spent in quiet solitude.

Although he wouldn't necessarily mind a few words with Emily over dinner. He had questions about some of his new acquaintances. Perhaps she knew them and could provide a bit of background.

Emily.

Twice that day he had thought of her. Wondered what she might think of his office. Wondered if she had taken her inheritance. Since her affianced had died, perhaps she had resigned herself to a life of spinsterhood.

Would she remain at Woodscastle the rest of her life, though? Or use some of her funds to purchase a seaside cottage? A thought of a townhouse in London didn't seem to suit his idea of her, but then, he barely knew the young woman.

Well, he could remedy that over a few more meals. If she didn't offer the information, he could ask as a means of keeping up his end of the conversation.

He finished washing his body and helped himself to a linen, his gaze sweeping the bathing chamber. Although Woodscastle was old, he knew this room had to have undergone a renovation. The plumbing was modern. The tiled floor and walls appeared as if they had been recently installed.

When he finished dressing, he was about to check his chronometer when he heard the sound of a bell in the distance. Drawing his comb through his hair, James took one last look in the mirror and then made his way down the stairs.

About to make the turn into the corridor that led to the dining room, he paused when he realized Emily was making her way down the stairs from the Grandby wing of the house.

His first thought was that Humphrey had lied to him. Emily had not only dressed for dinner, but she wore a gown that would have had every line of her dance card filled had she been wearing it to a ball.

With her dark blonde hair, light complexion, and height, the coral silk gown had her looking as if she were attending a court dinner rather than an evening meal in a country estate.

"You look lovely," he murmured as he offered his arm.

A blush colored her face as she joined him. "Thank you. I wish I felt as much."

"What's wrong?"

She glanced around, making sure there were no servants about. "The lady's maid who usually sees to my mother and I went to Cherrywood with my mother, and I've lost track of the housemaid."

"So... you have no lady's maid?" he guessed.

She leaned in toward him. "I've missed at least two buttons," she whispered as she jerked her head back over one shoulder.

"Oh, allow me." James was quick to move behind her, his bare fingers making quick work of the first two fastenings. The expanse of skin above the edge of the gown had him slowing his efforts with the last button, though, his forefinger tracing the fabric so he barely touched her. The temptation to do more—to allow his finger to continue its exploration—was almost too much. Instead, he pretended to check to be sure the top button was completely fastened.

"Tickling is not fair," she said as her body shivered.

Although he intended to claim it wasn't deliberate, James decided to own up to it. "Apologies. I couldn't resist," he teased as he stepped back to her side and afforded her a smirk.

"Thank you," she said with a grin. "I do hope dinner is to your liking," she added as they entered the dining room. "I rather like this new cook's recipes. A bit more daring than the one we had before."

"I like just about anything," he assured her as he held her chair for her.

She took a seat and motioned for the first course to be served. "Is all well at the bank?"

"It is. Much as I expected, although there are obviously some new people working there," he murmured. "Tell me, are you familiar with a Mr. Henry Simpson?"

Emily was about to lift her spoon from the bowl of soup. "Your cousin, you mean?" Perhaps the time spent reading Debrett's was worth it. "The clerk at the bank?" If Henry Simpson hadn't been her uncle, she would have welcomed him as a suitor. His excuses as to why he still wasn't married were much the same as Tom's.

James blinked and then made a sound of disbelief. "That's *Henry?*"

"You didn't know it was him?" Emily chided. "He's my father's half-brother, and he's been working as a clerk at the bank for at least ten years. He'll be head clerk when Mr. Streater retires in a few years."

"Now I feel ever the fool," James said before returning his attention to the soup.

"Were you introduced to him?"

"I was, and I thought he looked familiar, but…" He sighed. "He must think me daft for not realizing it was him."

"You cannot be expected to recognize or remember everyone," she said. "Our families are just too large."

"Thank you for your kind words. Now I'm almost afraid to ask about Mr. Harris."

Emily furrowed a brow. "The one that works at the museum?"

"That would be him," James replied, his eyes widening. "He happened to be at the bank today, and I mentioned I would be donating some Greek vases to the museum. He seemed… intrigued, but he didn't react with the same level of enthusiasm that Mr. Wellingham did."

Emily straightened. "Why ever would you wish to donate Greek antiquities?" she asked in alarm, just before she allowed a sigh and settled back in her chair. "I apologize. It's really none of my business, of course."

"You favor Greek vases?"

"Well, not especially, but they have become so valuable. Apparently Tom wanted one—"

"It arrived. He spoke of it last night," James explained. "As for the ones I have, I cannot believe they can be too valuable."

"Why ever not?"

He seemed reluctant to reply and then finally said, "I

won them in a game of whist from a baron who obviously could not afford to gamble."

The reference to gambling seemed to knock the air out of Emily. "Oh," she said on a sigh, turning her attention back to her soup.

James regarded her a moment. "Are you disappointed by my decision to donate the vases? Or is there another reason I have suddenly lost your good opinion?"

Blushing—she hadn't meant to leave him with that impression—Emily asked, "Do you enjoy gambling?"

Immediately taking her meaning, James was quick with his reply. "Not especially. I rarely gamble. I was at a house party and was invited to sit in on a set on behalf of someone else."

"Oh," she replied, heartened at his response. Perhaps he didn't share his late brother's proclivity for losing more than he could afford. "I do wonder why Mr. Harris didn't seem interested in the vases. Why, one of the museum's patrons is currently sponsoring a dig in Greece."

"Mr. Wellingham mentioned there are a number of Greek artifacts he is charged with cataloguing."

"I am so glad the museum was able to hire him. His interest is genuine, and he truly enjoys the work, I think."

"He'll have nine more vases to see to when my donation is delivered. Probably on the morrow."

"What makes you think they aren't particularly valuable?"

James allowed a shrug. "I cannot imagine Baron Bradford still owning anything of value. Why, he lost his home this past year."

Emily's eyes widened. "To the Earl of Wadsworth," she said with some excitement. At James' look of surprise, she added, "Bradford Hall is next door to Worthington House. In Park Lane. Sir Benjamin lives there. That's where he and Lady Angelica will live when they return from their wedding trip."

"I do hope Wadsworth didn't have to spend a pretty penny to make it livable," James remarked.

Grinning, Emily said, "Sir Benjamin had an observatory built in the back garden."

"Ah, yes. He's an astronomer. Discovered a comet, I think."

"He did," Emily affirmed. After a moment, she said, "You will have to let me know what Mr. Wellingham discovers with regard to the Greek vases. I admit to a certain curiosity about their value."

"I will," James promised. Relieved he seemed to have redeemed himself with the young lady, he returned his attention to his dinner.

CHAPTER 14

PUZZLES OF A DIFFERENT SORT

In the pottery restoration workroom, British Museum
Two days passed before Gabe dared pay another call on Frances Longworth in her workroom. The amphora he held between gloved hands had arrived the morning before, its provenance reviewed and its cataloging complete. Although only a very slight chip marred its top edge, he thought it best to bring it to the workroom for Mrs. Longworth to review before turning the vase over to the curator for display.

He was sure the single male depicted in black on the red pottery was that of Apollo. Apparently naked and his body in profile, it was possible his nether region would require some obliteration. Although Gabe had studied it closely, he couldn't make out anything that might be offensive to a typical museum visitor, but he trusted Mrs. Longworth to know.

Carefully cradling the two-handled pot in one arm, he knocked on the workroom door and waited. After what seemed an eternity, he heard Mrs. Longworth's familiar "Come" with what sounded like an exasperated sigh.

Girding his loins for a scolding, Gabe opened the door

and stepped inside, careful to close it behind him. No need for anyone to see him while he conducted business, nor did he wish to cause a scandal should another employee see them together in her workroom. "Good morning, Mrs. Longworth," he said with a slight bow.

He blinked as he stared at the potter.

Mrs. Longworth was seated before a spinning potter's wheel, her knees on either side of the wheel's vertical support. Her hands, wet and covered with gray slip, were held against both sides of a jar that seemed to form before his eyes. Despite his presence, her attention was fully on her work.

Gabe's first thought was that he wished he was the pot. From the way she held her hands, from the angle of her fingers, and the manner in which the gray water dripped from her wrists, he could only think carnal thoughts.

How could he not?

She was the vision of an enchantress, casting her spell on the damp clay with the slightest press of a finger or the firm push of her palms. The jar grew taller, wider, and then rounded before a neck formed beneath her touch. Then she pulled her hands away and the wheel slowed to a halt.

Gabe swallowed. Hard.

"Good day, Mr. Wellingham," Frances finally answered, her attention on what he held rather than on him. "What have you there?"

Remembering to breathe, Gabe did so, and then hoped she wouldn't notice his arousal. "An Attic pot that might require your... obliteration skills." He glanced down at Apollo and then frowned. Now that he looked at it in the brighter light of the workroom—despite being in the basement, the room did have a window near the ceiling—he questioned his earlier assessment.

Had Apollo's nether region already been painted over?

She gave him a quelling glance. "Oh, really, Mr. Wellingham," she scolded, dipping her hands into a bucket of water before wiping them on a rag. She moved to join him. "Place it on the table, and let's have a look."

Gabe did as he was told, but his attention was on what she had been creating. "Your krater is amazing," he murmured, lowering his head so he could see the profile of the pot against a darker background.

"Then I have failed, for it was supposed to be a volute," she replied as she briefly glanced over at her vase. Now that the shape and profile matched that of an ancient one, she intended to slice out pieces to match the voids she needed to fill in the other pot.

"It will be once the handles are added," he argued. "What, pray tell, is this for?"

"Potsherds," she replied absently, her attention on the figure of Apollo as well as the other images that decorated the amphora he had brought with him.

"Potsherds?" he repeated in alarm. "You... you're going to break this into pieces?"

"No. I will carefully cut out the pieces I am in need of and then..." She shrugged. "Then I'll reduce the rest into a lump of clay. I am in need of three pieces to complete the puzzle of the disastrous mess that arrived from Italy yesterday."

The word "disastrous" had Gabe tearing his gaze from her pot. "Whatever are you talking about?" But even as he asked, his attention went to a volute that sat on one of her shelves. Although it was in one piece, there were voids where pieces were missing, and from the craggy lines in the surface, it was apparent it had arrived as a pile of potsherds and been reassembled.

"Etruscan?" he guessed. The ancient civilization was by no means a specialty of his, but he had certainly studied it at university. He had been most struck by how much of what had been attributed to the ancient Italians appeared as if it could have been made by Greeks.

"That is what I was told." She straightened from examining the amphora he had brought and shook her head. "Is this an acquisition from another museum? Or part of a private collection, perhaps?"

Gabe shook his head. "No. Came from the same dig site in the Peloponnesus that those other amphorae came from earlier this month."

It was Frances' turn to blink. "Then someone at the dig site did the obliteration before they shipped it," she stated, using his word with disgust. "Did a passable job of it, though. The black paint matches perfectly, and the result is well done." She had pulled on a pair of gloves, and her forefinger was tracing the profile of Apollo.

"What?" Gabe joined her at the worktable. "That... that cannot be. We were assured that all the vessels would be shipped here after no more than a light cleaning of the exterior."

She shrugged. "Well, someone altered this."

Gabe furrowed a brow. "You are saying someone... painted the... the wiggly bits before it went into the crate?"

Frances rolled her eyes. "I cannot imagine anyone painting the 'wiggly bits' *after* it was in the crate, unless they were in there with it." She angled her head to one side. "Are you quite sure this didn't come from another museum?"

At the moment, Gabe was only sure that if he didn't get very far from Frances Longworth and very quickly, he was going to kiss her.

And he knew his advances would not be welcome.

"I have the providence papers that came with it," he claimed. "A lengthly description of where it was found, its circumference, its height, and a brief description of the decoration. It all matches." He dipped his head, struggling to keep his mind on the matter at hand instead of the intoxicating scent of the potter that had just drifted past his nose.

How could she smell of spring lilies when she should have smelled of earthy clay?

"What is it?" she asked, her dark brows furrowing.

"I think it best I leave and come back another time."

She made a sound of disgust. "If you think I'm gong to change my opinion of what has been done to this amphora just because—"

"I do not."

She continued to frown. "Then what is it?"

Gabe squeezed his eyes shut, hoping he could overcome his desire for her. Perhaps honesty would gain him an advantage with the prickly woman. "I wish to kiss you, my lady," he whispered. "I know it is wrong, but I cannot help it."

Frances took a step back from the table, her face displaying a look of shock. "Really, Mr. Wellingham. What is it about you and... and *kissing?*"

Lifting his gaze to meet hers, Gabe sighed. "I find I... I *like* you, Mrs. Longworth. Against my better judgment—and yours, I'm sure."

Frances blinked and wavered a moment, her eyes darting about as if she was looking for a means of escape from the workroom. "Well, I'm sure it's just a... a temporary situation," she managed to get out. Especially if he recognized it was against her better judgment. And his.

Should she feel offended by the remark?

Or flattered?

"I thought so, too, but... I find myself thinking of you at the most inopportune times," he replied.

Her eyes widened. "Inopportune?" She glanced at the door to determine if she could make it there before he could intercept her.

Except that he stood between her and the door.

She thought of screaming, but who would hear her down here in the basement? Mr. Peabody in Acquisitions was all the way down at the end of the hall. And even if he came quickly, what would he find? Her, in a compromising position with Mr. Wellingham? She couldn't abide a scandal. Not now. Not here at work.

Gabe nodded. "I apologize. I truly am sorry. I do not mean to embarrass you, nor do I mean to make you fearful of me."

Angling her head to one side, Frances neither bolted for the door nor took another step back. Instead, she regarded the archivist with curiosity. "What exactly... what exactly are your thoughts when you're... *thinking* of me?" The words came out in a whisper, and she cringed at the thought she might be encouraging him.

But she was curious.

Gabe straightened. "I think of how I wish to kiss you again, of course."

A frisson darting through her entire body, Frances sucked in a breath and cursed herself for the unexpected reaction. "Oh? Is that all?"

He shook his head. "I wish to take you to my home so that we might share a dinner and conversation."

"Dinner?" She took another breath, cursing her stomach at how it growled just then, reminding her she hadn't yet helped herself to the small luncheon of cheese and bread she had brought from her tiny room in the boarding house in Kingly Street. "And what would you expect in return?" Her query sounded of suspicion and contempt, although part of her wanted desperately to accept the offer.

When was the last time she had enjoyed a dinner with another adult?

He shook his head. "Nothing, of course," Gabe replied. "Other than a few servants, I am the only one in the house for at least another couple of months, and I find myself in need of companionship."

The word had her eliciting a heavy sigh.

Companionship.

He may as well have said "sexual intercourse" or offered *carte blanche*, because wasn't that what he truly wanted?

A mistress?

Before she could reply, he said, "I know you must be thinking the worst of me. That I am offering... *carte blanche*... or expecting some sort of favor in return, but I assure you. I only wish to share my dinner with you."

"And kisses," she countered, a bit too quickly. For some reason, the thought of his kisses was rather welcome just then.

Gabe's eyes rounded. "Only if you offered them freely."

Pausing perhaps a moment too long, Frances said, "I would never do such a thing, Mr. Wellingham."

Never? The word sounded ever so final.

"I understand. Dinner only, then. I have a town coach scheduled to arrive at six o'clock to take me home. After dinner, I will have the same town coach take you to... wherever it is you live. I can even escort you to your front door—"

"You will do no such thing," she whispered. Although she was ready to agree to having dinner with him, the very last thing she wanted was for the archivist to know where she lived!

Gabe jerked back as if she had slapped him across the face. "But, I insist you arrive home safely," he argued.

Her hands going to her hips, Frances sighed. "If you truly wish my company for dinner, then you will not see me home."

His face screwing up in a grimace, Gabe finally nodded. "Agreed." Even if she didn't tell him where she lived, he could ask his driver for the address once the man returned to Trenton House.

Frances swallowed. "Six o'clock," she said, her voice nearly a whisper.

"I will come for you then," he said, rather liking how their quiet words sounded in the workroom.

He was about to turn and take his leave when his attention went back to the amphora. "I suppose there is no reason to leave this with you."

"I suppose not," she replied. "But should you ever discover how it came to be altered, I hope you will share what you learn."

"You will be the first person I tell," he assured her, just before he scooped up the amphora, bowed, and took his leave.

Frances allowed a sigh as she regarded the back of her gloved hand.

He hadn't kissed it upon his arrival, nor had he done so before he left her workroom.

Would he do so later that evening?

CHAPTER 15

A WALK IN THE GARDEN

eanwhile, in the library at Woodscastle
"I missed you at breakfast this morning."
Emily gave a start at hearing James' comment as she entered the library. "Oh. Good morning," she said as she turned to find him regarding the shelves behind the massive desk. She couldn't have counted how many times she found her father ensconced at that desk over the years, pouring over stacks of papers and muttering to himself about inventors and innovations. "I slept entirely too late, but I should be excused since I was reading until nearly four o'clock this morning."

James pulled a rather thick tome from an upper shelf. "Sounds like you were reading a good book. Surely better than any I have had to read of late," he remarked.

"I finally finished *The Story of an Earl*." She moved to the mullioned windows at the front of the library and looked out. "Baron Sommers wrote it just after I was born. A piffle of a book, really."

James watched her as she leaned over the library table beneath the window, his reward a quick view of her ankles. He found her profile rather fetching as well. Her hair had been styled a bit differently, and her gown accentuated a slim waist. "Did you sort who all the characters were in real life?" he asked, allowing a grin at hearing her assessment of the book. "I hear that was the sport of the day back when it first appeared in bookstores."

She joined him at her father's desk. "I did. Especially Cousin Milton, of course, since he was the inspiration for the book." She paused a moment. "Are you perhaps one of his godsons?"

Milton, Earl of Torrington, was famous for having agreed to be a godfather to no fewer than one-and-twenty girls and nearly that many boys back when he was a younger man.

James allowed a chuckle. "Guilty as charged," he admitted, remembering his last encounter with the earl. As he always did, Torrington asked if James had finally married. When informed he had not, a sour expression and an admonishment had been offered along with a reminder that the earl had waited far too long to wed and had regretted it.

Up until this week, James had never paid much mind to the earl's scolds.

"And you? Are you one of his many goddaughters?" James asked.

Emily shook her head. "Uncle Thomas has that responsibility." Pointing to the book he held in his arms, she asked, "What do you have to bore yourself with next?"

He gave her a quelling glance. "Commodities," he replied as he aimed the cover of in her direction. The title, *Thoughts and details on the high and low prices of the last thirty years,* was imprinted with gold foil, along with the author's name, Thomas Tooke. "I don't suppose you've read it?"

"Actually, I have. Father suggested it years ago." When she noted his reaction of surprise, she added, "As a means of putting me to sleep. I had a terrible case of insomnia. Turns out, it was far more interesting than I expected, and I ended up finishing it without ever falling asleep once."

She sobered as she realized the time. "You're not at the bank."

"It's Saturday," he said simply.

"You don't work on Saturdays?"

"I do not. Although having to read about commodities will be work for me. What are you doing today?"

"I've already gone over menus with the cook and the household schedule with Mrs. Elliot, so I was thinking of taking a turn about the back gardens. I've been on the lookout for the first sign of daffodils. The weather looks rather fine today. Would you care to join me?"

Glancing towards the windows and noting the unusual blue skies, James said, "That sounds like a much better prospect than reading about commodities," he replied.

"I'll get my coat and a muff and meet you at the back door," she said, as she turned to make her way out of the library.

"Wait," James said. "Where... *where* exactly is the back door? You know, I've never been given a proper tour of Woodscastle. "

Emily inhaled sharply. "I shall have to remedy that when we return from the garden." She crooked her finger and motioned for him to join her on the threshold of the library. She pointed down the passageway that began on the east side of the stairs and led past the entrance to the dining room. "There, at the end of the corridor."

"Where you've been going after dinner every night?" he asked.

She nodded, surprised he had taken note. "Indeed. I like to walk after dinner. Get a bit of air."

James suddenly regretted having turned down her invitation to walk with her the night before. His mind had been on a number of matters, not the least of which was her. Although her offer had been tempting, he hadn't had the impression she really wanted him to join her. "So, do you always walk in the gardens at night?"

She allowed a shrug. "Usually. If it's not too cold, or if it's not raining hard, which I know makes it sound as if it never happens..." She arched a teasing brow.

"I'll get my coat and hat," he said as he gave her a brilliant smile, appreciating her sense of humor.

The two hurried off in opposite directions, although James paused on his way around to the front door and watched his hostess as she made her way toward the back door.

Despite the bell-shaped skirt of her bright navy gown, he could still admire her figure and the sway of her hips. He had been imagining those hips far too frequently these past few days. Imagining them without the skirt. Imagining her wearing nothing at all, her breasts free of stays and a chemise. Imagining her naked, beneath him, as he made love to her.

Had he really been so long without female company that he was forced to imagine his hostess in a compromising position?

Apparently.

Surely Emily would make a better lover than his mistress had been. He already knew she was better company than Marjorie had been. Emily had yet to show a disagreeable air. To put voice to a complaint about anything other than the time she had mentioned that one of her slippers was too tight during breakfast.

He could have countered with a comment that his trousers were too tight at the time—her delicate scent had wafted past his nose and set his mind to more carnal thoughts, but he had kept quiet.

What the hell was happening to him?

Four days at Woodscastle—not even entire days, given he was at the bank for most of them—and all he could think about was Emily.

Shaking his head in an effort to clear it, he took his great-coat from the hall tree and was about to pull it on when Humphrey appeared as if from thin air.

"Here, sir. Let me help you with that. Miss Grandby is ready for you at the back door."

Ready for me?

His mind immediately returned to the vivid image of her naked. The next thought of the butler helping to undress her had him snapping out of his reverie. "Already?"

At first, the butler seemed at a loss for words. "She is efficient, sir," he remarked as he settled the coat onto James' shoulders.

"Pray tell, how long has Miss Grandby been running the household?"

Humphrey gave it some thought and said, "About three weeks now, sir." He handed the man his hat.

James was about to ask if that was all, but then he remembered the rest of the family had been gone to Derbyshire about that same amount of time. Apparently she had learned in her mother's absence or been taught before Christiana Grandby took her leave with the rest of the brood. "Very good. Well, I guess we'll be in the gardens."

James hurried off to join Emily at the back door, and he grinned at seeing her bright red redingote. Should she ever be caught in a blizzard, she would be easy to spot. Her hands would not be, though, as they were hidden inside a white fur muff. A matching white hat covered most of her blonde hair.

Surprised at how his body responded to seeing her look so joyful, James was secretly relieved his greatcoat was long.

"It's a bit chilly, but it's not nearly as cold as it has been," Emily said as James opened the door for her and then offered his arm. Despite her words, their breaths appeared as clouds in front of their faces as they made their way along a crushed granite path behind the house.

"This must be quite impressive in the summer," James

remarked as he paused and took in the vista. Woodscastle's parkland extended all the way to the tree line to the east, but its north and south boundaries weren't readily apparent.

"It's gorgeous when it's green," Emily agreed. "There's some cattle, of course, and the horses. Father had stone fences built on the perimeter to help keep all the animals in."

Not seeing any evidence of the fences, James said, "They must be covered with snow." He noted the well-worn path that led into the gardens, the entrance marked by an arbor. Once they were under it, the path led off in two directions.

"Which way?"

"You choose," Emily replied. "For the most part, it's just a circle."

When he noticed the direction of a few footprints in the snow, James led them to the left. Although no flowers were apparent, there were several rows of boxwood hedges to mark the edge of the gardens, and fruit trees stood in the middle of areas in which roses and other perennials had been planted. Several yews had been shaped into spheres, their positions suggesting the garden had been set up as a *parterre*. "A formal garden?" James guessed.

"Oh, hardly," Emily replied as they made their way. "Mother likes it a bit messy, which is why it's not symmetrical."

"And if you had it your way?"

She angled her head in his direction, far enough so it nearly touched his shoulder. "I admit to preferring a symmetrical garden," she said. "But one small enough that I could see to keeping it up if a gardener wasn't available."

"So you're not afraid to get your hands dirty?"

"I wear gloves when I garden, of course," she countered. "And you? Did you keep a garden in Bath?"

James shook his head. "I lived in bachelor lodgings near the bank. There wasn't a garden anywhere nearby, but there were some beautiful places to walk and ride along the river."

"Do you miss it? Bath, I mean?"

Inhaling slowly, James considered it odd that not once in the past few days had he given his former town a moment's thought. He knew he wouldn't miss the entertainments nor the bank—he had stayed entirely too long—but he had come to realize over the past few days that he didn't miss anyone he knew there, either. "Not a bit," he breathed.

"No one at the bank? Friends? Or your mistress?" Emily prompted.

The sound of a grunt preceded James' response. He was about to scold her for mentioning a mistress—gently bred ladies weren't supposed to know of such things—but her query hadn't sounded the least bit judgmental. "What makes you think I had a mistress?"

Emily pinched her lips together, but only for a moment. "You are an unmarried gentleman. You held a position of some importance. I probably shouldn't know of such things, but I am aware how rumors can ruin an unmarried man if he... if someone were to suspect..." She allowed the sentence to trail off and made a sound of defeat, deciding not to mention his brother, Henry, had at one time been the subject of such rumors. She had wondered at one point if they were the reason he had finally made known his feelings for her.

"Would you think that about me?" he asked, pausing so Emily was forced to turn and face him. "If you didn't know me?"

For once, Emily was glad of the cold, for her blush was easily hidden in her otherwise rosy cheeks. "*I* would not, but I have known you since I was born," she reminded him. "I cannot imagine *not* knowing you. Besides. I saw you kiss Ariel behind the stables," she claimed, referring to her oldest sister.

"Wot?"

"Do not deny it."

James resumed walking, although a bit slower than they

had been going before. "I had a terrible crush on Ariel," he admitted.

"*Every* young man in London had a crush on her," Emily countered.

"How do you even remember that?"

She gave him a quelling glance. "I may have been very young, but I was not blind," she replied. "There were young bucks calling at the house nearly every afternoon. Mother rarely had to bring flowers in from this garden because there was always a new bouquet of hot house flowers arriving for Ariel," she claimed. "The same thing happened with Sarah. She basically had all of Ariel's castoffs paying calls on her—"

"That's not true. I knew better than to attempt a courtship with her," James stated, hoping he didn't sound too relieved at never having courted the second oldest daughter.

Emily was about to tease him, but something about his manner had her sobering. "It's good that you did not. I have always felt sorry for her husband." When James' jerked his head, she added, "Nothing he does is enough. Sarah is never satisfied. Had you married her, you would have ended up in the poor house."

His brows furrowing, James regarded Emily for a long time. "For a moment, I thought you might be jealous—"

"I am not. At least, not of her."

"—But instead I'm left wondering if you wanted her husband for yourself."

It was Emily's turn to stop. James realized almost immediately that their conversation had veered into dangerous territory. Her expression conveyed as much anger as it did hurt.

"I was *thirteen* when they wed. The only man I had a crush on back then was..." She stopped and swallowed the last word. A wave of sorrow swept over her, and she struggled to breathe. She took a deep breath and said, "Was too old for me. But it doesn't matter any longer."

"Who?" James' gloved hands gripped her shoulders. For a moment, he wanted her to say, "You." Perhaps she had held a candle for him all these years. Perhaps she had put off suitors thinking he might one day pay a call on her.

Something deep in his chest constricted at the thought that she might actually feel affection for him. But seeing how the memory had her nearly in tears, he thought better of it. "Emily," he whispered.

"He's dead, so it matters not," she said. "Besides, I learned I am probably better off without him." She managed to paste a pleasant expression on her face and inclined her head. "Shall we?"

James blinked, stunned by her simple words and by how quickly she seemed to recover. "Emily," he repeated in a whisper. "I'm so sorry. Whoever he was... he would have been very lucky to have you as his wife."

*E*mily stared at James. *How could he not know?* But then, except for Lady Andrew, Henry hadn't told anyone he had secured Emily's promise to marry him. They'd had three weeks in which to spend stolen moments together. A few days ensconced in a family cottage, neither having told anyone exactly where they were. He was already showing signs of acute illness that last day, and by the time he had returned to Merriweather Manor, he'd grown too sick to share his news. Even his thought to marry in a civil service at his bedside was too much for him at the end.

After he had given her the betrothal ring, they had shared a bed twice whilst at the cottage—it was his right, her mother had explained. But then influenza soon had him housebound. A few days later, he was unable to leave his bed, and by then, Emily knew she wasn't carrying his child.

The idea of becoming a wife and then possibly a widow in such short order held little appeal, especially since she wasn't pregnant. Instead, the rest of the Merriweather Manor families had been ordered to stay away from Henry lest they, too, come down with the disease. With them safely ensconced in their own apartments and unaware of her presence, Emily had simply sat at Henry's bedside and held his hand, sometimes reading to him and sometimes humming softly until he had finally died in the middle of the night.

She had wept that night, wept with grief as well as with relief, for she had come to learn far too much about Henry during those long days by his bed. He probably didn't even know he was telling her his deepest, darkest secrets while fever literally burned him to death. He probably didn't even know she was with him at the end.

When Emily had attempted to return the betrothal ring to Lady Andrew—she was sure it was a family heirloom and thought it best she give it back—the older woman had refused to take it. "It was his to give to the woman he loved, and he loved you," Jane had said that day at the small cemetery behind Merriweather Manor. The two of them had been the last ones remaining by Henry's grave. "He wanted you from the time of your come-out—before your come-out, I think—but he always thought he was too old for you. That you wouldn't want *him*," Jane had explained.

The words had come as a surprise. Although Henry had hinted he had waited for her to grow up before he made his intentions known, he had also said he feared Emily might marry another.

With four older sisters, each waiting until they were older to wed, Emily had merely bided her time thinking she might end up a spinster.

Perhaps Fate had intervened on her behalf. Intervened and then played its terrible tricks. She still wasn't sure if she should be sad she was spared a life with Henry or if she should be glad. Either way, she knew she had to move on.

She couldn't continue moping about Woodscastle as if she'd lost her best friend.

Even if she had.

Given her inheritance, she could afford to do as she pleased, and so marriage had not seemed so necessary.

It still didn't. Except she wanted a child.

The memory of having lain with Henry came to her late at night. She wondered if she would ever again enjoy the sense of security and joy she had felt whilst in his arms. The sense of being wanted. Of being needed.

"*I* wanted a child," Emily blurted.

James stared at her in surprise, her words entirely unexpected. "Well, it's not too late," he murmured. "Is it?"

Emily rolled her eyes and resumed walking. "Of course not." After a pause, she asked, "And you? Do you want a family?"

And there it was. The question that usually had James clenching his teeth and making excuses to take his leave. The query that had him avoiding the mothers of marriageable young ladies, even if it meant taking a longer route whilst shopping.

Except this time, the query didn't rankle.

Perhaps due to the way she had asked it, or perhaps because he was no longer in Bath and those with marriage on their minds weren't begging for his name on their proverbial dance cards.

If Emily had been the one to ask for a dance, though, he would have filled her entire card with his name, the two-dance limit with the same woman be damned.

"Oh, dear. I've gone and asked the question that does not yet have an answer," Emily remarked as she stopped and knelt at the edge of a flower bed. From between the dried, crinkled leaves partially covered with snow, a few green shoots appeared. She pulled a hand from her muff and pushed away the dead leaves.

Allowing a sigh, she glanced up to find James leaning over her in an attempt to discover what she had found. His head was mere inches from hers, but his attention wasn't on the new growth that portended a cluster of daffodils. He was staring at her.

"It had an answer. For a long time, it was a resounding no," he said. He straightened, pulling her up with him.

Emily gasped when she ended up pressed against his front, one of her hands gripping his lapel in an effort to regain her balance. Warmth suffused her entire body as she stared at him. "And now?" she whispered, struggling to remember what it was they were talking about.

"I don't know." He gave a one-shouldered shrug. "I... I don't know." When his eyes locked with hers, he must have seen what he was looking for.

An invitation.

For a moment later, his lips settled onto hers, her lips parted, and he kissed her quite thoroughly.

*J*ames reveled in Emily's willingness, her eagerness, in the feeling of her soft lips against his, in the way she held tight to him as he deepened the kiss. Then he claimed her mouth with his tongue, and any ability he might have had to think or reason was lost.

He thrilled at the taste of her. Her body pressed against his, and his manhood responded. Her soft moans urged him to continue the kiss.

He had never kissed his mistress. Never kissed any woman with such passion. Never allowed himself to simply get lost and not worry about how he might find his way back to reality.

So when he finally pulled away, he did so as if coming out of a dream. Not quickly, for he didn't want her thinking that he had decided he was making a mistake. Slowly, because he regretted having to end it.

When their lips were finally apart, he regarded her with an expression of bemusement. "I still don't know."

Emily gave him a brilliant smile, her teeth bright white against her reddened lips. "Well, I should hope you wouldn't base your desire to have a family—or not—on a single kiss," she scolded. "In my defense, I do not have much in the way of experience when it comes to kissing."

"Oh, the kiss had nothing to do with my answer," he countered, his humor apparent. "And despite your claim, your kiss was by no means one of *inexperience*."

She slapped her muff against his chest. "Liar," the word said with a grin as she hit him again with the muff.

James offered his arm, and they resumed their stroll, his mind on how easily she had returned his kiss. On how she seemed to know exactly what to do.

Well, she had been betrothed, he remembered. He was about to ask just who it was that she had agreed to marry, but she spoke before he had a chance to say anything.

"So, since you are not yet ready to take a wife and fill a nursery, will you look for a mistress in the city?"

About to admonish her, James instead asked, "Why? Are you offering?"

Not expecting the quick rejoinder, Emily stared at him a moment and said, "Maybe."

James let out a sound of disbelief. "If I were to take a mistress, and I am not saying that I will, I certainly wouldn't take an innocent to my bed."

"I am hardly an innocent," she replied, nearly regretting

the comment. When she saw his look of surprise, she added, "Remember, I was betrothed."

He made that sound again. Something between a groan and a growl. Emily had a passing thought that he might make the same sound when he was at the peak of his pleasure during lovemaking. At that point when his body went still, as if he were gripped with pain, and just a fraction of a second before he reached his ecstasy.

Henry had made that same noise. Just before his release had him lowering his slight body onto hers, just before he murmured words she couldn't understand, just before he went limp and fell asleep in her arms.

When he awoke, it was to apologize for having fallen asleep atop her. She wouldn't have let go of him. Especially after the second or third time they had made love.

"Oh. The one who died."

The words were said as if he finally believed she had been betrothed. Emily once again considered beating him with her muff. Maybe forgoing the muff and simply beating his chest with her fists. Or she could slap him across the face. Remove her glove to ensure it gave him as much pain as she would incur doing the slapping.

Instead, Emily simply stared at him.

James dipped his head. "That was wrong of me. I'm so sorry," he said suddenly. "I would not blame you if you slapped me as hard as you could." For a moment, he just stood there, not sure of what to do. He was fairly sure she was going to take him up on the offer of a slap across the face until he saw her lower lip quiver.

He gathered her into his arms and pulled her against him. "I cannot believe I said that."

"Did you say it because you are jealous of him?"

James made that groaning growling sound again, and his hold on her tightened. "Was it that obvious?"

Emily stilled in his arms. Perhaps she should slap him across the face. "Maybe just a little."

James dropped his face onto her fur hat, and he continued to hold her. "You will tell me all about him over dinner," he said. "But not before."

Emily lifted her head to say that she would not, but his lips once again covered hers, and she was lost in his kiss.

CHAPTER 16

A PERPLEXING POT

eanwhile, in the Roman and Greek exhibit hall, British Museum

"Might I have a word with you?" Gabe asked as he came upon Mr. Harris in the exhibit hall featuring the Greek and Roman artifacts.

The portly gentleman's attention went to the vase in Gabe's arms before he directed his spectacled gaze on the archivist. "Will it take long? I've an appointment with a patron soon. One who helps pay your salary, I might add."

Gabe shook his head as he struggled to hide a wince. He hadn't mentioned his relationship to the Earl of Trenton to any of his co-workers and had decided it was better that way. "It's about Apollo," he said as he moved to a nearby pedestal. A number of short columns had been arranged to accommodate the new acquisitions from the current excavation.

Mr. Harris' eyes widened behind his glasses as Gabe lifted the amphora onto a column, centered it, and stepped back. "What about Apollo?" the curator asked as he stepped up to the Attic pot.

"He's been... *altered*. Prior to shipment," Gabe replied. "The papers that arrived with this vessel appear correct. They claim this is one of the finds from the dig happening in Laconia. But Mrs. Longworth believes Apollo was already... painted," he explained as he pointed to Apollo's hips. "But according to the arrangements the museum made with the archaeological team, no alterations were to occur prior to shipment."

"His wiggly bits?" Harris asked as he bent to study the amphora. He pulled a small magnifying glass from his waistcoat pocket and examined the decoration. After a moment, he frowned and then straightened. "You're quite sure the documents weren't switched with another artifact?"

Gabe nodded. "If they were, it happened prior to shipment. But the description matches perfectly to this piece. I can't imagine how any mix-up could have occurred."

Mr. Harris shook his balding head. "Perhaps it was painted this way prior to glazing," he suggested. "The original artist may have slipped and simply made a fig leaf where the wiggly bits would go."

Gabe marveled at how the curator kept a straight face as he said the words. "Mrs. Longworth claims it was painted after glazing. By someone who knew what they were doing," Gabe argued.

At the mention of Mrs. Longworth, Mr. Harris screwed up his face. "A real sourpuss, that one."

Gabe gave a start, surprised that he wasn't the only one who had been left with that impression of the potter. "But her restoration work is excellent," he said in her defense.

The curator's eyes rolled up before he agreed. "True, but expected given her training."

Glancing around to be sure no one was within earshot, Gabe asked, "At Wedgwood's, you mean?"

Mr. Harris shrugged. "That, too, I suppose," he allowed. When he noted Gabe's arched brow of surprise, he added, "She was Longworth's daughter." When Gabe continued to stare at him, he sighed. "Before he died a few years ago,

Frank Longworth was one of the factory's very best artisans," he explained. "Besides his skills as a potter, he was a master at painting. Did some fabulous pieces for the Countess of Torrington."

Gabe's eyes widened. He had met Adele Slater Worthington Grandby. Had even had a crush on her only daughter, Angelica, at one time. "Was the commission done... a long time ago?" he asked, thinking Frances Longworth couldn't be more than five-and-twenty years old now.

Could she?

Or perhaps the commissions had been done before Longworth died.

"Oh, I suppose it's been eight or ten years ago," Mr. Harris said with a shrug. "Such a shame. He had a penchant for styling his pieces after the shapes of these Greek vases," he said as he indicated the amphora and then motioned to a krater he had just finished putting on display. "Why, I'm told he could create one in just a few minutes from a round lump of clay—do a dozen in an hour, and then paint them with exactly the same pattern, glaze them, and have them out of the kiln for sale the next day."

Gabe recalled the vase that Mrs. Longworth had been making when he interrupted her. Although he had only seen her alterations on the ancient pottery, he wondered if she had her father's skills as a painter. "His loss must be keenly felt at Wedgwood's," he commented.

Mr. Harris shrugged. "I suppose, especially since his death was so sudden. I had the impression he was a fairly young man."

"So... you never met him?" Gabe asked.

"Never had the honor. I'm told he was a recluse of sorts. Worked in a room by himself. I suppose Mrs. Longworth takes after him in that regard," he muttered as he turned his attention back to the amphora.

Gabe thought of Mrs. Longworth and wondered if she

had always taken after her father in that regard. She didn't seem ill at ease when he was in her workroom—just annoyed by his presence. Almost as if she thought he was there to berate her, or find fault with her work.

Which couldn't be further from the truth.

When Gabe moved to lift the amphora from the pedestal, Harris waved him off. "Leave it. May as well start loading in the exhibits as they come in. You'll run out of storage room otherwise, given all those crates that just arrived."

Gabe blinked. "All those crates?" he repeated.

"Yes. Nine of them. Sent to *your* attention, in fact. They were delivered yesterday. I think they've all been opened."

Gabe's eyes darted to the side and then came to rest on the Apollo in front of him. "Oh, dear. I think I may know what happened," he breathed.

Harris lowered his glasses on his nose. "A mix-up, perhaps?" he hinted.

"Those nine crates were a donation from Mr. James Burroughs," Gabe explained, deciding not to add how James had acquired them. He still wasn't sure how he would establish providences given they'd been won in a game of whist.

Frowning, Harris removed his glasses completely. "You mean the banker?"

"I do. Have you met him?"

"A few days ago," Harris replied. "He mentioned the donation. Said you knew all about." He pointed to the amphorae. "So... you're thinking this may be one of *those* donations?"

Gabe nodded. "I'm fairly sure of it, but I'll know more when I discover if there is another just like this one from the dig." He was about to lift the Apollo, but Harris shook his head.

"Leave it," he said. "You can switch it out once you know for sure."

"But… there's no label."

"I'll have the calligrapher make the label based on the paperwork," Harris said quietly. "And in the meantime, I shall make some inquiries of our lead archaeologist."

"Lord Henley?" Although Gabe had never met the viscount personally, he knew the archaeologist had done a number of excavations to uncover Greek mosaics in Sicily and southern Italy. His small family accompanied him on his trips but were usually in London between assignments.

"Indeed. Henley is usually very fastidious, so if this is a pot from his dig, I can't imagine this is his doing," Harris remarked. "So let's hope this is just a mix-up."

"Indeed. Now where might I find those crates?" Gabe asked.

"In the back. Last I saw, they were all lined up in our section of the receiving area."

Gabe thought of bringing up his thoughts on the origins of pottery credited to Etruscans, but decided he would have to be put off when he pulled his timepiece from his waistcoat pocket. "Very good, sir. My apologies. I've kept you entirely too long, sir," he said.

The time was nearly half-past five o'clock. If she hadn't changed her mind, Mrs. Longworth would be joining him for dinner that evening, which meant he had a half-hour to find nine crates and their contents.

"Oh, think nothing of it. I'm always up for a good mystery," he commented. "Which I suppose is usually the case with these Greek artifacts. Good evening."

Gabe made his way back to the receiving area, nearly running in his haste to find the crates.

As Harris had described, there were nine of them lined up, each with their lid slightly ajar.

One crate was empty.

"Dammit," Gabe breathed as he checked the contents of

the others. He quickly ascertained that every pot was authentic, all probably from the Classical period.

He also discovered that every pot that might have featured a naked man or a partially clad female had been painted to hide any nudity.

Remembering James' comment about a "bombastic baron" having been the owner of the pots, he thought to simply write to the banker and ask if he might learn the man's name. Perhaps the baron would know who had done the painting, and from there, he could let Frances know.

About to return to his office, he paused and stared down through the opening of one of the volutes. Sure he could make out something at the bottom, he removed his top coat, reached into the volute, and felt a pasteboard card. Pulling it out, he held it close to a nearby lamp and frowned.

What the hell?

He went to the krater next to it and discovered a card at the bottom of it.

The same calling card.

Every pot contained the same calling card.

He was tempted to run back to the Apollo amphora to discover if it, too, contained a card, but a quick glance at his chronometer showed it was nearly six o'clock.

With any luck, Mrs. Longworth would be joining him for dinner.

CHAPTER 17

OF MISTRESSES AND MORE

*M*eanwhile, back in the gardens behind *Woodscastle*

Emily and James resumed their stroll through the empty gardens, the sun doing its best to warm the winter air. They didn't mention their second kiss, nor did they speak of what had initiated it. As with their first kiss, neither one had made the move to end it, exactly. Both had simply pulled away when it seemed appropriate to do so.

So when they came upon the stone bench that marked the end of one crushed granite path and the beginning of another, Emily was surprised when James announced, "I will not be taking a mistress."

She moved to take a seat on the bench. "Should I be offended you didn't make me an offer of *carte blanche*?" she asked, trying hard to keep her voice light.

He joined her on the bench, once again making that growling groaning sound. "You should be glad. My last mistress complained bitterly."

Emily inhaled sharply. She almost asked the obvious question, but James was quick to give her a quelling glance. "Not about *me*, exactly," he said. "But it seems her life as a mistress was rather lonely. She was never satisfied with anything I gave her—"

"Not even flowers?"

"I... I don't recall ever giving her flowers," he stammered.

"Well, there was your problem," Emily said, a grin teasing the corners of her lips.

"Do not tell me flowers would have been more welcome than baubles. She made it known that gifts of brooches, bracelets, and earbobs were expected," he said in his own defense.

"Well, they are if she has someplace to show them off, I suppose," Emily argued. "What's the fun in having expensive jewelry if you cannot wear it so others might see it?"

Well, she had him there. But Marjorie always seemed so pleased to receive jewelry, her attentions for a time more amorous than usual. But she also begged to be allowed to join him for Society entertainments. "I couldn't take her to *every* event I was invited to," James said. "It wouldn't have been appropriate."

"I suppose not." Emily sighed, but she noticed he still seemed perplexed. "Did you feel affection for her?"

"Never once. In fact, by the time I ended our contract, I found I didn't even like her."

Emily sobered, surprised to hear his comment. "So, she wasn't amenable?"

"Not in the least."

After a pause, Emily sighed. "May I inquire as to why you employed her to begin with?"

He had a hard time speaking of a matter a young woman had no business knowing anything about. And yet Emily's queries were forcing him to come to terms with what had happened in Bath. With why things had ended so badly with Marjorie.

"I didn't choose her, of course," he said.

Emily made the groaning growling sound she had heard him make so many times during their walk. "James!"

"What?"

"If you didn't choose her, then how did she become your mistress?"

He allowed a heavy sigh. "These... *arrangements* are not how you're imagining them," he explained. "I let a friend know I was in want of a mistress, and he made inquiries on my behalf with friends of a mistress, and then those friends let her know someone was interested in her services, and then a contract was drawn up, and we met and decided on a term —a length of time—and the other details—"

"Details?"

"Housing, a modiste, pin money," he said in a huff. "And then when all was in agreement, we signed the contract."

"And then you went to bed?"

James guffawed. "Eventually, but it didn't happen right away."

A look of disappointment crossed Emily's face. "It all sounds so much like a business transaction. As if she were a... a commodity."

"It is," James concurred, wincing at her use of the word *commodity*. "She was. An expensive one."

"So there is no regard for one another? No affection?"

He sucked in another lungful of cold air and let it out slowly. "Sometimes. I have friends who love their mistresses," he said. "My uncle James, in fact—"

"The Duke of Ariley?"

"Yes. He *loved* his mistress. Lily bore him two daughters before she died. He loves them dearly, as do I. Daisy and Diana are two of my favorite cousins."

When he didn't offer more, Emily said, "Go on."

"For the most part, it is just a business transaction."

"So, sexual favors for money?" Emily half-asked.

He grimaced. "It's no different from employing a prostitute, I suppose, except a mistress is exclusive. You don't share her with another man. She is beholden to you and only you for the term of the contract, and she is available when she is supposed to be."

"And you say more expensive?" Emily guessed.

He made that growling groaning sound and said, "Yes."

After a long moment, Emily sighed. "I wouldn't need the money."

"Emily!" He turned to find she had a huge grin on her face. "You cannot jest about such things. I cannot believe we're even having this conversation." He threw up his hands in exasperation.

"Except that you've enlightened me on a topic of which I had an interest in learning more about," she argued. After a moment, she added, "But more importantly, now I think you know."

He furrowed his brows. "Know what?"

She gave him a quelling glance. "That you may not want a family, but that you *do* want a wife."

James swallowed and almost made that groaning growling sound again. He managed to suppress it at the last minute. "How ever did you come to *that* conclusion?"

She dipped her head and then regarded him with a wan smile. "You may not miss your mistress' constant complaints—"

"I do not."

"—but I think you miss having a woman in your bed."

"We were always in hers," he countered.

"You miss having a woman."

He inhaled as if he intended to put voice to a protest, but then he sighed. "I just want a quiet life, Emily."

"With a wife," she insisted.

He winced again. "Can she be a quiet wife?"

A blush colored her face. "Must she be quiet in bed, too?"

"Emily!

Giggling, Emily stood up from the bench. "Come. It's time for luncheon, and you have a book to read."

Reminded of the book about commodities, James offered his arm. "You are not to tell anyone about this conversation," he warned in a low voice. "If your father or... *worse*, your brother Tom were to hear that I spoke with you on the topic of mistresses, he would have my hide." He almost asked that she not tell anyone about their kisses, either, but he assumed she would know better.

Emily dared a glance in his direction and struggled to maintain a sober expression. "I wouldn't dare," she replied, suppressing the urge to giggle. "Although I've never seen your hide, I rather imagine I would like it just the way it is."

"Emily!"

She grinned the entire time it took for them to walk to the back door.

CHAPTER 18

DINNER WITH A RELUCTANT GUEST

A few minutes later, at the museum

Gabe straightened the papers on his desk and was about to take his leave of his office when Frances Longworth appeared on the threshold. A navy wool redingote covered her day gown, and a muff hung from one hand while a reticule dangled from her wrist.

"Perfect timing," he remarked. "I was just about to come for you."

"I came to let you know that I have changed my mind," Frances said, her eyes not making contact with his. "I think it best if we're not seen together."

"I don't see how we can avoid it given we are colleagues and our work requires us to speak with one another," he argued.

She huffed. "That's not what I meant, and you know it," she said in a quiet voice, and then seemed to change her mind again. "Outside of the museum. After work. There could be talk."

Gabe swallowed. "Then we will not leave at exactly the same time," he replied with a shrug. "Besides, it's dark out, and I've just come from speaking with Mr. Harris and discovering something very curious. I should like to tell you about it."

The words had her eyes widening with interest, so Gabe continued. "There should be a town coach parked directly in front of Montagu House. Four horses, all with white blazes on their foreheads. Simply get in, and I will follow you in a moment."

Frances stepped back and looked left and right before giving him a nervous glance. "This is rather improper, Mr. Wellingham."

"First and foremost, Mrs. Longworth. I am a gentleman," Gabe said as he joined her at the door. "You have my promise I shall behave as such. We are merely two colleagues sharing an evening meal during which we shall be discussing ancient pottery."

Her eyes darted to one side. "You promise you will have me returned to my home when we are finished with dinner?"

"I promise," he said. "Now, dinner is usually served at seven, so it's best we be on our way."

Frances still looked as if she would bolt at any moment, but she made her way to the stairwell and disappeared from view as Gabe held his timepiece and watched the seconds tick by.

How was it a minute could go by so slowly?

When it was finally time, he pulled his door shut, hurried down the hall and up the steps, his shoes making faint tapping sounds on the marble-covered floor. He forced himself to slow down as he made his way down the front steps of Montagu House, a thought crossing his mind that in a few years, it would be replaced by the last phase of the museum's expansion. The entire front—and the doors by which patrons would enter the museum—would look like a Greek temple.

Had anyone foresaw a century ago that the mansion

would be unable to hold all the British Museum's vast collections?

As Gabe made his way, he was glad for the gas lights that illuminated the entry area, and for the pools of light from the gas lamps lining Great Russell Street that marked the road's edge.

The coach-and-four was where he expected it to be. His driver was quick to meet him at the curb, pulling open the door. When Gabe glanced in, he let out a sigh of disappointment at seeing it was empty. He turned to his driver. "Did you see a woman come out of the museum a minute ago? Dark coat?"

The driver nodded and then pointed up the street. "Would you be referring to her, sir? I saw her looking over the horses. Thought she might have mistook this for a hackney—"

"Yes, dammit," Gabe said, finally making out the silhouette of Frances Longworth's figure walking south. "Meet us up the street and then take us to Trenton House," he ordered before he took off at a run to catch up to the potter.

Frances had paused at the next corner, waving in an attempt to hail a hackney. Gabe was quick to join her, offering his arm and an apology. "Perhaps a minute was too long for me to wait," he said as the town coach halted next to where they stood. Breathless from his run, he opened the door and held out a hand to assist her.

Appearing nervous, Frances finally placed a gloved hand on his and stepped up and into the coach. Gabe followed, making sure to take the seat opposite. "I spoke with Mr. Harris about our mysterious amphora," he said in preamble.

Her gloved hands smoothing over the velvet squabs, Frances took a moment before responding. "I hardly think it's mysterious," she countered, her eyes adjusting to the dim light from the exterior lanterns that hung on either side of the coach windows. She took an experimental sniff, impressed when her nose didn't detect the typical odors of a hackney.

"He said Lord Henley is in charge of the dig. He's a top-notch archaeologist, although I think he is best known for his work in uncovering mosaics," Gabe explained. "Spent several seasons on a dig near Agrigento on Sicily unearthing as many mosaic floors as he could."

Frances listened intently. "He does not sound like one who would try his hand at painting" she remarked.

"Exactly," Gabe agreed. "Because... well, I haven't confirmed it just yet, but I believe the Apollo amphora was actually from a different collection. One that arrived yesterday."

"Go on."

"I had drinks with a couple of gentlemen a few nights ago, and one of them said he had some Greek vases he wished to donate to the museum."

"That's awfully generous of him."

"It was. He sent them to my attention, but I wasn't informed they had arrived until I spoke with Mr. Harris, not even an hour ago," he explained. "So I hurried down to the receiving area and found the nine crates. One of those crates is empty."

"Oh, dear," Frances said, already imagining what might have happened.

"Exactly. At Mr. Harris' encouragement, I left the altered Apollo amphora on a stand on the exhibit floor. I'll have to go back and check it when I return to the museum," he continued. "But I am fairly certain it is the one that came from that crate."

"No paperwork on the donated items, I suppose?" she guessed.

"Not exactly," he hedged, not yet ready to tell her about the calling cards. "So here's where it gets a bit tricky," he continued on a sigh. "Somewhere, there is an Apollo from the dig. I have the paperwork. The description, the measurements, everything exactly matches that of the amphora I showed you earlier today."

"You think someone pilfered the one from the dig?" she asked in alarm.

Gabe blinked. He had been so surprised at finding the calling cards, he hadn't even thought of the original Apollo as anything other than misplaced. "I'm not sure now," he breathed.

Attempting to relax into the comfortable squabs, Frances was relieved to hear Gabe speak only of museum business. "Could it have ended up at another museum, do you think?" She could see him shake his head in the dim light.

"How would I have the paperwork and not the pot?" he countered.

"So you're sure the original Apollo's crate arrived?" she asked.

"Well, the paperwork did."

"How much do you suppose that amphora is worth? Say, if someone did take it from the museum and were to try to sell it? What would they get for it?"

Gabe gave a shrug. "It's doubtful a private collector would part with such a piece for less than... a hundred pounds," he reasoned. "Perhaps more."

A hundred pounds sounded like a good deal of blunt to Frances—she barely made two times that much in a year—but she also knew a well-preserved Grecian vase could cost well over five-hundred pounds. "Unless the seller is very much in need of money," she countered.

Gabe's eyes widened. The potter was obviously familiar with the other side of owning antiquities. Collectors were as passionate as they were quirky in their choice of what to buy and what to sell. "True," he murmured. "Mr. Harris said he will make inquiries of Viscount Henley, in the event this

Apollo *is* from the dig site and not from the donor, so we should learn something in a month or two."

"And in the meantime? Will you keep the altered piece in your office?" She wished she could spend more time studying the paint that had been applied to it.

"Mr. Harris already has it on display in the area designated for recent acquisitions."

"Without knowing for sure from whence it came?" Frances asked in surprise.

"For now, he is trusting the providence that came with the original piece," Gabe replied with a shrug. "Which is all he can do, I suppose. More crates were expected to arrive from the *Sea Breeze* this afternoon, and I don't recall seeing them, but then I wasn't looking for them, either."

He furrowed a brow, just then remembering that Tom's vase had also arrived on the *Sea Breeze*—several days ago. Surely the crates would have already been off-loaded. He supposed it helped that Wellingham Imports had seen to Tom's shipment. They no doubt expedited the crate's transport from the ship.

Frances nodded her understanding. "I will be ready for whatever comes," she said.

About to remark on how smooth the coach ride was compared to a hackney, she was stunned when the coach came to a stuttering halt and Gabe said, "May I escort you to the door? Or would you prefer to go up alone? Barclay will admit you, of course."

Frances was about to ask who Barclay was—she hadn't thought about the number of servants who might work in his townhouse—but she shook her head. "You may escort me."

Gabe opened the coach door and stepped out even before the driver was down from his seat. He offered his hand. Frances placed her gloved hand on it and gingerly stepped down.

She cursed herself for not having paid attention to just

where the coach had been going once she was in it. They might have traveled to Cheapside or Chiswick, Cavendish Square or King Street.

A quick glance up and down the gas-lit street confirmed it was a tony neighborhood even before she fixed her gaze on the townhouse in front of her. The round light from a gas lantern illuminated a dark green door. A wrought iron fence lined the pavement, and flower boxes, now topped with mounds of snow, hung below the ground floor windows. Although the exterior of the four-story structure looked as if it were made of white marble, she knew it was merely stucco that had been painted to appear as such.

Gabe directed his attention on the driver. "I will require the coach again this evening to take my guest home, but not for a couple of hours," he said as he held out his arm.

"Very good, sir." The driver bowed and saw to the horses as Gabe escorted Frances to the door.

It opened before they were up the two steps in front of it. "Evening, Barclay. Mrs. Longworth, one of my colleagues at the museum, will be joining me for dinner this evening," Gabe said as he divested himself of his greatcoat. "If you could let cook know there will be two of us."

"Of course, sir."

Gabe turned to Frances, noticing she hadn't yet started to unbutton her redingote. "Barclay will see to your coat and muff."

"Oh, of course," she said, her attention on the elegant hall and what she could see beyond in the great hall. If this was Mr. Wellingham's residence, then perhaps archivists were paid far better than she had thought they were.

"Is there any correspondence?" Gabe asked of Barclay.

"Only a note delivered by a courier late this afternoon. I put it in the study for you, sir."

"Nothing from Italy?" The words were out before he could stop them. Gabe winced, knowing the butler would have mentioned it if there had been word from his parents. Besides, there hadn't been enough time since his family's departure for word of their arrival in the Kingdom of the Two Sicilies to make it back to England.

"No, sir. Should I have coffee and walnuts brought to the front salon?"

"Please do. We'll await dinner in there," Gabe responded.

"In the meantime, would Mrs. Longworth like the use of a ladies' retiring room? Your sister's bedchamber is available," Barclay offered.

Gabe turned to the potter, who looked more uncertain than he had ever seen her. "I should like to wash my hands."

Barclay waved for a housemaid to join them and murmured instructions to the servant. With a nervous glance at Gabe, Frances followed the maid up the stairs.

When she was out of earshot, Gabe turned to Barclay. "There will be no gossip in this household regarding Mrs. Longworth and her presence here," he stated. "She works in the museum doing pottery restoration, and we've some matters to discuss regarding some recent acquisitions."

"I'll see to it the servants are apprised, sir." Barclay hung up Frances' coat and muff and hurried through the great hall beyond the door.

Gabe headed to the study, eager to read the missive that had been delivered. Although the writing on the white envelope was familiar—his cousin Tom Grandby had penned Gabe's name and "Trenton House" in his masculine scrawl—the brief note from Tom contained therein was accompanied by a tightly folded letter addressed to Thomas Grandby and the members of the museum board.

Dear Gabe,

I expect to retrieve the enclosed letter from you when next we meet, but I wanted you to be aware of some Greek pottery coming your way from Viscount Henley. Seems he made arrangements with another archaeologist to acquire some Greek antiquities that were taken from our dig site many years ago.

Lord Darius—you will know him as Dr. Darius Jones— knew of the missing pottery and negotiated for their purchase on behalf of the museum. Be assured they are legitimate and will arrive with their providences. Let us hope you find them as intriguing as Lord Darius did. I would hate to learn he had paid too much.

Will I see you at White's tomorrow night? I am otherwise engaged this evening with matters having to do with a horse. As you know, horses are not my area of expertise, so I am consulting an expert on the subject.

Sincerely,

Tom

His curiosity piqued, Gabe wondered if this had anything to do with the information he sought regarding the Attic pottery featuring Apollo. He also wondered at the reference to a horse. His cousin didn't typically ride for pleasure or for exercise.

Had his cousin decided to invest in a race horse?

Wanting to be sure Frances wasn't left to fend for herself when she came back down the stairs, Gabe moved to the better-lit great hall to read the letter from Lord Henley. As Tom had described in his brief note, Lord Darius had indeed not only negotiated the purchase of some ten Attic amphorae and volute-kraters, but he had made sure the providences were secured as well.

The reason became clear as Gabe continued reading.

The pottery had originally been discovered by Lord Darius while he was excavating in the Peloponnese on behalf of an Italian archaeological concern more interested in Roman ruins and mosaics than the Greek artifacts found at the site.

Determined to save the Attic pieces from an ambivalent organization, Lord Darius had simply removed the pieces to the home of a private collector where they had apparently been on display for the past two decades.

Gabe rolled his eyes. 'The home of a private collector' was probably Lord Darius' villa—the one he shared with his wife on Sicily.

The sound of slippers on the stairs had Gabe tearing his attention from the letter to find Frances making her way down the last set of steps, her gaze attempting to take in all it could of the townhouse's interior.

Without her redingote and the oversized apron she always wore at work, it was apparent to Gabe that Frances possessed a pleasing figure beneath the orchid gown she wore. Trimmed in white vandyke lace, the bodice was almost too modest, though.

"Your sister's bedchamber is quite well-appointed," Frances remarked in a quiet voice, as if she feared being overheard.

"Since she is the only daughter in the family, I think Mother spared no expense," Gabe replied with a twinkle.

"Is she no longer in residence?"

Gabe joined Frances at the bottom of the stairs. "Anne is on her wedding trip. She married not two weeks ago, and most of her things have already been moved into her husband's house, so I expect she will no longer require the use of her bedchamber."

Frances continued to study the artifacts on display in the great hall, immediately recognizing several pieces of Wedgwood pottery mounted on caryatids located between doors to the various rooms.

Gabe noticed her attention had been captured by the large vase on the round table located in the middle of the hall. The vase held an arrangement of hot house flowers, the last of those that his mother had ordered before the family's departure for Rome. Despite having been delivered nearly a fortnight ago, they were still in relatively good shape for cut flowers.

"My mother's favorite vase," he commented. "She dearly loves flowers, so my father had it made for her."

Frances tore her gaze from the porcelain vase, her eyes widening. "Oh. At first I thought it..." She shook her head but then once again glanced at the vase. "But it cannot be."

"What is it?" Gabe asked, noting her curiosity.

She allowed a sigh. "I just thought it might be from my former employer's studio."

Gabe straightened, understanding the reason for her startlement. "It is." Then his eyes widened. "Did your... did your father create it, perhaps? I understand he was quite an artist."

Frances stared at him a moment. "Who told you that?"

Furrowing a brow at her query, Gabe said, "Mr. Harris."

Frances gave her head a shake. "Oh, of course." After another moment, she added, "Yes, I believe it was one of his."

Gabe couldn't help but notice how the words were said without emotion. Without conviction. Perhaps she no longer mourned her father. "I suppose it is a shock to see one of his creations on display a hundred and fifty miles from where it was made," he said as he led her to the front salon. His mind raced to remember if there were any Wedgwood pieces in there.

"Especially one that was commissioned, which is why I was surprised to see it here."

Gabe motioned for her to take a seat in a floral upholstered chair. Given the color of her gown, he thought she looked perfect among the blooms featured in the fabric.

Then the meaning of her words hit him.

Commissioned.

The vase had been commissioned by his father especially for his mother. The design included her favorite flowers painted in minute detail on a background of green leaves and finished in a pearlescent glaze.

He took the seat opposite Frances just as a footman appeared with the tray of coffee and a plate of walnuts.

Should he admit he was related to the Earl of Trenton? He hadn't told any of his co-workers at the museum that he was the bastard son of Gabriel Wellingham, but then no one would expect a museum employee to be related to an aristocrat.

For the time being, Gabe decided to use the arrival of the coffee as a means to change the subject. When the footman had taken his leave and Frances had seen to pouring the coffee, Gabe cleared his throat. "May I ask why it was you sought employment at the museum?"

Frances offered him a cup and seemed to struggle with how to respond. "There are not many businesses where I could work, Mr. Wellingham."

"Call me Gabe. We needn't be so formal when we are not at the museum," he said as he held out the plate of walnuts.

Taking a few of the nuts, Frances said, "Gabe seems far too informal."

Her host allowed a shrug. "Gabriel is my given name."

"Gabriel," she said, as if saying the word for the very first time. "You may call me Frances. As for my position, I applied when I learned the former restorer was let go. An agent acting on behalf of the museum paid a call on Mr. Wedgwood asking if he knew of anyone who could fill the position."

"So... he recommended you."

She shook her head. "He did not, in fact."

Gabe furrowed his brows and then his eyes widened with understanding. "He did not wish to lose you and your skills," he guessed.

"As a woman, I was paid less than the men he employed, so I believe he did not wish to lose a cheap employee," she said, just before she took a drink from her cup. She seemed to savor the flavor, and Gabe wondered if she was used to the stout and bitter coffee served at the corner coffee shops in London.

"That hardly seems fair. Especially considering your skills."

Frances visibly colored. "I appreciate you saying so, Mr... Gabriel," she stammered.

Hoping he finally had her trust, Gabe asked, "So, did you make the move to London because your father died?"

Her eyes darted towards the fireplace, her quick gaze taking in the urn that sat atop the mantel. "That, and... well, there were other reasons," she replied. "How is it you came to be hired as an archivist?"

Gabe thought her method of redirecting the conversation rather deft. He almost had her telling him more about herself. "I did my studies in the Classics at Cambridge," he replied. "I've always been especially interested in Ancient Greece, so I was eager to accept the position when I learned of it from Mr. Harris."

"So... you were not already a clerk?"

Gabe shook his head. "I only finished university last June."

The tinkle of a bell sounded from out in the hall, and Barclay appeared at the door. "Dinner is served, madam, sir," he announced.

Setting his cup on the tray, Gabe stood and offered his hand, much like he had seen his father do hundreds of times with his mother.

For the first time that evening, he was nervous.

CHAPTER 19

READING AND RUMINATING

Meanwhile, in the library at Woodscastle James was sure he had stared at the same page of the book, *Thoughts and details on the high and low prices of the last thirty years* by Thomas Tooke, for over an hour. Every time he was sure he was absorbing the information presented—alterations in currency, or the effects of war, or the effects of seasons on prices—he would find his mind wandering.

A mention of furs reminded him of Emily's muff, of how she had used it to slap his chest, in perhaps the most ineffectual beating he had taken in his entire life.

A reference to leather had him remembering her gloved hand as she pushed away the dead leaves and snow from the daffodil shoots. Of how he had thought that hand might slap him hard across the cheek for his insolence.

The discussion of domestic silk reminded him of how she had looked in her day gown as they ate their luncheon of a cream-based lobster soup and a cold collation of meats and cheese. Of how her dark blonde hair had looked like silk under the candle-lit chandelier.

And, finally, the chapter on gold had him wondering just how much Emily Grandby might be worth.

He rolled his eyes.

Now he was thinking of *her* as a commodity. Which, on the one hand, she was. She no doubt had a sizable dowry. A decent inheritance. On the other...

She was a young woman.

At times, she seemed entirely too happy—at his expense. But at others, she seemed quite sad. The light usually dancing in her green eyes would be extinguished for a time, whatever the cause a mystery to him.

Then he remembered that she had every right to be sad— she was grieving. She had been betrothed to a man who had died before they could wed.

For the first time, James wondered who the lucky man had been. Some young buck, no doubt. Someone who probably didn't deserve her. Someone who probably planned to use his new-found wealth to buy a house in town for her and a hunting lodge in the country where he would take his newly-hired mistress and gamble every night.

No wonder she had put voice to so many questions about mistresses that morning!

Jealousy of whomever had gained her agreement to marry had James feeling anger.

Anger on her behalf.

Emily Grandby deserved a husband who would hold her in high esteem. Who wouldn't employ a mistress or frequent brothels. Who would give her everything she wanted.

Because wouldn't she do the same for him?

The thought of a cup of tea had him thinking the simple drink seemed to make even the most perplexing situation less so. Perhaps he could ring for tea, and the butler would serve him. Or he could serve himself. How hard could it be to simply pour a cup of tea?

As is by magic, a cup of tea appeared on the desk in front

of him, its saucer decorated with two biscuits. He glanced up to find Emily poised to set down a plate on which was a slice of cake.

"Is it time for tea already?" he asked in surprise. Had she read his mind?

"Indeed, but I didn't mean to disturb you," she whispered.

"Oh, I don't mind in the least. This is not my favorite subject," he replied, referring to the book.

"That's quite obvious. I cannot imagine which topic has you looking as if you could strangle poor Mr. Tooke."

James attempted to school his features into a more pleasant expression. "It was not the author I was thinking about."

"Oh, dear. Have I not been quiet enough?"

"What?"

"I was quite sure I didn't make a sound whilst reading yesterday's *The Times,*" Emily said, her hand waving toward the library table. Illuminated by the late afternoon light from the windows above it, the newsheet was spread out on the oak surface.

James shook his head. "You didn't. I didn't even know you were in here," he added, wondering how he could have been so unaware of her presence.

At the moment, he was too aware of her. The light scent of her perfume wafted past his nostrils, and he had to resist the urge to follow it as he inhaled. Like a puppy, begging for attention and a scratch behind the ears.

"Well, that is the point of being quiet," Emily replied, making room for the cake plate by moving aside the ink pot. "So, if not the author and if not me, then who had you looking as if you wished to strangle them?"

James settled back in the desk chair and regarded her a moment. "Your betrothed."

Emily jerked backwards, the comment so unexpected she

had to take a moment to remember how to breathe. "Why would you be angry with *him*? He's not even alive."

Knowing immediately that he had erred, James dipped his head. He didn't even know why he was angry about what a dead man had done. "He took your virtue."

"As was his right."

"Did he tell you that?"

Emily inhaled sharply. "My mother did, if you must know." Well, she hadn't said it to her, exactly, but she had said as much to her oldest daughters just before they wed.

Emily's hands went to her hips. "You would do the same if you ever saw fit to take a wife," she accused.

His eyes widened, but James found he couldn't argue with her, at least on that point. His hands gripped the edge of the desk in front of him. "Did you love him?"

She once again reeled, shocked by his tone of voice and glad he wasn't standing over her. She wasn't about to let him cow her into feeling guilt. "I did. For a time. And you should be ashamed. He loved you and your sister more than you could know."

James stared at her. "Henry?" he finally said in disbelief. "My older brother?"

"Well, of course," she replied, her dismay apparent in how her body shook.

"Henry?"

"How could you not know?" she asked, tears escaping despite her efforts to keep them at bay.

"He was old enough to be your fa—"

"Don't! Don't you dare," she warned. "He was eight-and-thirty, so yes, he was older than me by fourteen years, but he told me he loved me back when I was... but twelve or thirteen."

"We were living in Switzerland."

"You'd returned from the Continent almost a decade before that," she argued.

James struggled with his memories of the time when his mother still lived. All three of her children had been born in Zurich. First Henry, who favored their mother and suffered the same maladies as her over the years.

Then came James, who took after his father in both looks and manner.

Then finally Sophia was born. Her features were the best of both of her parents, and she had been the one to suffer the most when their mother died. She'd only been seven at the time.

Despite their mother's death in 1810, Sophia's temperament was most like hers. Four years of finishing school in Geneva with her best friend, Emelia Comber, had prepared Sophia for their move to England in 1817.

James knew why his father had decided to return to British shores. The woman he had apparently loved long before he had married Bess Craven had just come out of mourning. Lord Andrew made sure his return to England coincided with when Jane Vandermeer Fitzpatrick would be available to marry.

His father had never told him the history of how it was he ended up married to the only daughter of Lord Craven and his wife, Persephone. But James had never thought to ask. His parents had always seemed happy together. When his mother had died, his father had mourned her and then remained a widower for eleven years—despite well-to-do widows throwing themselves in his path at every social function. A banker in the world's financial center was considered a good catch, after all.

"We moved to London in eighteen-seventeen."

"I know," Emily replied. "I was only three, but I remember it quite well because my father would take me to Merriweather Manor to show me the renovations that your father was seeing to at the time."

"I don't recall you back then," he argued.

"That's because you went off to Eton and Henry went to Cambridge."

"How do you remember that?"

"I have two older brothers who were at Eton the same time as you," she reminded him. "Roger and Tom."

He allowed a wan grin. "Of course. How could I forget?" he replied, wondering how he might compel her to say more. "How long... how long did Henry court you?" James stammered. Although he hadn't received many letters from Henry during his time in Bath, he couldn't recall any of them mentioning a woman of note. There was no mention of courtships. No mention of a young woman who might have caught his eye. James had begun to believe that Henry might be a molly, if only because he was aware of the same suspicions about him given his lack of a wife.

If Henry was in love with Emily, then why hadn't he said anything about his regard for the youngest Grandby daughter in those letters?

As if Emily could read his mind, she said, "He waited until my older sisters had all married. The day after Christina's wedding, he paid a call here at the house and asked if I might join him on a ride."

James gave a start. "But that was only last spring." Although he had been in Bath, he had received an invitation to the wedding breakfast.

"Yes," she acknowledged.

"And then he died..."

She sighed. "A few weeks later, yes."

He reached for her hand and then pulled her toward him until she was forced to sit on his lap. His arms wrapped around her middle as he settled his head into the crook of her shoulder. "I am sorry for your loss," he whispered.

"As I am for yours." Her arms settled around his shoulders, and she inhaled softly.

His scent was so different from Henry's. There were no

hints of sweet florals or citrus but rather musk and amber, wool and man.

The body against which she leaned was different, too. Solid, with a thick chest and broad shoulders. Arms that were long and strong, while Henry's had been far thinner. Hands with long, broad fingers. Not bony, like Henry's.

When James didn't offer a reply, Emily asked, "Did you come home for his burial? I don't recall seeing you there."

He nodded. "I barely made it. Word was delayed getting to me in Bath, and then I had to be back there a few days later, and so I wasn't able to stay at the house very long." He paused a moment. "A relief, really. I could not abide the huge crowd at the house."

"You never did like it when we were being noisy children."

"It wasn't that bad back then," he argued.

"I'm quite sure you spent your entire time in our company cringing."

"Oh, it was that obvious, was it?"

"Indeed. I remember thinking you would be one of those fathers who never stepped foot in the nursery. Your son would have to be sixteen or more before you would even make his acquaintance."

James pulled a face, about to argue. But he understood why she would say such a thing. "I could abide an hour or two of my own children, I should think," he claimed.

Emily's manner sobered. "You could?"

Ignoring the hurt he felt at hearing her response, his attention went to the ring that hung from the gold chain around her neck. "I should have known it was him." He reached up and grasped the ring between his thumb and forefinger. "But I didn't recognize the ring."

Now he did. He had one just like it up in his jewel box.

"He claimed it was an heirloom, but when I offered it to

Lady Andrew, she told me to keep it," Emily explained. "Do you know who it belonged to?"

"Our grandmother."

Emily made a sound of disbelief. "The Dowager Duchess of Ariley?"

James allowed a wan smile. "Margaret Merriweather herself," he acknowledged. "And you should keep it. She intended he give it to his wife upon a betrothal, and you do not want to cross the old crone."

"James!" she scolded.

"You have met her?" he half-asked.

Emily admitted that she had met the woman. "A long time ago, back when she still had rooms in Merriweather Manor," she said. "I think she liked me because I'm one of Gregory Grandby's children, and she always felt sorry for my father because his mother disappeared when he was four."

James arched a brow. "Did she really, though?" he asked, rather liking how comfortable it was to simply hold Emily in his lap. His legs were growing numb, though, and soon he would have to ask her to stand.

"Father said she married the butler and moved to London," Emily replied, a teasing grin lifting the corners of her mouth. "I love that story."

"Ah, yes, the butler story. Do you really believe it?"

Emily gave him a quelling glance. "We're speaking of *my* grandmother here," she reminded him. "And yes, I believe it because her husband, James Simpson—Henry's father, by the way—told it to us every time we asked him to. He always adored us. Claimed he adored all the children at Merriweather Manor when he was the head butler there.

"But then he fell in love with my grandmother, and when her first husband died, he finally told her," she explained. "He would do anything for her."

James inhaled slowly and reached up with a hand to cup the side of her face. "You inherited her beauty."

He watched as her face pinked with her blush, but then she quite suddenly stiffened in his hold. A moment later, and she was standing next to the desk with the plate of cake.

Humphrey entered the library a second later.

"Do you wish for me to bring more tea, my lady?"

Emily turned to regard the servant with an expression of sadness. "Oh, would you, Humphrey? I'm afraid I was not quick enough to serve, and now the pot has gone cold," she replied as she moved to where the butler had set the tea tray.

Humphrey nodded and retrieved the tray. "I'll return shortly."

James quickly downed his lukewarm tea, marveling at his hostess' quick thinking. And then he grunted as the pins and needles of a limb gone to sleep suffused his leg.

He had more questions for Emily, but they would have to wait until dinner.

CHAPTER 20

DINNER INTERRUPTED

ack in the salon at Trenton House
Frances seemed to think twice before she placed her hand on Gabe's and allowed him to help her to her feet. "Would you be eating alone if I had not agreed to join you?" she asked in a quiet voice.

Gabe nodded. "Indeed. In fact, I have been doing so for a fortnight." He led her to the dining room, relieved that Barclay had placed her at his right instead of the opposite end of the long table.

Frances barely noticed the table, her attention on the long sideboard. She struggled to keep her mouth closed as she boggled at the sight of several small porcelain pieces displayed on the thin, top shelf.

Her gaze settled on the tall vase in the center.

"Did your father make that vase?" Gabe asked as he pulled out her chair. His eyes darted sideways as his suspicion grew. "Or did you?"

Frances nearly fell into the chair at hearing his query. "I... I believe I did, actually."

Gabe settled himself in the carver, remembering how she had reacted to seeing the vase on the hall table.

Remembering how Mr. Harris had referred to Frances' father.

Frank Longworth.

Before he could put voice to another suspicion, a footman appeared and poured wine while another delivered bowls of soup. When they were once again alone, Gabe said, "Now will you tell me the truth? Are you, indeed, Frank Longworth?"

Frances' eyes darted to the vase on the sideboard and then back to Gabe. "Only if you explain how it is *you* are in possession of a vase that was commissioned by an *earl*," she challenged, proceeding to eat her soup as if she didn't expect he would reply.

"I assure you, *I* am not in possession of any vases, my lady."

She gave him a quelling glance, which he took to mean he had to continue with his explanation. "This townhouse is an entailed property of the Earl of Trenton. The Wedgwood pieces were all gifts from the earl to his wife. His countess," he replied. He held up a glass of white wine, as if in a toast.

Frances held up her own glass, studying the facets in the Waterford crystal before she took an experimental sip. Of course it was good wine. She wondered how an archivist could afford such an extravagance, and then realized it was probably the earl's wine. "He has excellent taste," she murmured, referring to both the wine and the ceramics.

Gabe nodded as he sampled a spoonful of soup. "The countess is quite taken with all of the them. In fact, she would be honored to make your acquaintance, should you be the one who is responsible for having created her favorite pieces."

Pausing before finishing the last of her soup, Frances stared at him. "The honor would be mutual."

Allowing a slight grin, Gabe said, "I shall see to it when she and the earl have returned from Italy."

A pair of footmen appeared with the next dinner course and Frances was prevented from asking the next obvious question—*how did he come to live in their house?*

When the servants had taken their leave of the dining room, Gabe pulled out the letter he had received from Tom Grandby. "A letter arrived today. Seems we can expect more Grecian pots, but not from the dig site."

Her attention going to the white parchment he held, Frances wondered why he used "we" when mentioning another shipment of pottery. "If not from the dig, then from where?" she asked as she boggled at the selection of foods that had been set before her.

"A private collector, apparently." He was relieved to see the footmen had placed the platters on the table and then taken their leave of the dining room.

As he waited for Frances to help herself before he filled his own plate, Gabe was heartened to hear her murmurs of appreciation. He wasn't surprised at seeing the slices of ham, but he was impressed by the number of side dishes. "Please be sure to take your fill," he encouraged. "Cook is used to making meals for five and sometimes forgets to scale down the portions."

"This is more food than I have seen in a very long time," Frances commented, tucking into the creamed vegetables.

"So... you are usually forced to eat alone as well?"

She straightened, tempted to tell him that her usual dinner companion could barely eat solid food. "I am," she replied. Her gaze went to the letter Gabe had set down on the corner of the table. "I believe you were about to tell me of your letter."

Gabe finished a bite of ham. "Have you ever heard of Dr. Darius Jones?"

Frances shook her head, but then her eyes widened. "The archaeologist? Isn't he the Duke of Westhaven's brother?" Although she had never paid much attention to aristocrats and their families, she had come to recognize the names of those who had discovered the works on display in the museum.

"Indeed. He is married to an Italian woman and usually lives in Sicily," Gabe replied. "He knew of ten pots that had been removed from Lord Henley's excavation site many years ago, and he saw to it they were placed into the hands of a private collector—"

"For profit?" she asked in horror.

Gabe shook his head. "I doubt it. Lord Darius married a woman of some fortune, and I can't imagine he has ever profited from his work on other digs." When she seemed satisfied by his response, he added, "When he learned of Lord Henley's dig, he arranged for the shipment of those ten pots on behalf of the museum."

Although it wasn't so unusual for a patron to buy something on behalf of the museum, Frances was intrigued that an antiquarian had done so. "That seems rather generous of him," she remarked. Her attention on her food, she secretly thrilled at eating her fill of ham. She never purchased the meat unless she could buy only a slice or two from a butcher. "How is it Lord Darius knows Viscount Henley?" she asked then, thinking the two men were at least two decades apart in age.

"They have worked on excavations together for years," Gabe replied. "Henley is an expert in Greek mosaics, and Dr. Jones tends to prefer Roman relics, so their paths cross frequently," he explained.

"So... does he say anything about the alteration to the Apollo pot?"

Gabe furrowed his brows before he turned his attention to the letter. "I don't know." He unfolded the missive and quickly scanned the letter, thinking he might have missed that particular detail. "He doesn't mention the Apollo amphora, but that doesn't surprise me. What you sorted in the coach may very well be true—that the Apollo for which I have a providence has been taken with the hope that the one donated by Mr. Burroughs would take its place."

"Mr. Burroughs?"

"James Burroughs. He just returned to London to take a position at the Bank of England," Gabe explained. "He was in Bath for many years before that."

"Would Mr. Burroughs know who made the alteration?" she asked.

He shook his head. "I cannot imagine it. He's not a collector—he prefers pots made in Stoke, in fact."

"Well, if he's not a collector, then how—?"

"He won them in a game of whist," Gabe stated. "I'm quite sure he doesn't recognize their value. Every one of those pots is from the Classical period. They're all two-thousand years old."

Frances nearly recoiled at hearing his claim. "So... whoever he won them from probably did the alteration," she reasoned, wishing she knew what had been used in the way of ink or paint.

"I don't know. I suppose he might have."

"Who is *he?*"

"'A bombastic baron', is how Burroughs described him," Gabe said as he pulled one of the calling cards from his pocket and placed it on the table. "Are you familiar with this man?" he asked, a sigh following his response.

Frances lifted the pasteboard card and blinked several times. "James Holland," she said. "Yes, he's from Stoke. He's a painter. He usually does landscapes and flowers, I believe. From where did you get this?"

Gabe pulled the others from his pocket, and she furrowed her brows as she looked at each one in turn. "They're all the same."

"There was one at the bottom of every one of those donated pots," Gabe said.

She leaned back in her chair. "Which means there should be one in the bottom of that altered Apollo pot, if it's from this same collection," she reasoned.

"Exactly."

"No wonder the alteration was so well done," she breathed. Then her eyes widened.

"What is it?"

"Mr. Holland paints with oils and watercolors," she said with some excitement. "So it's probable he did the alteration using either oil paint or watercolor."

"Ah, so now that you have your answer regarding the kind of paint that was used—"

"If it was watercolor, I may be able to remove it." A brilliant smile appeared before she sobered. "Unless, of course, it's better to leave the alteration in place."

Gabe dipped his head. "I'm almost afraid to tell you this, but…" He allowed a sigh.

"What is it?"

"Eight pots. Eight cards. That means there are probably alterations on every single one of those pots," he said with disgust.

"I'll take a look at them. See what's what before those others arrive from the *Sea Breeze*," she assured him. "You must have been so pleased to discover these were as old as the others that have been sent."

Reminded that Tom's Attic pot had been on the *Sea Breeze* and was from the same era, Gabe said, "Indeed. I was recently asked to appraise a pelike—a sort of pot-bellied amphora—"

"I know what a pelike is," Frances said with a prim grin.

"Oh, of course. Well, a private collector, Thomas Grandby, in fact, asked that I take a look at his newest acquisition." He paused, remembering his reaction to the art on the pelike.

"Did it come from Greece?"

"Yes. And it's a stunning piece, Frances. No doubt it's from the Classical period—probably 350 BCE. It depicts the birth of Aphrodite, so both Hermés and Poseidon are included, as is Eros," he explained. "I must say I look forward to the day when I might be able to acquire one of my own. Although there were probably several versions done back then, I would love a copy of his version," he said. "Every element of artwork on that pelike is exceptional."

Frances regarded him a moment, gratified to know he truly appreciated the ancient Greek works. "When do you suppose the next shipment of the museum's pots will arrive?"

"I expect we'll see them Monday," Gabe said. At her look of surprise, he added, "They were sent on the *Sea Breeze*, which is already in the docks in Wapping."

Furrowing a brow, Frances asked, "How it is you know that?"

"Mr. Grandby's pelike arrived on that same ship three... four days ago," Gabe replied.

Frances nodded her understanding and continued eating until she suddenly straightened. "Today is Saturday?" she half-asked.

"Yes."

"Oh, dear," she whispered, her eyes widening. "I apologize, Mr. Wellingham—"

"Gabe."

"—but I really must be going. I cannot believe I..." She set her napkin on the table and pushed her chair back.

Frowning, Gabe asked, "What is it?"

She was halfway up from her chair. "Mrs. Hough will be angry. I cannot be late on Saturdays," she said, as if her response was enough of an explanation.

Gabe stood up and hurried to the door. "Barclay!" he called out. "Let the driver know we must depart as quickly as possible."

"You needn't come with me," Frances said as she passed

him and nearly ran to the vestibule in her haste to take her leave.

Following her, Gabe said, "I will escort you, of course. I promised to see you home safely."

Barclay helped her into her redingote and offered her the muff once she had the buttons closed. Meanwhile, Gabe had helped himself to his own greatcoat and top hat. "Barclay, give our apologies to the cook. I'll be back later this evening."

"Very good, sir," the butler responded as he and Frances rushed out the front door and climbed into the town coach.

The driver opened the trap door in the ceiling. "Where to, sir?"

Gabe looked to Frances, who appeared as if she was about to cry. "Number nine, Kingly Street," she called up. "And please hurry."

When the driver acknowledged the address, the door closed and the town coach lurched into motion.

"Is Mrs. Hough your... your land lady?" Gabe guessed. Perhaps Frances lived in a boarding house, and there was a curfew.

But Frances shook her head. "I suppose you could call her that," she replied, her eyes tightly closed.

Gabe noted her distress and moved to her side of the coach, an arm wrapping around the back of her shoulders once he was settled in the squabs. "What is wrong?" he asked in a whisper. "Tell me, please." He pulled a handkerchief from his waistcoat pocket and offered it to her.

"The time. I must be there by eight o'clock on Saturdays, or..." She allowed the sentence to drift off and shook her head. Tears dripped from her cheeks, and she finally accepted the square of linen from him.

"You lose your room?"

She shook her head. "No."

"She calls the constable and claims you're a thief?"

Frances' mouth dropped open, and she turned to stare at him. "No!"

Gabe furrowed both brows. "She assesses an exorbitant fine for your tardiness?"

Frances sniffled. "Possibly." After another moment, she added, "Probably." Fresh tears fell, and Gabe felt her entire body shake as she sobbed.

Gabe gently tugged on her shoulder until her head finally dropped onto his shoulder. "This is my fault," he said, lowering his hand to rest atop hers. "I insisted you join me this evening. I will make it right, I promise."

"You needn't," she whispered, the words barely heard over the sound of the coach wheels as they sped east in Oxford Street. "I should have remembered that today was Saturday. Had it been any other day, my later arrival would not be so bad, but Saturdays..." A sob escaped.

"Please allow me to do what I can," he urged. "I rather enjoyed our dinner together, and I would be bereft if it was to be our last over this... whatever it is."

The coach took a sharp turn to the right and slowed to a stop. "That was quick," Frances said as she straightened, her voice filled with hope. "What time is it?"

Gabe struggled to read his pocket watch in the light of the coach lanterns. "It's only a quarter past eight," he replied.

The door opened and Frances shot out of the coach as if shot out of a cannon, a muted, "Oh, no, no, no," sounding as she made her exit.

Gabe struggled to get up and out of the squabs, hurrying after the potter as she ran up to the front door of a townhouse. A series of them were located on both sides of the street, and Gabe was sure he had paid a call on one of them at some point in the past.

Before he could remember any details, though, the door opened and an older woman appeared. Her arms crossed as she angled her head and regarded Frances with what Gabe could only describe as a sour expression. From somewhere inside, the cries of a baby made their way to his ears.

"I apologize, Mrs. Hough. I was detained—"

"You know the rules, Mrs. Longworth. No later than eight o'clock—"

"I have told you there might be times when I would not be able to leave my position—"

"He's been the absolute *worst* this evening. Howling for the past two hours. I cannot even hear myself *think*."

Frances pushed past the old crone and disappeared from view. That's when Mrs. Hough's attention went to Gabe. Her eyes narrowed. "Oh, I see how it is—"

"Good evening, Mrs. Hough. Allow me to introduce myself. I am Gabe Welling—"

"Oh, I will not, sir! Remove yourself from my sight. Rakes are not welcome in this neighborhood. "

Gabe's eyes widened in disbelief. "Madam, I'll have you know I am not a rake. I am a gentleman, and I am employed by the British Museum as an archivist," he stated. "Mrs. Longworth's tardiness is entirely my fault, and you shall not hold it against—"

"*You* will not tell me what to do, and I do not care who you are."

Frances reappeared carrying a wrapped bundle, and a cloth bag hung from one arm. "He's soaking wet," she complained. "When was the last time you changed his nappy?"

Mrs. Hough's expression darkened, and Gabe watched in horror as she turned her wrath on Frances. "I'm quite sure I cannot recall. His incessant crying has been most *vexing*."

Frances recoiled, but then furrowed her brows. "Did you... did you feed him? I was sure I left enough for both his luncheon and his dinner."

"Leave this instant, or I shall never again look after him," Mrs. Hough threatened. "If I'd any idea you were a... a *whore,* I would never have agreed to take him in the first place."

Gabe was sure he had never seen Frances look so shocked, almost as if the hag had bodily struck her. "You apologize this instant for your slanderous comment," he demanded. "Mrs. Longworth is an expert in her field, gainfully employed at the British Museum."

"You will not tell *me* what to do," the crone spat out.

Determined she no longer be the target of Mrs. Hough's wrath, Gabe stepped forward and reached for Frances' hand. "Come. Let us be going. Mrs. Hough, be assured Mrs. Longworth will never again darken your door, and should I ever come across you again, you will suffer the cut direct," he warned.

Frances whispered a hoarse, "No!" even as he pulled her toward the coach. The light from behind them disappeared as the door was slammed shut, and the whimpers from the bundle Frances clutched increased to wails.

Gabe opened the coach door and did his best to help Frances into the coach. When he caught sight of her teary eyes, he knew why it was she had trouble making her way into the conveyance. He turned his attention up to the driver. "Tell me, Mr. Watkins, do you suppose your wife is still up and about?"

The driver nodded. "Of course. Much as she'd like our two to be settled in bed, she reads to 'em 'til eight... sometimes nine at night. And the Thompson babe is probably still awake as well."

Gabe allowed a sigh of relief. "Then we shall head back to Trenton House."

"Very good, sir."

Once Gabe was settled in the seat opposite Frances, the coach lurched into motion. His gaze settled briefly on the townhouse at Number Three, and he realized why it was he recognized the street. His cousin, Thomas Wellingham, lived there with his wife, Emma. On the other side of the street was the largest town home, that of Tom Grandby's grandmother, Sophia Simpson and her second husband, Henry.

His anger at Mrs. Hough having abated somewhat, Gabe took a deep breath and regarded Frances for a moment. Tears streamed down her cheeks, but the baby's cries had stopped. When he heard the tell-tale sounds of nursing, he understood why.

"You will not take that baby back to that crone," he hissed vehemently.

Frances let out a huff, obviously prepared for his attempt at chivalry. "And, where, pray tell, will I take him? Mrs. Hough was the only one I could find to look—"

"He can stay at my house. Mrs. Watkins would gladly look after him."

Frances gave a shake of her head. "I will not prevail upon someone I do not know—"

"I will introduce you. Tonight. She is quite qualified."

"Qualified?"

"She was my sister's nurse and now sees to a couple of the servants' children as well as her own," he explained, aware that the fight seemed to have gone out of his colleague. "Your babe's nappy will be changed, and he will be fed whenever he is hungry."

"At what cost?" she asked in a whisper. "I gave Mrs. Hough a pound a week—"

"Wot?!"

"I was desperate, Mr. Wellingham."

"Gabe, please," he corrected her. "I will not begin to guess how it is you can afford such an extravagance—"

"Must I remind you I have a position?" she countered, just before she seemed to crumple. Her head dropped back on her shoulders, and when she turned her attention back on him, she seemed to have regained her composure. "I live cheaply so that he can be well cared for."

Gabe wasn't about to argue that Mrs. Hough's care didn't seem *well* by any stretch of his imagination. "His care under Mrs. Watkins will be far better, and the cost much less," he said.

"How much less?"

Not expecting to have to quote an amount, Gabe lifted a shoulder. "You'll not have to pay more than a pound a *month*."

Frances gasped. "How... how can that be?"

"Mrs. Watkins is already employed at the house to see to the other children. We're simply adding one more, and she adores babies." In all the hubbub, he hadn't thought to wonder why it was Frances had a baby. He was sure she had never been married, but now he wondered if she was a widow. He angled his head to one side. "What is his name?"

Frances sniffled. "David."

"Was he named for his father?"

She shook her head. "He... he would have wanted nothing to do with me if I told him I was with child, so I..." She allowed the sentence to trail off and then sighed as fresh tears trickled down her cheeks.

His breath held a moment, Gabe swallowed. Her babe was a bastard. "He is why you left Staffordshire." The words were meant to come out as a question.

"His father threatened to tell everyone at the studio that I was a whore if I so much as hinted I was really Frank Long-worth. And I would have lost my position if anyone had learned about the babe." She seemed about to sob, and Gabe quickly moved to sit next to her.

"The worst of it was that I only had the position because I had to agree to... to... allow him..." The unmistakable keening of a woman in distress had Gabe wrapping his arm around her shoulders to pull her closer.

"Shh," he whispered as he felt her relax into his hold. He looked down to see two dark eyes regarding him with interest. Given the size of the bundle and the features he could make out in the dim light, he figured the babe was no older than six or seven months.

He would have to be, since Frances wouldn't have still been pregnant when she started at the museum.

Then he remembered her enormous apron and thought perhaps she could have hidden her condition behind it.

"He's quite a handsome little man. How old is he?"

"I gave birth to him in June, so... seven months, I suppose."

"So... you took some time off?" He hadn't yet been hired at the museum back then. He was still in Cambridge.

"Of course, not," she replied, sniffling.

Gabe jerked. "How is that... possible?"

She shook her head. "I brought him in a basket to work with me. I hid him under a blanket. He rarely cried. But after a couple of months, he was simply too hard to hide, so that is when I began paying Mrs. Hough extra to care for him," she explained. She suddenly glanced out the window. "Where...? Where are we going?"

"Back to my house."

"But... I need to go home—"

"Must you?"

Frances turned to stare at him. "You are doing this with the expectation of something in return. I understand," she whispered.

"I am not," he argued. "I merely wish to make up for what happened earlier. You will spend the night in a guest bedchamber, and David will be seen to by Mrs. Watkins."

"And in the morning?"

He hesitated before saying, "Breakfast. A rather elaborate affair on Sunday mornings. Not to be missed. And then... I shall see to it you are returned to your home." It was then he realized that they had just been to her home. Mrs. Hough wasn't just a caretaker for her baby, she was also her landlord.

The thought of taking her back to the old crone's townhouse had Gabe wincing.

"And if I want to go home tonight? Now?" she countered.

"Do you?"

Frances jerked in his hold, her gaze going to the parade of townhouses that passed by beyond the glass windows. After a time, she realized they were in Mayfair. She saw the sign for Curzon Street and knew then they were close to Hyde Park.

The thought of a sumptuous breakfast after tonight's dinner had her deciding she would accept his offer of hospitality. But only for the one night. Tomorrow was Sunday. Once Mr. Watkins took her home in the morning, she would have the entire day to spend with her son. Mrs. Hough would probably be away at church for half the day. "This is very improper."

Gabe sighed. "I suppose it could be construed as such, but we will know the truth, as will the servants. You are simply a guest. A colleague in need of a place to stay."

"You will not expect me to share your bed?"

"Of course not."

"And you will not expect me to share mine?"

Gabe winced. The mere question had him wishing he wasn't so damned honorable. "As I tried to explain to Mrs. Hough, I am a gentleman," he claimed. "As much as I wish I could share your bed—and I do because... I have no idea why—I have no expectation you will extend an invitation for me to do so. Therefore, I intend to spend the night in my bedchamber. Alone."

Frances stared at him, shocked by his claim that he wished he could share her bed. After everything that had happened this evening, and given what he had just learned about her, the very last thing she expected was for Gabe Wellingham to desire her.

CHAPTER 21
ABOUT A RING

*M**eanwhile, in the dining room at Woodscastle*
James had thought to wait for the dinner bell to chime before going into the long dining room at Woodscastle, but curiosity had him perusing the sideboard and other furnishings as he waited for Emily to join him.

He had changed into dinner clothes, glad for the excuse to set aside the book he had been studying most of the day. The mindless act of undressing and dressing had allowed him to simply think.

Without conscious thought, images of Emily filled his mind's eye. For the past few days, he found he had become obsessed with her.

He wondered what she was doing. What she was thinking. What she liked and disliked. What did she think of him? And why the hell had she agreed to become Henry's wife?

The thought reminded him that she had never said why it was she had agreed to marry Henry. Just that Henry had claimed to love her.

And why had his brother thought it necessary to wait until all the other Grandby girls were married before calling on Emily? Wasn't that an old-fashioned idea?

He stared at a porcelain figurine atop the sideboard, one positioned next to a vase featuring a feminine shape. The gentle curves of its silhouette had him wondering if Emily's were similar. He knew she had the slender waist and a generous bosom—her dinner gowns emphasized her charms—but her hips were always hidden beneath the bell skirts that had become so popular this past decade.

Damn the French.

"Do you frown at it because it displeases you? Or because you're thinking of something else?"

James turned and helped himself to Emily's hand. He raised it to his lips and kissed the back of the silk glove. "I was cursing the French," he admitted.

"Oh." She dipped a curtsy. "Liquor? Or fashions?"

"Why, fashions, yes, if you must know." His gaze dropped to her skirt—this one wasn't nearly as wide as some of the others she had been wearing. The shimmering peacock blue silk draped in soft folds from her waist—and he allowed a brilliant smile when the silhouette of one of her thighs was briefly in evidence. The same fabric sheathed her bodice, but was cut low enough to display the tops of her breasts.

The only item that appeared out of place was the gold ring that hung on the chain around her neck. The sapphire stone was at odds with the greener blue of the silk.

"You look stunning."

Emily couldn't hide her first reaction. "Now you have me suspicious," she warned as she moved to take her seat at the table.

"Rightly so. I was trying to imagine the shape of your bum."

She sat down. Hard. "If your intention was to shock me, Mr. Burroughs, you have managed to do so," she replied, barely able to suppress a grin.

James joined her at the table. "I cannot believe I just said that out loud," he murmured. "You must think me mad."

Pretending she had already come to that conclusion, Emily waved for a footman to see to the first course. "Really, James. You need only ask."

"You're joking," he accused, after a very long pause.

"You can ask me anything. At this point in my life, nothing except for what you just said would shock me," she claimed.

"Why did you agree to marry Henry?" The words poured out so quickly, even he was shocked at hearing them.

Given the footman was in the process of pouring wines, Emily was saved from having to respond right away.

After Humphrey appeared with the first course of soup and set it down, she said, "He claimed he had loved me for a very long time. And I felt affection for him. At the time," she quickly qualified. She turned her attention on her soup, knowing James would want to know more. Before she had finished her second spoonful, he cleared his throat.

"*At the time*," he repeated. "So... what happened that had you changing your mind?"

Emily was almost relieved at hearing the invitation to tell her side of it. No one else had asked, but then she had been very careful about keeping her betrothal a secret. "Lady Andrew paid a call. She asked if Henry had said anything about needing money. A loan."

James dropped his spoon into his soup and stared at her. "For what?"

Although she had been determined to remain calm should James ask anything more about his brother, Emily found she was torn about telling him what she knew. The man was dead now. But perhaps Henry had left a mess, and James, or worse, their father, would discover it the hard way.

"Gambling debts."

James stared at her, as if she might have grown horns or sprouted a tail. "Henry?" The name was said so softly, Emily barely heard it.

"Last winter, he went to Lady Andrew and told her he was in need of some funds. Wondered if she might be of help because he didn't want to bother your father at the bank."

"Go on," James said, his mind racing. As far as he knew, Henry wasn't a gambler. He played whist on occasion, but only at house parties.

As far as he knew.

"She spent some time in conversation with him in an effort to learn what might have happened. She claimed he was given a generous allowance—"

"He was. We both were," James said.

"But he finally admitted he had been duped in a card game and had lost it. And in his attempt to earn it back, he lost more than he had with him."

James inhaled slowly, knowing what she described was probably just the tip of a much larger problem. "Let me guess. It was not just the one time."

Emily shook her head. "I had already agreed to marry him, but I hadn't yet told my father—he and Tom were up north for some railroad negotiations or some such—so no arrangements had been made as to my dowry."

"Thank the gods."

"And, then, within the next week, Henry came down with what he thought was a head cold. Another week, and he was bedridden. It was as if he had given up on living. He couldn't get money from Lady Andrew—she refused him outright when she learned why he needed it—and I only considered it because I didn't know the truth of just why he needed it until she told me."

James listened intently, his gaze on how her hand gripped the ring that hung between her breasts.

"What did you do?"

Emily pinched her lips together and tugged hard on the chain that held the ring. The clasp gave way, and she allowed the ring and chain to fall onto the tablecloth. "It's paste," she said in a whisper.

Reaching for the ring as if it was a snake intent on biting him, James unthreaded it from the chain and examined it closely. "Pardon my curse, but it's a damned good copy," he murmured, noting the sapphire's color and the way the diamonds that surrounded it shimmered under the dining room chandelier. The gold band even looked as if it was made of gold.

"I had it made to replace the real one," Emily said, wiping a tear from her cheek. "While I still had the real one."

James dropped the ring. "What happened to the real one?"

Emily struggled to take a breath. "Forgive me. I knew it was your grandmother's, but I would have been satisfied wearing the copy, so I pawned it, and then I had a courier deliver the money to the man who threatened to kill Henry," she explained. "In the end, it didn't matter. He died a few days later."

"Oh, my God, Emily," James said in a whisper. He lifted the ring again. "Are you quite sure you pawned the real one and not the copy?"

Emily couldn't understand why James seemed so interested in the ring. "I've just told you that your brother was in debt due to gambling. I'm quite sure the money from the ring was enough to cover his debt to the one man, but what if he owed money to others? I have worried all this time that someone would come for your father or for you."

"No doubt there were others who held markers, but Henry is dead. Anyone holding a marker wouldn't dare try to collect from my father. He's a duke's son. A duke's brother."

"What if they come for you?"

James allowed a shrug. "I'm a duke's grandson. A duke's nephew," he reminded her. "His debt is not mine."

Emily straightened in her chair. "Oh. Well, that's a

relief," she replied, heartened by his response. She returned her attention to her soup, but finding it cold, she set down her spoon.

"Your chain is broken," James said as he lifted the end of the jewelry to find a link had pulled open right next to the clasp. "Should I have it repaired for you?"

Allowing a wan grin, Emily replied, "I will never wear it again."

James nodded, understanding just then that she had worn the ring for a far different reason than sentimentality. "Then I shall buy you a new one. One that will not make you feel as if you are wearing an anchor about your neck."

The light returned to her eyes. "You needn't do that. You shouldn't do that."

"But if I did?" he prompted.

Emily considered the ramifications. "I would wear it."

"And if someone asked you where you got it?"

A brilliant smile appeared. "I would tell them I received it as a gift from a man who wished to know the shape of my bum."

James' eyes widened. "You wouldn't dare!"

Emily giggled in delight. "Wouldn't I?"

Something deep inside James took a tumble, and he sobered slightly. "I suppose you would."

He was just about to lean over and kiss her, but the footman reappeared with the next course, and James was left to imagine far more than the shape of her bottom.

CHAPTER 22

A MOVE IS MADE

*B*ack at Trenton House

As Gabe and Frances shed their coats in the vestibule of Trenton House—an exercise that required Gabe hold onto David for a few moments while Frances not only removed her redingote but also surreptitiously buttoned up the front of her bodice—he apprised Barclay of the situation. "Please see to it a guest bedchamber is made ready for Mrs. Longworth," he instructed. "I fear her living situation has been put into peril this evening."

As was usual for the staid butler, Barclay managed to hide his alarm. "The Peach Room on the second floor has been made ready, sir."

Gabe blinked, wondering how Barclay had known they would be in need of it this evening. "Your efficiency is to be commended," he said dryly.

The butler looked as if he wished to say more, but instead he reminded them that they hadn't finished their dinners. "Cook insisted that the footmen leave the place settings, but he has returned the dishes to a warm oven should you wish to continue your dinner. There is still the dessert, as well."

Frances' eyes widened in surprise. When Gabe looked to

her for her opinion, she said, "I feel awful. He has gone to all this trouble for us?"

Gabe shrugged. "He is a good cook," he remarked. "And you needn't feel awful about it. You are my guest."

Appearing uncertain, Frances turned her gaze onto the bundle she held. "Let me see to my son first," she pleaded.

Giving the sleepy babe a chuck beneath his chin, Gabe said, "Of course. I'll take you up to the nursery straight away."

He escorted Frances up the three flights to the nursery. As Gabe expected, Mrs. Watkins welcomed David as if he were one of her own, despite his soaked gown and nappies.

"Why, he's an adorable babe," the older servant said in her thick Scottish brogue. "Six months, is he?"

Frances knew then the woman had children of her own. "I really need to bathe him," she replied. "I'm afraid the woman who looks after him whilst I am at the museum was not amenable to doing so this evening."

Mrs. Watkins furrowed a brow. "If you're in search of a new nanny, I would certainly be willing to see to him," she offered. "Mine are older now, and they no longer require me hold 'em much. Me husband says I've spoiled 'em rotten, seein' as how I don't like it when they cry. I like to hold 'em when they're upset. Figure they will grow up to have more compassion," she explained. "Which is why I like working here, because the—"

"Mrs. Watkins was my sister's nurse," Gabe interrupted.

"And your younger brother's," Mrs. Watkins reminded him. She turned her attention back to Frances. "That was before I had my own." She lowered her gaze onto David. "I'll just take him into the bathing chamber and see to it he has a bath before I put him into a fresh gown and nappies."

"You will bathe him?"

Mrs. Watkins blinked. "Well, of course. And I'll put him down for the night. There's a bassinet there in the corner," she said as she pointed to a white wicker basket suspended from a framework that allowed it to rock. Above it was a canopy of white ruched tulle.

"It's beautiful," Frances breathed as she moved to inspect the basket. "Far too fine for my son," she added in a whisper.

Mrs. Watkins joined her. "Nonsense. Babies deserve the best," she said quietly. "Seeing as how they don't always get it the rest of their lives."

Frances boggled at hearing the older woman's words. "Bless you," she murmured.

Mrs. Watkins blushed. "Now I'm sure you have better things to be talkin' about than babes. Why, the entire household is all in a twitter about hosting an artist this evening. I do hope you can stay. The house has been so quiet since his—"

"Thank you, Mrs. Watkins," Gabe interrupted. "We still have to finish our dinners this evening before Mrs. Longworth can retire to the Peach Room."

Mrs. Watkins' eyes widened. "The Peach Room? Why, that's the best guest bedchamber in—"

"Exactly," Gabe interrupted again. "We'll leave you to bathing David now," he added. "And I'm sure Mrs. Longworth will come back to check on her son before she retires for the evening."

"Oh, I will," Frances agreed.

"Good night, Mrs. Watkins," Gabe said as he offered his arm to Frances.

Frances took one last look at her son before she allowed Gabe to lead her from the nursery. "She seems very competent."

"She is," Gabe agreed as they made their way down the stairs. "Would you like to refresh yourself before we resume dinner? I know, I would."

"Could I?" she replied, just as they paused before a door on the second floor.

"Indeed. Mrs. Longworth, may I present the Peach Room?" Gabe teased as he opened the bedchamber door.

The room, lit with two gas lamps, was decorated in soft greens, from the Aubusson carpet to the velvet drapes that covered the two windows on either side of the dressing table. A deep green velvet counterpane covered the bed, and a green canopy draped like a cone from the ceiling overhead. Green silk moire covered the walls. At the head of the bed was a painting that gave the room its name, a still life of a bowl of peaches.

Frances let out a nervous giggle in her attempt to take it all in, and Gabe struggled to keep a straight face. "Do you think you can be comfortable here this evening?" he asked.

She turned and gave him a brilliant smile. "I do believe I can."

"Good. But should you need anything, please know that I am just..." he pointed to his right. "In the bedchamber next door." As he half-expected, Frances arched a brow in suspicion. "The two rooms are not directly connected," he quickly added.

Wondering at the sense of disappointment she felt just then, Frances did her best to appear shocked that he would even say such a thing. She did another quick glance around the room, searching for a pitcher of water. "Where is the nearest bathing chamber?" she asked. "I should like to wash my hands."

Gabe led her further into the room, and he pointed to a door near the corner. "Right through there. There are two pumps for water. You'll find the hot water—"

"Hot water?" Frances repeated, her eyes wide.

Angling his head back and forth, Gabe said, "It's a bit of an experiment really. Once we had gas brought into the house, Father saw to having a line brought in here so water in the bathtub could be heated directly. From there, the water can be diverted to the washing bowl, but you have to remember to put a plug into the drain hole, or it just..." He stopped when he noted how she stared at him. "I can show you, if you'd like."

Frances blinked. "Is there water in the bathtub... all the time?"

It was Gabe's turn to blink. "Oh, no," he said, understanding her query. "But the valve for the gas has to be turned, and then the flame for the gas has to be lit for the water in the tub to heat. A maid probably saw to it already."

"Perhaps you should show me," she said, peeking around the edge of the door to discover a rather large room lined in glazed tiles. A bathtub sat along one wall where a series of pipes snaked along the floor where it met the wall.

One pump fed water into the tub, and from there, into the pipe that went off to a pair of pumps mounted on the edge of a large bowl that was sitting atop a wooden stand. The stand also supported an oval mirror.

She could see tiny flames coming from beneath the raised tub and wondered how the entire floor wasn't on fire.

She was about to put voice to her query when Gabe said, "The gas burns at a lower temperature than wood, and there is a layer of concrete beneath the tub to keep the flames away from the floor."

"But it's not lit all the time?" Frances half-asked.

He shook his head. "No. Once you no longer need hot water, you simple turn this valve..." he moved to the end of the tub... "to the left, and then the gas is turned off," he continued as he showed her a contraption that was mounted at one end of the tub. "A maid will see to it it's turned on in the morning." He moved to the bowl and motioned to the pumps. "You might have to pump two or three times for the hot water to start coming through," he explained. Then he motioned to the hole in the bottom of the bowl and a round disc attached to a small handle. "Use this plug to stop the water from draining away."

Frances regarded the plug and then the drain hole. "But... where does the water go when the plug is pulled?"

Gabe furrowed a brow. "To the Thames, I believe. At least, eventually." When he noted her look of chagrin, he realized she was asking where the water went inside the house. "It goes into a pipe..." He pointed to the floor and then to the wall "...that hooks into another larger pipe that has several other pipes hooked into it, and that pipe drains into an underground pipe that leads to the Thames."

Frances seemed impressed but then asked, "Was the house built with all those... pipes?"

Grinning, Gabe sighed. "My mother would have preferred it, but no. The house is far older than modern plumbing, I'm afraid," he said with a shake of his head. "We weren't even living here when Father arranged to have the pipes installed. Then new interior walls had to be built to hide the pipes. They run in the outside walls of the house, so every room with pipes was made a few inches smaller once the renovation was complete."

Frances quickly surveyed the network of piping. "Is it like this for all the bathing chambers? How many are there?"

Gabe nodded. "There are eight that I know of, plus the pipes that were added for the kitchens at the back of the house."

"So... the servants don't have these in their chambers." She hadn't meant the comment to sound like an accusation, but she immediately dipped her head and appeared about to apologize.

"Actually, there are two up on the third floor. One for the men and one for the women," Gabe said, gratified when her eyes widened in wonder. "Father didn't think it would be very efficient to force the servants to haul water up there, and once the system was installed, it meant the chamber off the kitchens could be used exclusively by the stable boy and the groom. Gave them a place to sleep as well as to bathe. Which meant there was more room in the stables for hay. ”

"How civilized," Frances said as she studied the pumps that stood over the large porcelain bowl.

"Go on. Give it a go," Gabe encouraged.

Frances looked uncertain. "Do I plug the hole now? Or wait until the hot water comes?"

"I like to plug it first. Sometimes the hot water is hotter than I like, so the mix of tepid water with the hot is perfect."

Popping the plug into place, Frances lifted the hot water pump handle and pulled it down. Once she had done it twice, water began to fill the bowl. On the next pump, she could see steam coming from the water. "Oh!" she said in amazement. "It's working."

She lifted and lowered the pump handle one more time and stepped back to watch as water half-filled the bowl. A smile lit her face. "I shall be terribly spoiled after this night," she said with a giggle, helping herself to a ball of soap. She dunked her hands into the warm water and allowed a sigh.

Gabe watched her, a smile appearing at seeing her delight and hearing her giggle. At some point, he had thought her far older than him—perhaps thirty. But now, with her face lit by the flames of a candle lamp and her tears long gone, he thought she might be his age. He was about to ask, but she was drying her hands on a linen while marveling at the feel of the soft fabric.

"Would you like to use the water?" she asked. "It seems a shame to drain it when I've hardly..."

She wasn't able to finish the sentence. Gabe had closed the distance between them in a single step and covered her lips with his. One hand moved to cup her cheek and the other held onto her shoulder, as if he needed her for support.

Despite her initial surprise, Frances returned the kiss in equal measure. How long had she wanted him to repeat what he had done that day in the workroom? How many times had she relived that all-consuming kiss? Imagined it just before she fell asleep at night and woke up to having dreamed about it the night before?

When Gabe finally pulled away, he left his forehead resting against hers. "I have wanted to do that all night," he whispered, his eyes still closed.

"I cannot imagine why," Frances replied, her eyes wide open. "I've done nothing but cause you trouble—"

"My lady, saving your son from that poor excuse of a nanny was no trouble. I was glad to do it." His eyes opened slowly, and then he blinked. "I do hope you... you don't *live* in her house."

Frances allowed a sigh. "It is a boarding house, and yes, I have a room there," she admitted, deciding he would eventually discover where she lived.

Gabe pulled her into his arms. "You cannot go back there—"

"My things are there. Clothes, and—"

"I'll send a footman and a maid—"

"You'll do no such thing!"

"I will not let you live there with that—"

"Where would I go? I cannot afford anything more than a room—"

"Here. You can live here." Even as he said the words, he knew it would be unseemly for her to do so. He was a bachelor. At some point, his parents would return from the Kingdom of the Two Sicilies and expect life to go on as it had before his sister, Anne, had married. "Or we can find something better for you," he suggested on a sigh.

"Perhaps," she replied, although her manner suggested she wouldn't be doing such a thing. "We should go down to dinner. I shouldn't want your servants to have to work so late because of me."

"Of course." He stepped over to the bowl and helped himself to the ball of soap, rinsing his hands beneath a stream of water from the pump. With a murmured, "Thank you," he took the linen from Frances and dried his hands.

As they descended the stairs to the ground floor, he thought of what it would be like to do this every night. To walk down the stairs with Frances at his side, to eat dinner with her, to spend their evenings speaking of their day at the museum and of David. To spend their nights making love and then sleeping in one another's arms. To wake up …

He gave a start, realizing Frances was staring at him. "What is it?"

"I was about to ask you the same question," she replied. "You looked as if you were far away."

Gabe allowed an impish grin. "Apologies. I suppose I was."

Frances stared at him a moment and then dipped her head. "I am keeping you from your club."

Frowning, Gabe said, "You are not, actually. I hadn't planned to go on this night." He led her into the dining room. "I will go tomorrow night, but only because my cousin has requested I meet him there." He pulled out her chair.

Returning to her place at the table, Frances sat down and watched as Gabe took his. "But, don't you have to meet Mr. Grandby tomorrow evening?" she asked, remembering the letter he had read to her earlier that evening. She regarded the meal set before her, marveling at the selections as she lifted her fork.

"Mr. Grandby is my cousin," he said. "Second cousin, actually."

Her eyes widened. "So *that* is how you have a position at the museum," she said, as if the circumstances of his hiring had been puzzling her.

"What? Oh, no," he replied as he shook his head. "Tom had no idea I wanted to work in a museum until after I had already secured the position under Mr. Harris," he explained.

"And I rather doubt he would have used any influence he might possess on my behalf. Until recently, we didn't really know one another very well."

Frances relaxed and resumed eating.

"He had some say regarding your hiring, though," Gabe added after a moment.

"Mine?" Once again, Frances was on alert, her face paling.

Gabe chuckled. "He read your character and approved your hiring is all," he assured her.

"Thinking I was a man, no doubt."

Gabe bobbed his head back and forth. "Probably. But what does it matter? You're obviously a better artist than the last potter they employed, and the curator of the Roman and Greek antiquities knows it."

Once again, Frances looked surprised. "He does?"

Reaching over to cover her left hand with his right, Gabe gave her a brilliant smile. "He does."

Warmth flooded her belly at feeling his encouragement as his hand encased hers and gave it a shake.

"I think he is pleased with you as well." When she noted his anticipation at hearing more, she added, "Your predecessor was not nearly as learned as you, nor was he very... *interested*. He had no appreciation for antiquities."

Gabe stared at her. "Then why would he seek employment at a museum?"

She shrugged and replied, "He was a clerk. He couldn't understand why anyone would care to look at old stuff he claimed could be found in the homes of aristocrats."

Shaking his head in disbelief, Gabe was glad his father had never taken to collecting more than the usual reproductions of Roman statues that could be found in the halls of most townhouses. "Surely such blasphemy wasn't tolerated!" he teased.

Frances did her best to suppress a giggle, happy to know he could find humor in the situation.

She imagined what it might be like to do this every night. To sit at a table laden with rich foods and glasses of red and white wine knowing her son was being looked after by a nursemaid with a pleasant disposition. To spend her night in an elegant bedchamber in a velvet-clad bed. To bathe in a tub with warm water a phalanx of servants hadn't been forced to bring up in cans from the kitchens.

"Now who is the one who looks as if she is far away?" Gabe teased, just before he finished his main course.

Sure she blushed at having been caught ruminating, Frances shook her head. "I am glad you insisted I come back here."

"As am I," Gabe said, just as a footman appeared with a plate of cakes and dishes of ice cream. He kept his attention on Frances as she watched, wide-eyed, as the footman set the tray on the table and then took his leave. "Do you like ice cream?"

Frances tore her gaze from the confection and stared at him. "I've no idea. I've never… tried it."

Gabe chuckled, thinking she was fibbing. But then he realized from how she used a spoon to test the small mound of the confection that she probably hadn't eaten it before. "It's cold," he warned.

He loved seeing her expression of wonder as she took her first experimental taste. Loved seeing how her eyes closed briefly as she savored the flavor of bergamot.

If they had been anywhere but the dining room—anywhere the servants couldn't walk in on them—he would have kissed her. Kissed her and used his tongue to taste what she tasted.

He imagined what he would do if any dribbled onto the bare skin above the neckline of her gown. Of how the cream would taste mixed with the taste of her. Of how her milk-laden breasts would taste should his lips be allowed to move lower. To cover her engorged nipples and suckle them as his hands cupped her breasts.

"Your ice cream is melting."

Gabe blinked, her soft words pulling him from his reverie. He nearly cursed, glad the table hid the evidence of his turgid manhood behind his trousers' fly. Another moment, and he would have imagined stripping her bare. Licking and kissing her heated skin until she begged for him to make love to her.

Not that she would do such a thing. This was Frances Longworth. Prickly and particular. Proud.

"I'll just pour it onto my cake," he managed to get out without sounding like a frog in heat.

"Oh, that sounds delicious," she replied, collecting a sample of the lemon cake and then dipping it into her dish of ice cream. Once she had raised it to her lips and tasted it, she swallowed and made a murmur of appreciation.

Gabe swallowed. Hard.

"When we have finished our dinner, would you be amenable to staying here?" Gabe asked. "At the table? I usually have a small glass of port. Perhaps you would like one as well?"

Frances gave him an uncertain glance. "I've never had port."

"So this will be an evening of firsts."

"Indeed," she replied, wondering at the fluttering she felt in her chest.

CHAPTER 23

IN THE DARK OF THE GARDEN

*M*eanwhile, at Woodscastle

"Do you usually drink port?" James asked as Emily sipped the dark red liquor from a small cordial glass. He had been surprised when they had both been served the after-dinner drink the very first night he had eaten at Woodscastle. Now that it had happened again, he wondered if all the women who usually resided at Woodscastle drank the stuff.

"Most nights," Emily replied. "I like it better than brandy." She watched to see what his reaction would be, grinning when he gave her a look of disbelief.

"You shock me, my lady," he said with a grin.

"I think we've done quite enough of that tonight."

James was about to agree, but what harm would another incident cause? "Then I suppose I shouldn't ask if I might join you on your walk in the gardens this evening."

"But of course you should. I would love the company."

"You've not grown tired of hearing me prattle on about the bank?" he countered. He hadn't been speaking of it all that much, really, but he had found that Emily not only seemed interested, but she was able to answer several queries about some of the people who worked there. If she didn't know someone directly, she could at least suggest the name of someone who did. "My sister, Sophia, would have been bored to tears."

"Remember, both my father and Tom see to investments, and Roger is a banker. If they didn't speak of matters of money over dinner, I would think that either the country was about to collapse, or my father had lost his fortune," she replied, her manner so deadpan, James was left believing the latter was possible.

"You could have been a banker," he remarked.

"I could be many things, but my sex prevents it," she replied.

"Of course," he murmured. "Well, at least it doesn't prevent you from escorting me in the gardens."

Emily tittered. "I shall not only escort you, I shall protect you from the beasties that might appear," she claimed as she stood.

"Beasties?" James repeated, rising and then offering his arm. He led them from the dining room and then to the back door where her coat and muff were hanging.

"Mathilda may join us, even though she should be in the barn by now." Emily allowed James to help her with her redingote.

"Mathilda?"

"She's the milk cow," Emily replied as she walked with him to the front door, where his greatcoat hung on a peg. "There are usually at least two rabbits, and if there are not, it's because of the dog."

James pulled on his greatcoat with Humphrey's assistance. "I don't recall having seen a dog about."

"That's because we don't have one," Emily said as she pulled on her gloves. She watched as Humphrey lit a small lantern.

James was about to ask the next logical question—if not

their dog, then who did it belong to?—when he considered another possibility.

A wild dog.

"Is it feral?" he asked in alarm, accepting the lantern from the butler.

A brilliant smile lit her face. "I should hope not. He's an Old English Sheepdog," she said before she paused and then added, "Well, I suppose he *could* be feral, but he's such a darling—just a big round bundle of fur—no one would taken him seriously if he attempted to bare his teeth. Why, I don't think his teeth would even show if he did, given all that fur on his face. Besides," she added after another pause, "I truly think it's Bernard."

James gave a nod to Humphrey, who seemed to have trouble keeping a straight face just then, and he offered his arm to Emily. "Bernard?" he repeated.

She nodded. "He belongs to Sophia," she said as she took his proffered arm, delighting in James' look of confusion. "Your sister. You do remember her—you spoke of her over port. A year or so younger than you?" Emily went on as they left the house through the back door. "Lives at Merriweather Manor?"

The darkness that engulfed them faded as the firelight from the lantern surrounded them, and after a moment, the glow reflecting from the snow on the clouded skies cast the gardens in an ethereal glow.

Allowing a deep chuckle, James said, "In my defense, I haven't seen Sophia in a very long time." His comment was accompanied by a slight cloud that quickly dissipated from in front of his face.

Emily sobered. "She wasn't at Merriweather Manor when you last had dinner there earlier this week?"

"She had already left for Brighton to pay a call on one of our aunts."

Pretending to shiver, Emily said, "Although I enjoy

Brighton in the summertime, I cannot imagine spending the winter there."

"Me, neither," James agreed, "but Aunt Jane has taken to living there year-round. When were you last there?" he asked as they passed under the arbor.

Emily made a sound of disappointment. "For the opening of the Anthaeum. That was over five years ago."

"Oh, no." James' arm stiffened beneath her hold. "Was your father an investor?" he asked, referring to the huge conservatory that had been constructed in Hove.

"No, although I think he would have been tempted to invest in another if the Anthaeum had been a success," she explained. "But he had heard the stories of the problems with construction, and when the engineer quit the project, he nearly cancelled our holiday."

"So, were you there when it collapsed?"

Emily nodded. "Father had already let a townhouse nearby, so as many of us that could go went along with him —we had quite a caravan of coaches—and we made a holiday of it."

"Such a spectacular disaster," James remarked. When he noticed Emily's quirked brow, he quickly added, "The collapse, I mean. Not your family's holiday, I hope?"

"Despite all my siblings and the grandparents and aunts and uncles, we all got along swimmingly," she claimed. "Just a few days before it was scheduled to open, we drove by the site. It was immense. The dome was a hundred and sixty-five feet in diameter. The installation of the glass had only just begun, and there were workmen climbing all over scaffolding both inside and out, but it looked spectacular," she recalled with some excitement. "Imagine our shock when we arrived for the opening on August thirtieth only to discover the entire structure was in a heap, half buried in the ground. Father said that was because the iron braces were so heavy and that they fell from such a height as to practically dig their own graves."

Although James had heard similar tales from others who had witnessed the wreckage, he loved listening to Emily's version of it. Despite the darkness around them, her face was lit with enthusiasm.

"It's a wonder no one was hurt," James said, secretly glad he had been in Bath and that none of his clients had been investors in the project.

"Oh, but poor Henry Phillips. He was the botanist who arranged for its construction, and he was left blind," Emily argued.

"Blind?"

"From the shock of seeing what had happened," Emily explained. "From seeing his lifelong dream crushed into the ground, both literally and figuratively."

They had reached the stone bench, and James allowed Emily to sit before he settled next to her and set the lantern on the ground. "I suppose seeing your life's work—your dream project—all in a shambles would be a shock."

"At least none of our shocks on this day have been so monumental," Emily said.

James had thought to bring up a topic that she might find shocking, but he was prevented from doing so when a slight whine reached his ears. "Did you hear that?" he asked as he tensed.

Straightening on the bench, Emily glanced around. "Bernard?" she called out.

A moment later, a huge hairy sheepdog ambled toward them from the other crushed granite path, his tail wagging. When he spotted James, he stopped and cocked his head to one side. He let out a quiet 'woof'.

James let out a guffaw. "So this is Sophia's dog?"

"Indeed," Emily said as she held out her hand in the dog's direction. Tentative, Bernard made his way to stand in front of Emily, his attention clearly on James, as if he didn't trust the man.

Once Bernard was seated before her, Emily took his head between her gloved hands and used the tips of her fingers to scratch behind his ears. "And how are you this evening, you big beastie?"

The dog let out a mournful whine.

"That bad?" Emily pulled a napkin from her pocket and unwrapped the linen to reveal a slice of meat and a boiled potato. The dog happily finished off the treats in just a few swallows.

"You're feeding him?" James asked, his voice tinged with rebuke.

"I've no idea if he's been staying here in Sophia's absence, or if he walks here every night from Merriweather Manor," she replied. "But it's no trouble for me to see to it he has some food."

James allowed the dog to sniff his boots, but he didn't make a move to pet him. "I suppose if I had that much hair in front of my eyes, I wouldn't be able to tell where I was."

Giving him a grin, Emily said, "Well, it appears someone has been seeing to him. He looks as if he's been brushed."

"And judging from his size, I should think he's being fed, as well." James turned his attention on the dog. "Bernard, it's time for you to go home."

Bernard's ears lifted, and he turned to face Emily.

"You heard your uncle. Go home now."

A grunt of amusement sounded from James, but the dog took off, disappearing over the boxwood hedge in the direction of Merriweather Manor. "Uncle?" he repeated.

He knew he would find her smiling at him even before he turned to face her. The odd sensation in his chest had him taking a quick breath.

"You don't like being an uncle, do you?"

James furrowed his brows. "It's not that I don't like it,

exactly. I just find the children sometimes make me nervous," he said quietly. "I'm always afraid I'll curse in their presence or say something inappropriate, and then their mothers will be admonishing me over dinner in one breath and then wondering why it is I haven't take a wife in the next."

Emily stared at his profile for a moment, finally understanding something she had wondered about in Henry. Neither man sought to marry on their own accord. Henry had only done so because circumstances—the need for funds—required him to take a wife. He probably would have remained unattached had he not gambled away his allowance.

Would James ever be forced to marry? And if so, what would compel him to do so? He had no need of money. No real need of an heir.

He did need a companion, though. Emily was sure of it. As sure as she knew she wanted a child.

"You won't be like that with your own children, of course," Emily said.

Allowing a short laugh, James asked, "How do you know that?"

"You won't have a need to meet them for the first time until they return from university, all grown up and ready to collect their inheritance."

James wasn't sure if she was teasing him. "I'm quite sure I would want to at least hold the babe a moment before I leave him in the nursery. Until he's old enough for Eton," he argued. "I might even speak with him on occasion before that."

Emily dimpled. "And if it's a girl?"

Looking as if he'd been slapped across the face, James just stared at her.

"Perhaps you could teach her to dance," she suggested.

"I would hire the very best governess for her, of course,"

he said, his voice so quiet Emily could barely make out his words. "I rather doubt I could play patty-cake, though."

"I'm surprised you know what that is."

"I'm really not that bad with children," he argued.

"I believe you."

"Enough that you would take a chance with me as their father?"

Trying hard to suppress a look of shock at hearing his query, Emily allowed a wan grin. "Enough, yes." She paused and inhaled slowly. "More if you kissed me, of course."

She wasn't really ready to be kissed, but once her words were out, James had his hands on her shoulders and his lips on hers. From his quick move, she expected it might be a punishing kiss, hard and fast and unforgiving.

Had he felt pressured into proposing a marriage he didn't want? Into facing life with children when he didn't really want them?

But it was nothing like that. His quick move belied how softly the pillows of his lips pressed to hers. How gentle his hands were as they steadied her shoulders and then trailed down her arms. How slow he inhaled as he pushed his tongue into her mouth and tasted her. How intoxicating his scent was as it enveloped them both.

She didn't know how long they sat there, kissing one another in the dark, but at some point, Emily knew they were no longer alone. The air around them had changed, and the sense of being watched had her slowly, regretfully, pulling her lips from his.

James had noticed the change as well, and he was the first to turn and regard their intruder with a mixture of surprise and humor. "You must be Mathilda."

Emily couldn't help but giggle as the cow seemed to nod in agreement and then make a mooing sound.

"I suppose you have a treat for her, too?"

"Actually, I don't," Emily replied. At his look of disbelief, she added, "I wouldn't know what to feed her."

"So... how do you get her to leave?"

"Oh, I just walk with her until she's headed in the direction of the barn."

"I suppose it is getting a bit chilly out here," he murmured.

"Just watch your step," she warned as they stood. "In case she's dropped any pies in our path. Or there's a rabbit."

Mathilda turned and made her way slowly out of the garden on the same path as she had entered it while James and Emily took the other. Once past the arbor, Emily urged Mathilda to continue on as James held the door for her.

Once inside, James wrapped his arms around Emily and kissed her quickly. He knew the butler would appear at any moment to take their coats.

"We'll make plans tomorrow," he said when he finally stepped away from her.

"And in the meantime?"

"Perhaps I'll finish that book tonight. Sleep well." And then he headed up the stairs.

Emily watched him go, a heady mix of happiness and relief and disappointment making her wonder how he could think of sleeping at a time like this.

There was more shocking to be done on this night, and she was determined to do it.

CHAPTER 24

SECRETS REVEALED IN THE DARK OF NIGHT

*B*ack at Trenton House
Their port long finished, Gabe suggested he and Frances head upstairs. "I didn't mean to keep you from your son for so long," he said as they made their way to the stairway.

"I didn't mind. I cannot recall ever having such a grand dinner. And you were right. The port was very good."

When Gabe continued up the steps after reaching the second floor, Frances said, "There really is no need for you to come to the nursery."

"Oh, but I insist," he replied. "I'd like to be sure the youngest guest I have ever hosted is settling in."

Frances had a fleeting hope he might do the same for her, which reminded her she had no clothes with her. No night rail. She would, of course, simply wear her chemise to bed, but she didn't want him seeing her in it.

"Barclay saw to it a lady's maid delivered some night clothes to your room," Gabe added, just as they reached the door to the nursery.

"He needn't have done that."

Gabe gave her a quelling glance. "We are speaking of a

servant who prides himself on thoroughly seeing to his duty. There would have been no getting around it, I assure you."

Frances rolled her eyes before she hurried to the bassinet. David was covered in a soft blanket, his eyes closed and his chest rising and falling with his even breaths.

"He looks like a little cherub," Gabe whispered.

"A bald one," Frances countered, sighing with relief at seeing he was asleep. "And given the events of the night, I rather expect he will sleep through until the morning."

She allowed another sigh, and Gabe noticed how she looked as if she might be about to cry. "What is it?"

Her dark brows furrowed, and Frances gave a shake of her head. "To think that at one time, I had no intention of keeping him."

"What?" Gabe struggled to keep his surprise under control.

She reached out and touched a fingertip to her son's cheek. "I didn't think I would want him. I was going to leave him at the Foundling Hospital, but then, when the midwife gave him to me, all wet with his face scrunched up and his hands curled into fists, I could not bear the thought."

Gabe reached an arm around her shoulders, turned, and pulled her against the front of his body. "I often wondered if my mother had the same sort of plans for me."

Frances stared at him. "Whatever do you mean?"

Allowing a one-shouldered shrug, he said, "Once I learned I was a bastard, I mean. Before that, I had no reason to wonder."

Blinking, Frances shook her head. "But—"

"Oh, my father married my mother, once he found out about me, but that wasn't until I was David's age." Gabe's eyes darted to one side when he realized to what he had admitted. He hadn't intended to tell her he was illegitimate, but everyone in the *ton* knew. At some point, she might have learned it from someone else.

Her look of shock turned to consternation. "So, why would she have even told you? It seems as if it wouldn't have mattered."

Gabe winced. He had never begrudged his younger brother's right to the earldom. To the title he would eventually inherit. How could he when his father had accepted him so readily? Choosing to marry Sarah Cumberbatch despite her position as a commoner? Despite the circumstances under which they had first met? Despite her holding a position as the manager of a coaching inn the second time they met?

How could he bemoan his position in Society when his father had recognized him as his own and was so generous with his inheritance?

"It doesn't matter to me," he finally replied in a quiet voice. "Just as I hope it does not matter to him," he added as he nodded in the babe's direction.

Frances glanced over at the bassinet before returning her attention to Gabe. "That has been my worry ever since he was born. I can claim I am a widow—that his father died in a war or... or an accident—but I have no papers to prove a marriage. No way to account for him. Nor would I ever wish anyone to know the identity of his real father."

Gabe hugged her harder before he stepped away. "Then that is the way it shall be," he whispered. "Your secret is safe with me. Come. It's late. Let me escort you to your bedchamber."

Frances wondered at the sense of disappointment she felt at hearing his words. For a moment, she had thought he would be taking her to his bed, and for a fleeting second, she knew she would go willingly.

She would no doubt regret it in the morning. She had promised herself she would never again allow a man to bed her unless she was wed—even if he did threaten to tell everyone he knew she was a wanton or a whore.

"Should I send a lady's maid to help you undress?"

Frances wondered what it would be like if he undressed her. Wondered what it would feel like to have his fingers undo the buttons of her gown and slip the sleeves from her shoulders. What it would be like to have him pull the tie on her stays. Lower her petticoats to the floor. Remove her shoes and roll down her stockings.

Had he done such a thing before? Or had his lovers already shed their clothes and been wearing a dressing gown when they joined him for their trysts? Had there even been trysts? She nearly put voice to the query when she realized he was waiting for an answer.

What was the question?

Something about a lady's maid. "There's no need," she whispered, hope her reddened face wasn't apparent in the dim gas lighting in the corridor.

They stopped in front of her bedchamber, and Gabe lifted her hand to his lips. "Sleep well, my lady."

"You as well." She dipped a curtsy and watched as Gabe bowed and disappeared behind the door to his bedchamber. When she heard the latch click into place, she did the same in hers.

A single candle lamp on a nightstand lit the room in a golden glow, and as if in slow motion, Frances undressed and pulled on the frilly night rail that she found draped over the end of the bed. She reveled in the soft fabric, and then gave a start when she caught her reflection in the looking glass above the dressing table.

How could a single evening have her looking years younger? Closer to her own age?

Could a single kiss really be the reason there were no longer frown lines embedded between her brows? Why there were no longer lines at the outer edges of her lips, where her perpetually pinched expression had etched them over the last couple of years?

Or was it because, for just this one night, her son was safe and sleeping soundly, tucked into a comfortable bed instead of the bottom drawer of a broken bureau? And because she was about to climb into a large bed covered in elegant velvet?

Whatever the reason, Frances grinned as she took the pins from her hair. She shook the brunette locks until they fell past her shoulders and halfway down her back.

Using the ivory hairbrush from the dressing table, she smoothed the waves of her hair until they felt like silk. Not finding a ribbon to bind it, she let it be and settled into the turned-down linens.

Of course the bed was comfortable. Of course the small fire in the fireplace kept the chill away. Was this not the most comfortable bedchamber in which she had ever had the pleasure of sleeping?

The bed was perfect, but sleep eluded her.

Despite having turned down the lamp and covering herself in the cotton bed linens and blankets, Frances felt restless. She found her thoughts drifting to Gabe. Imagining what it might be like to share his bed.

Would they sleep apart? Or would he hold her in his arms? Would he wake in the middle of the night and kiss her? Use the tips of his perfectly manicured fingernails to incite tickles beneath her skin? Use the flat of his hand to skim over her heated skin? Touch the tip of his tumescence to the swollen bud that ached at the top of her thighs?

Frustrated, she threw back the covers and headed for the door. Perhaps she could make her way down to the kitchens and find some milk. Warm milk. Surely that would help.

She opened the door and nearly let out a yelp.

Gabe, garbed in a dressing gown left open at the top, stared at her in surprise.

"Were you... were you going somewhere?" he asked in a whisper, his gaze taking in her changed appearance by the dim light of a hallway sconce. With her hair down, she looked years younger. Softer.

Desirable.

Frances shook her head, but said, "I thought I might find some milk, but…"

His expression betraying his own uncertainty, Gabe nodded. "If that's what you want," he replied, turning as if he intended to lead her to the kitchens.

"It's not. Not really."

His brows furrowed. "What is it you really want?"

Without a word, Frances took a hold of his hand and pulled him into the bedchamber.

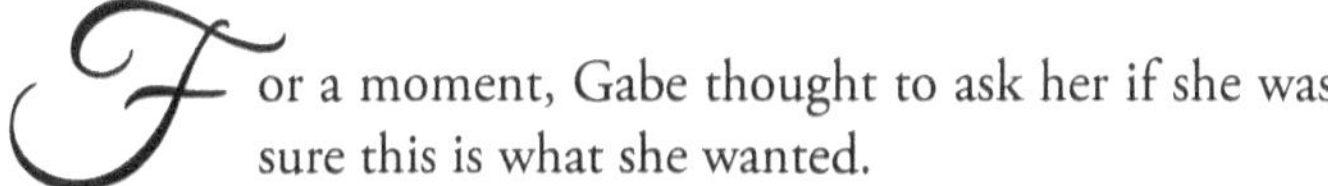

or a moment, Gabe thought to ask her if she was sure this is what she wanted.

But he would be a fool to do so.

She had been on her way out of the bedchamber, possibly on her way to his.

The door shut behind him as he took her lips with his own. Willing lips. Eager lips that returned his kiss measure for measure.

His hands moved down her back to cup the globes of her bottom through the cotton fabric of her night rail. Then he slid them up her sides as her arms lifted and wrapped around his shoulders. He felt her fingers slip through the curls at the back of his head, and his scalp shivered in delight at the same moment his thumbs rubbed over her nipples.

Her soft inhalation of breath interrupted the kiss, but only for a moment. Taking small steps, he soon had her backed against the edge of the bed. Sliding his hands back down to her bottom, he hitched the hem of the night rail up to her thighs and lifted her up onto the bed.

He sensed she was about to turn over, and he wondered if she thought he intended to take her from behind. Was that how her baby's father had impaled her? Bent her over the edge of a bed to have his way with her?

Probably not even a bed. A table or a chair.

Well, he had no intention of treating her as anything other than the lady she was. The lady she would be after she agreed to wed him.

The sudden thought of matrimony had him pausing a moment. Long enough to see that she didn't know what to do. Long enough to know this wasn't the time to be mentioning a betrothal.

Determined to prove he would see to her pleasure before taking his own, he gentled his hold on her legs. He slowly moved his hands to beneath her knees and spread them apart.

With his own feet still on the floor, he was the one who bent down. He moved a hand to her quim and felt her jerk as a finger parted her folds. A whimper sounded as the tip of his tongue searched for her womanhood.

He finally felt the engorged bud, and he flicked his tongue across it before pushing it into her over and over. Her whimpers increased to soft cries and mewling, her hips bucking with every thrust of his tongue. At some point, she had pulled the night rail farther up her body, or perhaps his hands had done so as they explored her heated skin, exposing her belly and the undersides of her breasts.

Dizzy with his own desire—his manhood throbbed and strained against the velvet counterpane—Gabe finally straightened and pulled her hips to the edge of the bed. He sank himself into her on a sigh of relief and held himself still until he was sure she was ready for more.

He lifted her knees to his hips, and from there, she seemed to know to wrap her legs around him.

When he slowly pulled out of her, he heard her soft whimper. "Am I hurting you?" he asked in a hoarse whisper.

"No, but I don't know what to do."

He thrust into her, and he heard a soft gasp as he sucked in a breath between his teeth. "You needn't do anything, my love." His breaths quickened with each rhythmic thrust as his hands gripped her hips. Then he remembered to pleasure her again. One thumb slid down her mons to where their bodies met, and he rubbed her womanhood.

Perhaps he had pressed too hard, or she was already on the verge of her release, but all at once, he knew he could hold on no longer. The contractions of her orgasm pulled his manhood in and gripped him, over and over, as his seed spilled into her and stars appeared before his eyes.

Unable to hold himself up, he lowered his torso to hers, kissed both her breasts, and settled his head between them.

When her breathing finally returned to normal, Frances moved her hands to Gabe's shoulders and then to the back of his head. She was sure he was sleeping, but how he could do so when half his body was still over the edge of the bed, she knew not. And with the night rail bunched up, she couldn't see anything beyond his shoulders.

She managed to pull the garment off over her head, feeling relief when her struggles to move had Gabe waking up from his brief nap.

He lifted his head and gazed at her. A grin lifted the corners of his mouth. "Do you have any idea just how beautiful you are?"

A blush colored her cheeks, and she blinked several times. "I feel... young," she whispered. "And I'm trembling all over, but—"

"You're probably freezing," he countered in alarm, lifting himself until he was standing. He was still wearing his dressing gown, although it was wide open in the front.

"But I'm not cold," she argued, managing to pull her knees together in an attempt at modesty. Gabe didn't seem the least bit concerned for his own, she noticed, for he didn't attempt to close the robe.

And why should he? He had the body of a Greek god, his torso sculpted much like those naked statues that stood in the museum. He could have been Cupid's father, given his crown of blond curls and blue eyes.

Frances watched as he hurried around the bed, leaning over to take her body in his arms so he could place her on the downturned linens.

"Would you mind terribly if I... if I stayed?" he asked. "I'd like to hold you for a time, and besides, I don't think I'd have the strength to make it back to my bedchamber if I wanted to."

She couldn't help the humor she felt at hearing his words, especially since he had just lifted and easily carried her to the other side of the bed. She couldn't help but delight in the shivers that coursed through her body. Her entire being felt alive, all tingly and sensitive, warm and wanton.

She grinned as she moved over and lifted the bed linens in invitation. She watched as he shed his dressing gown, his skin golden in the firelight. His manhood, still semi-erect, bobbed about as he climbed onto the bed and then took her in his arms. He kissed her on the mouth and then the forehead before he settled back onto the pillows and promptly fell asleep.

Marveling at his ability to sleep when she felt as if she were wide awake, Frances settled her head into the small of his shoulder. Beneath her cheek, she could feel his pulse, steady and slowing as the minutes ticked by. One of her hands moved to rest on his chest, and she was soon fast asleep.

CHAPTER 25

THE SHAPE OF A BUM REVEALED

*M*eanwhile, at Woodscastle

James stopped in the library to retrieve the book *Thoughts and details on the high and low prices of the last thirty years*, before he headed up to his room. A quick glance at the massive desk reminded him of the time he had spent there holding Emily, of the tale she had told about Henry.

Once he and his brother had grown and gone their separate ways, he hadn't expected they might also grow apart. That Henry wouldn't think to come to him for help bothered James. That Henry instead first went to Lady Andrew rankled. That he then thought of a marriage to Emily as the solution to his problem angered James.

Or perhaps Henry had thought to come to him first and then thought better of it.

How would he have reacted at learning his brother was in financial straights? Would he have loaned him the money to clear up that debt that their grandmother's ring had apparently paid off?

Which brought him back to thoughts of the ring.

He lifted the bauble from the nightstand and regarded it under the light from the nearest candle lamp. He was sure it wasn't paste, as Emily claimed, and now he wondered if it was even a copy.

Perhaps she had mixed up the rings when she pawned the one. Which meant whomever gave her the money for it wasn't a jeweler. Or a goldsmith.

He sighed and placed it back on the nightstand. Perhaps he would pay a call in Ludgate Hill. Discover from a jeweler its worth.

Would he give it to her as a betrothal ring, though?

He moved to the dressing table and opened his own jewel box. Pushing aside cravat pins and cufflinks, he pulled out a ring and compared it to the one he held.

The sapphires appeared identical, as did the diamonds that surrounded them. Even the number of tiny stones matched. The gold was the same. The bands were the same width. And the goldsmith marks inside the bands and under the center stones were the same.

He chuckled, wondering just how many identical rings his grandmother might have owned and who had them all now.

Had she commissioned them for this very purpose? So that every grandson might have the same ring to bestow on their brides? Even in death, Mary Margaret Merriweather was as manipulative as she was in life.

Bless her heart.

James set aside the two rings on the dressing table and quickly doffed his clothes. Given the fire and the warmth in the guest bedchamber, he eschewed his nightshirt in favor of simply climbing into the crisp bed linens naked and reading the book until he could fall asleep.

He had just settled in and begun the fourth part of the book when a firm *knock* sounded at the door. "Come," he called out, thinking Humphrey was there to let him know he would be retiring for the night.

So he was entirely shocked when Emily opened the door, quickly stepped in, and then closed the door behind her.

James blinked. At first, he thought he might be dreaming, for her dark hair was no longer pinned up but flowing freely. It did so over a gown the likes of which he had never seen before—not even on his mistress.

The fabric, shiny and ivory in color, clung to her curves and outlined the fronts of her thighs. It might have also displayed the swell of her hips, but a dressing gown of the same fabric hung from her shoulders and hid them.

Just below the hemline, two puffs of fur appeared, apparently the tops of her bedroom slippers.

"I thought a gentleman was expected to stand up when a lady entered a room."

Jame swallowed and set the book on the nightstand. "I thought so, too, but I'm not sure if he can still be considered a gentleman if all he is wearing are bed linens."

He watched as Emily instantly changed from seductress to the woman he had spent the day with. She lifted a hand to cover her mouth as she tittered.

"Wherever did you get that gown?" he asked, his gaze once again taking her in from head to toe.

"Suzanne's in Oxford Street," she replied. "It's French."

James gave an approving nod. "Now I'm rather sorry I cursed them earlier today," he replied, sounding a bit breathless. He sat up straighter on the bed. "Are those the rabbits you mentioned earlier?" he asked, pointing to the slippers she wore.

Emily looked down at her slippers as if seeing them for the first time. "Oh, dear. Do you suppose that's why they weren't in the gardens earlier this evening?"

He quirked a brow. "I suppose I shouldn't assume why it is you have come here this time of the night," he said. Then his eyes widened. Perhaps she was merely there to see to it he was comfortable, although she hadn't done so any of the other nights he had stayed at Woodscastle. "Or do you always wear such a gown to bed?"

Emily finally stepped farther into the room, her attention going to the book on the nightstand. "I don't. At least, I never have before."

For a moment, James thrilled at the thought that his brother had never seen her like this. "That's a relief."

"I thought you wanted to learn the shape of my bum," she said as she lifted a hip, bent her leg slightly, and settled on the edge of the bed. She left her other foot pressed firmly on the carpeted floor.

James swallowed. "I most certainly do. Among other things."

She let out a sigh of relief. "Oh, good, because I nearly turned around and went back to my bedchamber three times whilst on the way here," she replied. "Have I shocked you?"

"Thoroughly, but I rather doubt it's the last time you're going to do it on this day."

Emily gave him a quelling glance. "You're not having second thoughts about marrying me, are you?"

He shook his head. "If I'd had any, they most assuredly would have flown out the window when you appeared at the door," he murmured. "For a moment, I thought I was dreaming, or else I had died and you were the angel that appeared to take me to heaven."

Her eyes darted to one side, as if she were trying to decide if what he described was a welcome scenario or a frightening one. When she noticed how the corners of his lips lifted, she said, "Oh, well that's a relief." She sighed. "Tomorrow is Sunday, and since you don't have to go to the bank, I thought tonight would be a good night for you to... to teach me how to make love to you."

If he hadn't learned so much about her this past week, James might have been further shocked at hearing her comment. Instead, he felt relief at not having to be the one to bring up what could be an awkward situation on their wedding night. Especially considering she had lain with his brother.

He leaned forward and took one of her hands in his, the edge of the bed linens falling from his chest. "Will you then teach me how to make love to you?"

Her eyes widened at seeing the exposed expanse of his chest. Whorls of dark, crisp curls covered most of it. "I was rather hoping you might already know," she whispered.

"Well, I suppose there's only one way to find out," he said as he tugged her hand.

She leaned toward him, but took a moment to shed the satin dressing gown. Before she could do anything else, his hands had moved to her hips to pull her atop him.

Emily inhaled as she felt his hands smooth over the sides of her satin-clad body and down and around the globes of her bottom. She felt the vibration of his growl through the bed linens that still separated their bodies. "Does that mean you like the shape of my bum?" she asked in a whisper.

The vibration beneath her increased, and a chuckle sounded before James moved his hands to cup her face. "Very much," he murmured. His lips took hers in a kiss of passion.

Emily expected he might take her as Henry had always done. With Henry, there had hardly been a warning of what he intended to do. No preparation. No foreplay. Just a few kisses. He hadn't even undressed her completely those three times, claiming he could wait for that until after the wedding.

So she was surprised when James finished a kiss and then pulled the bed linens aside so she could settle onto the bed. When one of his hands smoothed over her shoulder to push down the sleeve of her gown and then cup her breast, she inhaled softly. The circular motions of his thumb were replaced with his lips, and she reveled in the sensations his tongue created. A moment later, and he treated her other breast to the same pleasure.

"What do I do?" she asked in a whisper interrupted by a slight gasp. One of his hands had smoothed down her side to grasp the hem of her nightgown, and now it was moving back up her thigh.

"Allow me to remove your gown," he replied, his whisper hoarse. "I don't want to tear it since I rather adore you in it."

The thought that he might rip the gown from her body brought as much excitement as whatever it was his hand had been doing between her thighs only the moment before. "Of course," she agreed as she struggled to sit up.

He helped in divesting her of the satin, the gown tossed onto the puddle of the matching dressing gown already on the floor by the side of the bed.

Emily marveled at how carefully he held her. At how the pads of his fingers barely touched her skin as his hand once again made its way, this time down the front of her body.

When it reached her mons, she parted her legs and inhaled sharply when she felt a finger invade her most private place. Slick from her honeyed folds, his thumb pressed against her womanhood, rubbed around it, and flicked over it. She gasped and struggled to remain quiet as one of her hands pressed against his chest for support.

James leaned over her and took her lips once more. This time, he barely pressed his to hers. When he pulled away slightly, it was to ask if she wanted him to continue.

"Yes," she managed between labored breaths.

"You needn't be so quiet," he whispered, aware from the way her chest pressed into his that she was nearing her ecstasy.

A mewl sounded from her throat.

"More?" he asked, pressing just a bit harder until he felt her entire body lift from the bed. Her mewling increased, her breathing ceased, and her neck arched back.

His lips sought the hollow of her exposed throat, his tongue delving into it as he flicked his thumb over her swollen nub.

The cry she let out excited him, and James quickly moved atop her. He kissed her lips and then reached down to lift her knees—she had already spread her legs wider in anticipation of what was to come.

Her knees gripped his thighs as his turgid manhood entered her, bit by bit, as her hands skimmed down the sides of his body to his hips. She pulled him in farther, a move that surprised James and only reminded him that she had done this before. He gave into her pull, growling when the base of his manhood collided with her quim.

Deep inside her, his manhood throbbed with need, but he was determined to regain some semblance of control. "Am I hurting you?" he managed to get out, aware of how her body trembled beneath his.

"No," she replied on a breath. "Please don't stop."

Stop?

It was far too late for that, and he was about to tell her so, but he couldn't waste his breath on words. Not when his entire body begged for what was to come.

James kissed her once more and then pulled out of her— almost all the way. When she mewled in protest, he pushed back into her.

Emily understood what to do, her hips meeting his with the thrust. But this was nothing like what Henry had done with her. While Henry had been somewhat careful at first, his motions had quickly turned chaotic, hard to follow. He had cursed and grunted, and never once had he paused to ask if she was in pain.

With each of James' early thrusts had come a moment when he paused to either kiss her lips or a nipple, or to murmur how beautiful she looked. And then, when the rhythm was established and his movements had quickened, he could only kiss or suckle one of her breasts.

Emily reveled in watching his powerful body above hers. Reveled in watching how his arm muscles bunched with each thrust. Reveled in seeing the cords of his neck strain when he lifted his head and suppressed a groan. Reveled in how one of the hands he'd been using to hold himself over her reached down between them to where they were joined and set off a wave of pleasure in her unlike anything she had ever experienced before.

Her cry came just before James' growl, just before his entire body seized and remained suspended over hers.

Her fingers gripped his back as she pulled up to meet him, her back arched so her breasts could press into his chest as wave after wave of pleasure crested and broke inside.

When James collapsed onto her, she wrapped her arms around his back and held on, afraid he might roll off of her. She needed his solidity, though. Needed an anchor to hold onto lest she be swept away.

At some point, she remembered to breathe. Remembered where she had left her arms and legs. Smoothed her hands up and down his back. Mewled her satisfaction.

His head buried in the space between her neck and shoulder, James napped for a time atop her soft body. He didn't awake with a start or wonder where he was. The sensation of her fingertips sliding up and down his back brought him out of his brief slumber, and he allowed a sigh that had his warm breath washing over her neck.

Emily turned her head and placed a kiss on his forehead as one of her fingertips raked through his hair. She felt his entire body shudder at the touch, and she kissed him again.

"I think I shall enjoy being married to you," he said on a sigh.

Emily hissed as he pulled his manhood from her body and rolled off of her.

"Did that hurt?"he asked, suddenly serious.

She gave him a pretend pout. "No, but you could have stayed another moment or two."

He leaned over and kissed her before he reached over to turn down the candle lamp. "I feared you would be smothered," he countered as he lowered his head onto the pillows and then turned his body to face hers. "Will you stay? Just in case you want to make love to me in the middle of the night?"

Emily blinked, just then comprehending his earlier words about marriage. Even though his invitation was couched in what she could have interpreted a jest, she knew he didn't mean it like that. He wanted her. He wanted her to stay. "Well, I'm not going anywhere when you put it like that," she murmured sleepily.

James grinned and wrapped an arm around her waist. He pulled her against his body as he rolled onto his back and promptly fell asleep.

A moment later, Emily joined him in slumber.

CHAPTER 26

THE REALITY OF MORNINGS

V ery early the following morning
The sound of a baby's giggles had Frances emerging from a deep sleep. She was sure she heard it in her dream, just after the briefest of kisses touched her cheek. The bed in which she slept had grown cold for a time, but was now once again warm.

A giggle. There it was again.

She struggled to capture the image in the dream and finally gave up, opening her eyes to a most unusual sight.

Gabe was holding her son on his broad chest, tummy side down. Then he lifted the babe, held him aloft, and then lowered his top half until he could kiss David's forehead.

David's giggles once again filled the bedchamber as his legs kicked, and Frances felt her chest tighten. Never had she seen her son so happy. Never had he made sounds such as these.

His biceps bunched, Gabe once again lifted the boy and was waving him through the air, as if he were a chubby bird. David caught sight of her as he briefly hovered over her, and he once again giggled. "Mama," he said, his legs kicking beneath the fresh gown he was wearing.

Frances sat up, torn between scolding Gabe or kissing him for entertaining her son. She didn't have to decide, though, for Gabe lowered the boy to his chest and held him with one hand while he lifted his torso with the other, leaned over, and kissed her.

"Good morning," he whispered. "I hope you don't mind. I knew you would want to check on him first thing, so I... I went and got him."

Frances blinked. "In your robe, I hope," she replied, noting he was naked from the waist up. The rest of him was beneath the bed linens, but a quick look confirmed he wasn't wearing anything down there, either.

Gabe chuckled. "Of course. Mrs. Watkins wasn't the least bit surprised to see me."

Color suffused Frances' face. Did all the servants know Gabe had spent the night in the guest bedchamber?

"It's still quite early, but she was up with her children."

"Is he wet?"

Frowning, Gabe lifted the boy again. "I don't see how, given Mrs. Watkins just put on a new nappy. She was dressing him when I arrived, thinking you would want to feed him first thing."

"Dada."

Gabe and Frances both turned to stare at the baby. "He's never said that before," Frances claimed.

David reached for Frances, and she took him from Gabe's hold. The babe immediately latched onto one of her nipples.

"I didn't mind," Gabe replied. "In fact..." He paused and redirected his gaze to Frances. "I wouldn't mind if he thought I was." He turned his attention back to the nursing boy, wondering if his own father had felt the same way he did the moment he had learned he had a son.

Lifting himself to a sitting position, Gabe leaned over and kissed Frances' shoulder. "Would you?"

She stared at him until David pounded on her chest, and

she was forced to turn her gaze back on the nursing babe. "What are you saying?"

"Marry me, Frances. Marry me, and I'll recognize him as my own."

Frances inhaled sharply and then shook her head. "This is all a dream, isn't it? I simply ate too late, and now I'm..."

She couldn't finish when Gabe leaned over again and kissed her mouth. Kissed her until David gave up his hold on his mother to say, "Dada dada." A chubby arm reached up, and Gabe absently caught it between a thumb and forefinger before the babe could pound it against her chest.

When he finished the kiss, Gabe turned his attention to David and said, "Finish your breakfast, young man. I wish to make love to your mother, and I cannot do it with you in the way."

But the babe's eyelids were already heavy, and his suckling slowed to a halt.

"Now look what you've done," Frances scolded. "He hasn't even started on my other breast."

"He can finish when I'm done with you," Gabe teased, gently pulling the babe from her hold to place him between two pillows.

"I haven't yet bathed," Frances argued, even as Gabe's hand slid between her thighs. She inhaled sharply, stunned at how her body responded to his touch.

With anticipation. Desire.

"I'll give you a bath when we're done," he promised, at exactly the same moment his thumb rubbed over her womanhood. "But until then, I wish to show you how all of our mornings can be if we wed."

Frances settled back in the pillows, deciding she had best not argue. With his mind on carnal matters, Gabe wasn't expecting she would give him an immediate answer to his earlier demand. It was hard to think of his words as anything else.

Marry me.

But then it was hard to think of anything as his ministrations brought her to ecstasy. A moment later, and he replaced his finger with his manhood, slowing pushing into her, allowing her body to pull him in with every waning wave until his cock was completely buried inside her.

At some point, she had lifted her knees, her thighs gripping the sides of his, and he murmured, "Bless you."

That was the moment when everything went still. When even their breaths were held in anticipation as his face hovered over hers.

And then he moved. Pulled out and pushed in, ever so slowly. He kissed her, pulled out, and kissed her again, increased his rhythmic thrusting until he could no longer hold on.

Warmth filled Frances as the muscles in his arms bunched, as his head lifted and his entire body seemed to go rigid. Just when she was sure he would collapse atop her, he did something—she wasn't even sure what he did—and pleasure suffused her entire body.

She hadn't expected sensations so intense. So unlike anything she had ever felt before. She struggled to breathe. Struggled to silence her mewling and soft cries lest she wake the entire household.

When Gabe finally settled onto her, it was only a moment before he rolled off of her and ended up on his back, his eyes closed and his breathing labored.

She glanced over at David, wondering if he had paid witness to what had just happened. His attention was on one of his feet though, one he seemed determined to stuff into his mouth.

Even as the waves of her orgasm were still abating, she reached for the babe. Although he wasn't fussy, she knew he was still hungry.

"Wait another moment, or you'll frighten him," Gabe said, pulling her back down with a heavy arm.

"What?"

Gabe sighed. "Your heart. It's still beating fast. He'll feel it and think you are in distress."

Frances furrowed her dark brows and stared at him. "How is it you know this?" She jerked, as if she intended to sit up even with most of him now holding her down and his lips having attached themselves to the side of her breast.

A sudden thought had her gasping. "Do you...? Have you a—?"

"I have only a younger brother and sister," he assured her, realizing why she might have thought him already a father. "But I was old enough when my brother was born to understand I wasn't to hold him unless I was calm." He pushed her back down onto the bed and once again lowered his lips to her breast, this time her left.

He held them there a moment. "And now you are." He rolled off of her, but left an arm sprawled over her thighs as she sat up and took the babe back in her arms.

Her heart rate might have returned to normal, but her body certainly hadn't. She wondered what it might be like if she allowed Gabe to bed her this way every morning.

Wouldn't he grow tired of her, though? He was a young man—far too young to be considering matrimony.

Wasn't he?

If she agreed to marry him, how long would it be before he took a mistress? Before he lost interest in her, or found another woman with a babe to save from their worldly woes?

"I will honor my marriage vows," Gabe whispered "I promise you that."

Frances gave a start, wondering if he could read her mind. She didn't dare look at him, though. If she did that, she would give in. She would agree to anything he asked—he had just tumbled her, leaving her unable to think straight. Or think at all.

Much like he had managed to do in the middle of the night. Slowly. Without a word. His hands smoothing over her heated body until every nerve ending awakened in bliss.

Had that been a dream?

"Your son will want for nothing," Gabe continued. "He'll be educated, and he will go to university, just as our other boys will, and they will be raised as I was. In a good home."

He heard her make a sound of disbelief, and he imagined she had probably rolled her eyes at hearing his words. "Our girls will have the very best governess. Beautiful clothes. Their pick of handsome men to marry, although…"

Frances moved David to her shoulder and began patting him on his back. "Although?" she prompted, finally warming to his vision for their future.

"I shall be very choosy as to whom they can take as husbands."

She couldn't help the moment of amusement she allowed to show before she once again sobered. Sobered and then sobbed. Could she trust this man? She barely knew him! "And you expect to do all this on the salary of an archivist?"

Even before he lifted his head, Gabe knew she was weeping. "At first. But when I am five-and-twenty, I shall come into some money. There will be enough for a generous settlement for you and our children."

Our children. He spoke the words so easily.

"You're too young to be thinking of marriage," she replied, sure he was younger than she was.

"As are you, but I will have you," he vowed. He glanced over at the nightstand beyond where she lounged, David asleep on her shoulder. The ring from his father's mother, a gold band topped with an emerald, lay where he had left it earlier that morning. Next to it was one from another grandmother, a sapphire mounted on a gold band and surrounded by diamonds.

On his way back from the nursery with David, he had stopped in his bedchamber and rifled through his jewel box. His grandmother, Charity Fitzsimmons Wellingham, might have been the youngest daughter of a viscount, but she had made a proud and cunning countess for the cruel and philandering Graydon Wellingham.

When she had offered the emerald ring to Gabe, she had done so with the words, *Worry not, for it was not a gift from your grandfather but rather a purchase I made for myself during my first month as a widow. One of many, for I decided I should possess at least as many pieces as he gave his doxies. But know this, young man. Quit your mistresses before you wed, and never return to them, or your marriage shall be as fraught with pain and sorrow as mine was.*

Gabe could imagine the Countess of Trenton scandalizing the jeweler in Wolverhampton—and the late earl's man of business—for indeed, the emerald ring was not the only piece of jewelry she had acquired that day. Upon her death, which he imagined wouldn't come for another decade or more, there would be an entire collection of necklaces, bracelets, earbobs and brooches Gabe could bestow on whomever he wished.

As long as it wasn't a mistress. His grandmother had made that provision quite clear.

As for the sapphire ring, he only knew of its intent—to be used as a betrothal ring. Surely giving both to Frances would ensure a positive response.

Instead of crawling over Frances to get at the rings, he rolled off the bed and walked around to the other side of it.

Frances watched as he did so, cursing her body's reaction at seeing him, naked, in the brighter light of morning. She was about to ask if he was leaving when he moved to sit next to her. She placed the dozing David on the bed. Suddenly feeling vulnerable, she turned to regard him, nearly pulling the bed linens up to cover her own nakedness.

He lifted the rings from the nightstand and held them each between a thumb and forefinger. "I want you to be my wife. I want your son to be mine," he said in a quiet voice. He took her right hand in his and slid the sapphire ring onto her finger. Then he took her left hand and slid the emerald ring onto it. "If you cannot give me an answer now, I understand. I can be patient. But I will not let you go back to that awful woman's house. You will live here as long as it takes for you to—"

He couldn't finish. Frances' lips covered his as her hands went to the back of his head. When she pulled away, she said, "You're a very stubborn man."

"So sayeth the prickly woman," he said as he arched a brow, wondering how she would react.

Despite her attempt to hide her reaction, Frances couldn't help the wince that crossed her face. "Prickly?" she repeated as she blinked several times.

"And proud and perfect," he replied quickly. "None of those are traits for which you should apologize, Frances."

"Pride? I do not—"

"I meant you are a proud woman," he argued. "Although, yes, you take great pride in your work, which is to be commended." When she didn't respond, he added, "Always in the pursuit of perfection. I cannot help but love you for it."

This time, Frances did flinch. "Thank you for noticing."

He inhaled and then sighed, a grin finally touching his lips. "I should go get dressed. I'll send a lady's maid—"

"You said you would bathe me," she reminded him, deciding she could display a bit of her prickliness just then.

He displayed a brilliant smile. "So I did," he agreed.

It was another hour before he summoned a lady's maid.

CHAPTER 27

THE WONDERS OF A MORNING

*M*eanwhile, at Woodscastle

Despite the dark drapes covering the windows of the guest bedchamber, a sudden sliver of gray light had Emily rolling over and into James' hold.

"I don't want it to be morning," she murmured.

"It's not yet. Not really," James replied, his eyes closed. They opened suddenly when Emily's hand slid down the front of his body and met his manhood, which most definitely knew it was morning.

"Is it all right if I touch it?"

A sort of growling groan was his initial response. "Only if you are prepared for what will happen next."

Her eyes widened in wonder. "Oh! What might that be?"

James did his best to suppress a chuckle. "I'll make you climb on top of me and demonstrate your riding skills," he warned.

"With this as the pommel?" she asked as her hand wrapped around his morning tumescence.

At first, James thought she was teasing and was about to admonish her, but her expression of wonder was too real. "Perhaps for a start," he murmured. When her eyes rounded, he knew she understood what she would be expected to do. "Have you... done it like that before?"

She swallowed and shook her head. "No, but I've read all the books about sexual congress that we have in the library."

"Oh. Have you now?" he muttered. "I suppose you looked at all the color plates in them, too?"

"Oh, I did that first," she admitted.

James couldn't help but grin. "What makes you think I'll be able to teach you anything new?" The hand holding his manhood slid up and gripped a bit harder, and he inhaled sharply.

"Reading about something isn't the same as *doing* it," Emily argued. Her hand slid back down, but only after her thumb had caressed the sensitive skin at the very tip of his rod.

James stiffened both in body and cock, and he said, "I do believe it is in this case." He took another labored breath. "Time to ride," he whispered, "but not sidesaddle."

"I've never ridden astride," she replied as she climbed over him, her long hair tickling him as it dragged over his chest.

He jerked beneath her, and she paused a moment before settling into place. "Now what do I do?"

Aroused and ready, James was on the verge of simply rolling her over on the bed and repeating what he had done the night before, but he took a moment to gaze at her.

"Allow me to just look at you a moment," he said, quickly taking her hands into his so she couldn't cover anything.

Embarrassed, Emily glanced away, her gaze taking in the dressing table and then the nightstand and finally James as he stared up at her. "Am I... lacking anything? Compared to your mistress, I mean?" she asked.

He shook his head in the pillow. "Not a thing, my sweet. Besides, you have made me forget her completely, and I thank you for that." In the gray light, her erect nipples were partially hidden by locks of her dark blonde hair. The shadows revealed more than they hid, for her breasts were rounder than James had first thought.

Emily was about to argue, but she saw how his gaze raked her body, how his chest rose and fell with his quick breaths. Felt how his cock lengthened in her hold.

Would this happen if he didn't find her desirable? "You're welcome," she whispered. "Now tell me what to do."

"Lift your hips and take me into you." His hands moved to grip her hips, though, to prevent her from coming down onto him. "Wait. Are you... are you ready?" he asked. He slid a hand between her thighs, gratified when he felt the slickness along her feminine folds.

"I wouldn't have woken you up if I wasn't," she said. "I've been wanting you the entire night."

James thrilled at hearing her words. "Why didn't you wake me?"

Her eyes darted to the side. "Well, I didn't want to seem *wanton.*"

His body vibrated beneath her as a guffaw escaped, and she took the opportunity to lift her hips and impale herself on his sword—all the way to the hilt in one swift downward thrust.

James growled in both relief and shock. "My lady. When we are together like this, you can be as wanton as you wish," he assured her, one of his hands holding her hip while the other slid up her body to cup a breast and tease the nipple. He half expected she would ask what to do next, but she lifted off of him slightly and lowered herself back down as he murmured something in a language he hadn't spoken since university.

She repeated what she had done while she said, "Why, I think I should be offended, but perhaps the way you said it suggests you do not mean for me to take offense."

"Oh, I meant no offense," he assured her, his breaths short and growing shorter as her motions increased in speed and his hips thrust up to meet hers.

When he pressed a thumb against her swollen womanhood as she was separating her body from his, he watched as her back arched and her head fell back.

The sight of her in her ecstasy was enough to send him into his own, his seed spilling into her as her body slowly fell down atop his.

His arms fell over her back as a sea of stars passed before his eyes and he passed out.

Boneless, Emily had known James would break her fall, or at least slow it with his powerful arms. Now he, too, seemed to have lost his strength, his body as limp as hers as she settled her head onto his chest and listened as his heart beat a quick tattoo.

After a time, his breaths settled into a regular pattern, and she finally fell asleep.

"After that, I'm left wondering if we might marry on the morrow."

Emily purred as she used a finger to trace a whorl of hair on his chest. "I'm certainly old enough," she replied. "But isn't a special license required for a quick wedding?"

"It is. And I really should bring up the matter with your father," he whispered. "Or Tom." Despite her protests, James slid her from his body and settled her on his side. He then lifted himself onto an elbow and regarded her a moment. "You have done this before, I know, but..." He paused, wondering at his need to be compared to his brother.

"It was nothing like this, James. Nothing like it has been between us," Emily said with a shake of her head.

"Nothing?"

She sighed. "From what little of what my sisters have told

me, I knew to expect pleasure at some point, but I never experienced it with your brother," she said quietly.

James felt a surge of pride, but at the same time, he wondered why his brother wouldn't have seen to Emily's pleasure before taking his own. "Perhaps I am just the better lover."

"Oh, there is no doubt of that," Emily agreed. "But then, you are both so *different*. Which is to be expected, I suppose."

His brows furrowing, James asked, "Why do you say that?"

Emily turned onto her side to face him, one hand pressed onto his chest. "With only your mother in common, it's only logical you two would have different bodies. Different ways of doing the same thing."

James blinked. "What are you talking about?"

Emily stared at him, and her grin disappeared. "Henry's father—"

"*My* father," James interrupted. And then his brows furrowed. "Are you saying Henry's father was *not* my father?"

Her eyes widening, Emily wondered how to respond. "I thought you knew."

James sat up and struggled to control his breathing. "I didn't. If my father, Lord Andrew, wasn't his father, then... then who was?"

Emily sat up alongside him. "He told me his mother had been violated by a rake, Lord Brougham, after a night at the theatre."

James winced and sucked in a breath between his teeth. "Go on."

"Well, despite your father's age at the time—Henry said he was only eighteen—he married your mother knowing she carried another's baby. Henry said he often wondered if it was because Lord Craven had bribed Lord Andrew with a huge dowry, or if his father truly felt affection for his mother."

"He felt affection for her," James insisted. "Father told me that many times after she died of pneumonia." He winced, not having thought of that awful day in 1810 in a very long time. Elizabeth Smith-Jones Burroughs had been a beautiful woman and a wonderful mother to her three children. The thought that she had been forced into a marriage she might not have wanted didn't seem possible.

"How did Henry find out?" James asked in a whisper.

"Just before your mother died, she told him because she said—"

"My father would never tell him," James finished for her.

She nodded. "Something like that." She placed a hand on his arm. "I'm so sorry. I thought you knew all of this."

James shook his head on a sigh. "It explains much," he commented. "Henry was so much like Mother. He was always so sickly, just like her, and he looked almost nothing like me and certainly not like any of our cousins on the Burroughs side," he recalled.

Emily leaned her head against his shoulder. "But in knowing he didn't share you and Sophia's father, I think Henry no longer felt as if he *belonged* quite as much. Especially when he returned from university to discover his father had remarried."

"He was surprised by that," James agreed.

"But you were not."

James settled back onto the pillows and urged her to join him. He wrapped an arm behind her shoulders and pulled her so she was half atop him. When she lowered her head into the small of his shoulder, he kissed the top of her head.

"Before I left for university, my father and I were deep in our cups one night, and he told me how much he loved Jane Vandermeer. Since I'd never met her, I had no idea who he was talking about."

Emily angled her head. "I cannot imagine you—or your father—foxed."

"It is rare," he said just before he yawned. "Makes me wonder if he would have told me about Henry if we'd kept drinking that night."

"Perhaps he did, and you just didn't remember," she suggested.

James inhaled slowly and let the breath out in a *whoosh*. "Possibly," he murmured. "I cannot believe everything that has happened today."

"It has been a day full of shocks," Emily agreed. "Mostly for you, unfortunately."

James almost considered telling her about the rings, but decided the topic could wait for another day.

"May I stay?" she asked. She doubted she could move if she wanted to, every limb so relaxed, she felt limp all over.

He gave a start. "I'm not letting you out of this bed," he replied as he moved to take her into his arms. He had her turned over on her side and bent so her back was against his chest and his knees were tucked in behind hers. "Besides, when you finally do have to get out of this bed, I want it to be light enough so I can see your lovely bum as you walk away."

He felt her body quake with a giggle as he pulled the bed linens over their prone bodies. Warmth immediately enveloped them both.

Closing his eyes as a grin appeared on his face, James fell asleep.

Meanwhile, Emily's thoughts and questions whirled about inside her head, not the least of which was why were there two identical rings atop the dressing table?

CHAPTER 28

A TRUTH IS REVEALED

he guest bedchamber at Trenton House

Wearing the night rail she had shed the night before and drying her hair by the fire, Frances pondered her future. So much had happened in only a day.

Less than a day.

Her thoughts on a marriage to Gabe banged about in her head. There was so much she didn't know about him. That fear of the unknown was quickly countered with what she did know.

He was honorable.

Mostly.

He had, after all, been about to come into the guest bedchamber at the very moment she had opened the door to go to his.

Or perhaps he had merely been on his way to the kitchens, too. She had been the one to pull him into her room. She groaned at the thought of what she had done.

Did he think her a wanton? If he did, would he ask for her hand in marriage? Or had he only done so because they had spent the night together, and he felt honor-bound to wed her?

While most men rarely seemed interested in their children, Gabe was certainly good with her son. She had never seen David so happy. Never heard him giggle in such delight as he had that morning.

And most important of all, Gabe was gainfully employed. If they married and lived in this house, she knew David would have the very best care. And an education.

But just who was the master of the house? The mistress? What would life be like if she had to answer to another woman? Did Gabe merely have a room here? Or the run of the house?

The immediate alternative—returning to the boarding house and leaving her son in the care of the horrible Mrs. Hough—was more unsettling. If she could afford a better place to live, and the salary of a live-in nanny who could see to David, then life in London would be so much easier.

A knock at the door brought her out of her reverie. "Come," she called out.

A young housemaid appeared, her arms laden with several gowns. She curtsied and said, "Good morning, miss. Name's Thompson. I'm here to dress you—and your hair, if you'd like."

Frances blinked. "On a Sunday?" she asked in surprise. She had always thought servants had the Lord's day off.

Thompson shrugged. "Oh, I don't mind, miss. Mr. Wellingham asked if I might bring some gowns for you to try."

"I have my own," Frances replied, indicating the one she had worn the day before. "The rest will…" She paused, not sure when or how she would retrieve her things from the boarding house.

Or even if she would.

"Mr. Wellingham has already seen to arranging for your things to be brought from the hotel where you were staying.

Barclay has sent a maid and a footman to fetch them. You must be so relieved to be finally moving into a real house, if you don't mind me saying so."

Frances gave a start at hearing the young girl's words.

Hotel? Whatever had Gabe told the staff?

"I am," Frances acknowledged, deciding to play along. "It was very kind of Mr. Wellingham to invite me to stay," she said as Thompson held up each gown in turn. Frances nodded at every one.

How could she not? Every one was beautiful. Every one looked as if it were fresh from a modiste's shop. "Who do these belong to?"

"Well, *you*, if you like them," Thompson replied.

Her eyes darting to one side, Frances wondered how it could be Gabe would have women's gowns—very nice gowns —available on a moment's notice. "Does Mr. Wellingham employ a modiste? Here at the house?" A sensation of dread filled her just then. She was probably just one more in a long line of women Gabe Wellingham had invited home for dinner and then seduced.

What else could explain the gowns?

"These did belong to the countess, but the earl prefers she wear gowns more suited to her... title. He has to remind her she's a countess on occasion. Which is probably why the staff here all like her so much."

Frances blinked again. "The countess?"

Thompson nodded. "The Countess of Trenton."

Her eyes darting to one side, Frances recognized the name. The urn and vases downstairs had been commissioned by the Earl of Trenton on behalf of his countess. "She... lives *here?*"

Thompson angled her head to one side. "Sometimes. When she is not at the manor house near Wolverhampton... or at the coaching inn in Stretton... or in Italy. That's where she is now," the maid explained, her smile broad. "I hear it's warm there this time of the year."

But Frances was thinking of the maid's reference to Stretton.

A coaching inn? In Stretton? Why would the countess go there if she usually lived in Wolverhampton? Stretton was northeast of Wolverhampton—not on the way to London at all.

Frances thought back to that day she had received word she had the position at the museum. The day she had hastily packed, left a note of apology at Etruria saying she would no longer be available to work there, and climbed aboard a crowded coach bound for Peterborough. She would have taken the mail coach to Wolverhampton and then changed to a coach bound for London, but it was too late in the day.

She had made it as far as Stretton that first day and then spent the night in a tidy inn.

"A coaching inn?" Frances prompted.

Thompson smiled. "The Spread Eagle. I've not been there, but I hear it's quite popular. Clean, it is, with a taproom and good food, but I would expect nothin' less given her ladyship sees to the place. Have you heard of it?"

Frances managed to hide her surprise at hearing this last bit of news and nodded at Thompson's reflection in the mirror. "I stayed there once, and you are right when you say it is clean."

Beaming, the maid said, "I hear that's where the earl met the countess."

"Indeed?" Frances was about to imagine under what circumstances that event might have happened when she realized she had best get dressed.

She moved to take the nearest gown from the maid, a sprigged muslin in bright yellow, along with her own stays and chemise. She moved to the corner dressing screen. "Will she be... returning any time soon?"

Thompson took the other gowns into the dressing room and hung them on hooks. "I don't think so, miss. They just left a few weeks ago, just after Lady Anne married."

Pulling on the gown, Frances sighed at seeing the expert stitching and styling that had gone into making the bodice. She couldn't fasten the buttons on her own, but she was certain it would fit fine. She stepped from behind the screen and the maid grinned.

"I'll do up the buttons for you," Thompson offered, making quick work of the fabric-covered fastenings. She stepped around to face Frances, checking the fit and the length. "The countess is tall, but then, so are you. I thought I might have to take up the hem, but..." She shook her head and went to collect Frances' shoes from near the fireplace.

"Who is Lady Anne?"

Thompson brought the shoes and knelt down. "Why, she's the only daughter, but she married a future earl, so his lordship was quite pleased with the match."

An earl's daughter marrying a future earl seemed like a perfect match, Frances thought as she stepped into the shoes. She allowed a grimace at seeing her serviceable shoes with such a beautiful gown. Although she owned a pair of slippers, even they would detract from the gown should her feet show whilst she walked. "And what of the... heir?"

"That would be William," Thompson said as she straightened. "He still has a year or two of university, I think, but he's with the rest of the family in Italy."

"And the spare?"

Thompson shook her head. "The countess hasn't yet conceived another boy," she said sadly as she indicated Frances should take a seat at the dressing table. She picked up the comb and began pulling out the tangles that surrounded Frances' face.

"So... how is it Mr. Wellingham has come to live here?"

Frances asked as she watched the maid's reflection in the mirror.

"Well, seeing as how he's the oldest son, he hasn't had much of a choice in the matter, I suppose."

Frances blinked. "The son of the *earl?*" She blinked again. Gabe Wellingham was the son of the Earl of Trenton?

The bastard son.

He had said he was illegitimate.

Frances held her breath as she struggled to think. Think of everything she knew about the young man that had kissed her quite thoroughly at the museum. The man who had asked her to share his dinner, rescued her son, and then made love to her.

Proposed marriage.

They had only known one another for a fortnight!

Thompson nodded, unaware of how Frances stared at her own reflection in the mirror. "And the countess. 'Gabe the Younger,' many call him, because he looks just like his father."

"Indeed?" Frances managed to answer.

"Seein' as how he has a position here in town, I expect the countess would prefer he stay here at the townhouse when she and his lordship return to Trenton Manor. That's their manor house near Wolverhampton," she clarified. "Her ladyship isn't fond of living in London, you see, and besides, she sees to the coaching inn."

"I see," Frances murmured. "One of the earl's businesses, perhaps?"

"Hmm," Thompson nodded. "He bought it for her. Sort of an odd gift, if you ask me, but she was running the place when he married her, and she's determined to keep it going."

"I suppose that's where Mr. Wellingham was born."

And probably conceived.

"Why, I suppose you're right," Thompson agreed as she twisted Frances' hair into a loose bun atop her head. She used the pins that Frances had left on the table the night before to secure the bun in place, but then used the comb to pull some tendrils down at her temples. Although they weren't curly in the fashion of ringlets, they were wavy.

Frances regarded her reflection in surprise. She usually did her own hair in a tight bun at the back of her neck, but the higher, looser style was much more flattering. "It's beautiful," she breathed.

Thompson stabbed a few more pins into the bun and then stepped back to survey her work. "That should do for now, but I'll do it up more fancy for dinner this evening."

Not having thought beyond breakfast, Frances gave a start. *Dinner?* "Thank you. I'll just head downstairs now," she said as she stood up.

"Would you like to wear your earbobs, miss?"

Her hands going to her earlobes to discover she wasn't wearing any, Frances turned and noticed a pair of emeralds lay on the dressing table. "I don't even remember removing them," she said, her words more of a means to cover her surprise. She was sure those weren't there when she had prepared for bed the night before, which meant Gabe had left them.

She glanced at the emerald ring he had slid on her finger earlier that morning. The stones were an exact match, of course.

"Probably took 'em off when you bathed and just don't remember," Thompson said as she helped secure the earbobs into place. "They're quite lovely with the gown. Picks up the bit of green in the embroidered leaves perfectly," she said as she regarded Frances for a moment. "If that will be all?"

Frances was still staring at her reflection, though, barely recognizing the woman who stared back at her. She had youthened, her eyes now a bright green and her cheeks pinked, no doubt from what she'd been doing with the bastard earlier that morning. She finally managed a nod. "Yes, thank you, Thompson."

The maid bobbed a curtsy and took her leave of the bedchamber.

Frances stared after her. *Whatever have I gotten myself into?*

CHAPTER 29

BREAKFAST FOR TWO

*I*n the breakfast parlor at Trenton House
Although an ironed copy of *The Times* sat next to his place setting at the round table, Gabe hadn't yet opened it. He was pacing the breakfast parlor, his gaze occasionally going to the sideboard and then to the door.

The usual array of breakfast foods were set out in covered salvers, the china dishes bearing the Trenton crest. A coffee set was arranged on one silver salver to the left, and a tea set was set up on the right. Had Gabe even noticed the display, he might have asked Barclay why the offerings were more elaborate than usual. Despite his hunger, none of those items had Gabe's attention on this day.

Never before had he noticed the porcelain statues that decorated the top shelf of the sideboard. Each figurine was delicate, painted in muted colors and depicting a scene from the prior century. He stopped and lifted one, turning it upside down in an effort to see if there were any manufacturer's markings. Although he could make out a primitive indentation in the clay, he couldn't read the signature.

"They are not my designs," Frances said quietly, joining

him at the sideboard. "I only ever made vases and urns. Bowls and vessels that could be turned on a potter's wheel."

Gabe gave a start. "I apologize. I didn't hear you come in." Then his gaze took in her appearance. She looked so young, her face glowing in the light from the room's gas chandelier.

He leaned over and bussed her on the cheek. "The yellow is very fetching on you, as is your new hairstyle," he said as he returned the figurine to the shelf.

"I cannot believe the Earl of Trenton would find fault with this gown," she replied, her breath held in anticipation of his reaction. "Or any of the others the maid brought me this morning."

Gabe allowed a one-shouldered shrug. "He prefers that my mother wear more... elaborate gowns," he replied. "Practically forces her to order a new wardrobe every Season even though they only spend a few months here. So he can attend Parliament." Then his eyes widened. "Who said my father didn't like this gown?"

Not wanting Thompson to suffer for having told her about the Earl and Countess of Trenton, Frances asked, "When were you going to tell me you're the son of an earl?"

Gabe allowed an audible sigh, and he led her to a chair next to his at the table. "After you agreed to marry me."

Frances jerked back as if she'd been slapped. "Why not... last night, or... or when I first met you?"

Returning to the sideboard, Gabe dished up a plate for her, selecting one of everything—coddled eggs, ham, a rasher of bacon, roasted tomato—and then adding a slice of toast from the rack. Her eyes rounded as he set the feast before her, and she was about to put voice to a protest when he said, "I didn't want you to know."

He returned to the sideboard and dished up a plate for himself. "Would you like tea? Or coffee?"

But Frances had already moved to his side. "What would you like?"

"You, to be my wife."

"I meant coffee or tea?"

He sighed, resisting the urge to be cross with her. If he just gave her some time, she would tell him why she hadn't yet given him an answer to his earlier proposal. Even better, she might accept the offer. "Coffee. With a lump of sugar."

Gabe half-watched as she prepared his coffee and then made a cup of tea for herself. She set the cups on the table and retook her seat. "Are you ashamed of them?"

"What? No!" Gabe sat down—hard—and then shook his head. "Of course not. They are two of the very best people I have ever had the pleasure of knowing."

"Then... why ever would you keep them a *secret?*"

"They are not a secret," he argued. "At least, not to those who know me well." The words were out of his mouth before he could stop them, and he caught Frances' wince. "I meant the other offsprings of aristocrats, of course," he amended. "I merely..." He sighed again. "I don't wish to be judged because I come from a life of privilege," he finally explained.

Frances sipped her tea, his words reminding her of comments she had made with respect to those who were her betters in Society. "Is that why you took a position?"

He shook his head. "I wanted to work. I have seen what a life of leisure does to some of those who do not have to work, and I do not wish that for myself. Besides, I like being an archivist. I find it interesting, and it's a perfect use of my education. In fact, someday I think I would like Mr. Harris' job."

Frances regarded him with a grin. "I think you would be better at it than he is."

Gabe's eyes widened. "Really?"

She nodded. "I don't believe he has the same sort of *passion* you do for antiquities."

"Would you believe it if I told you that I feel even more passion for you?"

She shook her head. "No."

But a smile teased at her lips, and Gabe merely rolled his eyes as he tucked into his breakfast. He considered how he might frame the question that had him most concerned. When he swallowed, he finally asked, "If you had known I was the son of an earl, would you have come for dinner last night?"

Frances set down her teacup and said, "No."

Surprised by her quick response, Gabe stared at her. "Here I feared that if you did know, then I would never know if you married me because you felt affection for me or... or because I am the son of an earl."

"You don't think it could have been a bit of both?"

Gabe eyed her with suspicion. "You just said you wouldn't have come to dinner if you'd known I was the son of an earl," he argued. "How will we ever end up married if you do not allow me to court you?"

Frances struggled to keep a straight face. His earnestness was on fine display this morning. "Just as you feared being judged because you come from privilege, I feared being judged because... because I do not, and because I have a bastard son," she added in a hoarse whisper.

"Which you now know makes little difference to me," Gabe said, his voice quiet. Despite his request that no servants wait on them this morning, he could just imagine two or three of them on the other side of the door to the butler's pantry, listening in anticipation of some tidbit of gossip. He suddenly straightened. "That's not entirely true."

Frances paused the forkful of eggs that were halfway to her mouth. "What isn't?"

"Your son. I find I am rather enamored with him." The comment was meant to be a tease, but he knew immediately that she didn't take it that way.

Lowering her fork to her plate, Frances narrowed her eyes. "You cannot have him," she warned.

"I don't want him if I can't have you," Gabe countered.

She relaxed, realizing she might have overreacted, and she resumed eating. After a time, she said, "I can understand why you must be wary of women who would only marry you for your..." Rethinking her comment, she gave a huff. "Your *what?* You don't have a title. You *won't* have a title. Why would you be concerned I would only marry you because your father is an earl?"

Gabe drained his coffee and settled back in his chair. "For the money, I suppose. Although, in the interest of full disclosure—in the event you would marry me for money—I cannot collect my inheritance until I am five-and twenty."

Frances blinked. "How old are you now?"

"Two-and-twenty." He leaned forward. "Old enough to marry without my parents' permission," he added, giving her a wink. "Are you old enough to do so?"

She managed to suppress a laugh. "I fear I passed that requirement two years ago."

Three-and-twenty. Old enough to wed.

"Good. Then I can procure a license on the morrow, and we can be wed in a few weeks."

"But I've not yet given you an answer."

He reached over and covered one of her hands with his own. "Then ask me whatever it is that has you hesitating."

A blush colored her face, and Frances wished a servant would interrupt. Or that a caller might arrive. Or that Mrs. Watkins would require her help with David.

But no such interruption occurred, and Frances was forced to give him a reply. "I know you cannot help but be honorable, but I do not wish to marry you if the only reason for your proposal was because you feel... honor-bound to wed me."

"Honor-bound?" he repeated. He appeared confused a

moment before his eyes widened. "Oh, you mean because we shared a bed last night?" The edges of his lips turned up, but he quickly sobered when he saw that she wasn't the least bit amused.

That, and the butler had just appeared on the threshold.

"What is it, Barclay?" Gabe asked of the butler. "I'm attempting to goad Mrs. Longworth into marrying me." He was secretly glad to hear Frances' gasp of surprise. "I don't suppose you have a suggestion as to what I might do to convince her I would make a suitable husband?"

Barclay blinked. "Have... have you proposed, sir?"

"I did that first, of course."

"Did you... give her a ring?"

"Two of them, actually." Gabe reached over and lifted Frances' right hand. "My grandmother's emerald. The stone is perfect and goes quite well with her eyes, don't you agree? The other is a sapphire, of course, because that's to be expected."

Frances seemed impressed by his comments but turned her attention to the butler, curious as to what he might come up with next in the way of a suggestion.

"Did you tell her you would be an excellent catch?"

Turning his gaze onto Frances, Gabe said, "Not exactly, but I think she knows."

"Oh, I only *suspect* he might be," Frances corrected, her attention still on the butler.

Barclay sighed. "Have you told her you hold her in high regard and that you pledge your undying love to her until the day you die?"

"Oh, he hasn't done that," Frances said with a shake of her head, rather enjoying the butler's antics.

"But I do, or.... or I... I will," Gabe argued, his attention going from Frances back to Barclay. Suddenly frustrated, he asked, "Barclay, did you have some *reason* for interrupting our breakfast this morning?"

Stiffening, the butler said, "You have a caller, sir. Mr. Tom Grandby wonders if you might be in residence?"

Gabe blinked. Sunday morning callers were rare. Either Tom was simply in the neighborhood, or something was wrong. "Bring him here, and he can join us for breakfast." He reached out and snagged one of Frances' hands before she was halfway up from her chair.

"You have a guest, and I should check on David," Frances murmured, attempting to escape his hold.

"I have *two* guests," Gabe corrected her. "*Three*, actually," he amended, wondering how David was getting along in the nursery. He urged Frances to take her seat, and after a moment, she did so. "Perhaps Tom can talk you into marrying me," he added.

Frances was about to respond, but Tom Grandby appeared in the doorway, and Gabe stood up to greet him, Frances immediately following suit.

"Good morning. I do hope you're here for breakfast," Gabe said as he shook Tom's hand.

But Tom had noticed Frances, and he gave her a deep bow, an impressive feat given his height. "Good morning, my lady," he said.

Frances dipped a quick curtsy. "Good morning, Mr. Grandby."

"Have you met Mrs. Longworth?" Gabe asked as he directed Tom to the chair across from Frances.

"I've not had the pleasure. It's good to finally make your acquaintance, seeing as how I am familiar with your work at the museum," Tom said as he took the proffered chair. "I have read your character, of course."

Frances' eyes widened. "May I ask how you were privy to the document?"

Tom removed his gloves and set them on an adjacent chair. "I am on the board of directors for the museum. I, in fact, recommended you be hired after both my youngest sister and I read your character."

He gave Gabe a curious glance when his cousin set a filled plate before him and asked if he wanted tea or coffee. "Coffee, please." Then he grinned. "I forgot that it's Sunday. No wonder you're playing at being a footman. For a moment, I thought you'd gone and dismissed the staff."

Gabe gave him a quelling glance as he set a cup of coffee next to Tom's plate. "So, you're not here because something awful has happened?" he half-asked of his caller as he settled himself in his chair. He darted a quick look at Frances and was relieved to see she had resumed eating, although he could tell she was nervous.

Tom shook his head. "At first I thought to let you know that contrary to what I wrote in my note to you yesterday, I wouldn't meet you tonight at White's, but perhaps we should still do so."

His eyes widening with concern, Gabe asked, "Has something happened?"

"Oh, nothing bad, I assure you," Tom replied. "But I thought I should take a ride out to Woodscastle and check on my sister. Maybe spend the night in my old room." He turned his attention to Frances. "Emily is my youngest sister —about your age, I should think—and she has been staying at the family estate all alone whilst everyone else went off to Derbyshire for the holiday."

Frances angled her head to one side. "She is not yet wed?"

Tom shook his head. "I've often wondered if she will ever take a husband. I learned only recently that she was betrothed, but apparently the young man died before they could arrange a wedding."

"How awful for her," Frances commented, at the same moment Gabriel let out a gasp of disbelief.

"I didn't know anything about it until Burroughs

mentioned it at the bank on Friday," Tom said, turning to Frances to add, "James Burroughs is a mutual friend of ours who just recently returned to town from Bath."

"The same one who made the donation of the Greek pots to the museum," Gabe put in.

Frances nodded her understanding.

"Emily offered him a guest room at Woodscastle until he can arrange other lodgings," Tom explained, his comment again directed to Frances.

"How kind of her," she replied, his words reminding her that Gabe had done the same with her. She liked how the older gentleman included her in the conversation. "May I ask how it is you both know Mr. Burroughs? I only ask because I believe I might have met him at the bank this past week."

Tom allowed a brilliant smile. "He's my age, as blond as I am dark-haired, but not quite as tall."

"He's actually a cousin of Tom's," Gabe said. He angled his head, just then remembering how Tom and James were related. "In fact, we were very near to Tom's grandmother's house just last night. She lives... only a few houses from where you have... *had* your rooms."

Curious, Tom turned his gaze to Frances again. "Have you met my grandmother? Mrs. Simpson? Mrs. James Simpson?"

Frances' eyes widened. Although she had only been intro-duced the one time whilst passing the older woman in Kingly Street, Frances had learned from that chance meeting that Mrs. Simpson was the same Mrs. James Simpson that was included in the list of the museum's most generous patrons. That her grandson would hold a position on the board now made perfect sense. "Sophia Simpson?" she asked, just to be certain.

"Indeed! She is my grandmother. My father's mother. Her twins were born the same night as my oldest sister," Tom happily explained. "Rather odd having an aunt and uncle who aren't much older than me," he said with a shrug. "But I suppose it works out fine for Emily, given she's so much younger," he mused, his manner sobering somewhat. He turned his attention to his breakfast.

Still thinking of Emily and the dinner party, Gabe said, "I must not have known Miss Grandby's betrothed, for I don't recall learning of anyone's death among our acquaintances. Well, other than Henry Burroughs." He turned to Frances and said, "He was Mr. Burroughs older brother, and he was always a bit on the sickly side. He died of influenza last spring," Gabe added.

"How awful."

Gabe waited a moment, thinking Tom might offer a name, but when his cousin continued eating, he added, "The last time I saw Miss Grandby was at Worthington House. Last month, when we learned Hexham had proposed to my sister, and Sir Benjamin was about to propose to Lady Angelica."

Tom guffawed. "A rather momentous night, that was," he said. He turned his gaze on Frances. "We refer to the Grandby twins—my cousins by way of the Earl and Countess of Torrington. They are both married now and on their wedding trips."

"They should have made it to Rome by now," Gabe remarked.

"How nice for them," Frances said. "And your sister, Emily? Is she... still in mourning?"

Rather surprised by the question, Tom had to give it some thought. "If she is, she hides it rather well."

Emily had always been more reserved than her sisters. Less apt to display her emotions. But she had taken to spending more time in the library of late. "I think she has become a bit of a bluestocking, what with all the reading she does these days," he added. "It's good of you to ask. I think you two would make fast friends."

"She's sounds lovely," Frances replied.

Tom glanced in Gabe's direction before he redirected his gaze on Frances. "May I inquire as to what brings *you* to Trenton House on this fine morning?"

Frances struggled to keep from blushing. "The promise of a very good meal," she replied as she indicated her nearly empty plate. "And a long discussion about Greek pottery. If we should have a need to get into the museum this afternoon, would you know of a way we might accomplish that?"

Staring first at her and then turning his attention on Gabe, he asked, "What's this about?"

"Burroughs' donation. It's possible one of his pots may have been used to hide the theft of another just like it," Gabe said. "But I have to the check the bottom of an amphora just to be sure."

"Some of the personnel live there," Tom warned.

"I know," Gabe said. "But I'd hate to bother any of them on a Sunday."

Tom sighed but pulled a key from a waistcoat pocket. "Only works on the front door to Montagu," he warned as he passed it over to Gabe. "And I want it back just as soon as you can give it to me."

"Understood. Hopefully, this is all just a mistake. That both versions of the Apollo are there and one has just been misplaced," Gabe explained.

"If not?"

Gabe rolled his eyes. "We'll be in search of an amphora that may already be in someone's private collection."

"Probably purchased from a museum employee for a hundred pounds," Frances added with a look of disappointment.

Tom shook his head. "Keep me apprised," he said on a sigh, his brows furrowing as he turned to regard Frances. "I cannot imagine this is what you expected to be doing when you accepted an offer of breakfast."

"Not exactly, but it is a curious situation. May I refill your coffee?" she offered.

"This morning has also been an opportunity for Frances to see how my mother displays her fine creations," Gabe said before Tom could reply. He stood and reached for the coffee pot. "Vases and pots that my father commissioned." He directed his next comment to Frances. "Do not be concerned, for Mr. Grandby will appreciate knowing the truth of the matter." He set the pot down on the table as he retook his seat and then pulled Tom's letter from his pocket. He extracted the letter from Viscount Henley and gave it to Tom, remembering the missive was intended for Tom and the other members of the board.

"Oh? And what matter might that be?" Tom asked as he straightened with interest and took the letter.

"I don't think that's a good idea," Frances said, her eyes widening with fright. She reached over and poured more coffee into Tom's cup and then into Gabe's, hoping her hand wasn't shaking enough for them to notice.

"But you deserve the credit for your creations, Frances."

Tom narrowed his eyes. "You've made some pottery on commission?" he half-asked.

Frances looked as if she were about to cry. "I did, yes. But it was while I was still at Wedgwood, of course," she replied. "I assure you, I haven't done any of my own at the museum. I only work on museum pieces whilst I'm in my workroom."

"Of course," Tom murmured, wondering at how quickly she had paled. "No one is accusing you of impropriety," he assured her.

"The pieces she created are some of my mother's favorites, including the vase on the hall table," Gabe said, completely missing why it was his words had Frances so worried. When he saw how Tom was regarding Frances with a strange look, though, he cleared his throat. "Now see here, Cousin. Frances is already spoken for."

Tom turned to regard him, a slight grin touching his lips. "As I recall from her character, the young lady is not married," he replied carefully. "

Gabe's eyes darted to one side.

Should he further the fiction that Tom had first suggested at White's? That she had suggested the night before? That Frances Longworth was a widow? The claim would help her case when Tom learned she had a son.

He was prevented from saying anything, though, when Frances answered on her own behalf.

"I am a widow, Mr. Grandby," she stated. "However, Mr. Wellingham has surprised me by proposing—"

"Just this morning," Gabe said, a huge grin on his face. Then he remembered the bet that Tom and James had placed at White's. He desperately hoped Tom wouldn't blurt out anything about it.

Tom's eyes widened and then his brows furrowed in confusion. "And I interrupted?" he guessed.

Frances shook her head. "You arrived in the nick of time."

Gabe sobered. "She has yet to give me her answer."

"Which is her right," Tom said, barely able to hide his humor. He was still a bit bothered by the earlier talk of commissions, though. Francis—Frank—Longworth was supposed to have been the potter responsible for some of the studio's most prized custom pieces. Mrs. Longworth's character had not mentioned that she, too, had been an artist of commissioned works whilst at Wedgwood.

He turned his gaze back on Frances. "Let me guess. Gabe didn't tell you he was Trenton's son."

Frances' eyes widened in surprise. "He did not," she affirmed. She was about to mention she learned it from a maid, but then thought better of it. There was no reason for him to know that she had spent the night at Trenton House.

"He didn't mention that he's to inherit a fortune upon his twenty-fifth birthday?" Tom went on.

"Hmm. He mentioned an inheritance, although he didn't say it was a… was a *fortune*, exactly."

"Oh, it is," Tom said matter-of-factly. "And will be even more so when he's of an age to claim it."

"How do you know?" Gabe asked, shocked his cousin would say such a thing.

"Because your father had me invest it on your behalf," Tom replied. He turned back to Frances and said, "I'd list all the railways in which he has a stake, but I don't wish to bore you."

Frances was about to encourage him to do so when Gabe made his familiar sound of surprise. "Railways?" he repeated.

"There's a shipping company, of course," Tom went on, "and I thought it wise for you to have a stake in Wellingham Imports, seeing as how your father's cousin has done so well with that business."

Rather enjoying Tom's banter, Frances said, "That does seem ever so wise." Then she noted Gabe's continued look of shock, and her grin widened.

"Did he tell you he is illegitimate?" Tom asked, *sotto voce.*

"Thomas!" Gabe scolded.

Frances ignored Gabe and said, "He did. Before any of the rest of it, I'm afraid."

"He doesn't sell himself well, does he?" Tom continued, acting as if Gabe wasn't sitting just a foot away from him.

"He does not," Frances agreed. "But it's quite refreshing in a man, really."

"And he probably hasn't yet plied you with words of love and affection."

Frances blinked, once again feeling as if she were being led into a trap. "Well, not exactly. But he did give me two rings," she added as she held up her hands.

It was Tom's turn to blink, and he sobered considerably.

He turned to stare at Gabe. "How long have you been planning this?"

Gabe rolled his eyes. "I do believe I mentioned my... *attraction* to Mrs. Longworth the last time we met at White's."

While Frances had already turned her attention on Gabe—his comment suggested his regard for her had begun far sooner than the day before—Tom turned to stare at Gabe in disbelief. For perhaps a moment too long, for he remembered that conversation. *Attraction* wasn't exactly the word Gabe had used to describe the pleasant young woman who sat across from him now, her manner at times overly sober and skittish and at other times downright playful.

He almost wished he had met her first.

"So you did," Tom replied slowly, just then remembering how they had teased Gabe. How he and James, in their half-drunk states at the time, had placed bets on a wedding taking place. He turned his gaze back on Frances. "So, Mrs. Longworth—

"Call me Frances, please."

"So Frances, when is the wedding?"

Frances took a careful breath. "Well, if Mr. Wellingham can secure a marriage license on the morrow, then I suppose the ceremony can happen in... a few weeks?"

"If he springs for a special license, you can be wed in a few days," Tom countered. Then he remembered the terms of the bet. "Or you could wait six months."

Tom had to suppress the urge to yell out in pain as Gabe's foot impacted his shin.

"Six months seems rather a long time," Frances commented.

An odd sensation filling his chest, Gabe reached out and covered one of her hands with his. He turned back to Tom and asked, "Will you stand with me?" He wanted nothing more than to be rid of his cousin so that he might take Frances into his arms and kiss her senseless.

"Just let me know when and where," Tom said as he stood up, his expression suggesting he had just remembered something very important.

Something about James Burroughs. About his sister. And Henry.

"What is it?" Frances asked, rising to her feet.

"Something tells me I should head directly to Woodscastle," Tom replied as he quickly pulled on his gloves.

"Is something wrong?"

"My sister is hosting James Burroughs at Woodscastle until he can find suitable lodgings in town," he reminded her. "And other than a few servants, there is no one else staying there."

Frances' eyes darted to one side. "She doesn't have a companion?"

Tom shook his head. "Given she's never been left at home alone before, it's not been necessary."

"You don't believe James will do anything... inappropriate?" Gabe asked, remembering the banker's conversation at White's.

"Probably not." Tom's response wasn't said with much conviction, though. He gave a bow, and Frances dipped a curtsy. "So good to meet you, Frances. I look forward to welcoming you to the family," he said, just before he took his leave.

Gabe watched him go and was about to move to Frances' side, but Tom's sudden change of character had him following his cousin instead. "Pardon me. I'm going to see him out."

"Of course."

When Gabe caught up to Tom in the hall, he said, "If you're worried Burroughs would do something... untoward, I rather doubt it's in his character." They continued to the front door, Tom's pace quickening.

"It's not what *he* would do that worries me," Tom replied.

Gabe stared at him, and then he inhaled slowly. "I think I know who her betrothed was."

"The only dead man of our acquaintance who *might* have proposed to her was Henry Burroughs," Tom whispered.

"James' older brother," Gabe said as he nodded, but then his brows furrowed. "Surely James would have known his brother and your sister were betrothed."

Tom shook his head. "*I* didn't know she was betrothed." He took his hat and coat from Barclay. Despite a blast of cold air, he slowly made his way out the door and into a flurry of snowflakes to his town coach.

CHAPTER 30

BREAKFAST FOR THREE

n hour later, at Woodscastle

Barely conscious, Emily saw light on the other side of her eyelids, and she knew the sun was fully above the horizon. The staff had enjoyed an early breakfast and had already departed for church, so the entire household was eerily quiet.

She opened one eye to regard the clock on the mantel above the fireplace and had to open the other to confirm that it was nearly ten o'clock in the morning. She inhaled, not intending to wake the man on whom she was mostly covering with her body.

"Is it after noon?" he asked in a whisper.

"No," she said as her lips curved into a grin.

A distant *thud* had her on alert.

"What is it?"

The same *thud* occurred again. The front door opening and shutting. A male voice. Humphrey's baritone.

Emily scrambled off of James and out of the bed. She bent to retrieve her night clothes. "I must go. Tom has just arrived," she whispered.

Not nearly as alarmed as Emily, James watched her as she

made a hasty retreat, not through the guest bedchamber's door, but to a panel in the wall near the north corner of the room. "I adore your bum," he said in a hoarse whisper.

Emily gave him a quelling glance as she pressed a spot in the panel along the wood trim.

James watched in fascination as the panel swung open and Emily disappeared behind it.

He had half a mind to follow her, and then remembered her comment about the secret passages that had been discovered in the house when her father had seen to renovations. That was back when Gregory Grandby took Christiana Wellingham to wife.

The year James had been born.

Settling back into the pillow, James inhaled slowly, reveling in the scent Emily had left behind. He wished she were still tucked up against him, her sleep-warm body a welcome addition to his bed.

He dozed for a bit, but opened his eyes when footfalls sounded on the steps leading up to this part of the manor.

When the hard *knock*—and then a rather impatient *knock-knock*—sounded at the door, he called out, "Come," and wasn't the least bit surprised when Tom Grandby opened the door and stepped into the room.

"Good morning," James said as he sat up.

"No doubt it has been as good for you as it apparently was for Gabe," Tom remarked, his manner most severe. His gaze swept the room, and he turned his attention back on James. "Where is she?"

Never having seen Tom so incensed, James blinked. He knew he could feign ignorance, but he had decided just the moment before that in this case, it wasn't necessary. He already intended to bring up the topic of Emily and when he might marry her, so he thought to simply get the embarrassing part out of the way. Admit he had ruined Emily—even though he hadn't—and asked when he might wed her.

And he was about to do so when Emily appeared behind her brother, fully dressed and with her hair done up in a bun atop her head. "Tom?" she called out. "Are you bothering our guest?" She moved up to stand just behind him.

Tom whirled around and stared at his sister. "Where have *you* been?"

Emily jerked back as if she had been slapped. "In the kitchens. I was just letting cook know to start breakfast. Would you care to join us? I can let him know there will be three of us."

Tom glanced between her and James, relieved that James had at least lifted the edge of the bed linens so his bare chest was no longer on display. "I... I had breakfast with Gabe at Trenton House," he finally replied.

"Oh, and how is our cousin?" Emily asked as she stepped up next to her brother. She winked at James.

"Betrothed."

Emily's eyes widened, and James let out a *whoop*.

"Really, James. You sound as if you've won a wager," Emily scolded.

"That's because I have," he said, the bed linens no longer covering his chest. "Just a small one," he added, remembering the issue with gambling. "Well, that is if he is marrying the potter."

Emily glanced at him and then at her brother. "Is he referring to Mrs. Longworth?"

"Indeed," Tom replied, his face displaying a reddish cast due to embarrassment at having barged in on his friend and now because James was doing nothing to hide his nakedness. "She was at Trenton House for breakfast this morning, and she was trying to decide if she was going to accept his offer."

Emily knew immediately that if the young woman was there for breakfast, then she had probably spent the night at Trenton House. "He must hold her in high regard," she said.

James angled his head. "Why do you say that?" he asked

as he stepped out of the bed and moved into the dressing room.

Tom boggled and quickly lifted a hand in front of Emily's eyes. "James!"

"Oh, really Tom. It's nothing I haven't seen before," Emily said with a grin, rather excited at finally getting a glimpse of James in his naked glory. If only the drapes had been open, the room would have been lighter.

Tom's eyes rounded, and his attention darted back to the dressing room door.

"I have four other brothers besides you," Emily added on a huff, leaning casually against the door jamb. In a slightly louder voice, she said, "Although I don't believe any of them can claim such an attractive bum."

"Emily!" both Tom and James scolded.

She ignored them and said, "As I was saying, Gabe Wellingham must find Mrs. Longworth especially appealing. He wouldn't consider a woman to be his wife unless she was as fetching as his mother and just as industrious."

"Wellingham did say as much at White's the other night," James remarked, his head poking out from the dressing room.

"Well, she is that," Tom murmured, his gaze turning back on his sister. "Although maybe from a more artistic standpoint."

Emily gave a shrug. "She worked at Wedgwood's studio, so I would expect her to be. Have you seen any of her ceramics?"

"I may have one in my office, in fact," Tom replied dryly. "But as it happens, some of her best work is on display in Trenton House."

"Really?"

He nodded. "Commissioned pieces," he added in explanation. "Vases, urns... quite beautiful pieces."

"Well, good on her," Emily said with a nod. "And good

for Gabe. He's a bit young, but he's got a position and an inheritance to fall back on should he decide he doesn't wish to work for his living." Her attention went to the dressing room door. "Darling, do you need any help with your buttons?" she called out.

James peeked around the corner again, his head angled sideways. "Thank you, love, but no. I'll just be a moment."

His mouth dropping open, Tom stared at his sister. "Have you...?" he eyed her with suspicion.

"Have I *what?*" Her response sounded more like a challenge than a simple question, which had Tom's brows furrowing.

His voice lowering to a hoarse whisper, he asked, "Have you been *entertaining* our guest?"

Emily's eyes blazed as her hands went to her hips, but before she could reply, James stepped out of the dressing room, fully clothed but for socks and shoes. "You be careful what you say to the future Mrs. Burroughs," James warned. "Or I'll meet you out back for a row in the snow."

Tom's eyes widened, and then he blinked. "Future Mrs. Burroughs?" he repeated, his gaze going back to Emily.

She displayed an ever-so-prim grin. "He proposed last night. In the gardens. Bernard and Mathilda were there to make sure everything was above board."

"Who's Bernard?" Tom's expression had changed from anger to one of confusion.

"My sister's dog," James said as he pulled on his socks and tied the garters.

"And Mathilda is our cow," Emily offered helpfully.

"I know who Mathilda is," Tom replied in a huff. "How long has this been—?"

"I fell in love with your sister over tea that first day I came here," James said as he pulled on his shoes. "But I didn't realize it until a couple of days ago."

Emily regarded him with wonder. "Likewise," she agreed.

"But I must admit I feared you thought only to do right by your brother."

"What about his brother?" Tom asked, once again confused.

"Oh, I was betrothed to Henry," Emily admitted, deciding it was no longer necessary to keep it a secret.

"Over my dead body," her brother replied, his anger once again apparent.

"You mean his?" James put in, coming to his feet to regard his future brother-in-law with a look of resignation.

"No. I mean mine," Tom argued. Then, as if he realized he might have overreacted, he dipped his head. "Apologies. I didn't mean to speak ill of the dead."

From the look she saw crossing his face, Emily knew then that Tom had knowledge of Henry's debts. There was no other reason for him to be so angry about the man.

James stepped over to the dressing table and scooped up the two rings. He shoved them into a pocket and then moved to stand before Tom. "Perhaps we can finish this discussion over breakfast. I'm starving."

"Of course," Tom said with a nod.

James offered Emily his arm, and she placed hers on it. Wordless, the three made their way down the stairs and into the dining room just as Humphrey appeared with dishes for the sideboard. Coffee was poured and plates were filled, and once the three were seated, Tom was the first to speak.

"Who knew you were betrothed to Henry?"

Emily allowed a sigh. "Only Mother and Lady Andrew. You and Father had left to go up north the day after Christina's wedding, so there was no one for Henry to speak with."

"I remember that day," Tom said. He looked to James. "Did *you* know about your brother?"

"About the gambling debt?" James countered, deciding he could get to the crux of the matter. At Tom's nod, James indicated Emily and said, "Not until yesterday."

"*You* knew?"

Emily nodded. "I knew something was wrong. One week he was the happiest man in all of England, and the next week, he looked as if he wanted to die. The week after that, he did," she explained. "But he told me when he first fell ill that his life was in danger. That he needed money to pay off a debt."

"Emily thought to save him by hocking the betrothal ring he had given her," James explained as he took up the story. "But she had a copy made first." He pulled the two rings out of his pocket and placed them on the table.

"*What?*" Emily put her fork on her plate as she regarded the identical rings. Although she had seen them on his dressing table the night before, she hadn't realized one was hers.

"Isn't one of those the ring you've been wearing on a chain recently?" Tom asked. Then his gaze lifted to meet James'. "I recognize those rings."

"No doubt. There must be... ten or fifteen of them in our family alone."

"What?" Emily asked again. "Which one is which?"

James gave his head a shake. "It doesn't matter. They're all the same."

"But the one I was wearing was a *copy*," she argued.

"A copy, yes. But it's not paste as you thought." He lifted each one in turn and showed her the marks on the insides of the gold bands. "See here? This is the mark of the goldsmith who fashioned the piece."

"But... I didn't pay that much to the jeweler who made it," she claimed.

James considered her words a moment. "He probably didn't have to make anything. He just pulled out another from the stash he already had on hand." He regarded the ring he still held and then reached for her right hand. "If it's all right with you, I'll give you this one for now, but find something unique to give you for when we wed," he said as he slid the ring onto her fourth finger.

Emily stared at him and then turned her attention to the familiar ring. "I don't understand," she said with a shake of her head.

"I think I might," Tom said as he plucked the other ring from the table. He regarded it in the light from the overhead chandelier and made a sound in the back of his throat. "I'd wager there are, hmm..." He held out a hand with his fingers splayed out and started counting as he murmured names, all of them descendants of Margaret Merriweather Burroughs, Duchess of Ariley, and Mary Margaret Merriweather Grandby, Countess of Torrington.

The two sisters had at least fourteen sons and grandsons between them, and since Tom had one in his jewel box, he figured all the great-grandsons had them as well. "At least twenty of these," he finished, finally having lost count of the great-grandsons.

James chuckled. "So you think both my grandmother and your great-grandmother gave these to all the boys to use as betrothal rings?"

"They did indeed," Tom nodded. He settled back in his chair and allowed a chuckle. "And the reason I know that is because I saw that same ring just a couple of hours ago."

"On Mrs. Longworth's finger," Emily breathed.

"Indeed." Then Tom sobered. "You said you hocked one to pay Henry's debt?"

Emily nodded. "A few days before he died. He told me everything whilst he suffered a fever. I thought he would recover, and I just wanted him back to the way he had been that first week he courted me." She sighed. "But then the more I discovered about him, the less I wanted to marry him."

"And yet you've agreed to marry his brother," Tom teased.

"Half-brother, yes," Emily replied.

"Half?" Tom furrowed his brows and turned his attention to James. "Dare I ask?"

James shook his head. "A tale for another time," he sighed. "I only just learned of it. I'll tell you about it tonight at White's."

"Gabe will join us there," Tom said. "I rather imagine he will have much to explain."

The three resumed eating their breakfasts, and conversation ceased until Tom asked, "Have you a date in mind to wed? The rest of the family probably won't return from Woodscastle until the end of February."

"I'm not waiting that long," Emily stated.

"I'm not getting any younger," James added.

"Special license?" Tom guessed.

James nodded. "If you'll give your blessing, yes."

"Won't Mother be upset?" Tom asked, directing his gaze on his youngest sister.

Her eyes widened and then she allowed a giggle. "Don't you mean *relieved*? I'm sure she's had quite enough of weddings in this family." She paused a moment. "But I know she would dearly love to see *you* exchange vows with some lovely young lady."

Tom's eyes widened, but the words reminded him of the woman he had just met the day before. "I'm sure she would," he murmured.

He wasn't about to say anything else.

CHAPTER 31

A WOMAN SAYS YES

The hour before, in the breakfast parlor at Trenton House

"Surely he doesn't believe his sister will do something scandalous," Frances said when Gabe returned from having seen Tom to the door.

Gabe didn't return to his seat at the table but rather moved to stand next to her chair. Leaning over, he kissed her first on the cheek and then on the lips. When he finally pulled away, he allowed a long sigh. "I have wanted to do that since before he arrived," he complained.

The corners of her lips lifting at hearing his words, Frances said, "Something tells me you're not a patient man."

He pulled his chair over so he could sit next to her. "I am when it comes to most things in life. But not with you. If you did not agree to wed me until... next year, I could go on just fine knowing I would eventually have you at my side, for the rest of my life," he explained quietly. "But if you hadn't given me an answer, or... or if you had told me to sod off, my lack of patience would have had me doing some rather pathetic pleading and cajoling and behaving in a most immature manner." He noticed how she didn't argue. "And you would, of course, tell me I was being an idiot."

She grinned. "I would, although I would couch it in much more polite terms," she agreed. She leaned over and kissed him, rather liking how shocked he looked, his eyes wide open. When she pulled away, the grin returned to her lips. "You didn't close your eyes," she accused.

"Neither did you," he whispered, pulling one of her hands to his lips so he could kiss the back of her knuckles. "What would you like to do today?"

The query was filled with what sounded like mischief, but Frances could only think of practical matters just then. "Are you certain you wish me to live here? Before the wedding?"

"Absolutely."

"Your neighbors—"

"Are mostly gone from London this time of year," he interrupted. "And for those that are still here, I will have Barclay remind the staff that you are a colleague and staying at the behest of the earl. Just until we're married."

Frances gave him a dubious glance. She knew she would be unable to talk him out of allowing her to return to Mrs. Hough's house for more than just her things. Then she remembered what Thompson had said about the footman and maid who had been sent to pack her belongings. "I should go home and help with the packing."

"It's already being done," Gabe said, his gaze darting to the door. "In fact, I expect the footman and maid who were dispatched earlier this morning will return shortly, if they haven't already."

If Thompson hadn't told her earlier that morning, Frances knew she would be shocked at hearing his words. "But, Gabe, how will they... how will they know what is mine and what belongs to Mrs. Hough?"

"They know not to bring any of the furnishings, of

course, but everything else in your room belongs to you, does it not?"

"I… I suppose."

"And Mrs. Hough would not allow them to take anything that belonged to her."

She furrowed a brow and finally nodded. "True. You needn't have troubled your servants on a Sunday, though. I feel awful about causing them extra work."

"Neither attends church services, and I have seen to it they will earn a bit extra for their work today."

Frances sighed. "You're incorrigible."

"Not usually."

She gave a huff. "I should like to take David for a walk if it isn't too cold."

Gabe brightened at the mention of the babe. "We can go to the park," he murmured. "There's a pram we can use. I'll have Barclay see that it's made ready."

"A perambulator?"

He nodded. "I think Mrs. Watkins has used it on occasion, but she always said it was too fancy for her children. I think it was my sister's."

"Sounds as if it will be too fancy for David."

"Nothing will be too good for him," Gabe replied.

"I will not have you spoiling my son—"

"*Our* son."

Frances couldn't argue further when Gabe once again kissed her.

"Is that how you always intend to shut me up?" she asked when he finally ended the kiss.

"Will it work?" he asked, a brilliant smile appearing.

Frances dipped her head as a blush colored her face. "Probably."

Gabe pulled the museum key from his waistcoat pocket and held it up. "Later, I shall go to the museum and look for the Apollo amphora."

"I'm coming with you," she said. "The search will go faster if there are two of us searching for it."

"If you'd like," he agreed, heartened she had offered. "Come. Let's go up to the nursery and see what David is doing." He stood and offered his arm, but Frances was regarding the dishes.

"I should like to clear away the breakfast—"

"Barclay will see to it," Gabe replied. "There is much we need to discuss, and I wish to learn your opinion on a number of matters."

She regarded him with curiosity. "Opinion?"

He nodded. "Housing first. I cannot yet afford to let a townhouse, but I have been told by my father that I can continue living here until such time that my brother inherits the earldom," he explained. "My mother may have had something to do with his offer. Now that I have a position in town, she wants me to..." He allowed a shrug.

"Remain close?" Frances offered.

"Indeed," he replied. "I think she fears me taking lodgings in a building of bachelors. Spending my nights at gaming hells or..." He allowed the sentence to trail off, knowing he shouldn't suggest he might spend time at a brothel. "Are you amenable to remaining here until I can use some of my inheritance to buy us a house?"

Frances allowed a grin as they climbed the stairs. "I am more than amenable." She furrowed her brows. "Do we then share *your* bedchamber?"

Gabe shook his head. "Oh, no. If you like it, you can remain in the Peach Room. Which I hope you'll do, because there is a connecting door to my suite by way of the dressing room."

She allowed a gasp. "You said the two rooms weren't connected," she accused.

"The bedchambers are not. Just the dressing rooms," he countered, managing to keep a straight face.

"You could have come into my room that way last night."

"I almost did," he admitted. "But I feared you might clobber me with the fireplace poker." They rounded the stairs to go up to the next floor.

"But if I'm using the guest bedchamber, then where will future guests stay?"

"In one of the others."

Frances stopped mid-flight. "*One* of the others? How many guest bedchambers are there?"

Gabe seemed to count in his head a moment. "At least three, but Barclay would know for certain." He urged her to continue climbing. "I'll have him see to hiring a lady's maid for you—

"What about Thompson? It seems a waste to hire another maid if she's able to do it."

"If you like her, and if she has the skills required—"

"Skills?"

Gabe nodded. "Well, it's evident she can style your hair, but she'll have to be the one to see to your clothes, help you dress, and prepare for bed. Help you bathe—"

"You mean you will not?"

Gabe was so surprised by her question, he stopped mid-flight. "If I'm allowed, I would gladly do so," he replied, his manner rather serious. "But I must warn you that there may be occasions when I will end up in the tub with you—"

"You say that as if you think I will mind."

"—Because we'll both need to be ready to leave for the museum at the same time in the mornings, so we can ride in the town coach together."

"No dawdling, of course," she said.

"Well, maybe an occasional dawdle," Gabe argued as he resumed climbing the stairs. His expression remained serious despite his teasing words.

"I look forward to it," Frances replied, a grin touching her lips. "What else must we discuss?"

"I should like to hire a modiste for you."

"But why?"

"You'll need dinner gowns. A ball gown or two. Something for the theatre."

Frances was about to put voice to a protest—she hadn't thought of what might be expected of an earl's son with regard to social engagements. Instead she asked, "Do you expect we'll receive invitations for such events?"

"Well... I already do," he replied. "My legitimacy, or lack thereof, has little bearing when it comes to social engagements. My father has recognized me as his son, so I am afforded the same regard as my younger brother. More so, perhaps, since he is still in university."

Nodding her understanding, Frances stayed abreast of him as they turned to climb the next flight of stairs.

"Do you ride?" he asked.

"Not since I was a child."

"Did you like it?"

"Yes, of course."

"Then I can see to acquiring a horse for you, although Anne may not take her mount with her to Worthington House. I'm sure Hexham has a decent horse for her in his stable."

"I suppose I don't need to mention my lack of riding clothes," Frances said as they made it to the third floor.

"The modiste can make you a riding habit or two," Gabe said as they approached the nursery. "And until then, we can simply ride in the barouche or on my father's phaeton."

"Or walk," Frances suggested.

Gabe grinned. "Or walk."

The door to the middle of the three rooms was open, and the high-pitched voices of children filtered out.

They paused at the threshold, and Frances inhaled softly. There, in the middle of the floor was her son sitting atop a blanket, his gaze captured by the antics of two young children involved in building a tower with brightly painted wooden blocks.

When the tower wavered with the addition of a block on top, the young girl—Frances guessed she was about six—sucked in a breath. Meanwhile the boy, at least that old and perhaps older, scurried backwards and groaned as the tower crumpled and the blocks scattered everywhere.

David giggled as a block tumbled toward him and came to rest against his foot. Sure he would lift it to his mouth, Frances was about to step in when Mrs. Watkins knelt and offered him a rattle instead. The boy retrieved the block as David's attention went to the rattle.

"Is he always this happy?" Gabe asked.

Frances shook her head. "Until today, I never heard him make such a sound."

"But he has smiled before?" he half-asked.

She nodded. "When I've returned from work. I just thought he did so because he knew he was about to get his dinner."

"I'm of the same mind as him with regard to your charms, but for a very different reason."

"Gabe!" she scolded, a flush coloring her cheeks.

"Good morning, Mrs. Watkins," Gabe said when the woman noticed them at the door. "We've come to get David."

"Ah, Mrs. Longworth, Mr. Wellingham, good morning," the older woman said as she made her way toward them. "One of the footmen is seeing to the pram right now. I expect it's already in the front hall for ye."

Frances and Gabe exchanged quick glances. "I hadn't had a chance to speak with Barclay about the perambulator," Gabe said.

"Och, I saw to mentioning it to him first thing, when I took my own tykes out whilst you were busy with the babe.

Chilly morning, but those two don't seem to mind," she added as she indicated her own children.

"Do you take care of other children besides your own?" Frances asked, remembering there were more rooms off the nursery.

"Oh, aye. One of the housemaids has a toddler. He's with her today seein' as how it's Sunday," Mrs. Watkins said as she lifted David into her arms. "Now, he's got a fresh nappy on, so he should be set until you return."

"Thank you," Frances said as she took the babe into her arms. His grin widened as he regarded her, the rattle making noise as he shook his hand in excitement.

"We won't be gone long," Gabe said to the nanny.

"I'll be here when you return," she replied as she pulled several small blankets from a bureau. "Take these to keep him warm," she instructed, "and by the time ye return, I should have his nursery all set up proper like." She indicated the room next door.

Frances blinked, her gaze following the nanny's to see that there was, indeed, a room set up for a baby. "*His* nursery?"

"Oh, aye. His things arrived from the hotel just a few minutes ago, and the footman saw to moving the bassinet in there for me. I just have to put away his clothes and set up a bucket for his nappies."

Curious, Frances stepped into the small room, her attention quickly going to a valise. Inside were David's gowns, nappies, blankets, and other clothes.

"Is everything there?"

Frances gave a start as Gabe wrapped an arm around her waist. He took David from her, relieved when the babe settled onto his bent arm without complaint.

"It looks like it," she said as she knelt down. "I never dreamt he would have his own room." She rummaged through the valise, relieved to see that the housemaid had managed to find all the baby things. *But of course she would*, she thought as she remembered there was only the one chest of drawers. The boarding house room offered little in the way of furnishings and only included a single cupboard for kitchen items.

When David squealed, she gasped and looked up to see Gabe lifting the babe into the air above his head, much like he had done earlier that morning. She nearly burst into tears.

"What's wrong?" he asked as he bent down, David tucked against one shoulder.

"Nothing. Nothing at all," she whispered. "It's just that, at any moment, I'm going to wake up, and it's not going to be..."

She couldn't finish when Gabe pulled her to standing with his free arm and settled his lips over hers. When he finally ended the kiss, he left his forehead pressed against hers. "This had better be real," he murmured. "For what else would explain why my sleeve is wet beneath your son's bottom?"

Her eyes widening, Frances pulled her head from against his. "Don't you mean *our* son?" she asked as a grin touched her lips.

Gabe smiled and kissed her quickly.

"I do."

CHAPTER 32

A PERPLEXING PLOT OVER
A POT

ater that day, in the Roman and Greek exhibit hall, British Museum

Using the key Tom had given him that morning, Gabe opened one of the front doors of Montagu House and slipped inside. Frances followed, cringing when she heard Gabe's boot heels tapping on the marble floor.

"You were wise to wear slippers," he whispered, as they made their way to the hall where the recent Greek and Roman acquisitions were on display.

"Are we expecting anyone to be here?"

"The east wing includes quarters for some of the employees," he replied. "So only if they decide to look at the exhibits."

Frances gave a huff. "I would have liked the option of living here."

"Then you would have had to have been a curator or a keeper," he replied. "Or a custodian." After they turned a corner and were near the Greek exhibits, he added, "I rather doubt those quarters can hold a candle to the Peach Room."

Grinning, Frances agreed.

Gabe hurried up to the amphora featuring Apollo. With

Frances' help, he removed his top coat and shoved his arm through the narrow opening at the top, his fingers just barely grazing the bottom of the pot. He felt the pasteboard card and sighed.

"Is it in there?" Frances asked. She had the other calling cards in her pocket, rescued from the dining table in Trenton House.

Gabe pulled it out and held it between two fingers, his disappointment obvious.

"So this is from the collection that Mr. Burroughs donated," Frances stated.

"Which means the other one that is very similar to this one is missing," Gabe murmured. "The one for which I have papers."

"Papers but no pot. Do you think it's stolen?"

His expression displayed confusion. "Before I show this card and the empty crate to Mr. Harris, I think I should do a thorough search. Your shelves, my office, Mr. Harris' office, the receiving area," he listed as a hand raked through his curls.

"It would be terribly hard to hide given its size," Frances remarked. "But if it looks like this—"

"It does," he affirmed.

"Then at least I know what I'm looking for," she said. When she noticed his expression, she added, "You needn't look so glum."

"I would hate to think that someone who works here is a thief," Gabe said, pulling on his topcoat and readjusting his sleeves. "But if we cannot find that amphora, then I will have to report it as missing."

They hurried back to the basement and parted ways, Frances immediately moving to her shelves to look for the amphora. Nothing stored there was as large as the Apollo, though.

Meanwhile, Gabe entered his cramped office, cringing at

the papers that lay scattered on his desk. He'd intended to leave it more tidy, but he'd run out of time. Frances had appeared at his door to let him know she had changed her mind.

Had that only been a day ago? He glanced at his chronometer.

Almost exactly.

What if he hadn't insisted she join him for dinner?

She would have arrived at No. 9 Kingly Street well before her deadline, and the issue with her landlord would never have occurred.

Her landlord would still be an old crone, though.

Poor David!

"You'll never find it staring at your desk," Frances whispered from the doorway.

Gabe gave a start. "Of course not," he murmured, quickly seeing to the matter at hand. He checked under the desk and then perused the set of shelves that took up one end of the room. Only a few artifacts were there, though. Small pots waiting to be catalogued. Nothing as large as the Apollo.

His gaze went to a cylindrical ceramic container, obviously modern. Before he could examine it more closely or look at the paperwork that sat beneath it, Frances stepped in and shut the door behind her.

"What had your attention so completely just now?"

"Thoughts of you, of course," Gabe replied, finally turning away from the shelf. "Of how different today would have been if I'd let you get away last night."

Her expression of amusement disappeared. "Are you having second thoughts?"

He shook his head. "I am not. I'm wondering how I would have convinced you to give me a second chance." He joined her where she stood. "Make that a first chance. I fear if I had attempted to kiss you again, you would have slapped me across the..."

He couldn't finish his thought. Not with her lips colliding with his. Not with her entire body pressed against his front. When she finally pulled away and her heels once again touched the floor, she angled her head and said. "Or I might have just done that."

Staring at her a moment, Gabe pondered her response. "Oh," he said as he blinked several times. "Oh! Still, I am rather glad it happened as it did."

"Me as well," Frances admitted. She glanced around the office, knowing there was no way the Apollo could be in the cramped space. "What next?"

Reminded of why they were in his office, he said, "The receiving area. I'd like to check any crates that have been opened."

Her eyes rounded. "You do know that's a lot of crates?"

Gabe considered the comment. "Perhaps," he admitted. They took their leave of his office and headed up the stairs and toward the back of the building. At no point did they come across anyone as they made their way as quietly as they could manage.

In the receiving area, the nine crates of pots that had been donated by James Burroughs were where Gabe had found them the night before. "I think it would be a good idea to return the cards to these pots," he said. "Just in case something happens to another pot."

"I can do that whilst you look around," Frances said as she pulled the calling cards from her pocket. She dropped one into each pot as Gabe surveyed the rest of the wooden crates, some of them haphazardly stacked and others neatly arranged. Not a single one of the easily accessed crates contained a Greek pot, which had Gabe rethinking his strategy.

"You've worked here longer than I have. Has this sort of thing ever happened before?" he asked as he rejoined her and then led her in the direction of a stairwell that would take them back to the basement.

Frances angled her head to one side and said, "Only once that I know of."

"Was it found?"

"Indeed." She paused mid-step.

"What is it? Or rather, what was it?"

Her eyes darting toward the ceiling, Frances seemed to think another moment before she said, "It was more of a mix-up really. One of the keepers had Mr. Peabody order something for his office. A blackboard." At seeing Gabe's furrowed brow, she added, "You write on it with chalk."

"I know what a blackboard is," Gabe replied.

"Oh. Well, it arrived, but then was delivered to the archivist for the African exhibits. He had no idea why it was brought to him, but he thought it might come in handy, so he had it mounted on one of his office walls and began to use it to track incoming artifacts."

"That sounds reasonable."

"Meanwhile, the keeper who ordered it wondered why he had received a black mask—one from an African king or some such—since he was the keeper of the ancient Egyptian exhibits."

Gabe took in a slow breath, just then remembering the modern terra cotta cylinder he had seen on the shelf in his office.

"As it happens, the young man who was seeing to deliveries at the time couldn't read very well. He saw 'black' and just mixed up the two items."

"Frances, you're a genius," Gabe said, his steps quickening as he headed toward his office.

"I am?" She watched as he took off at a run, disappearing into his office.

Before Frances reached the door, he was back out again, carrying the cylindrical pot. "What is that?"

"One ceramic plant container, manufactured by the Apollo Pot Company," he read aloud from the paper that had been underneath it. "Stoke-on-Trent."

Frances gasped. "I've heard of them, of course," she said. "But... who ordered a plant container?"

"Well, *I* certainly didn't, and I rather doubt Mr. Harris did." Having a difficult time supporting the pot while trying to read, Gabe offered her the paper. She took it and read it, finally allowing a sigh of frustration. "It only has Mr. Peabody's name here at the bottom," she said.

"Then that is where we shall start," Gabe said as he headed to the other end of the hall. Although the door to the Acquisitions Office was closed, the handle lowered and the latch gave way.

Frances entered first. She stepped aside to reveal the Apollo amphora sitting on the floor next to Mr. Peabody's desk. A small potted palm, still in its plain nursery pot, had been placed over the mouth of the amphora.

Gabe set the pot he held on the man's messy desk and held his breath as he removed the potted palm from the top of the amphora. "Is there already soil in there?" he asked, an expression of pain crossing his face.

Frances peered inside and grinned. "None." She moved the Apollo to the side and motioned for Gabe to set down the other pot in its place. Once he had it in position, he dropped the potted palm into it—the nursery pot nested perfectly inside the cylindrical pot.

"Well, that makes for a rather attractive display," Frances murmured as she stepped back to admire the palm. "I wonder if Mr. Peabody could find a palm for my workroom."

Gabe gave her a quelling glance. "Do you think he truly intended to put that tree into my Apollo pot?" he asked in dismay.

She shook her head as she placed the paper onto the middle of Mr. Peabody's desk. "Darling, if he had, he would have already done so," she replied. "Although your Apollo is far too large for the palm, the neck is too small for its trunk, so he couldn't have used it as a planter for this tree if he had wanted to. You had nothing to be worried about."

Gabe hefted the Apollo pot into his arms. "This belongs in the exhibit hall," he said as he stepped out of the office.

"Actually, it belongs in my workroom," she countered. "There's a bit of painting that has to be done on it, remember?"

Wincing, Gabe asked, "Oh, must you?"

"I'll be sure it's removable," she promised. "Just think. A hundred years from now, some poor potter is going to have to restore all these Attic pots to their original condition because genitals will be in fashion again."

"You managed to say that without blushing," Gabe remarked.

"That's because you're a bad influence," she accused.

He set the pot on Frances' worktable and arched a brow. "Does that mean I don't have to worry about you obliterating mine?"

Her eyes rounding, Frances did blush that time. "As long as they do my bidding, you've nothing to worry about."

The two took their leave of the museum in a hurry.

CHAPTER 33

A CONCLAVE OF COUSINS AT WHITE'S

ater that night at White's Men's Club, St. James Street Gabe found Tom Grandby where he usually sat, a glass of brandy in one hand and a letter in the other. He waited until Tom noticed him before he moved to join him.

"Thank you for meeting me," Tom said as he stood up and shook hands with his second cousin. "I half expect James to join us. I invited him when I spoke with him this morning."

"Thank you for the invitation," Gabe replied, noting a footman was already seeing to his drink. "I take it all was well when you arrived at Woodscastle this morning?"

Tom rolled his eyes. "It was. I may have overreacted."

"What exactly did you expect to discover?"

"Emily, in bed with James."

Gabe blinked and then allowed a shrug. "Although I do not know Mr. Burroughs well—I've only met him here the one time—I do know Emily. Why, I think she would make a fine match for him."

"You are right, of course. It's just, something happened last spring, and ever since, she's been... *different*."

Gabe seemed to think on the comment a moment before he asked, "Did you discover if she was indeed betrothed to Henry Burroughs?"

"She was," Tom said quietly. At seeing Gabe's look of pain, he added, "I confirmed it with her this morning."

"Poor Emily," Gabe breathed. "She never said a word of it."

Tom pinched his lips together. "Knowing what I do about him now, I have to admit I am relieved she was never his wife." He went on to explain the situation, Gabe listening intently.

When he finished, Gabe murmured, "So... he needed Emily's dowry."

"Indeed. And I cannot say that I would have discovered the truth before they said their vows. If he had not died, Emily would have been in an impossible situation."

"Surely you or your father would have helped," Gabe suggested.

"We would most certainly have seen to an annulment, but that would have left Emily ruined. She wouldn't have been able to make an advantageous match," Tom insisted.

Gabe gave him a quelling glance. "You underestimate your sister, for I have always found her agreeable," he said quietly. "If I had never met Frances, I would have been glad to take Emily to wife."

Tom considered his words for a moment. "Thank you for saying so." He took a deep breath and nodded to the footman who delivered their drinks. Then he leaned back and regarded Gabe with an arched brow—a brow that then waggled in a tease. "Frances did say *yes* this morning, did she not?"

Gabe inhaled. "She did."

"So what, pray tell, happened last night?"

"We had dinner together."

"And yet she was there for breakfast this morning."

Gabe nodded. "Yes. I invited her for breakfast." There was no need to mention the fact that he had seen to it she was now living in Trenton House.

Tom angled his head to one side. "I recall not even a week ago that when James and I placed our bets, you were quite adamant that you were not considering her for marriage at all."

"That's because I wasn't."

At that moment, the two became aware of a rather tall man standing next to their chairs. They looked up in unison to find James regarding them with an expression that suggested he had news.

"Did I hear the word *marriage*?" he asked with a grin.

Gabe stood and shook hands with the older gentleman. "You did. Within a week, I shall owe you some money."

"And what about me?" Tom asked as the three took their wing-backed chairs.

"Your bet was for six months. His was less than four," Gabe reminded him.

"Is this the same woman you said was *prickly*?" James queried.

"She... had a reason to be, but I believe I have seen to it she will no longer be." Gabe paused. "Prickly, that is. I still expect she will be *particular*. Which is a necessary trait in our line of work."

James leaned forward. "What have you done?"

Gabe inhaled before he said, "I proposed. This morning. She finally accepted, and we're to be married. Soon, I hope."

James looked to Tom. "Well, it seems you were telling the truth this morning at breakfast."

Tom gave him a look of chagrin. "Of course I was. And I'd like to think I helped Gabe gain an advantage with the young woman—"

"Advantage?" Gabe repeated. He turned to James. "He made me out to look like a fool."

"I did my due diligence," Tom argued. "I had to see to it that she understood just how good a catch you were."

Confused, James shook his head. "What the hell happened?"

Gabe said, "We had dinner together last night. We spoke of many things, and... well, let's just say I'll be a father a bit sooner than I ever expected. Gladly, though. Her son David is—"

"Not yours, I hope," James interrupted in a whisper.

"Oh, no, of course not. But, I will recognize him as my own, just as soon as I can."

"How old?"

"About seven months."

"Seven months?" Tom struggled to keep his voice down. "How can that be?"

"She was with child when she started work at the museum," Gabe replied, keeping his voice low.

"No one said anything about it," Tom claimed.

"That's because no one knew."

Tom glanced around, as if he feared eavesdroppers. "Why in the devil would she leave Staffordshire if she was with child?"

Gabe hadn't wanted to explain too much, but Tom was family, and he had a stake in Frances' position at the museum. "She applied for the position at the museum because she had to get away from her situation in Staffordshire. Away from a man who threatened to give away her secret if she didn't... accommodate him."

James' wince matched Tom's. "Whatever secret could a woman possess that would be worth that sort of... of blackmail?" James asked in a hoarse whisper.

Gabe directed his answer to Tom. "If I tell you, you must promise me she will not lose her position at the museum."

"I cannot do that if she's done something illegal," Tom argued.

"She has not. Well, other than misrepresent her identity."

Draining his brandy, Tom gave a nod. "All right. I promise she will not lose her position."

Gabe inhaled slowly. "She was Frank Longworth."

Tom narrowed his eyes. "I knew it," he said.

"What? How?"

"When you spoke of her having done commissions for your father. Those vases were most definitely done by Frank Longworth."

Clearly not understanding the importance of Gabe's claim, James furrowed his brows. "Who was Frank Longworth?"

"Frances Longworth," Gabe replied.

"Not the daughter... or... or the widow of Frank Longworth?" Tom half-asked.

"Daughter of," Gabe replied. "But when the real Frank Longworth suffered an apoplexy and could no longer create pottery, she took his place at the potters' wheel."

"And this Frank is important... how?" James queried, obviously still confused.

"He... *she* created pottery on commission at Wedgwood's studio up in Staffordshire," Gabe replied. "Beautiful pieces. All attributed to Mr. Francis Longworth."

"I have one of Longworth's vases in my office," Tom commented. "A stunning example of the perfect shape and artistry."

Gabe said, "My mother has at least *five*, including the large urn on the table in the front hall. All of them were commissioned by my father."

Tom gave a nervous laugh, and then he sobered. "She must have been rather proud to see one of her pieces so prominently displayed."

"She was not."

When Tom frowned, Gabe added, "She couldn't understand how it was that pieces she had created under commission ended up in a house to which she had been invited to dinner."

"Surely she knew she was in Trenton House," Tom remarked.

Gabe didn't reply, but James allowed a guffaw.

Rolling his eyes, Tom remembered their discussion over breakfast. "You hadn't told her you were Trenton's son."

"I hadn't, but she knows now."

Another brandy appeared at Tom's elbow, and he was quick to take a drink. "Prickly, was she?"

"Damn you," Gabe countered.

"Oh, good God," James said suddenly. "That's probably when you had to tell her you're a bastard and won't inherit the title."

"Oh, I already had," Gabe said. "I mean, I had told her I was a bastard, but that was before she learned who *my* father was. *Is*."

Tom leaned forward. "How did the topic even come up?"

Gabe regarded his brandy a moment before a brilliant smile lit his face. "David is about the same age I was when father found out about me," he said in a quiet voice. "Which brings me to the reason I came tonight, even though I would much rather be at home with them."

"Oh?" Tom and James weren't sure if they should be offended or impressed.

"I was wondering if you might consider being his godfather?"

A laugh erupted from Tom before he sobered. "I am honored, of course," he murmured. "But... I am not married—"

"Your cousin Milton was not, either, but he took on over twenty godsons and goddaughters before he took a wife," Gabe reminded him.

Dipping his head, Tom said, "True." He gave the request a

moment of thought. So far, none of his siblings had requested he be the godfather for their offspring, but then, he was already their uncle. "Perhaps it's time I consider such matters."

Gabe straightened in his chair. "From the manner in which you just said that, I have to wonder if changes are in *your* future."

Looking ever so uncomfortable, Tom finally shrugged. "Possibly," he hedged.

"You mentioned in your note that you had to see someone about a horse."

"Indeed."

"And?"

Tom pretended the matter was of little consequence. "A potential client is all. I received a request to meet with someone regarding their investment opportunities," he explained. "They have a fortune that must be protected. They also happen to train horses for the racing circuit."

"Are you buying a race horse?" James asked in surprise.

"No." The word held the sort of finality that suggested James shouldn't inquire further, which instead had him furrowing a brow.

"What's her name?"

His mouth dropping open, Tom straightened in his chair. "Whatever has you asking *that*?"

"If it had been a *man* looking to protect a fortune, you would have said so," Gabe accused, reminded of his expectation of M. F. Longworth. Of course he had thought she would be a man. Mr. Harris expected *she* would be a *he*. Even Tom had assumed it from having read her character before she was hired by the museum.

"You know that I cannot disclose my clients' identities," Tom stated. "Besides, I haven't yet decided if I will take her on."

"Because you have feelings for her?"

"What? No!" Tom appeared a bit too exasperated and said, "No," one more time.

Gabe's eyes widened in delight, and he said, "Perhaps I should pay a visit to the betting book," he teased.

"Don't. You'll only lose," Tom warned with a shake of his head.

James exchanged glances with Gabe, and the two were up and out of their chairs in an instant, hurrying off to the room in which the book was mounted for all to see.

Rolling his eyes, Tom glanced down at the letter he still held.

A letter of apology.

It was the very last thing he had expected to receive from the woman he had met with the afternoon before, but it meant he had a decision to make. Take her on as a client, or walk away.

There was another option, of course, but he couldn't think about that just now.

Gabe and James returned, huge grins on their faces.

"You and I have exactly the same problem," Gabe announced.

Tom frowned. "And what is that?"

"We're in love."

James cleared his throat, which had both Tom and Gabe turning to regard him. "I probably should mention that I, too, have proposed marriage on this day."

Gabe stared at him before he chuckled. "Emily?" he guessed with a huge grin. His gaze quickly turned to find Tom displaying an unreadable expression.

"I thought to speak with you about it this morning —*before* you learned I planned to marry her," James said in his own defense, "but then Emily interrupted us, and I didn't get the chance."

Tom dipped his head. "And I didn't have the chance to ask if you are only doing this because she was to marry

Henry?" Their earlier conversation would have been different had Emily not been present. They might have very well ended up in a row in the snow.

James winced. "Of course not. Truth be told, I had already made up my mind about her before she told me about Henry. And what a shock that was."

"So, *you* didn't even know she was going to marry your brother?" Gabe asked.

The younger brother shook his head. "My stepmother, Lady Andrew, knew. So did Emily's mother. As far as I know, they kept the betrothal a secret from everyone else."

"But why?" Gabe asked.

Tom inhaled sharply. "They must have known about Henry's debt."

"They did," James confirmed. "Or, at least Lady Andrew discovered it and then shared what she knew with your mother," he added as he nodded in Tom's direction.

"But how did *Lady Andrew* find out?"

"Henry needed money. He wouldn't have gone to Father," James replied. "He knew better. But he always had Lady Andrew's ear, because she knew his secret."

"Secret? You mean that he had debts?" Gabe queried.

James shook his head. "The other secret. Turns out, my brother was actually my *half*-brother. His real father was some rake who took advantage of my mother after the theatre let out one night. When her father, Lord Craven, learned a child was on the way, he negotiated with my father for a quick wedding to save her reputation."

Tom's mouth dropped open as he stared at his cousin. "However did you discover this?" he asked in a whisper.

Not wanting to admit he had learned it all from Emily only the night before, James said, "It seems Lady Andrew and my father were in love even before my parents wed. But her father had arranged for her to marry the Earl of Stoneleigh, so my father accepted Lord Craven's offer."

"Well, this certainly explains why you and Henry were so *different* from one another," Tom murmured.

Gabe's brows furrowed. "Do you think he asked Lady Andrew for the money to pay his debts?"

"Oh, I am most sure of it," James replied. "And when he couldn't get the funds from her, he courted Emily."

"Which is why Lady Andrew told my mother," Tom guessed. "And why she kept it a secret from all of us."

The three men regarded one another in turn.

"What other secrets do you suppose these women are keeping from us?" James asked as he settled back in his chair.

Gabe finished off his brandy and allowed a wan grin. "I cannot imagine Frances having any more secrets, but I shall endeavor to learn them all. Starting tonight," he said as he stood up. He pulled the museum key from his waistcoat pocket and offered it to Tom. "Mission accomplished. The Apollo amphora has been found—"

"Where?"

"In the Acquisitions Office. Mr. Peabody's order for a plant container from the Apollo Pot Company ended up in my office and the real Apollo ended up in his."

"And the pots that I donated?" James queried.

"All unpacked and accounted for. Are you quite sure you wish to donate *all* of them?"

James allowed a shrug. "Of course, unless... why do you ask?"

Gabe regarded Tom a moment before he said, "Your Apollo is a close copy to the one that was missing."

"So... it's not worth much then," James guessed.

"Oh, it's from 350 BCE," Gabe countered. "And in far better shape than the one I was in search of."

James and Tom exchanged glances. "I've already made the donation, but if... if the Apollo is in your way, I suppose I can find a home for it somewhere."

Gabe arched a brow. "I think I can ensure it's considered superfluous."

"I will take it, then," James agreed.

Giving the two older men a bow, Gabe said, "Gentleman. I am going home, and tomorrow, I'm paying a call in Doctors' Commons for a marriage license."

James straightened in his chair. "If you'd like, I will join you on the morrow in Doctors' Commons." He drained his brandy and dared a glance at Tom. "I think I, too, will be taking my leave so that I may learn all of Emily's secrets," he said as he stood.

Tom rose and straightened to his full six-foot, two-inch height and said, "And I will come learn with you. About time I spent a night at Woodscastle," he said, one eyebrow arched.

Giving him a quelling glance, James said, "I am not going to like you as a brother, am I?"

Tom shook his head. "Probably not."

CHAPTER 34

A QUIET NIGHT BEFORE BED

A half-hour later, at Trenton House

After Gabe had peeked into the Peach Room and found it unoccupied, he made his way up to the nursery. Although the three rooms were quiet, he stepped into the baby's room and held his breath.

The oddest sensation gripped his chest, and he knew he had made the right decision when it came to Frances. The woman might be a force to be reckoned with in the workplace, but she was also a good mother.

Dressed in the frilly nightrail she had been wearing the night before, she sat in the rocking chair, David held in her arms. He had been nursing and was now sound asleep, and after a moment, Gabe realized she was as well.

Recalling the number of times they had made love the night before and then again that afternoon when they had returned from the park, he thought she deserved to sleep. He had been selfish, he decided, even though she had been a willing participant. An enthusiastic lover after their first coupling had proved to her how pleasurable making love could be.

Moving to stand by the side of the rocker, he carefully lifted the babe from her arms and placed him in the bassinet.

Then he turned and was about to lift Frances into his arms when she awoke with a start. "Shh," he whispered. "I just put him down, and it looks as if you require your bed."

Frances stared at him. "What time is it?"

"Half-past ten o'clock," he replied.

"And you're home already?"

"Well, of course. I'd rather be here with you, and besides, we must be at work in the morning."

She allowed him to help her stand and was gratified when he took her into his arms and hugged her. When he kissed her on the temple, she asked, "Did you even have anything to drink?"

"Just a brandy," he said as he led her out of the nursery and to the steps. "If I drink two, I get terribly tipsy, and I talk too much."

Frances suppressed a giggle. "I shall remember that."

"It seems we are in good company when it comes to our nuptials."

"Oh?"

"James Burroughs—"

"The one who donated the Greek pottery?"

"Yes, that's the one. He has asked Emily Grandby for her hand, and they plan a quick wedding," he said as he opened the door to the Peach Room.

"And you think they will make a good match?"

"I do. He's older than Emily by... oh, a dozen years, but I sometimes think of her as an old soul." He paused a moment. "Would you like me to ring for your maid?"

"No," Frances replied. "She already helped with my buttons earlier this evening."

He glanced around the room, noting there were items on the dressing table that hadn't been there in the afternoon. "Did Thompson already see to putting away your things?"

Frances nodded. "She did. And she mended two hems and a hole in one of my stockings."

"We can get you some new ones."

"But—"

"Then you can give the others to her."

Frances was about to put voice to a protest, but then understood what he was trying to explain. "Is that true for other clothes as well? The maids get the hand-me-downs?"

"Gowns, at least," Gabe acknowledged. "Does that bother you?"

She shook her head. "I am glad to learn they are not discarded."

Gabe glanced over at the bed, noting that Thompson had turned down the bed linens, and the lump at the end of the bed suggested she had placed a warm brick beneath the linens and blankets.

"I wrote a letter to Mrs. Hough to let her know I would no longer require lodgings in her house," Frances said as she moved to climb into the bed.

"Barclay will see to its delivery," Gabe said as he pulled the bed linens over her. "Did you gloat?"

"Of course not!"

"Not even a little bit?" he teased as he sat on the edge of the bed.

Frances allowed a sigh. "I said that I accepted the offer of a room and a nursemaid at the house of one of the museum patrons," she explained.

"You didn't tell her you had accepted an offer of marriage?" he countered.

Frances allowed an impish grin. "I didn't wish to gloat."

Gabe grinned and then leaned down and kissed her. "If you prefer, I will sleep in my own bed—"

"I do not."

Blinking, he regarded her a moment. "I was terribly

selfish last night. I thought perhaps you might want a full night's sleep."

"You thought wrong," she replied. "Now, do you need help with your buttons? You *are* going to join me in this bed, are you not?"

For a moment, Gabe struggled to keep a straight face, for her tone of voice and words of insistence were exactly how his mother sounded when she was in want of something.

Frances Longworth might not look like his mother, but she was most certainly much like her in other ways.

"Yes, my lady," he replied. "But I can see to my own buttons."

Glancing down, he realized she had already undone the ones on the fly of his trousers and was working on those at the bottom of his waistcoat.

"Or not," he added with a happy sigh.

CHAPTER 35

MONDAY MORNING MURMURS

The next morning at Woodscastle

"I cannot tell you how glad I am that there are secret passages in this house," James whispered as he practically fell onto Emily.

She giggled softly, her sleep warm body now tingling from their early morning lovemaking. "I shall have to make use of the longest one at any moment. I expect Tom will awaken soon."

Emily had pretended to sleep in her own bedchamber the night before, but stuffed her bedcovers with pillows and then sneaked around the house via the hidden passageway to Emma's bedchamber. From there, she made it into the guest room and James' bed.

"Will I see you before I leave for the bank?" James asked as he rolled off of her, heartened to hear her mewl of protest. He propped himself up on one elbow and watched her with heavy-lidded eyes.

"I'll be down for breakfast."

He kissed her lips and then the back of one of her hands. "I'm going to join Mr. Wellingham for a trip to Doctors' Commons today. To buy a marriage license," he said before he kissed one of her nipples. "To think, a week ago I hadn't given a thought to marrying at all."

"I blame that on your mistress," Emily remarked, rather enjoying his attentions.

James furrowed his brows, wondering if he had heard her correctly. "My mistress? What did she have to do with it?"

"Her constant complaints had you believing that all women behaved like she did."

Regarding her with a frown, he allowed a sigh. "There are certainly many who do," he argued.

"Why do you say that?"

"I pay mind to some of the comments made by my fellow men. Those who have been married for some time."

"But what man would wish to take a wife if that's his expectation?" she asked in a whisper.

"None, I suppose," he replied. "But there are other considerations. Obligations."

"Heirs, yes, but until Henry's death, you weren't under any pressure to marry, were you?"

He shook his head, his tongue darting over one of her nipples.

"Then, are you marrying me because... because you now have the obligations that Henry once had?"

Realizing she might be leading him into a trap from which there would be no easy escape, James paused in his ministrations and pretended to think. "Now that you mention it, that might be one of the reasons."

She jerked under his touch and made eye contact. "There are others?"

He chuckled, which had the entire bed vibrating. "Shall I list them all?"

"Oh, please do," she encouraged. "And don't leave any of them out."

"You're a saucy wench, you're more wanton than is proper, you have a beautiful bum, and I love you."

Emily giggled, but then her mouth formed an 'o' as she peered down the front of her body. "So my breasts don't figure into it?"

"Oh, yes. Did I not mention those?" he teased. He sobered and then settled back onto his elbow. "I will admit Lady Andrew gave me a bit of a push in your direction, but I could think of nothing and no one but you that first day you invited me in for tea," he murmured. "I was quite smitten."

"I'm so very glad I left a good impression," she replied.

"Which begs the question. Why would *you* wish to marry a man who is half again as old as you?" he teased.

Emily gave him a brilliant smile. "For your fortune, of course. And for the tumbles," she replied, dimpling.

"Not for my bum?" He leaned over and kissed her on the cheek.

"Oh, that, too. And because I love you, and I want you to be the father of my child," she added, kissing him before she slipped out of the bed. She scooped up her bedclothes from the floor. "See you at breakfast, darling," she whispered, just before she disappeared behind the panel in the wall.

James settled back onto his bed and allowed a chuckle. It seemed married life would be quite different from what he had expected it would be.

CHAPTER 36

AN UNWELCOME VISITOR

ater that morning, at the British Museum
Edward Cooper stepped out of the smelly hackney and turned his gaze onto Montagu House. Despite the rain, or perhaps because of it, a number of people were making their way into the sixteenth century building.

From this vantage, it was hard to believe a rather large—and growing larger—museum was located within. He double-checked the dog-eared note he carried in his waistcoat pocket, confirmed the address, and made his way to the entry doors.

Once he was in the first hall, he paused. The sheer enormity of the place had him boggling. If Frances truly worked here, as her father had insisted when Edward had paid a call on the man the week before, then he would have to find an employee and inquire as to her whereabouts.

The visit to Frank Longworth's cottage on the edge of Stoke had been a lark. He had half-expected to find Frances still living there, even though several of the potters with whom she worked claimed she was no longer in Stoke.

"Gone to the capital," one of them told him. "Pro'bly to get away from the likes of you," another said.

Although the words had been said in jest, Edward bristled and threatened to fire the man.

He had the power. He was in charge of production at one of the studios.

The thought that Frances Longworth could simply leave Stoke without a backward glance—and barely a note of warning to her studio—had barely registered with Edward.

At first.

There were other women he could compel to his bed with threats. None were as comely as Miss Longworth, but it hardly mattered if he didn't have to look at them as he had his way with them.

But then Frank Longworth's absence—or at least his artistic talent—had been noted by others farther up in the company. After a few more months and an angry exchange with one of his superiors, Edward was warned he had to find a suitable replacement. Someone who could churn out the highly valued pieces commissioned by the wealthy. Someone who could paint them with the same deft hand.

Edward already knew Frank Longworth had suffered apoplexy—discovering Frances had essentially taken his place gave him his leverage over the woman—until she suddenly resigned and took her leave of Stoke.

Well, he had to get her back.

He was prepared to offer her higher pay than she had received the year before. How much could she be making working at a museum?

"Pardon, sir, but might you know where I can find Miss Longworth?"

The museum guard shook his head. "Couldn't tell you."

Edward furrowed his brows. "Couldn't? Or won't?" he challenged, dipping a hand into a waistcoat pocket in search of a shilling. Surely bribery would work to gain the information he needed.

The expression on the guard's face suggested he wasn't the least bit impressed by Edward's tactic. "Can't," he replied. "Don't know who you're talking about."

Sighing, Edward said, "The potter?"

A glimmer of recognition seemed to pass over the guard's face then. "Oh, the lady who fixes exhibits?"

Not exactly sure what Frances did for the museum—Frank had merely said she worked here—Edward said, "That would be her."

The guard shook his head. "That area is off limits to patrons, sir."

"Then who do I need to speak with?"

His gaze slowly traversing the hall and then the stairs leading to the floor above, the guard said, "Mr. Harris, but I don't see him out here."

Edward stepped away from the guard. Armed with a name, he made his way through the crowd until he reached the opposite wall. He noticed a well-dressed young man coming from the direction of a stairwell.

He pulled a card from his waistcoat pocket and held it out. "Might you direct me to where I can find Miss Longworth?"

Angus Peabody took the card and gave it an assessing glance. Noticing the reference to pottery below Edward's name, he said, "We already have a source for her supplies."

"Of course. I'm an old friend. Just in the city for the day and thought I would pay her a call."

Screwing his face in annoyance, Angus said, "Don't be long. A whole shipload of crates just arrived, and she's probably buried in work."

"I'll be but a moment," Edward promised.

"Downstairs. Third... or fourth door on the right, I think," Angus said, hurrying on with his own errand.

Edward watched the man take his leave before he made his way to the stairs. As he descended, he passed a blond gentleman making his way up. Edward was about to say something to him, but merely nodded in his direction when he noticed that the man seemed distracted.

But then the blond man stopped on the stairs and said, "Pardon me, sir. You cannot go down there."

"Oh, but I've an appointment. With Miss Longworth," Edward said as he waved his calling card.

Gabe Wellingham furrowed his brows. He had just come from the workroom, a brief stop to remind Frances he was headed to Doctors' Commons. She hadn't said anything about an appointment, but then her worktable held three kraters and a rhyton from that morning's delivery.

"Well, then, good day." Gabe continued on his way toward the front doors, his mind on finding a hackney. The guard near the front door caught his eye, though, and he made his way to the large man.

"What is it, Mr. Thompson?"

"My sister tells me she's become a lady's maid for a new guest at your townhouse."

Gabe did his best to maintain an impassive expression. "Ah, yes. Mrs. Longworth was in need of a new situation, so it only seemed prudent to offer her a room. It's not my townhouse, though. I just have rooms there."

The guard gave him a knowing glance. "You're secret is safe with me, sir."

"Secret?"

"That you live in an earl's home. According to my sister, it's quite a lovely place."

Gabe inhaled. "Yes, yes, I'm very fortunate to live there."

"Some bloke just waved his card saying he was looking for Mrs. Longworth."

Gabe nodded, wanting to be on his way. "I passed him as he was about to go down the stairs."

"Didn't like the looks of him," Thompson stated. "Besides, what's a man from Stoke doing here looking for her?"

Inhaling sharply, Gabe faced the guard. "Stoke?" he repeated. "What was his name?"

"Edward Cooper. Something having to do with pottery."

But Gabe was no longer listening. He was already making his way though the crowds and to the stairwell.

CHAPTER 37

A NECESSARY CONFRONTATION

*M*eanwhile, downstairs in the pottery workroom

When yet another knock sounded at the workroom door, Frances didn't bother looking up. Three deliveries had already been made that morning, the treasures from the *Sea Breeze* arriving on a series of dray carts from Wapping.

Her attention on a small crack in the Apollo amphora, she called out, "Come," as she used a tool to determine how deep the crevice extended into the clay.

"So *this* is where you've been hiding."

Frances straightened so quickly, she nearly sent the pot toppling over the edge of the worktable. "Mr. Cooper?"

"In the flesh, as they say," he replied, his brows waggling.

"What are you doing here?"

Edward's attention went to the shelves of pottery and then to the antiquities that nearly filled the worktable. "Looking for you, of course. You left and didn't even say good-bye."

She allowed a shrug. "The coach schedule didn't allow for the niceties that day."

A hand going to his chest, Edward affected an expression

of hurt. "You didn't really think you could just leave and not expect me to look for you?"

Frances pinched her lips together, tempted to say something entirely unladylike. Instead she managed to say, "I didn't give a thought to you at all, actually."

Edward's face darkened. "Really, Frances—"

"Mrs. Longworth," she corrected.

"Oh, is that how they know you here?" he asked as he waved a hand.

"It is. Now, if you would be so kind as to leave, I have work to do."

"Work?" he repeated, his voice mocking. He waved at the pots on the worktable. "A bit beneath your skills, are they not?" He took a step in her direction and paused, pretending to study the krater.

"Not usually," she replied, turning her attention back to the cracked pot.

"Not a very welcoming place to ply your craft," he went on. "Surely you miss the studio?"

"I do not."

"Miss the pay?"

She gave him a quelling glance. "As I recall, I was paid half of what you paid the men who worked on the regular line."

"Well, that's why I am here. To offer you your old position at *double* the pay."

"And which position would that be?" she responded tartly. "The one at the studio? Or the one I had to assume when you were blackmailing me?"

Edward's eyes widened, a hint of anger appearing. "Now, see here—"

"Leave, Mr. Cooper, or I shall have you escorted out," she demanded.

"If you think I'll allow you to insult me like this, think

again, Mrs. Longworth," he countered, taking another few steps in her direction.

Her eyes darting to a nearby pot, Frances wondered if she might have the strength to lift it and then hurl it at the cur who was essentially blocking the only way in or out of the workroom. "Insult?" she repeated in the most pleasant voice she could manage. "Why, I'm surprised you would even know what that is, Mr. Cooper."

About to advance on the potter, Edward gave a start when the door flew open.

Breathing heavily from having run from the bottom of the stairs, Gabe stared at Frances and then turned his gaze on the caller. "You said you had an appointment," he said in as calm a voice as he could manage.

"I did," Edward replied. "I was offering Mrs. Longworth a position. Her old position. At twice the pay," he claimed.

"Does that include an appointment for continued blackmail as well?" Gabe asked.

Edward turned a steely gaze on Frances. "What *lies* have you been telling these people?"

"Nothing but the truth," Frances stated.

"She's lying," Edward said to Gabe. "I employed this woman as a potter in Stoke."

"And threatened to expose her as Frank Longworth if she didn't warm your bed," Gabe countered.

His eyes blazing, Edward seemed about to deny the claim and then changed his mind. "Beds were rarely involved," he hissed.

"Ah, so you admit it." Despite his immediate urge to smash a krater over the man's head, Gabe turned to the door. "Thompson!" he called out.

The burly guard appeared at the door and peeked into the workroom. "Yes, Mr. Wellingham?"

"Hold this man until either a Runner or a Peeler gets here. I wish to press charges—"

"Charges?" Edward repeated. "But I've done nothing wrong."

Gabe's attention went to Frances. "Where shall we start?"

Frances inhaled slowly and realized this was her chance to get even with Edward Cooper. "Embezzling from his employer will garner the most interest, I should think," she said as she crossed her arms. "I'm sure they will be interested in hearing the stories I was told by Mr. Cooper before I left their employ."

Struggling to hide his reaction at hearing this new accusation, Gabe said, "And then the blackmail?"

"Yes," she agreed. "By now, I expect there are other women who have been forced to keep their silence by his threats."

"And then there's trespassing," Thompson said from where he still stood filling the doorway.

Edward stared at each one of them in turn. Knowing his exit was blocked, he lifted a pot from the shelf and held it out in front of his body. "If you don't let me go this instant, I'll drop this," he warned.

Gabe hissed as the guard paused in his advance. Frances merely arched a brow. "Really, Mr. Cooper. Have you no regard for ancient antiquities?"

"None."

Frances allowed a shrug. "Then I guess you'll have to drop it," she said.

Trapped and now incensed, Edward let go of the pot as Gabe yelled, "No!"

The guard quickly moved to grab Edward, pulling his arms behind his back as the amphora smashed into what seemed like a thousand pieces on the concrete floor. The shards scattered about, finally coming to a halt a few seconds later.

His hands on either side of his head, Gabe stared at Frances and wondered at her expression.

With her arms crossed and her arched brow, she looked as prickly as he had ever seen her. "Frances?"

She turned her gaze on him and gave him a brilliant smile. "It was one of mine," she said with a shrug. "Now I have the potsherds to fill in the missing pieces," she said as she indicated an identical amphora on the shelf. "This has to be my favorite puzzle of all," she added as her gaze scanned the floor. After a moment, she dipped down and then straightened, holding a triangular-shaped potsherd. "Here's one of them," she said as she held it up.

Gabe's gaze went from the amphora with several voids to the floor, where the rest of her matching pieces were indeed among the rest of the shattered amphora. "You minx!" he murmured, a grin slowly appearing.

"I'll see to this cretin," Thompson said as he pushed Edward out the door.

Careful not to step on the shards that littered the floor, Gabe rushed over and pulled Frances into his arms. "Are you all right?"

"I'm fine, really," she whispered. "But thank you for coming when you did."

Gabe nodded. "When Thompson said a man from Stoke was here to see you, I..." He paused. "I don't know what came over me, but I just knew I had to come. You're under my protection now."

Frances lifted her head from his shoulder. "We're not even married yet."

His eyes widened. "The license! I was on my way to Doctors' Commons when I ran into Thompson," he said, stepping out of her hold. Then he gave her a quick kiss and made his way out of the workroom, gingerly stepping around the potsherds as he took his leave. "I'll be back."

CHAPTER 38

REASONS TO MARRY

An hour later, in Doctors' Commons

"Fancy meeting you here," James said as he joined Gabe on the pavement outside the archbishop's office and offered his hand. "I was beginning to think you might have developed a case of cold feet."

Gabe shook his hand. "Apologies for the delay. We had an incident at the museum—"

"Is everything all right?"

"It will be. A Peeler was being summoned when I was finally able to leave," Gabe replied, remembering how Thompson was still man-handling Edward Cooper while another guard was sent to fetch a constable.

"Did someone try to steal something?" James asked as they made their way into the building.

Gabe was about to reply in the negative, but he allowed a grimace and said, "Some*one*, as a matter of fact. The cur was there for Frances. Her blackmailer," he added in a quieter voice. Before James could respond, Gabe held up a hand. "He thought to bribe her to return to Stoke. Offered her the same position she had at twice the pay."

"She didn't take it."

"Of course not," Gabe replied. "I'd been warned by one of the guards that a man had asked about her, and I raced off and managed to get down to her workroom..." He stopped speaking, his breathing labored from just having relayed the incident.

"In the nick of time, it would seem," James murmured. "Look, we don't have to do this today," he said, about to turn around and lead them back out the door.

"Oh, yes we do. *I* do," Gabe argued. "I cannot tell you how... *frightened* I was for her. I am her protector now."

James narrowed his eyes. "It would seem you were frightened for yourself as well."

Gabe jerked as he regarded his new friend. "What are you saying? *I* was not in any danger."

Angling his head in an attempt to be sure they weren't being overheard, James whispered. "Maybe not you, but your heart?" At Gabe's sound of disbelief, he added, "What if she had taken the offer?"

"She wouldn't have!" Gabe replied, trying hard to keep his voice down. "If she was frightened of him, she surely did not display it. At least, not after I got there."

"Standing up to him, was she?" James suggested.

Gabe blinked. "He brought forth her *prickly* side," he affirmed. "If he hadn't dropped a pot, she no doubt would have dropped one on his head. Probably kicked him in the balls, too."

James winced. "So, she was never in any real danger?"

"I don't know that," Gabe replied. "She surely was in the past. He violated her. He got a child on her."

"You met the man who was responsible for your betrothed's move to London," James stated. "It's a wonder you didn't kill him."

"Hardly."

"Face it, Wellingham. You never would have met Frances Longworth if she hadn't been forced to leave her situation in

Stoke," James said quietly. "Perhaps meeting her nemesis was a good thing for you."

"Good?" Gabe's anger once again surfaced. "What are you saying?"

"Now you know," James replied. "You'll never have to imagine what he's like. Never wonder if he was jilted or deserved to be left behind. You'll always know he was a dishonorable man. You'll always know Frances was telling the truth about him."

"I already knew that," Gabe murmured.

"So... you still wish to marry her." It wasn't a question.

"I do. Today, if I can."

James held up a staying hand. "Perhaps we can make arrangements to marry at the same time. Prevail upon Grandby to act as one of our witnesses," he suggested. "I can make arrangements to take a day from the bank, and you two can take a day from your positions at the museum."

"That sounds reasonable," Gabe replied. He glanced towards the clerk's desk and was about to head in that direction but then paused. "I know we spoke briefly of this at White's, but *are* you marrying Emily out of a sense of honor? Because she was betrothed to your late brother?"

"Of course not," James replied. "I knew I wanted her to be my wife before I even learned about the two of them," he claimed. "What's this about?"

Gabe rolled his eyes. "I have known her almost my entire life. She is friends with my sister. I just... I don't want to see her hurt."

Anger lit James' eyes. "I assure you, I have no intention of hurting her," he ground out. "How can you even—?"

"I only feared you were trying to do right by your brother, in which case you would eventually feel ensnared by a trap of your own making," Gabe explained.

"I am not, I assure you." The mere reminder of a trap—

hadn't Emily voiced the same concern?—had him on the defensive.

"You're much older than she is. More worldly."

"Oh, she's more worldly than you think," James replied, remembering the words he had used to describe her earlier that morning. "And I love her dearly for it."

"You'll get her out of Woodscastle?"

James frowned. "What's wrong with Woodscastle?"

"She's the youngest daughter. If you continue to live there, she'll have to see to her mother in her dower years," Gabe reminded him.

"I'm buying her a townhouse as a wedding gift. In Mayfair," James replied. "But even if she does have to see to Mrs. Grandby..." He paused and allowed a guffaw. "You do *know* Mrs. Grandby, do you not?"

Gabe gave a slight shrug. "I have met her, of course," he hedged. "She's a cousin of mine."

"No one will have to take care of that woman in her dower years. She'll want the entire house all to herself," he said with a grin, one that was quickly matched by Gabe. James glanced over at the clerk. "Now, have we put voice to all our concerns?"

Allowing a sigh, Gabe said. "We have. At least until Tom decides to marry, and then we'll have to repeat all of this with him."

James gave him a huge grin. "Then let's do this. I'm not getting any younger, and you're... you're so damned young. Are you sure you wish to get married?"

"I am positive," Gabe replied.

Pulling their purses from their waistcoat pockets, the two made their way to the clerk's desk.

A half-hour later, they emerged from the office and hailed hackneys headed in opposite directions, wedding dates in mind and marriage licenses in hand.

• • •

hen Gabe returned to the museum an hour later, he met with the constable who had been summoned. Although Thompson had been able to relay the charges as he remembered them, the Peeler insisted on speaking with Gabe.

"I can only charge Mr. Cooper with trespassing," the constable explained in a quiet voice. "I don't have any jurisdiction over anything he might have done in Stoke," he added. "But I rather imagine if you sent word to his employer about the embezzling, he would have him charged up there."

Disappointed, Gabe asked, "Can he be put in gaol? For a night or two, at least until we can send word ahead?"

The constable seemed to think on the query for a moment. "I suppose if he makes a move to escape or tries to take a fist to my face, I could ask my commander to keep him locked up for an extra day," he suggested.

Gabe winced. "I'd rather you not get hurt, sir."

"Oh, I don't intend to. Got his hands locked up tight and a wagon on the way to collect him," he replied. Then he gave Gabe an exaggerated wink. "We'll make sure he's on the first coach out of town, but not for a couple of days," he added.

Gave shook hands with the man and hurried to the pottery workroom. He wanted to kiss Frances before returning to his office to pen a letter.

CHAPTER 39

A WEDDING GIFT OF MONUMENTAL PROPORTIONS

A few days later, outside of St. Paul's Church
Tom Grandby regarded the two newly-married couples who stood before him, the women both clutching rolled-up marriage certificates and small bouquets of hot-house flowers while the men exchanged glances that might have held as much sudden terror as they did happiness.

"Well, I'd suggest meeting you two at White's tonight, but something tells me you will not take me up on the offer," he said with a grin.

"I think I might be available Monday night," James suggested, his eyes darting sideways to see how Emily would react.

"I promise I will not mind as long as you come home," she replied, her face beaming with happiness.

Gabe dared a glance at Frances. She blushed and managed a shrug. "I shan't mind. I have another man at home I can spend my time with," she teased.

"Monday night then," Tom said. "Congratulations to all of you."

He moved to step away when James said, "You really must consider doing this, and soon, Grandby."

Tom paused and regarded his friend with a pained expression. "We'll see," he replied. Then he tipped his hat and hurried off toward his town coach.

James and Gabe exchanged quick looks before they shook hands and murmured their congratulations to one another.

"We're off to Trenton House for a late breakfast," Gabe said. "And we'll probably do a wedding trip in the summer."

"We'll be staying here in town," James said, his comment eliciting a look of surprise from Emily.

"But... I didn't bring a valise."

James merely grinned. "None needed, my sweet. Good day to you both," he said as he led his new wife to their town coach.

Gabe chuckled as he watched them go, knowing exactly where they were heading.

*M*eanwhile
"Are we going to a hotel?" Emily asked when James finally climbed into the town coach and took a seat next to her. He'd been conversing with the driver, but not loudly enough for her to overhear their conversation.

"We are not," he replied as he settled an arm around her shoulder. The coach lurched into motion.

When he didn't offer more information, Emily furrowed her brows. "Are we going to a coaching inn?"

James chuckled and realized he needed to tell her something. "We are not."

"Are we going to a friend's home? Or... or one of your relatives' houses?" There were so many Burroughs who lived in London, they could end up in Cavendish Square or Westminster or Mayfair.

"We are not. I do think you will like it, though."

Emily shoved out her lower lip. "Something tells me

you'll like it even more, since I won't have any other clothes to wear, and I'll be forced to be naked whilst there."

James made the growling groaning sound. "Oh, my sweet. Now you've gone and put an image in my head that I do not wish to erase," he whispered.

She crossed her arms as a giggle erupted. "Where are you taking me?"

He inhaled and let the breath out slowly. "This was supposed to be a surprise. We are going to your wedding gift," he finally answered.

Emily's eyes darted to one side. "It must be a rather *large* gift," she reasoned.

James seemed to consider the comment for a moment, as if he were counting in his head. "Four floors, nine... no make that twelve rooms, not counting the servants' quarters, of course—"

"You bought me a *house?*"

"In Curzon Street, yes," he replied. He was about to say more, but she was suddenly kissing him, her body repositioned so she was practically sitting atop him in the cramped coach. He wrapped his arms around her waist and held her as she continued to kiss him.

When she finally pulled away, mostly because she had to take a breath, James murmured. "I was planning to give you a tour, but something tells me—"

"Library first. Then the bedchamber," she said before she resumed kissing him.

James was the first to pull away when that kissed ended. "The library?"

Emily blinked several times. "There is a library, is there not?"

Struggling to remember the rooms in the house—he had only been there the one time prior to arranging for its purchase—James said, "First floor. I apologize, but there are no windows in there," he warned.

A brilliant smile lit her face. "Well then, it will be perfect." She resumed kissing him, and James realized the library would soon become his favorite room in the house.

CHAPTER 40

A WEDDING GIFT OF
MODEST MEANS

ack at Trenton House

"You seem awfully anxious to be home," Gabe teased as he paused before the front door of Trenton House.

"I am. I want you to open your wedding gift," Frances replied. Despite the gray skies, she displayed a smile and the rosy blush of a newly married bride. She also carried the marriage certificate, carefully rolled up and secured with a ribbon.

Barclay opened the door, and Frances was about to step in, but Gabe put out an arm to stop her.

"What is it?"

"I wish to carry you over the threshold," he replied, lifting her into his arms.

"Oh!" she cried out, giggling as Gabe carried her into the house.

He set her on her feet and gave his hat to the butler. "Barclay, I am a married man."

"Congratulations, sir. My lady," the butler replied as he took Gabe's greatcoat.

"Thank you," Frances said as she removed her redingote, her excitement palpable. "Come. Your gift is in the study."

Gabe gave Barclay a glance of curiosity, annoyed when the butler pretended he hadn't heard her comment. "You didn't have to buy me anything," he said when Frances took his hand and pulled him toward the study.

"I didn't *buy* it," Frances replied. "I made it."

Pausing just inside the door, Gabe stared at the huge pasteboard box that sat atop the mahogany desk. A red satin ribbon adorned the top. "Frances," he breathed.

"It's a bit heavy, so—"

"Then how did you manage it?"

"Barclay helped, of course," she replied, practically bouncing on her toes. "Open it."

Gabe leaned over and kissed her cheek. "I will, but then it will be my turn to show you your gift," he said.

"But, you already gave me two rings," she protested, holding out both hands, palms down.

He wasn't about to tell her that in addition to a wedding band, James had bought a townhouse for Emily. Just down a few doors and across the street from Trenton House.

Grinning mischievously, Gabe regarded the box another moment before he untied the ribbon. Then he noticed the box had no bottom—only sides and the top. "Hmm," he murmured.

"You just have to lift it off," she said, nearly ready to do it herself. "Straight up."

Gabe placed his hands on either side of the box and did as he was told, his manner sobering as the gift was revealed. "Frances," he breathed. "You made this?" He set aside the pasteboard and leaned in close to the examine the pelike, an exact replica of the one in Tom Grandby's office. "How?" he asked in awe.

"I remembered what you said about Mr. Grandby's pelike. That you would be happy to have one, even if it was a copy," she said as she studied his reaction. "So I sent a letter to him asking if I might see it. He not only allowed me to pay a call to his office to take measurements, he had it delivered to my workroom so that I could copy it exactly," she explained.

"He never said a word," Gabe whispered.

"Well, I did ask him to keep it a secret," she said. "Do you... like it?"

He turned to her and allowed a brilliant smile. "I love it," he said. "Not as much as you, of course."

She smiled as he took her into his arms. "Now I'll have to decide where I wish to display it," he murmured. "I can hardly wait until we have our own house. This can be the featured piece in the front hall," he claimed with some excitement."

"I made sure it can hold water if you wish to use it as a vase," Frances said.

"No water," he said with a shake of his head. "I shouldn't want to risk it. If a servant were to break it while they filled or emptied it, I would be sick," he replied. "No, this will eventually have a special place in my study."

"Well, I'm glad you like it."

Gabe finished perusing the pelike and then stepped back. "Now it's your turn, but I hardly think you'll like my gift as much as I do mine."

Hesitant, Frances took his proffered arm, and Gabe led her down the corridor toward the back of the townhouse. "I feared it wouldn't arrive on time, but it was installed just yesterday," he said as he paused before the last room, one that was opposite the kitchen.

"Installed?" Frances repeated. Both of her dark eyebrows arched. "Whatever could you...?"

She stopped speaking when Gabe threw open the door. What had been a storeroom was now a pottery workshop, complete with a potter's wheel and a kiln. There was a workbench along with wooden shelves already stocked with clay, pigments, glazes—Frances couldn't begin to take in every-thing all at once.

"Do you like it?" Gabe queried. "I had help, of course, because Barclay had to find a carpenter to do the shelves and build the table," he explained before his face screwed up in a grimace. "I feared this might be a bad idea, given it's your daily job, but you seem to take such joy..." He had to stop speaking when her lips collided with his, her kiss as enthusiastic and as thorough as any they had shared before.

When Frances finally released Gabe, she said, "I love it. I do. But not as much as I love you."

Gabe took her into his arms and hugged her hard. "I have something for David, too," he murmured. "Some *things*, rather."

Frances leaned back in his hold. "*Things*? As is more than one?"

His eyes darted to the side before he said, "Yes."

"You're going to spoil him rotten, aren't you?"

His eyes darted to the other side. "Yes," he admitted before his dimple appeared and he nearly laughed.

Frances grinned as tears spilled down her cheeks.

"Oh, don't cry, my sweet," he said as he took her back into his arms. "They're just things. A few toys. A rocking horse. A high chair. Things he can share with his younger brothers and sisters when they come along."

Frances buried her face against his shoulder, her own heaving with a sob. "Just adopting him has been enough."

"Ah, about that. I spoke with my father's solicitor, and I only need claim the child as my own. I have done so with the marriage settlement—"

"Marriage settlement? But... but I have no dowry," she argued.

Gabe shrugged. "I didn't require one. But everything has been put into writing," he replied. "David's education and a settlement for you when I die. Should something unusual happen that leaves me destitute, the solicitor has assured me the earldom will see to your welfare. It's part of what my father settled on me when he acknowledged me as his son."

She gasped. "Nothing unusual had better happen to you," she said in alarm.

He grinned. "We'll remind my mother of that when she returns from the Kingdom of the Two Sicilies and discovers I've married without her as a witness," he said jovially.

"She'll hate me, won't she?" Frances asked on a sigh.

"Oh, no. She'll love you for having taken me off the Marriage Mart before some destitute baroness can force her daughter on me," he teased. When he noted her wince, he added, "And because you're Frank Longworth."

"You're sure?"

He nodded. "Now, let's go see to that son of ours and then get to work on the next one."

Frances allowed a brilliant smile. "Lead the way."

Six weeks later, at Woodscastle

The crunch of coach wheels in the crescent drive had Emily lowering her book onto her chest. Given her husband's head was in her lap—he'd been napping on her and the large sofa in the Woodscastle library since their return from church that morning—she had to wiggle her thighs to rouse him.

"What is it?" he asked as he blinked awake, attempting to peer at her from beneath her bosom.

"Someone's just come into the drive." The sound of another coach made its way through the front window, and Emily inhaled. "They're home."

Humphrey had given her a letter from her mother that morning with word that the family was departing Cherrywood and would be on their way home the next day. That was four days ago. She had been expecting her family's arrival at any time.

James groaned. "I suppose that means I must give up this particularly interesting view of you and prepare for lots of people," he complained. He sat up and regarded his wife with a look of worry.

"There aren't that many of them that still live here," Emily assured him. Her parents, her oldest brother's family, and her youngest brother numbered just eight. "It won't be as chaotic as was at Merriweather Manor, and we'll leave for our home tonight if it's too much for you."

They'd had dinner at Merriweather Manor the night before, and given the late hour, they had elected to stay at Woodscastle rather than returning to their townhouse in Mayfair. By the time they made the short trek to Woodscastle at nearly midnight, Emily and James were both exhausted.

"I'll be fine," he said as he offered her a hand and then pulled her up from the sofa and into his arms. "We'll be fine," he amended. "But I do love that we can spend the night in our own home tonight."

Emily took a deep breath and let it out before she kissed him. "I look forward to it. Did you know we're across the street and only a few doors down from Gabe and Frances?"

"And close to the park," he said, as they made their way to the front door. They hadn't yet taken advantage of their proximity to the park, but would do so when the weather improved.

And when they weren't spending so much time in the library. Or one of the bedchambers. They still hadn't decided which one they liked the best.

Humphrey already had the door open, and several children spilled into the house, their faces happy at seeing their youngest aunt, each one taking turns to meet their new uncle.

Next came Roger, whose boisterous laugh and good-natured ribbing reminded Emily that James and Roger had attended university together. His raven-haired wife, Helen, the daughter of their uncle's business partner, Todd Vandermeer, pulled Emily into a hug and bussed a startled James on the cheek.

He barely recognized the willowy woman who was nearly

as tall as her husband, despite having been introduced to her a number of times during his university days.

Emily's youngest brother, Milton, came next, his hands spreading out on either side of his body as he gave his sister a brilliant smile. He shook James' hand, vowed he would follow in his cousin's steps by not marrying until he was in his forties, and announced he needed to take a piss. He sauntered off as James struggled to keep a straight face.

"Well, he's not changed a bit," they both said in unison, and then they laughed.

Emily inhaled and turned her attention to the last of those who stepped into the house. "Welcome home, Mother. Father," she said, always amused by the fact that her father was well over six feet tall while her mother was barely five.

Christiana Wellingham Grandby, her curly hair cut short and streaked with gray, regarded her youngest daughter with a happy sigh and then turned to look up at James. "I never thought it would take you this long to snag one of my daughters," she scolded. "But you did end up with the best one. And if you repeat that to any of my older girls, I will deny it."

Chuckling at his wife's comment, Gregory Grandby gripped James' hand in a firm handshake. "Thank you," he said. "You received the settlement?"

James nodded. "I did, thank you. I've seen to arrangements for Emily, of course, and I bought a townhouse in Curzon Street."

"So soon?" Christiana mewled. "When will you move?"

"I already have, but you can pay a call anytime when you're in town to shop," Emily offered.

"Oh, I'll do more than that," Christiana countered. "I'll take a room there for respite." She quickly added, "I'm only teasing, of course," her comment directed to James. "I know I said I wanted ten children, but then I forgot they would eventually come with offspring. Now it's as if motherhood has started all over again." Then she sailed off in the direction of the Grandby wing.

James gave Emily a sideways glance, and she gave her head a slight shake. "Not until we're sure."

Gregory caught the words but merely dimpled. "Any news from Trenton House?"

James and Emily exchanged looks of surprise. "Like what?"

Her father grinned. "I hear the earl and countess are returning from their holiday today."

Emily inhaled sharply. "Gabe will be introducing them to his new wife," she breathed. "Poor Gabe."

James furrowed his brows, his jaw dropping. "You mean 'poor Frances', do you not?"

Understanding his meaning, Gregory guffawed and then made his way to the library as Emily gave her husband a brilliant grin. Then she glanced around and realized they were once again alone.

"Well, I'd offer my lap again, but Father is in there," she said as she tilted her head toward the library.

James dared a glance up the stairs. "I could admire the shape of your bum."

Giggling, Emily didn't answer but lifted her skirts and hurried up the stairs. Attempting as calm a manner as possible, James followed her.

He took the last few steps two at a time.

M eanwhile, at Trenton House
Having spent most of the gloomy Sunday afternoon in her workroom, Frances had finished washing and was changing into a day gown when she became aware of a commotion downstairs.

Thompson inhaled sharply and said, "They're home."

Frances stared at the maid and then at her reflection in

the dressing table mirror. "I'm so nervous, I think I may be sick."

"Her ladyship is not one to be frightened of, my lady," Thompson assured her. "Now, let me just pin up this one lock of hair, and you can go down and meet her."

Frances settled onto the chair and watched as Thompson tidied her hair. She thought of the series of small bud vases she had finished firing that day, all identical but for the floral pattern she had painted on each. Surely the gift of them to the countess would help smooth her way with the woman.

Gabe had written to his parents with word of their marriage, but the next correspondence he received from his mother had obviously been penned prior to her receiving his note. Frances now wondered if the countess even knew her oldest son had married.

"I really wish Gabe was here."

A knock at the door nearly had her jumping out of her skin. "Come," she called out, her voice tentative.

Had the countess come upstairs already?

Gabe stepped in and gave her a brilliant smile, David sitting in one of his arms. "Your wish has been fulfilled," he announced.

Frances ran to him, hugging him hard. "I didn't expect you home for hours." She moved to take the baby, but Gabe indicated he would hold him.

"I came just as soon as I heard the *Sea Breeze* had docked," he replied, offering his arm.

"Isn't that the same ship that brings the finds from Greece?" she countered as they made their way to the stairs.

"One of them, yes. My parents weren't the only valuable cargo aboard. We're expecting a few crates at the museum tomorrow."

"But... I thought the earl and countess were in Italy," she replied.

"Well, they started there and then made their way to

Greece. Sort of a Grand Tour. Their itinerary had them in Athens until last week. They would have taken the *Sea Breeze* out of Piraeus, the port nearest Athens," Gabe explained. "Perhaps my father was able to acquire a vase or two for his study."

Frances stiffened as they descended the stairs. She could hear unfamiliar voices in the hall below. She wondered if bringing the babe down with them was such a good idea, and was about to ask Gabe why he thought to do so when a sudden hush fell over the house.

They had reached the top of the last flight of stairs to discover several sets of eyes aimed in their direction.

"Breathe, Frances," Gabe said in a quiet voice, his face displaying a brilliant smile as they continued down the rest of the stairs.

His gaze fell first on his mother. From the way she glowed, she looked as if she had been sun-kissed. If there was any gray in her hair, it didn't show now.

Meanwhile, his father, an older-looking version of himself, was most definitely tanned from the sun. His golden blond curls, streaked with a few lighter strands, looked as if they hadn't been combed in a fortnight.

William, his arms crossed and displaying an expression that could only be one of humor, looked as if he'd grown a few inches. He was as tan as his father and nearly a twin in appearance to Gabe.

Frances took in a shuddering breath and, upon seeing several smiling faces aimed in her direction, found it easy enough to form one of her own.

"Welcome home," Gabe called out.

"We're so glad to *be* here," Gabriel Wellingham, Earl of Trenton, replied, stepping up to take Frances' hand. "It's not every day I get to meet a new daughter." He leaned over and brushed his lips over her knuckles at the same moment Sarah, Countess of Trenton, hurried up to kiss her son on the cheek and take the babe from his arms. William stood back and waited until he could follow his father in greeting Frances.

"Mother, Father, William, I'd like you to meet my wife, Frances," Gabe said, realizing almost immediately that his mother would be in possession of David for some time.

"It's so good to finally meet you," Sarah said as she grasped Frances' hand with her free one and gave it a shake. "I am just in *awe* that Gabe found you. An artist whose works we already own! And David. Such a good looking little boy," she added. "Oh, isn't he just a darling?"

David stared at the countess for a moment before he gave her a huge grin and then lowered his head to her shoulder.

"My first grandchild," Sarah sighed. "You'll have a cousin very soon, I expect," she added, her eyebrows waggling in Gabe's direction.

"Anne is already expecting a baby?" Gabe asked in awe.

Gabriel cleared his throat. "She is not the only one. Seems Rome is the place to go if you're in want of a child."

"Trenton!" Sarah scolded, quickly adding, "We're not yet positive."

"Mother?" Gabe's eyes rounded in shock.

Frances covered her mouth with a hand in an attempt to hide her humor.

"I've wanted another ever since William went off to university," Sarah replied as she turned her attention back to David. "But if I don't have one, I suppose I can just shower my attentions on this little man."

David once again grinned, his four teeth gleaming under the light from the chandelier.

Relieved at how quickly Gabe's parents had accepted her and David, Frances said, "You're welcome to do so whenever you wish, my lady."

"Careful, there, or you'll never have a chance to hold him

again," Gabriel warned. He turned his attention on Gabe. "Any trouble while we were gone?"

Gabe shook his head. "None. But I have made a slight modification to the storeroom at the back of the house," he said as he waved toward the corridor.

"Oh?"

"I must take a look," Sarah said, as she made her way toward the back of the house. "It's well past time something was done in there." She angled her head toward David. "I always thought it would do as a pantry, but cook didn't like that it had windows."

Frances' eyes widened—she hadn't yet had a chance to tidy it since she had pulled the vases from the kiln. "I fear there's a bit of a mess in there," she whispered to Gabe when he drew up alongside her.

He bussed her on the temple. "Shh. It can't be any worse than your workroom at the museum," he chided.

Sarah stopped short at the threshold, and those behind her were forced to stop in their tracks before she gingerly stepped in.

"Apologies for the mess," Frances said once she had made it into the room.

The four bud vases, set up in a straight line on the work-table, were the first things Sarah noticed. "Oh, these are beautiful. Did you make these?"

"For you, yes, my lady," Frances answered. "I was going to wrap them in tissue and put them in a box—"

"For me?" Sarah handed David to Gabe. She lifted one and examined it closely. "This floral pattern looks just like one I have on the sideboard in the dining room," she commented.

"That's because it is the same, Mother," Gabe said. "Frances made that one, too."

Sarah straightened and exchanged a glance with her

husband. "You commissioned those pieces from the Wedgwood studio, did you not?"

"I did," Gabriel replied. "The vase in the hall as well." His eyes narrowed a moment before he faced Frances. "Mr. Frank Longworth, I presume?"

Her face pinking, Frances dipped a curtsy. "Indeed, my lord. I'm very honored to make your acquaintance."

"And I yours," he said with a grin. He turned to his son. "You *do* realize what this means?"

Gabe regarded his father with a look of confusion as William grinned behind him.

"With a famous ceramist in the house, your mother may never allow her to return to the museum. She'll keep her here to show her off to all her friends and have her busy creating ceramics—"

"I will not," Sarah said emphatically. She dared a glance at Frances and added, "Well, maybe an introduction or two, if you're willing." After a pause, she added. "I'm so very glad Gabe found you."

Her lower lip trembling, Frances said, "Oh, I believe it was the other way around, my lady."

"She speaks the truth," Gabe said, remembering the day she had found him in the receiving area at the museum, when he was sure a two-thousand-year-old rhyton had seen its last days. "But once I knew where to find her..." He paused and then allowed a guffaw when he remembered something he had said at White's. "I chased her until she caught me."

Gabriel displayed a brilliant grin. "Like father, like son," he said.

AUTHOR'S NOTES

Bastards and Adoption

During the time in which this book takes place, a child was considered a bastard if he was born out of wedlock. Even if his parents married after his birth, he was still considered a bastard. For purposes of inheritance, the father could recognize the child as his own and provide a settlement for him, but *the child could not inherit any aristocratic titles.*

Although adoption and fostering have occurred on an informal basis for centuries in England, *adoption wasn't legally recognized until 1926.*

BCE

The use of BCE for Before Common Era (in place of BC for Before Christ) is correct in 1839. In 1635, derived from the Latin form *vulgaris aerae*, the expression *Vulgar Era* emerged. *Vulgar* in its original meaning was 'of the common people'. By the early 17th century, this expression had begun to take the variant form **Common Era**, which was introduced more widely by Jewish academics in the mid-eighteenth century.

Pottery Restoration

Most ancient Greek pottery is terra-cotta, a type of earthenware ceramic, dating from the 11th century BCE through the first century CE. The word *Attic* in black-figured pottery refers to its origin of the Athens region of Greece.

The usual restoration method started with reassembling vessel fragments. Missing fragments were replaced with new glazed and fired pieces of pottery and then gaps were filled in with plaster. The surface was then painted, sometimes extensively.

The materials used in these restorations included shellac, protein glues, oil paints, gypsum, plaster of Paris, barium sulphate, calcite, clay, kaolin, and waterglass (calcium silicate).

Depending on the tastes of contemporary society and collectors, decorative imagery was censored and painted over. Common examples include a fig leaf to cover genitals.

Bethrotal Rings

During the Regency and Victorian eras, sapphire rings were highly valued, more so than diamond rings since sapphires were considered a much more valuable gemstone. DeBeer's, the firm credited with having created the market for diamond rings, wasn't founded until 1888.

Family Relations - The Burroughs and the Merriweathers

If you're curious about the extended family to which the Grandbys and Burroughs belong, there is a family chart available on my website (https://www.lindaraesande.com/family_charts.html). Here's what I could have included in the chapter where Emily is reviewing the familial relationships in *deBrett's.*

Emily's paternal grandparents' place in the family included Mary Margaret Merriweather, Fourth Countess of Torrington, as its matriarch.

The countess' youngest son, Roger, had married Sophia Burroughs in 1770. The daughter of William Burroughs II, Duke of Ariley, and his duchess, Sarah Pendleton, Sophia had been a sort of feather in the countess' cap.

With two older brothers, there was no hope Roger would ever inherit a title, but having the daughter of a duke for a wife lent a bit of caché. It also helped cover the less than advantageous match made by the oldest daughter, Lucy.

Too bad Roger died of pneumonia after siring only one son. That son had been Gregory, Emily's father.

Meanwhile, the oldest boy in that family, George, who had inherited the earldom in 1759, sired Milton, the current Earl of Torrington, and Michael, who died young.

Emily traced the line from her grandmother, Sophia, back to the Burroughs' tree.

Sophia was the youngest in a family of five, where the oldest boy, Henry, had been the sixth Duke of Ariley. While married to Margaret Merriweather—the niece of Mary Margaret—Henry had sired five children, the youngest of whom was Andrew Maximillian.

James' father.

The oldest was also named James, and he was the current Duke of Ariley.

So Emily and James are second cousins, straight across.

ABOUT THE AUTHOR

A self-described nerd and student of history, Linda Rae spent many years as a published technical writer specializing in 3D graphics workstations, software and 3D animation (her movie credits include SHREK and SHREK 2). Getting lost in the rabbit holes of research has resulted in historical romances set in the Regency-era as well as Ancient Greece.

A fan of action-adventure movies, she can frequently be found at the local cinema. Although she no longer has any tropical fish, she follows the San Jose Sharks and makes her home in Cody, Wyoming.

For more information:
www.lindaraesande.com
Sign up for Linda Rae's newsletter:
Regency Romance with a Twist
Follow Linda Rae's blog:
Regency Romance with a Twist